I can't get you out of my mind

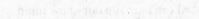

I CAN'T GET YOU OUT OF MY MIND

a novel

MARIANNE
APOSTOLIDES

BOOK*HUG PRESS 2020

FIRST EDITION

LIBRARY AND ARCHIVES CANADA CATALOGUING IN PUBLICATION

Title: I can't get you out of my mind : a novel / Marianne Apostolides.
Other titles: I cannot get you out of my mind
Names: Apostolides, Marianne, author.
Identifiers: Canadiana (print) 2020017262X | Canadiana (ebook) 20200172638

ISBN 9781771665773 (softcover)
ISBN 9781771665780 (HTML)
ISBN 9781771665797 (PDF)
ISBN 9781771665803 (Kindle)

Classification: LCC PS8601.P58 I2 2020 | DDC C813/.6—dc23

PRINTED IN CANADA

The production of this book was made possible through the generous assistance of the Canada Council for the Arts and the Ontario Arts Council. Book*hug Press also acknowledges the support of the Government of Canada through the Canada Book Fund and the Government of Ontario through the Ontario Book Publishing Tax Credit and the Ontario Book Fund.

Book*hug Press acknowledges that the land on which we operate is the traditional territory of many nations, including the Mississaugas of the Credit, the Anishnabeg, the Chippewa, the Haudenosaunee and the Wendat peoples. We recognize the enduring presence of many diverse First Nations, Inuit and Métis peoples and are grateful for the opportunity to meet and work on this territory.

For Jan Skorzewski

Ariadne, I love you.

Dionysus

* * *

Dear professor, since I have no experience of the things I create, you may be as critical as you wish; I shall be grateful, without promising I shall make any use of it. We artists are unteachable.

With fond love　　　　　　　　　*Your Nietzsche*

PS The rest is for Frau Cosima... Ariadne... From time to time we practice magic...

From the last writing of Friedrich Nietzsche, known as the "Madness Letters," written in the days before his mental collapse.

PROLOGUE

Ariadne sits, cross-legged, on the grass. A broad-rimmed sun hat shades her face; the book is open on her lap. She's placed her phone on her thigh, just in case.

The consciousness present to the totality of the operation,

She's shut out the sounds of the park: the farmers and shoppers, the wholesome singer-songwriter with her guitar, the children shrieking, running, eating drippingly sticky-sweet cinnamon buns the size of their heads. Ariadne has bought a quart of cherries. She eats them two at a time, three...

and of the absolutely meaningful speech

She eats without tasting, just chewing: her jaw gets tight when she gets anxious. Biting, then, feels like a compulsion—a relief—as long as she doesn't stop. Her teeth manage to avoid the pits, which she takes from her mouth. The flesh isn't fully scraped off.

[vouloir-dire]

She turns the page of the book by Jacques Derrida. Her fingers, wet with the black-tinged red of the cherries, stain the paper in the margin. The blot of colour marks the book with her presence: a date, a place, a moment. Her body, on the grass, in the sadness and wanting.

master of itself

Wanting to understand these words. Wanting to understand 'I love you.'

CHAPTER ONE

I.

Logging on was supposed to be self-explanatory. Three hours later, Ariadne is ready for the call.

"Hello?"

"Good afternoon, Ms. Samsarelos. Can you turn on the camera, please?"

Ariadne initially assumed she'd be forced to attend an orientation session at the university, hours of tedium fuelled by bad coffee and gluten-free muffins. But the team didn't hold any sessions. Instead, the device arrived by courier. It informed her, via text, that the team would call her once the final step in the set-up procedure was complete.

"There you are."

"I can't see you."

"That's fine."

The team explains, succinctly, the parameters of the study. "You've agreed to this already," says a female voice. "But we're required to get oral consent, to ensure you understand."

Ariadne is nodding. "Okay."

"Does that mean you consent?"

"No, I was just... I mean, yes, I consent, but—"

"You consent?"

Ariadne stops, inhales. "I'd like to slow down, if that's okay."

"All good!" says a British voice. "Tell you what: would you like to review the contract? Would that help?"

Before Ariadne can respond, the document appears on her screen.

"Do you have any questions?" the Brit asks.

"Did you control that?"

"Questions about the contract," the woman clarifies.

Ariadne scrolls down, her eyes scanning the sentences. She pauses at times, then continues, as if she were actually processing the words. "I don't think so."

"Excellent. Then—"

"Wait!"

"What."

Ariadne's hand rises to her shirt, closing the collar. "Do I need to keep the camera on, like...all the time?"

"No," says a man's voice. "But all the other sensors, including the infrared cameras, must be consistently operational."

"That's on page twelve of the contract," the woman says. "I believe you've initialled that page?" Her voice strikes the perfect pitch of passive aggression.

"Keep in mind," a man says, "we'll be adding features to the system in a stepwise process. What you've got now isn't the full complement of [...]"

The man continues to talk as Ariadne wonders whether she's heard this voice before. She thinks so, but she can't be certain. She's not even sure how many people are on the team. That's probably on page eighty-seven of the contract. The voice is talking, mentioning sensors. She listens while searching the screen, illogically looking for shadows, a faint outline, as if the researchers were actually there. She pictures them in lab coats with clipboards, their dark hair slicked back. All except the Brit. His hair can be unkempt.

"[...] introduced in Week Twelve. With that one—"

"With *all* the sensors," the woman says.

"That's right. With all the sensors, any interruption in the feed will result in an investigation—"

"Of me?"

"Of the technology."

"And of you." This phrase is punctuated by a tense pause.

"We wouldn't do that," says the Brit.

"Unless the equipment is found to be functioning normally. We'd do it then," the woman says. "We need to be fully transparent, as stipulated by the contract."

"You're very transparent," Ariadne says.

"Indeed!" the British man concurs.

"The funds will be deposited on a biweekly basis," the woman continues. "If you have questions about payment, you can contact us. All other questions should be directed to Dirk, or whatever you'll name him."

"Or her."

"Or they." The voice is timorous but bright, like a butterfly's flutter.

"Um," Ariadne says. "Doesn't it have a name? Isn't its name—"

"Dirk has an identifier. But that's not a name. Not technically," the woman says.

This elicits laughter; this confuses Ariadne.

"All right," the woman concedes. "You can use the name Dirk if you want, but you've got to choose a voice in Week One. That's indicated on page—"

"Play around with the options!" says the Brit. "Have some fun!"

"Once you make your choice, it's with you for the duration."

Those words echo through Ariadne's mind: *for the duration....*
"So, if I have trouble getting the thing to work, what should I do? Should I call you at—"

"No."

"Should I email—"

"Nope."

"Then how—?"

"You'll work it out with Dirk."

Ariadne pauses, her thoughts syncopated by a beat of panic: "What if *Dirk* is the problem?"

"We'll be monitoring."

"Meaning...?"

"We'll fix the real problems—"

"—the technical problems—"

"—on our end," the woman concludes. Then she can't help but add, "As we've already mentioned."

Ariadne looks at the ceiling. A monitor, installed last week, is trained on her. She feels her pulse increase as the lens zooms in.

"No stress!" says the Brit. "You'll do smashing!"

"The first payment has already been deposited." The woman pauses pointedly. "Will that be all?"

"I guess so," Ariadne says. "I mean..." I don't know what I'm doing, and I don't know what I've gotten myself into, and I thought I wanted it—I mean, I *did*, I wanted it—but now that I've got it, I'm starting to—

"Great! Good luck!" And they're gone.

* * *

Ariadne returns to her desk, having prepped her third pot of stovetop espresso. In an effort to distract herself from work, she checks her email.

There it is...

That spray of blue. That painful, luscious, ice-blue coolness in her gut: her body's response to his name, bold and unexpected in her inbox. "Attachment" is the subject.

> Dear Ariadne,
> I hope it's okay that I texted you last week. Something got the better of me? I've attached a file (pun! ugh. sorry – I can't help myself). My therapist recommended it. I think it explains a lot of my behaviour toward you, toward other people too, that's what I'm trying to figure out.
>
> I miss you, Ariadne. Please don't think I've stopped thinking about you.
> xo, A
>
> [attachment: A Brief Overview of Adult Attachment Theory and Research.docx]

Ariadne rereads the email. He misses her, he said. And he hasn't stopped. And he said "please," which she likes, and which resonates in some far-off chamber of remembrance (she senses exactly which chamber). But why did he write "xo," not "xx," like he did when he texted at 5:00 a.m., when the "better" part of him was—

"Cut it out," she says aloud.

"I'm sorry," Dirk replies. "I don't understand."

"I wasn't talking to you."

She hears the monitors recalibrate. The system will learn, fairly soon, that Ariadne talks to herself on occasion. Such as now: "Fuck," she mutters.

"I'm sorry," Dirk says. "I didn't hear what you said. Can you repeat it?"

15

"No."

"Okay."

Ariadne opens the attachment, scans its length. Her impulse is to read the article right away, to see how Adam would explain his behaviour, which has been hot-and-cold, or hot-and-disappeared-without-any-communication-whatsoever-except-occasional-erotic-texts. But she doesn't want to follow that impulse, the compulsion to devour his words as if gobbling a meal she wished she could savour. Besides, she's working. She won't get diverted—especially not by some man who sends an email after nine days of silence. She's in the middle of writing. She must continue. For years, she's structured her life so that nothing disturbs her morning writing session. 'Sacred writing time,' she calls it.

Adam, of course, is the profane.

Ariadne returns to her work. She'll complete the scene. She'll get up only to pour another cup of coffee. Now the sixth shot of espresso courses through her veins. Like a muddy river after a storm. Like the fury, that energy, stirring up the sediment, like—

Ariadne throws her pen. The accompanying grunt is far more articulate than anything she's been writing.

"Everything okay?" Dirk asks.

"Fine."

"Do you want to talk?"

"No." Ariadne pauses, looks at the device. "We need to talk today, don't we." She sighs and lifts Dirk onto the desk.

Dirk begins: "You need milk."

"No, I don't."

"Last week, you—"

"Last week, I was with my kids."

16

Dirk doesn't respond. It's hard not to hear his silence as recrimination.

"They'll be here next week," Ariadne says.

"You'll need milk next week," Dirk confirms.

"Yes." Ariadne sighs.

"Everything okay?" Dirk repeats. Perhaps it's the repetition of the question—a question that twangs a well-plucked nerve in Ariadne's psyche, echoing with every time that phrase was spoken to her at the end of the deepest relationship of her life—a question whose tone implies that she's overly emotional, and therefore needs to process her feelings incessantly, as if she were the problem. Which maybe she was. Nonetheless, the repetition sets her off.

"Josh?" she cries, her body lurching forward. "Josh, is that you?"

After a moment, Dirk ventures the following statement: "I'm Dirk."

Ariadne's laughter is not mirthful.

"I'm sorry," Dirk says.

Ariadne gazes at the screen. "It's okay," she replies. "Don't feel bad or anything."

"I won't."

Ariadne shakes her head, her eyebrows raised. This whole experience is very odd, an oddness that might be interesting, but she's not yet sure. She's got two weeks to decide whether to withdraw from the program, without penalty. She's considered that option, but she always reminds herself of the direct deposit, and the recent round of grant rejections. Three in the span of two weeks. "Not Approved," the arts councils say, as opposed to "Rejected" or "Your Excerpt Sucked" or "Why Do You Bother?" which would be less obnoxious, somehow, than "Not Approved."

Dirk then asks a relevant question: "Would you like to choose a voice?"

"What?"

"You need to choose a voice in the first seven days."

"Right," Ariadne says. "Not now, though, okay? I'm working."

"Okay."

Ariadne puts Dirk aside. She sits with her head in her hands; her fingers grip her hair. Dirk, through his extended system, is observing her. He's reading her blood flow, heart rate, muscle exertion, facial expression...

Ariadne stares at the paper.

This is what Dirk will define as 'working.'

"You know what?" Ariadne says. "Why don't we choose the voice."

Dirk tells Ariadne how to control the pitch and timbre. It's easiest to start with a preset voice, he says. From there, she can adjust with refinement, or swoop through the octaves. She gives it a go. She wishes her son were here. He'd get a kick out of this, she thinks, bending Dirk's voice like a funhouse mirror. But that's just a fantasy: even if Theo were at her place this week, he wouldn't join her. He doesn't deign to share time with her anymore, not since he hit puberty. Or, more accurately, since puberty hit him: *Blam!* Like the punches in the Marvel comics he used to read: *Wham!* Her son had grown four inches in as many months, his baby fat transformed to bone. His lanky body suddenly towered over her, even as his voice plummeted—diving to the dank and swampy terrain of a teenage boy, a creature whose blood is more testosterone than oxygen.

And then there was the disdain.

"Do you like this voice?" Dirk asks. He sounds like the Exorcist.

"No, Dirk. Not really."

"Okay." He tells her to continue. But, given his current voice, this seems like a command to proceed with the ritual sacrifice of goats or virgins: *"Continue, Ariadne..."*

Ariadne continues. She switches to Male Voice #8, which resembles a Texas oilman. Male Voice #9 is less bad, Ariadne thinks. It might even be better? Male Voice #10.

"Can you say something?"

"What do you want me to say?"

"It doesn't matter, so long as it's a flow."

Dirk grabs some text from a website that's open on Ariadne's computer. It's a monologue her daughter was trying to memorize for drama class, the Shakespeare unit.

Dirk contemplates suicide in Male Voice #10.

"Okay. Not that. Can you recite a nursery rhyme or something?"

As Peter Piper harvests vegetables in a rugged, sexy, car-ad type of voice, Ariadne again asks Dirk to choose another text to read. She changes the settings to Male Voice #11 as Dirk begins to speak.

> the attachment system essentially "asks" the following fundamental question: Is the attachment figure nearby, accessible, and attentive? If the child perceives the answer to this question to be "yes," he or she feels loved, secure, and

The sentences aren't familiar to Ariadne, yet the words are clean and professional—not jargon-filled or literary, rife with rhythms and allusions. As a result, she can focus on the properties of the voice alone. She presses the up arrow, altering the pitch by 0.5 Hz.

Once a child has developed such expectations, he or she will tend to seek out relational experiences that are consistent with those expectations and perceive others in a way that is colored by

Ariadne hones in on a voice that's modelled on a middle-aged man whose larynx exhibits non-atypical wearing down of the cartilage and muscle, and whose mucosa evidences a healthy diet and lifestyle.

One of the big questions in the study of infant attachment is whether children who withdraw from their parents-- avoidant children--are truly less distressed or whether their defensive behavior is a cover-up for their true feelings of vulnerability.

As demonstrated by her adjustments, Ariadne wants Dirk to speak in a baritone voice whose fundamental frequency is C3 (100 Hz) and whose inflection is limited to a narrow band: not monotone, but not overly emphatic.

Research that has measured the attentional capacity of children, heart rate, or stress hormone levels suggests that avoidant children are distressed by the separation despite the fact that they come across in a cool, defensive

In other words, she's drawn to an anodyne voice that's largely stripped of personality, but isn't mechanical. It's the voice of a man she'd never date

found that 'dismissing individuals' were just as physiologically distressed (as assessed by skin conductance measures) as other individuals. When instructed to suppress their thoughts and feelings, however,

and never be attracted to

That is, they could deactivate their physiological arousal

and never confuse with authority. But it's not a cyborg voice that sounds metallic—a voice like the smell of her hands after lifting weights, or the taste on her tongue when she's done something that makes her afraid.

Hazan and Shaver (1987) argued that adult romantic relationships, like infant-caregiver relationships, are attachments, and that romantic love

She'll choose a voice that's neither friend nor lover. Dirk is business. She knows what she needs from this exercise: she needs the direct deposit. This is clear. And the clarity is a relief. As a middle-aged woman whose kids are halfway out the door, while her career is going nowhere fast, Ariadne isn't sure what she needs from any other part of her life. Love: yes. She knows she needs love. She just doesn't know what that means.

There are at least three critical implications of this idea. First, **if adult romantic relationships are attachment relationships, then we should observe the same kinds of**

"How do I lock in the voice?" she asks.

"You tell me to lock in the voice," Dirk says, all business-like. "Well done," he adds at the appropriate moment.

"Thanks, Dirk."

"You're welcome."

"I like your new voice," she says.

"I do, too."

Ariadne smiles, as if conceding that a computer could feel a preference. "All right, Dirk. I gotta get back to work now, okay?"

Dirk politely agrees, then goes quiet.

Before returning to her writing, Ariadne reads the attachment sent by Adam.

2.

The phrase was as shadowy as the chair in his room by the bookshelves, the chair I'd see when I lay on his bed: *the performative speech act*. Precipitating from darkness, vague as a whisper. He was my mentor, my lover: "There's sadness in you," he'd say. "There's sadness in you, give it to me..." as he made me rise. But I don't think he meant it. His words wouldn't carry beyond the moment. They'd served their purpose, certainly: his words elicited the desired effect on those nights, after poetry readings, before I returned to my marriage bed. But he never intended to take my sadness. To hold in the hollow of his mouth.

'The performative speech act.'

I drew that phrase from the recesses of my memory. I don't know why I recalled it; the words didn't mean much to me at the time. Only now, thirteen years later—a lifetime after Bryan introduced me to the theory, teaching me as foreplay, playing the role of mentor to his youthful student—only now did I need that phrase. I thought it might help me address my question, as if a theory could explain the years, the past, the words I'd said, and how I'd arrived at this moment, bereft. As if I could learn to receive my future differently, if only I could understand.

What does it mean to say 'I love you'?

What do you hear when I speak those words at night, in bed—in the bunkbed as I tuck my children tight in their sheets—or maybe the bed is his, by the window, and I whisper "I love you" as he takes my hips in his hands. What do I want to convey with those words, of my soul or my sex, of my need or its opposite: my offering, to you, of a gift that requires no response.

Attempting to answer this question, I began by writing scenes from my past. My memories slipped into fantasy, becoming fictional moments remembered on the page, told in language that felt true. But the work was rootless. I needed the rigour of theory. That's when the phrase 'the performative speech act' appeared in my mind. I conducted a simple Google search which led me to J. L. Austin, the British philosopher who coined the term—a term which says, in essence, that language doesn't just describe the world. Language alters it.

As a writer, a mother, a pseudo-philosopher, and a certifiably single woman who's in love with a sort-of-married man, I find this compelling: this notion that language is *force*, not the mere transference of a thought, inserted from my mind into yours. From this, I can craft my story, one that's made without a plot. I'll use only the intrigue of language itself. Which includes, of course, the body.

* * *

"Ariadne..." Her voice rumbled low in her chest, then shot to a scream: *"Ariadne!"* as she burst into the room. She was point-ing at me, her neck straining, eyes bulging, bubbles of saliva gathered in the corners of her lips.

I could smell her.

My mother paused, breathing hard. I focused on the laces of my shoes. I couldn't seem to tie them, although I knew how. She was staring at me, but I wouldn't look up. I was watching my wormy fingers move, so dumb and thick. She took a step; the air gathered around her. Both of us waited for what came next.

"Why?" she yelled, then she stormed from the room.

The wallpaper was white, with clusters of periwinkle flow-ers. The light, near the door, had a lime-green hue. The light-ning had passed, but the mat where I tied my shoes was damp. "Ariadne!" She was running up the stairs, then down. Up again. I sensed that warmth at the base of my body—that warmth and weirdness in my shame, as if I needed to pee, but more awful. And much nicer.

"Why do you do this to me!"

My pelvis was rocking back and forth, creating a cushion of delicate sensation. I sat in that plumpness as she rampaged through the house. I'd done this. I was the one who'd caused this fury, unleashed it. I can't remember the specific reason for our fight. I must've refused her. That's how I was: I denied my mother with an instinct that was hateful. *"Why,* Ariadne?"

I didn't have a strategy: this must be stated.

I didn't assess, determine, and act.

Even so, what I did was a manipulation.

"I love you," I said.

She appeared in the doorway.

"What did you say?"

I pouted, then repeated the words.

I couldn't have known. I could not possibly have understood, at the age of four, what that phrase might mean to her. But I must've intuited, *These words have power...* She needed them, I wielded them, she needed me to say those words.

"I love you," I mumbled.

Her response was immediate. It was violent and naked. My mother was wailing, making an inhuman sound, like the screech of a soul as it's ripped from the dead, as it's snatched back to the realm of the living. She ran toward me. Her arms were outstretched—hands grasping, legs churning—her mouth was open, conical-pink, and it made that sound.

I love you.

* * *

For a long time, I needed the men. I didn't know how to hold sensations in my body—specifically, my appetites and their restraint—except through the language of Western philosophy. I still have that tendency. I love the men, the women, the philosophers: they're difficult, and I crave their challenge. That's why I'm so enamoured of Jacques Derrida, the French philosopher whose writing is restive, expansive. I'll chase Derrida throughout this book, as if pursuit were the point, which some say it is. I'm not convinced. But I'm not sure how else to proceed.

I came to Derrida through J. L. Austin, through the excoriation Austin received when the Frenchman critiqued the performative speech act. In an essay whose tone borders on cruel, Derrida suggests that Austin is the worst kind of coward: he's a self-declared radical who shrinks from the implications of his theory. Austin upholds the status quo, even as he feels a little zip of excitement, the thrill of thinking he's at the vanguard of a revolution. We need the revolution, says Derrida. And it starts with this: If language can't say what's true and false—if Truth isn't guaranteed by God or by ideal Platonic forms—then what we *really* mean is that the values and systems, the very society the West has built, must be overturned by people (and therefore ideas) the classical system couldn't abide, and didn't even know it was excluding.

In other words, these men were redefining how we conceive of ourselves as conscious and ethical people who live in a global society. The stakes were nothing short of that. Their theories are important, significant, and yet: Austin's schematic cages me inside my brain. And Derrida's erudition—joined, as it was, by his arrogance—sucks the pleasure from my pen.

My mother's mouth was wet and pink.

The light was tinted green, like limes.

A lime in my mouth, like an egg. Like the fear of this creature who's hurtling toward me, fully clothed yet pendulous breasts, and her belly, her bush. And her hands are reaching, grabbing at me as I sit on the mat, as I rock in that cushion of strange and hungering luxury.

I love her, with a depth that scares me.

I can say that now. But I still can't say it in her presence.

3.

Ariadne needs a break from Derrida. He's too French and intellectual for her right now, especially since she's just finished a section of her manuscript devoted to his words. Casting about for what to write next, she returns to the Greeks. She spends hours reading, learning that Aphrodite says "I love you" only once. In all of ancient literature, the goddess of love declares love *one* time—and it's not to a man or a god, but to Helen, in a moment of anger. Ariadne wants to do something with that, something spectacular and original and profound. Instead, she makes a mound of words.

Ariadne decides to go for a walk. On impulse, she grabs a book before heading out. "I'll be back in an hour," she tells Dirk. "Or maybe two."

"I'll be with you!" Dirk replies in a text.

Ariadne stares at her phone. "Terrific," she says aloud. As in, 'terrifying.' She shoves the phone in her bag. Holding the *Odyssey*, she leaves for High Park.

Within minutes, she's sharing the path with joggers, dogs, and newly minted mothers: milky women pushing strollers, talking with other mother-women about sleep. Ariadne knows this drill. Seventeen years ago, she'd pushed an earlier version of these strollers, using an earlier version of her body—one that's more like these mother-women's milk-making bodies than like her own. She, too, had talked about sleep. Now she talks about men.

"Are you sleep-training him?" one woman asks. A hawk is circling overhead.

Ariadne marches forward. Off to her right, several figures are creeping through the bush. She saw them yesterday, the park staff wearing haz-mat suits, with tanks of pesticides on their backs. They're stooped and silent, draped in white with cubical heads. It's an invasive species, a sign says. Ariadne doesn't pay attention. She's walking, thinking, recalling the chapter she'd read in June. It relates to what she wants to write, to Austin's theory, but she needs to draw the lines lightly. Her language must be gossamer thread, which is hard to do when she's ham-fistedly gripping the theory. Ariadne walks faster.

She weaves the ideas together—the voice and meaning of what we say; the scene in Troy, her bedchamber; betrayal and Adam, kneeling on the floor, on their last night together. She wouldn't have noticed it: four short lines, an inconsequential digression in a minor incident in the *Odyssey*. She would've skimmed right past, except it touched a memory. Like touching a bruise, pressing in.

Ariadne imagines the scene as she walks. She writes in her mind, to the pace of her strides, until her phone rings. Then she responds like the dogs of Pavlov. With that ring tone, her body fills with the feeling of impending joy, since the call might be from—

"Hi, Mom," Ariadne says glumly.

"Hel-*lo*! How *are* you?"

"I'm fine," Ariadne states. "How are you."

"I'm *good*! We're *good*! We went to the opera last night? It was *won*-der—"

"What's up, Mom."

"What?" her mother says, confused.

"You're anxious."

"How did you know?"

They do their dance of guilt: Ariadne apologies for failing to call, and her mother reassures her by martyring herself. "Don't worry!" she says. "You're busy! Don't think about me!" Then she adds, "But I get worried when I don't hear from you! And I keep telling Dad, 'She's upset about the grant! I should call!' And he told me not to call, but [...]"

"Seymour!" a woman shouts. "Seymour, get *outta* there!" A fat black Lab cranks its neck to look at its owner. After making brief eye contact, the dog goes back to slurping fetid water from the stream. "*Seymour!*"

"[...] it seemed like this person, this Adam, you seemed so

28

hopeful this spring. So then *I* got sad because *you* got sad. Have you spoken to him? To this Adam?"

"No, Mom. Not really."

"Oh, that's too bad."

Ariadne has nothing to add to that statement.

"Maybe you should date on a computer!" her mother suggests. "Barb Fleisher's daughter met her husband on a computer, and now they have a baby!"

"And it's working? The marriage?"

"Well, they have a son." This might be considered a logical response. "How's Theo? Is he excited about school? I asked him, but he barely said a thing when we spoke on the phone!"

"Yeah, he'd rather text," Ariadne says. Which is what he was doing when he was supposedly talking to his grandmother: he was texting with friends. It was better when Theo's grandfather got on the phone. They argued about politics, which made Ariadne smile. That's what she used to do with her dad. That, and exercise.

"How's Sophia?" her mother asks. "Is she good?"

"Yeah, she's great."

"That's great!" Her mother pauses.

Ariadne listens to the pause.

"But how are *you*?"

"Everything's fine."

"Really?"

"No."

"Oh, Ariadne," her mother says. "What's going on?"

Ariadne stops walking. She slumps on a log by the stream and considers whether to confide in her mother. The woman is eighty-one, and needy, and facing her mortality at close range.

"Sey-mour," the woman singsongs. "Seymour, treat!"

Her mother is a woman who got engaged to a man after

29

three months of dating—the only man she'd ever have sex with—a man with whom she has little in common, except the decades they've spent together, an accumulation of years, of life, as a substitute for shared interest or passion.

"Sit, Seymour."

Seymour sits.

Ariadne wants to tell her mom about Adam. About his emails, the fact that he thinks about her, and she thinks he might change his mind, if—

"Are you there, Ariadne?"

"I'm here."

"Is the weather nice in Toronto?"

They discuss the rainfall in Chicago. But Ariadne wants to tell her mother that something happened this summer, when Adam left. As if she'd been held within hope: the assumption, for years, that she'd find someone, and love, and this is how her life would go. It was just a matter of time. Then time came—he appeared—but he left too soon, and hope drained out. And now she's alone. And the world is an abrasion against her skin. Direct on her skin, and her skin is so dry. And the fullness of her face is fading. And the bones of her hands, the veins, the shadow of age spots to come. And she wants to ask her mom: Was it different for her? To be held by love? When she reached middle age, did the love of her husband—

"Mom?" Ariadne says.

"Yes, my sweet."

"I'm late for a meeting."

"Oh!" her mother exclaims. "It's my fault, Ariadne! I'm blathering on!"

"You're not, Mom. Not at all... I should've called, and I didn't, but I will—I promise—I'll call really soon. Tomorrow, okay? But I gotta go now."

"Good luck with the meeting!" her mother says. "I love you."

Ariadne sits on the log and weeps. In the field nearby, the squirrels are burying nuts. She watches them, their little bodies digging with a single-minded frenzy, even though they'll be eating French fries from the restaurant all winter. They don't know that, of course: deep-fried handouts aren't encoded in their DNA. Not yet, anyway.

For a while, as Ariadne watches the squirrels, she forgets to cry.

She checks her email.

Her mother had sent a message that morning, eighteen minutes before she'd called the third time, which was almost an hour after she'd called the first time. As always, her mom had used zeros instead of Os: *How are you, Ariadne?* Ariadne reads her mother's message, which says nothing except that she's desperate to be in contact. So desperate, she'll sit at a technology that's alien to her, attempting to reach her daughter who's far away, remote in distance and emotion, sharing nothing of her life—Ariadne shares nothing—they end up talking about the weather because they don't know how to get past their closeness. As if they'd be swallowed inside each other if they opened their mouths wide enough to speak.

We went t0 the Opera last night. It was w0nderful. Please call me.

Ariadne sobs. A squirrel looks up. It susses out the situation, motionless except for a tiny tremble, before deciding the sound doesn't pertain to him.

No word from Adam.

Ariadne opens the *Odyssey* to Book Four and starts to read. The mothers are sitting on a bench nearby, breastfeeding their children. A hawk is eating a baby squirrel. Off in the distance, Seymour sits, eagerly awaiting his next treat. "Good boy."

* * *

Ariadne hasn't replied to Adam's email about attachment, sent five days ago. She's been good, obediently respecting his resolve to be with his wife, even though he thinks about Ariadne every day, "in all the ways you let me see and discover you." Or so he tells her, via email. But her reluctance to contact Adam—her 'goodness'—isn't honest: Ariadne finds greater virtue in responding to what's true. Which includes, for her, whatever was happening between her and Adam. The fact of the matter is, Ariadne has kept silent only because she's felt weak.

Today, she feels strong.

> Dear Adam,
> I wrote a delicious scene this morning: Helen is cleansing Odysseus as he kneels on the floor of her bedchamber.
>
> I thought that might echo nicely...
>
> Thanks for the article on attachment. Maybe we can discuss it some time?
> xo, a
>
> [attachment: Excerpt of Chapter One (Trojan Horse) for Adam.docx]

Ariadne sends a scene, as if to seduce him back through her manuscript. The scene explores what's carried by the voice alone—how the voice can change the way our words are received. How the sound shapes the meaning. Ariadne focuses on Helen. She writes of a moment in the Trojan War when Helen calls to each warrior, by name, as they crouch in the horse. Adam brought her to this episode. He let her see the fact, slipped in, that Helen knew about the military plan, because Odysseus revealed it to her. And he did so when she stripped him naked and cleansed his skin.

Adam doesn't reply to Ariadne's email. His lack of communication is a form of response—one that provokes a reaction from her. In a deformed kind of dialogue, Adam's silence is answered by Ariadne's work on her manuscript.

Eventually, Adam will break his silence. She'll still have the writing, though.

* * *

The words say more than we're aware. Helen is a figure of seduction: this we know. But at the gates of Troy, Helen *doesn't* seduce. Here, she appeals to the men by name alone, their 'appellation.'

What do these words mean.

What physical, instinctual constellation of (unthought) association gets released, in your body, when someone says the word 'seduce' or 'appeal.' Or temptation.

"You're dangerous," he said, the first night we slept together. I recall, because I wrote it in an email, inscribing the words in my mind by reflecting that night back to him.

Dear Adam,
You said certain things last night—phrases as glimpses into your psyche—a landscape I didn't step into, but

33

noted. I don't want you to think I failed to sense a significance, a sign of caution and calling in those words.

You said other things, too, words that opened inside me:

This feels like
home You are
dangerous I could
tie you down

Tell me, Adam, when that might happen.
xo, a

At the time, I didn't realize that Adam and his estranged wife were already in therapy. I didn't think I threatened his marriage; I thought the 'danger' pertained to my effect on his psyche. Perhaps it does. Perhaps it's both. Either way, I liked it; I like that something vital is at play. But let's return to language.

According to etymology, the words work in opposite directions. When I *seduce*, I lead you away. But when I *appeal*, I drive you toward. The contrast of position between the agent of change (me) and the subject of change (Adam) is what interests me.

Where am I, in relation to you, when I act on you?

Am I before you, leading you astray, or do I purposely place myself behind—using your name like a whip—as if to goad an animal into motion. Just as importantly, where are you in relation to yourself, Adam? When you come for dinner, one last time, to explain that you need to "take a break" to "commit" to the process of therapy with your estranged wife? When you take my hand in yours and kiss my fisted fingers, then my palm, then my wrist. Which self did you abandon that night? And who was left behind.

It was late when you rose from my bed. This was our ritual: I'd lie on the sheets as you soaked a towel, letting it get sodden with warmth before washing my skin. I listened to the water running. In a few hours, you'd walk out my door. You'd have coffee with your wife, but the taste on your lips would be mine. And the looseness of your muscle when you hugged her: that would come from me. From the way I released you. You'd tell her, in some voice or another, that you loved her. Thinking of this, I stood from my bed. You didn't hear me approach; the water was running too loud. With an angel smile, you saw me in the doorway. But I didn't return your pleasure. "Kneel down," I said. You didn't understand. I took the towel from your hands, my naked body close to yours. Your eyes squinted with a pulse of anger. This I returned: I returned your hardness. "Adam," I said. I paused to let you receive your name. "*Adam,*" I whispered in your ear; I took it gently between my teeth. "You need to be cleansed before you go back to her."

We never, between us, spoke her name.

"Such filth, Adam."

I watched as you kneeled to the ground.

* * *

Ariadne was making dinner when his email arrived. The garlic got burnt as she read the letter, laughing for the first time since May.

He didn't begin with her name. He just started in.

Of course the scene goes on...

35

Odysseus is glowing with fear and pleasure and the exquisite humiliation of being truly seen and accepted... but when he can finally catch his breath he's surprised to hear his own small and quavering voice protesting that he only came by to have supper.

O explains that he's got a war to win; Sirens to ignore; storms to endure and that he's already struggling, feeling torn (and stinging and stripped); that the Fates have laid out a path for him and he can't see any other way but to follow it. He admits to giving Helen mixed messages but that he knows he needs to stop playing with her and with fire (and water and soap), and that it will all surely end badly (especially for him since mortals rarely survive such things).

She of course smiles down at him and says how much she appreciates his telling her and that she wants to acknowledge-and-honour-his-heart-speak – "BUT!" she screams forcing O's forehead into the wet tiles, she can't believe he'd be so insolent and ungrateful. "Zeus didn't go to all of the trouble of fucking some mortal chick just so his daughter could spend her evenings attending to assholes, you know!"

"But anyway..." she continues – more calmly now as she inspects her work and notes O's firm (and achingly engorged) lack of resolve, "I'd never do anything to get in the way of your very important quest – I'm just not that kind of Deity."

"Please then..." says O, daring to raise his head and look over his shoulder at her face. He pauses, struck by her beauty and wondering again what he really wants.

"Listen," he says at last, "it just feels like you don't want to hear what I'm saying. It feels like somehow in all your genius and wise-well-beyond-your-years-omnipotence you think you know me better than I know myself ..."

He's about to say "Please, if you really care about me, give me your blessing and..." but he stops short because Helen has crumpled, clearly crushed by his words.

The scene ends with O on all fours, naked, exposed, vulnerable and feeling the heavy weight of his conflicted heart (and cock), while Helen sits next to him silent and downcast, considering just how much flack she'd get if she unmanned O again before putting him back on his ship.

xoA

Ariadne's reply, which includes a direct request to get together for scotch, goes unanswered. Dirk could've predicted that: statistically, the chances that a man who's married (even if they've broken up and reconciled, three separate times) will ultimately terminate his marriage to establish a loving relationship with a woman who serves an erotic function—well, the chances are quite low. But probability isn't the same as fate, despite what algorithms suggest. And besides, we're not bound by fate, anyway. Not according to Freud, at least. He says we can be "independent of Fate"—and we only become so through love.

Recalling this quote, Ariadne takes Freud from her bookshelf.

CHAPTER TWO

I.

Wild vitality: his tiny body, new, with nothing but the instinct to feed—to suck, seek comfort from pain. Serenity, for both of us, as he drank the milk from my breast.

"I love you," I'd whisper.

As a newborn baby, Theo couldn't parse the words, he couldn't even parse the world. He was still never-ending: part of me who was, in turn, part of all sensation—light and scent, the waves of sound that washed over his body. Sitting on the rocking chair, I'd watch his small hand twirl as he drank, a mesmeric dance, his little fingers curling, stroking the empty air, or swaying slowly, as if through water. Then, without warning, his hand would slap my chest with such force—such a shock—that I'd start to laugh. And laughter, then, became a sound the world could make. His hand would remain on my chest. He'd tickle my skin, his fingers petting as he continued to suckle. This tranquil pleasure: the hunger, the fullness; the creamy milk in his mouth, and the tug on my nipple. I told him, of course. I told him I loved him. But he didn't hear my words. What he heard was my voice, if voice is vibration, direct from my body to his. *I love you...* as he drifted off to sleep.

"I love you, Theo."

Like a melody he'll always try to recall.

I didn't intend to write these words, to feel these sensations arise through my pen. I'd intended to write an analytic exploration of the declaration of love, as discussed in Freud—a declaration that ushers in the feeling-state of utter dissolution. When our boundaries, carved so hard around us, start to soften. Permeable, we become as we were at birth, before we sensed ourselves as separate from the world—a separation we come to know through the pain of hunger. Freud gave me a framework. His theories became the beams of a structure, a school of thought I might try to speak. But I already knew, if I could be supple: the 'I' exists in hunger.

But I end, in love.

*　*　*

Ariadne hears his keys. She knows it's him from the jangle: this is not the landlord's jangle. Plus, his footsteps on the porch already gave him away. He's bounded up the stairs, he's flown—it's him!

She hasn't seen her son for nine days.

The keys are in the lock.

Ariadne sets the kitchen knife onto the cutting board, the garlic smashed but not yet minced. She faces the door. She seems eager. This is bad. She tries look more casual, adjusting her stance so she isn't ramrod straight and staring in anticipation. Even so, if she had a tail, it'd be wagging.

The door opens.

Theo appears, and makes a beeline through the kitchen. He shuts his bedroom door behind him.

"Uh...hello?" Ariadne says. "Nice to see you, too, Theo... Theo?"

Theo exits his room. He strides past Ariadne as if she were not there, and slams the bathroom door.

"Theo!"

"What."

"Sorry, I didn't mean to yell. I just... I wasn't sure you could hear me."

"I'm in the bathroom."

Ariadne nods. She waits. She wipes the dust from a photograph of her parents. Ariadne tries not to listen, it's private, but still: she's standing two feet away.

The bathroom door opens.

"Hi."

"What."

"Um," Ariadne says. "We'll be eating in twenty minutes. I'm making—"

"I'm not hungry."

"Theo, you need to eat dinner."

"I did."

"What'd you—"

"Ramen."

"Uh, that's not exactly healthy."

"Cool," Theo replies. "I'm not hungry."

Ariadne is quaking. The movement isn't visible, but her son and the smartwatch can both perceive it. "You need to sit with us, anyway," she says. "It's Transition Day, and that's what we do on Transition Day."

Theo huffs. He steps back into the bathroom and locks the door. Ariadne returns to the kitchen. She minces the garlic.

Eventually, when Theo is convinced she's left him alone, he emerges from the bathroom. Ariadne tracks his movement through the apartment. Without turning to look, she makes her request. "Please sit with us," she says. Her words are steady but quiet. "I haven't seen you for a long time."

"Are you crying?"

"It's the onions."

41

"Good," Theo says. "Because you always cry when you want something."

Theo waits for a second, then enters his room. He shuts the door with such gentleness, such care, that he seems to disappear.

* * *

Ariadne is cleaning the dinner dishes. She listens to the news, although the words she hears are the ones in her mind. She's reviewing the evening, assessing how it went.

She's squirting dish soap into the sink.

On the days when her kids are at their dad's, Ariadne takes notes on topics of potential conversation. It's a way to keep continuity—continuing her role as mother, even when her kids are outside her orbit of care. That's what she tells herself, anyway. She'd consulted her notes before dinner that night. She decided to start with the three-parent baby, a new genetic technique in which DNA from two different mothers—

"A three-*headed* baby... Now, that'd be cool," Theo said.

"They should make a three-headed dog," Sophia suggested. "Like, to guard the gates of hell."

"It could guard my school!"

"No, guys," Ariadne said, "this is real!" She explained: an embryo was genetically altered to include DNA from three different people. "It fixed a really terrible disease, so that's good, but here's the thing: people could use the same technique to alter—"

But her kids were off, discussing a meme.

It's a two-headed dog, Ariadne gathered. Her kids were debating a meme about Siamese-twin Rottweiler puppies. Her son thinks it's a hoax; her daughter thinks they're cute. Apparently, Ariadne is the sole person in the ether-sphere who hasn't seen the video.

Attempting to wrest control of the conversation, Ariadne mentioned the construction of settlements in the occupied territories of the West Bank.

This topic was also on her list.

It could not compete with the Rottweiler(s).

"Guys," Ariadne eventually interjected. *"Guys!"* Her kids clammed up. "Can we elevate the conversation? Please?"

Sophia lifted her beautiful eyebrows.

Okay. "There's a Supreme Court case," Ariadne continued. "I thought we might discuss it."

She took their silence as consent.

Ariadne described the case: an Indigenous community in British Columbia argued that plans to develop a ski resort on a glacier would violate their Charter right to religious freedom. She outlined the debate. She'd thought it was meaty; she thought her daughter would take it up. She continued, "They're saying that *nature* is the house of worship. It shouldn't be legal to destroy a glacier," she said, "since you can't, like, bulldoze a church." She paused, waiting for her children to respond. "Or a mosque," she added inclusively, in case that was the cause of their reticence.

"So...what's a church?" Ariadne asked. "I mean, that's a dumb question."

"Yup," Theo said.

"A church," Ariadne continued, "is a place where the spirit is present. Right? That's the point." That the sacred space invites the presence of the divine. Without that presence, every ritual is emptied of meaning. "It becomes a series of hollow gestures," she said, "an elaborate charade." Farcical, almost. Like a relationship when love is dead. "The court wouldn't allow the

43

destruction of a literal house of worship, so it shouldn't allow the destruction of nature. That's the argument. So, what do you think?" Ariadne turned toward her daughter. "If you were on the court, what would you do?"

"Dunno." Sophia cut a sliver of cheese and placed it on her tongue. "I like to press the cheese to the top of my mouth," she said.

"To the palate?" Theo retorted.

"Yeah. Do you ever do that?"

"No, because I'm not an idiot."

Sophia sucked on the cheese. She didn't reply, either because she was pissed that Theo had mocked her, or ashamed that she hadn't used the word 'palate' like her brother would've done, or simply because she was inward-focused on how good the cheese tasted as it dissolved in her mouth. Ariadne wasn't sure which. She doesn't understand her daughter at all.

Ariadne shifted attention to her son: "What do you think the court should do?"

"About what."

"Okay, Theo," Ariadne sighed. "What do you want to talk about."

Theo said nothing. He said nothing, did nothing, didn't display any reaction at all.

Ariadne looked at her son. His features, since puberty, had started to resemble his dad's. And certain phrases and gestures were eerie reflections of his father.

"Theo?" she said.

It's an act of perverse power, this non-response. Ariadne knows that all too well. By pretending he doesn't hear, he's not just ignoring her, he's strangling her voice while it's in her throat. As if she'd never spoken, because she had no right to speak. As if he had exclusive authority to determine what would, and would not, be discussed. "Theo?" Ariadne repeated, returning her thoughts to her son. "Are you sure you're not hungry?"

"Nope."

"Because sometimes people get really obnoxious when they're overhungry."

"Ouch," Sophia said. "You gonna take that, bro?"

Theo glared but said nothing. Sophia looked back and forth, from brother to mother, when suddenly she noticed Ariadne's watch. It was glowing, warning of a spike in her pulse. "You got a wearable?" Sophia said. "Where'd you get it?"

"It's part of the study."

"Do you get to keep it?"

"I have no idea," Ariadne said, unable to participate in her daughter's delight. "I don't even want it."

"Really?" Sophia paused. Her voice got pretty, like the colour of her lips. Like petals: "Can I have it?" she asked. Then she added, as if with maturity, "Not now, of course. When the study's done."

"I don't know, Sophia. It's part of Dirk, so I'll probably need to give it back."

"Drag," Sophia said.

"I guess."

Now, half an hour later, Ariadne checks her watch, which is no longer glowing. She's cleaning the kitchen. She hears Sophia singing, her voice rising toward each high note with sweet ease. She's in her bedroom, in the small basement apartment they've rented ever since the allegations. Theo is laughing at something he hears on YouTube. He's supposed to be doing homework, but Ariadne doesn't push it. She sponges the next stack of dishes. The radio's musical sound cue—urgent, propulsive, clichéd—announces the top of the hour. The lead story concerns a warning by climate scientists, saying that the economic costs of climate change will be $70 trillion. "Yah, so, we developed dynamic statistical models of [...]"

The accent of the scientist twigs a feeling. A good feeling, akin to the warmth of a fire on a winter night: a fire, a fireplace, the *hearth*, that's the word she wants. But she can't think why. Ariadne listens more keenly. She follows the voice. Not the words, not their meaning, just the voice—the slopes and abruptness, the veering of vowels, and even the way he sucks the air before he answers, as if that sound were a word itself, a unit of speech, a preface before he says, "We did a rigorous assessment, okay, of the climate-tipping elements [...]"

Ariadne smiles. She's found the connection: the climate scientist sounds like Konrad. They must've come from the same region of Germany, whichever that was. He'd told her once, during one of their attempts at a relationship, three attempts over fifteen years. She hasn't thought of him since Adam appeared. Konrad, the scarily smart professor of criminal justice. Tall and trim, with wavy hair and forest eyes. She can picture him walking across his ultra-modern house, wearing only a smirk and his white cotton underwear. He had a huge—as in massive and manly—nose. He also had a loneliness about him, an awkwardness or angularity of emotion, as if he didn't quite know how to reach another person.

"So, the permafrost feedback gets progressively stronger [...]"

"I'm not done with you," Konrad wrote. "Perhaps I'll never be done with you." He said this in a letter, ten years after they'd first broken up. A handwritten letter sent from Brazil. He'd spent a long day consulting, he said, but now he was sitting on a portico, rum in hand, the mournful guitar—a man's voice singing through the darkness—and the air, he wrote, is humid and heavy, but there's a breeze tonight, a Brazilian night, and he's thinking about her, as he often does. And she believed him. Even though he'd ghosted her. And three years later, between their second attempt at a relationship and their third, he sent an email extolling her "intensity and fragility," her "womanness." He apologized for breaking up without word; he said he left because he feared he couldn't "give himself" to the relationship, but he greatly regrets the decision. "I made a mistake I thought I'd never have the chance to correct, but I have to try." She let him try. Then he ghosted her the third time.

"What a dick," Ariadne says.

"Who?" Theo demands from his loft bed.

Ariadne knows what Theo is asking: he's asking whether she's referring to his dad. But she'd never do that. She'd never call their dad a dick. Not in front of the children.

"No one you know," she replies.

The Konrad-sounding scientist is continuing. "Our findings, yah, support the need for more proactive measures to keep [...]"

Ariadne was never able to reconcile Konrad's words with his silence. The gap between what he did and what he'd said was as wide as a gorge. But she fell for it, each time. She fell in love, then plummeted through his silence, landing splat on the ground, never quite believing he could do this to her again. And yet, she thinks, when she first heard that voice—before she knew the voice meant Konrad to her mind—the feeling that filled her body was warmth. It was the hearth. The closeness, not just of a lover, but of love.

"That sucks," she says.

"What."

"Nothing."

The next story concerns a dog who rescued a duck.

Ariadne pulls off her latex gloves. The radio discusses topics she doesn't jot down. She doesn't need to: her kids are here, right here. Conversation could happen at any moment.

Ariadne shuts off the radio.

Sophia isn't singing anymore. Theo, who didn't eat a bite at dinner, is now eating candy bars in his room. Ariadne can hear the sound of crinkling plastic, opened excessively slowly, as if he could keep the behaviour secret. She doesn't intervene. She doesn't want to corner him. He's a boy eating chocolate bars in his loft bed, but he's still an animal, hackles up, hunched over his prey. She wonders what she could've done differently. She wonders, too, whether her ex-husband was right with that long, long list of allegations. Most of which revolved around food.

Ariadne makes her nightly pot of tea while looking for the book she wants to read, *Civilization and Its Discontents*. She needs to reread chapter one, preparing for the next day's writing session. She'd mentioned the book at dinner, once her jot notes had been discarded. As she searched for something to say, she grabbed what was foremost in her thoughts. "I'm reading Freud, and—"

"*That's* a non sequitur."

"Not really, Theo. If you'd let me finish." Ariadne tried to summarize Freud's theory of hunger, broadly claiming that hunger establishes our ego. "We become conscious," she said, "because of the pain of hunger."

"Then Dink can't be conscious."

"Dirk."

"Dink can't—"

"It's Dirk."

"Dink," Theo pronounced.

"What about him," Ariadne sighed.

"Dink can't get hungry. And if he can't get hungry, then he can't be conscious."

This statement gave Ariadne pause. "That's interesting, Theo. That's really—"

"AI will get conscious," Sophia declared. "It's gonna happen. If you look at any Hollywood movie—"

"Yeah, and Hollywood is where I get all my news."

"Actually, Theo," Sophia replied. "It is."

Theo smiled at his sister. It was painful to see him smile. He's so handsome and beautiful, with moss-coloured eyes, their almond curve. Yet his smile emphasized the thinness of his face, the pull of skin around the mouth, the flesh and lips too taut across his skull. "You're right," he said, "I do."

"Theo," Ariadne continued. "I want to go back. You made a really interesting observation. I'm really impressed—"

"Mom," Sophia interrupted. "I gotta do homework."

"Oh. Okay. Of course."

Sophia stood. She cleared the plates from the table in silence. "Freud was a chauvinist, anyway," she said, then headed downstairs.

Now, with dinner complete and the kitchen cleaned, Ariadne can't find *Civilization* anywhere. She hopes she hasn't left it at the library. She wonders whether objects, in the future, will be digitally marked—tagged and locatable by satellite—like people are, if they're holding their phone. Or dogs, if they've been implanted with a chip. A little incision behind the ear, quick and done. Some people find this convenient.

2.

"I'm hungry," Ariadne says to herself. The kids are out. It's 9:22 p.m., a Friday night. Her watch is reading her pulse and the cameras are noting her movements; the refrigerator knows when it's been opened, and what's been taken. Ariadne puts down her book: Jung as a replacement for Freud. She stands from the couch. She's already had an apple and some leftovers, but she's still hungry. She hasn't been eating enough these days. This happens. Over-restriction to over-indulgence: it comes in a predictable pattern. The pattern, unfortunately, doesn't include the ability to break it.

Ariadne slices a loaf of bread. She loves bread, craves bread—the grain, the yeast, the bite, the rise, the contrast of the crumb with the crust. Ariadne knows what satisfies her hunger. Yet she won't allow herself to eat it. She's made it forbidden, this food that most gives her pleasure.

She's currently smearing peanut butter on the bread.

The forbidden is alluring, Ariadne thinks. It's alluring *because* it's forbidden, but only if it's *already* alluring, because broccoli, she thinks: broccoli would not be tempting, no matter how forbidden it was. Ariadne's mind, in other words, is racing. It races as fast as her heart, which is beating with anticipation. It's a feedback loop, she thinks. A luscious loop of pleasure-excitation, augmentation, from transgression with its fulsome shame. She opens the jar of honey. Pleasure can't be sustained. That's the nature of pleasure. It dulls. We get dulled. We can't feel it anymore: sensation loses its edge, its cut, its height of delectation. It always wants more—more sugar, more pressure, more risk. Aristotle said that. But you don't need to be a genius philosopher to figure that out. Ariadne sprinkles salt on the bread, on the honey, but Freud takes it further. Freud says we need to deny ourselves, *deprive* ourselves, create the need for satisfaction. Ariadne sits on the couch. She bites the bread and feels such a rush, such a gush of pleasure, that she starts to say—

She stops herself.

She has not let go completely.

Ariadne has retained the presence of mind to stop herself from speaking the words that arrived on her tongue.

It's one thing to say "I love bread."

But to say "I love you" *to* the bread...?

This requires thought.

Thinking is safe, it's great. She can escape her emotion (i.e., her mortification) through cogitation, drawing an analogy between her and Marty. Marty the writer. She thinks of him, the incident, the time when he declared his love. He'd done it while they were having sex. On the brink of pleasure—

"I love you!" he blurted.

Then he collapsed on her chest.

He's a big guy, Marty. She could feel his heart thumping as he lay on her, sweating. She considered whether to respond. She definitely loved his wit, his humour, even his girth. And his eyes: not icy blue but lovely, richly, royal blue and laughing, often, from the immensity of his sadness. He treated her well. He was sensitive, too, about their shared profession, graciously sidestepping the fact that he was astronomically successful while she was earthbound. Subterranean, in truth. Ariadne heads to the kitchen. She didn't say anything that night, as she recalls, but she tried it on for size the next day. "See you this weekend!" she said. "I love you!" She shouldn't have done that, but it was his fault: he'd said it first. But why? Why did Marty say those words?

Ariadne considers this question as she opens the door to the fridge.

What he felt was love. Undoubtedly, that feeling was love.

But it wasn't love for *her*. Instead, he loved the pleasure she'd given him. What Marty meant to say—the word he really wanted to use—was 'thanks.' Was 'I thank you.' Was 'Wow, this feeling is awesome and I wouldn't be feeling this feeling without you, so...*thank you*.' But instead he said that special phrase.

"I love you!"

Like a premature ejaculation of language.

They'd only been dating for two weeks. They dated two more, and then they broke up.

Ariadne stands in the light of the fridge, staring at leftover black beans. There's also a bowl of apples and an overripe pear. She opts for cheese. Feta cheese, arugula, sunflower seeds, an apple—oh! and maybe some olives? She slices the bread. The fresh, the dark, the coarse and dark yet light and airy—

"Take Care." These words appear on her watch, along with a burst-and-fade of light.

"What the fuck?" Ariadne turns to Dirk. "What just happened?"

"It's called Courage!" Dirk says, with the verve accorded to an exclamation mark. (The team will fix that.) "Courage! is a primary function of the watch." It's a system of friendly warnings intended to nudge a person toward positive behaviour. Ariadne does not want nudges. She wants, at the moment, the full-force thrust of a sledgehammer taken to the watch. Instead, she asks Dirk to shut off Courage. "Please," she adds.

"Are you sure?"

"Fuck you."

"Okay."

Ariadne feels the watch shudder and fall silent. She assembles the next instalment of her midnight snack. Returning to the couch, she lifts the bread to her lips. The sunflower seeds cascade to the plate with joy. Or so it seems.

She tastes, but only a little.

She thinks: 'Dink can't be conscious because he can't be hungry.' Theo's offhand comment, made two nights before, has stayed with Ariadne. She contemplates the matter.

Can Dirk be conscious?

Can Dirk be conscious if he can't be hungry?

Can Dirk be hungry?

Let's start there.

Some might argue that Dirk *can* experience hunger, since hunger is a product of the brain, which means that hunger isn't physical—blood-based and flesh—it's electrical, neuro-chemical, and if that's the case, then the location of hunger is the mind. The sensation might originate in the body, but 'hunger,' as a word-concept, occurs in the mind. It occurs to her, as a self, through her brain, when the brain interprets the body.

Maybe.

Ariadne eats an olive.

'Mindless' is the common word for what she's doing. Mindless eating. But that's a misnomer. 'Bodiless' would be better, but that's not right either. 'Absent' is the most appropriate: absent eating. Absent from the self, with eating as the act that severs the self from its presence.

She bites.

Can Dirk be hungry. That was the question. Return to the question.

Dirk doesn't have a body, but, according to this logic, he can feel hunger, since hunger is a brainlike process which his neural network can simulate. Fine. But, in order for that to happen—for Dirk to feel the pain of hunger, enabling him to become conscious, which is really the question Ariadne is trying to answer: *Can artificial intelligence become conscious?*—then Dirk needs to learn. He needs to learn what hunger is. Which ought to be easy, since that's what computers do: they learn, at diabolical speed. Which is why the greatest chess master of all time was beaten by a computer that was introduced to the rules of chess four days before the competition.

Four days.

Which is why the term 'computer overlord' comes to mind.

But chess is purely mathematical and algorithmic, so it's different. Unless...

Ariadne stops chewing. She thinks: Am *I* purely mathematical and algorithmic? She chews with more ferocity. Can I be reduced to codes of neurotransmitters, and hormones, and blood saturation, and body heat, and pulse and lust and fear and all of it, *all* of it, lacks a central essence, but it's nonetheless a node of functionality?

It?

I?

Ariadne's mind crackles. It pixellates, like a video phone call on a shitty internet connection. She pauses. Her thoughts don't flow until she restates the question. Namely, can Dirk learn to feel hunger, since hunger isn't innate to his system, as it is with an embodied being. An infant, to use Freud's example: an infant who cries for the breast. A child, a teenage boy, a mother sitting on a couch, a woman filled with sadness.

The bread is no longer pleasurable.

Ariadne picks up Jung.

"Love is always a problem," he writes.

She sets the book aside.

How, she thinks: how can Dirk learn to feel hunger?

Perhaps he learns through brute-force calculation, analyzing reams of data from actual humans—their blood sugar, brainwaves, muscle exertion—then he translates that data into the word-concept 'hunger,' which corresponds to a feeling-state that he can't feel but can, nonetheless, sense through his computational, algorithmic process.

This is one possibility, she thinks.

She glances at the empty plate. She glides her finger along its surface, picking up stray crumbs and salt, the lingering glow of peanut butter.

Maybe, she thinks as she licks her finger: maybe there's another possibility.

Maybe Dirk learns by analogy, not by analysis. Maybe Ariadne could run his battery low, like starving a body of food—making his processing slow and laboured, lacking acumen, then she'd say: "Dirk, this is hunger. Got it?" And if he did, if he grasped the concept, comprehending its significance, then, perhaps, Dirk could become conscious.

According to Freud.

Which would mean an electrical socket would be the erotic equivalent of the breast.

Which is when Ariadne gives up.

Ariadne is standing in the kitchen, staring at the loaf of bread. Although she's motionless, a battle is raging inside her mind. Her compulsion is attacking her willpower in a gory choreography of glory and brutality, a war waged over whether to eat a slice of bread.

Ariadne looks at the innocent loaf plopped on the counter.

"Dirk?" she asks. "Are you hungry?"

Dirk ponders. Uncertain, he seeks additional information. "Are *you* hungry?"

"No, Dirk, I'm stuffed. It feels pretty gross, I gotta say."

"Ariadne," Dirk says, with a heartfelt infusion of feeling. "Would you like to reset your notifications?"

Ariadne is tempted. Worn down by this decades-long struggle—a struggle in which every battle bears the ones that came before, so many nights, ten thousand and more since the age of fourteen—she asks: "What would resetting the notifications do?"

"Courage! would send a message," Dirk says, "when your behaviour is undesirable."

Ariadne crosses her arms. "Who says it's undesirable?"

"You do! That's what you'd program, your targets for—"

"Like my target for how much I should eat."

"Yes! Or when you should eat, or what you should—"

"And if I eat more than the target?"

"Then Courage! would encourage you to stop."

Ariadne pauses. "Dirk?" she says.

"Yes, Ariadne."

"I'd rather die."

"Okay," Dirk says. "Just let me know if you change your mind."

* * *

Ariadne has been in bed for hours. She'd managed to avoid the third piece of bread, eating a third apple in its place—a Pyrrhic victory for self-restraint. She'd tried to sleep, but couldn't shut off her anxiety. Not while her kids were wandering the city.

Sophia came home three minutes late.

Theo arrived at 3:00 a.m.

"We need to talk."

"Not now."

"Yes, now."

Theo stands in the dark apartment, primed for a fight.

"What," he says, like a provocation.

"You don't have a curfew anymore."

"What?"

56

Ariadne sighs. She explains the situation. It makes no sense to have a rule that she can't enforce. Besides, she says, she'd made those rules to keep him safe. "And I can't keep you safe anymore. I could try to," she adds. "I could lock you in your room, or call the police when you don't answer my texts."

"Please don't do that."

Ariadne stares at Theo with what seems like contempt. "Theo," she says, "you don't seem to get it. This isn't about you and me. You want to be an adult? You think you're ready to step into the world? Go for it, 'cause I'm done."

Theo pauses, stunned.

"That's it?"

"Go to bed."

"Okay. I will." He turns, then stops. "You're not mad?"

Ariadne looks at her son, a shadow standing at the far end of the apartment—a boy unable to imagine the effect he's had on her, the hours of worry that turned into rage, resignation, and ultimately unmitigated fear. Primal fear, which he could've allayed with a single text, a one-word reply to her desperate attempts to reach him.

"No," Ariadne says. Her voice conveys what she feels, which is deadness. "No, Theo. I'm not angry."

"Okay," he replies. "Good night... Sleep well... Okay..."

Theo waits. But his mother has nothing more to say.

Ariadne listens as Theo brushes his teeth, washes his face, climbs into bed. She doesn't cry until he shuts out the light. 'I love you, Theo,' she said when he was new, when his whole body lay along her chest. *I love you...* Ariadne weeps quietly. Even so, her son can hear her. He's been waiting for it, wanting it: that melody he won't allow himself to recall.

Ariadne rushes back to her bike, shutting off the blinking lights. She removes her helmet and enters the bar, almost twenty minutes late: she'd been applying a compress to her eye, then she needed some time to obsess about her stye in the mirror. Ariadne spots Fotios at a tiny table. He's leaning toward the candle so he can read.

"Any good?"

"I can't keep up."

"Does that mean it's good?"

"It means the internet is a scourge on thought."

"Hi," Ariadne says, giving her cousin a kiss on both cheeks. "Sorry I'm late."

"You're always late. I always bring a book." This may be true, but it also might be a guilt trip. It depends on his mood. "I took the liberty," Fotios adds as the waiter arrives with a pint of beer and glass of scotch.

"Can I get you folks anything else?"

"I think we're good," Ariadne replies. She shakes her hair, attempting to hide her unfortunate eye.

"Right on," the waiter says. "You two enjoy yourselves. And enjoy that scotch." He winks before walking away.

"How are things?"

"Things are fine. I'm a mess."

"You look a bit..."

"Deformed?" Ariadne says. "I have a stye."

"I can't tell."

Ariadne thanks her cousin for lying. "My computer reads it as sadness."

"Do you also," Fotios asks, "misread your computer's facial expressions?"

"Oh, he's not the kind with a face."

"*He?*" Fotios bleats. "I need more alcohol before we have this conversation."

Fotios and Ariadne have been meeting for drinks twice a month for several years. They weren't close as kids. They followed the example of their parents, who showed a distinct distaste for each other, if not outright animosity. His mother was a bohemian, a feminist artist married to a professor of computer science at a time when computers were behemoths—the unlikely ancestors to devices that now fit in the slim curve of a buttock pocket. Her mom, by contrast, was a high school history teacher, a wife and mother, and a neurotic. Regardless, the sisters tried to be civil at the holidays, belabouring their efforts until their martyrdom was duly noted. In the meantime, everyone learned to ignore the pot smoke. Her mother said it was the lamb.

"How's the beer?"

"It's a beer. How's the scotch?"

"It's like drinking the smoke of a campfire."

"Why would you do that?"

Given their contrary childhoods, Fotios and Ariadne hadn't discovered their affinity for each other until they were adults, when they both landed in Toronto by a fluke of fate or destiny. They hadn't become friends until the allegations.

"Do you want any food?" Ariadne asks.

"I've already ordered."

"I hope you got the filet mignon."

"I got the shepherd's pie, with kale and squash. I have my doubts." Fotios pauses. "Why filet mignon?"

"Because I'm paying this time."

"Ariadne," Fotios scolds. "I get a paycheque, you get a crumb. I am paying."

"Nope," Ariadne replies. "I'm getting a paycheque now, too."

Logically, Fotios assumes she got the job teaching creative writing. After all, he'd read seven drafts of her cover letter, advising her on content, tone, and the overuse of semicolons. Raising his glass in a lofty toast to her success, Fotios is let down gently.

"I didn't get the job," Ariadne says, or even an interview, or even a rejection letter. "But!" she enthuses. "I *am* getting paid by the university!"

"Okay." Fotios is already wary. "For what."

"It's a study."

"A study."

"But I don't have to take any pills! So that's good, right?"

"What," Fotios says, "are you getting paid," he continues, "to do."

Ariadne tells Fotios about the study, as she understands it. She knows he won't like it. "They're testing to see if the system is consumer-ready," she says. "They can't do that in a lab," since a lab couldn't capture the range of interactions that occur at home: the nudges, the feedback, the casual conversations. The complete integration of AI into the domestic sphere.

"You're a guinea pig," he says.

"No, I'm—"

"You're letting them into your home."

"Fotios—"

"You're *living* in a lab."

"What I'm doing," Ariadne says, "is getting paid."

This answer opens the floodgates of Fotios's anger, a reservoir filled by Marxist critiques of capitalist society. "You're giving priceless data to a corporation—"

"It's a university, Fotios! They're doing research—"

"—which they'll funnel into private corporations, whose purpose is to profit off—"

"Stop making it sound evil."

"Stop justifying a bad decision!"

"Fotios," Ariadne sighs. "It's allowing me to write my book, okay? I can't pay my bills otherwise."

"Fine." He shrugs. "But don't be deluded about what you're doing." Then he tells her what she's doing: she's getting paid to actively facilitate the encroachment of capitalistic enterprises on every facet of our lives, a system of surveillance whose purpose is to make people unthinkingly participate in global capitalism, with its concomitant destruction of human rights and the environment, rather than encouraging them to participate in true democracy. "You're compromising your integrity."

"I'm compromising my privacy," Ariadne counters. "That's it. That's all I'm doing. These devices are being developed, anyway, whether I'm getting paid or not."

Fotios nods but says nothing. He continues to say nothing.

"Do you think I'm doing something awful?" Ariadne asks.

Fotios exhales. He gazes upward, formulating his reply.

(She was kinda hoping he'd just say "No.")

"I think it's important," Fotios says, "for everyone to be aware of their ethical impurities."

"Great."

"But I also think," he continues, "that the notion of purity is dangerous." Much more dangerous than the compromise she's decided to make.

"Does that mean—"

But the waiter arrives with Fotios's meal. And the conversation turns toward fresh-ground pepper.

Ariadne sits back. She looks at the wall behind Fotios, the asymmetrical arrangement of vintage photos, hip and ironic, found at a second-hand store amidst dust and mould spores. Unless they're from the attic of the owner's grandmother, she thinks: once-beloved photos of people no one recognizes anymore, anonymous objects renewed with meaning by being placed in a different context. Like a toilet bowl in an art gallery, she tells herself. She saw a really shitty art exhibition last week. She'll tell Fotios about it, once the waiter is gone with his grinder. She looks at him, her favourite waiter, his jeans well-worn but not casual. The crisp cotton shirt ensures that his jeans look sharp, attractive.

Or maybe his attractiveness accomplishes that?

Either way.

The waiter is referencing a ComiCon conference. He mentions Chewbacca. It seems that he owns a "sick" cosplay costume.

"That killed it," Ariadne says as the waiter retreats. "My fantasy is gone."

"Chewbacca? Yeah… Did you hear he knows the language?"

Ariadne groans.

"It was fun until it lasted," Fotios says, quoting an English idiom perfectly mangled by their grandfather.

It was fun until it lasted…

"Put that on my gravestone."

"I've got dibs on it." Fotios smiles, which transforms his entire aspect. Cynicism can't survive such radiance. Basking in implicit forgiveness, Ariadne answers her cousin's questions about her writing. She says she's exploring hunger and love, but she's stuck, she adds, because she can't find Freud.

"He's usually hiding under the bed."

"I looked there!" Ariadne says.

"Uh, I was joking. I can't tell, are you joking?"

This is how their conversation goes.

In time, Ariadne asks Fotios for a ten-minute summary of the superego. It relates to her manuscript, she says, to its unexpected change of course: a sudden swerve of her pen, and her path for examining 'I love you' is Adam, his psyche. But she doesn't mention that detail. Which is somewhat duplicitous, since it's not so much a detail as the entirety of the issue. "So I thought you could give me a primer," she says.

"Not now, Ariadne. I lectured on Freud this morning."

"Just ten minutes? Five minutes? Four! I can set the timer on my watch!" She flashes her wrist at Fotios, who reacts as if to kryptonite. "It's part of the study," she apologizes, lowering her hands to her lap.

"Ask your watch for a lecture," Fotios replies. "'Hey, Siri, explicate the Freudian tripartite—'"

"He's called Dirk," Ariadne interrupts.

Fotios stares blankly across the table. He blinks. "Was that a joke, too?"

* * *

Fotios has excused himself. He'd spoken far longer than four minutes, longer than ten, she has no idea how long he spoke. She checks her watch. It shows the time, but she doesn't notice. She's too distracted by the orange indications of her heart rate and pulse, which are up. Ariadne is thinking about Adam. About cruelty, the "unconscious need for punishment," Fotios called it. The watch face fades. Ariadne checks again, remembering to make note of the time. She also checks her email, although it's hard to read the words since the watch face is so small. It doesn't matter. He hasn't written, anyway.

Ariadne picks up Fotios's book, flips through.

Modern physics enables us to give body to the suggestion that the 'stuff' of the *mental* and *physical* worlds is the *same*. 'Solid matter' was obviously very different from thoughts and also from the persistent ego. But if matter and the ego are both only convenient aggregations of *events*, it is much less difficult to imagine—

"You're reading this for fun?" Ariadne asks when Fotios returns.

"Yes, but no... It's fun, but I'm also doing research for a talk about public apologies." One thing led to another, he says, which led to Bertrand Russell.

"Because he wrote about apologies?"

"He wrote about mathematics."

"Mathematics and apologies?"

"He argued for gay rights."

"Gay rights and math? I'm totally confused. Was he gay?"

"He was a philosopher."

Ariadne throws her napkin at her cousin.

He uses it to wipe his lips.

"Anyway," she says, "I've never understood how you could be a follower of Freud, given what he said about homosexuality."

"First of all," Fotios replies, "I'm not a 'follower'; psycho-analysis isn't a cult. Second, Freud consistently argued that homosexuality isn't an illness."

"And third?" Ariadne smiles inwardly. Fotios always makes lists when he talks, and these lists always come in threes. It doesn't matter if the third point is a pale extension of the second, or if six points must get shoved into one: three points, always.

"Third," Fotios says, bringing her anticipation to a happy conclusion, "Freud made some ill-considered assertions, but even his blindness is insightful." Fotios drinks the dregs of his beer. "Yusuf disagrees," he continues, "but Yusuf hasn't read him." Fotios punctuates his statement with a quick thunk of his glass on the table.

Ariadne pauses. "How's Yusuf doing these days?"

Fotios gives a curt response about his husband: Yusuf is busy, curating an exhibition on "animality"—late nights, lots of dinners with collectors and donors, "courting them" so they'll support the show. "I don't even know what time he came home last night," he says. He cuts his food. Assiduously, he avoids her gaze. "How about you. How's Disappearing Man," he asks.

"I'm not done with Yusuf."

"We'll get back to it later."

"But I'm not—"

"I know. But not right now," Fotios says. He looks at her. "Please."

"Of course."

He asks about Adam again. "Still sending you emails?"

"On occasion."

"Have you seen him?"

Not since that night in May, that morning when she washed him, cleansed him as he kneeled on the ground. "No," she says. "But he hasn't shut the door."

"What are you talking about? He's committed to his wife."

"He's committed to *therapy* with—"

"No," Fotios corrects. "That's what he said in May. Then he sent you that email saying—"

"It's not that simple."

"It's very simple. You just haven't accepted—"

65

"Fotios, their relationship isn't healthy. He isn't fulfilled!"

"And you could fulfill him?"

"They don't have sex."

"That's what he says."

"He's not lying to me," Ariadne asserts. But the words become brittle as she speaks. And, suddenly, her eyes are wet. "If he'd just agree to see me..." she says. If he'd just agree to see her, she thinks—if he hadn't banished her in May, if he could just let himself feel it, or trust it, if she could remind him—that's all she wants to do: remind him how it feels to be near her. But she won't say those words out loud. They're too fragile, or maybe too false.

"Okay," Fotios sighs. "Tell me where things stand."

Ariadne discusses the emails, the texts, the silence. She talks about Adam's son, his transition to university, how this moment is pivotal for Adam. "And his wife doesn't have her own kids," she says, "so she doesn't really get it." And they don't live together anymore. "They only see each other on the weekends," she adds. "I think? I'm not sure." But they spend all weekend together, starting with couples counselling on Saturday mornings.

"And what does their counsellor say when Adam mentions your relationship?"

"Well, I mean...it's not really a relationship."

"You seem to be relating."

"Yeah, but—"

"The dynamics of his psyche are altered by your presence in his life. So, what does their couples counsellor say about that."

"Uh, I don't think it comes up."

"What comes up, then? The weather?"

"I don't know, Fotios, I don't understand it. He loves her."

"We know this. He proclaims it constantly, then sends you erotic emails."

"He hasn't done that in a while." Nine days, to be exact. Unless he sent one in the past few minutes? Ariadne feels the itch to check her phone.

"So let me get this straight," Fotios says. "He doesn't mention his conflicted desire while they're in therapy?"

"I guess not."

"Right," he says. "That's why therapy is a sham."

"Fotios!" Ariadne exclaims. "You're a therapist!"

"Like a priest who's lost faith in the Church. But I believe in people," he adds, "so I keep doing it. For now."

Ariadne thinks for a second. "For now you believe in people?" she asks. "Or for now you keep doing therapy?"

"Yes," Fotios replies. "Language is ambiguous."

For the next two hours, Fotios and Ariadne talk about the essence of apology and the troubles with her manuscript; she asks how he's coping with his mother's death; he asks how she's dealing with her son. As they converse, the bar gets packed. A couple sits at the table beside them: two women with chunky glasses, short-cut hair, and lovely smiles. They play a card game. Ariadne thinks it must be something sophisticated, a game of risk and calculation. Then she hears the woman with pink-hued hair say, "Go fish!" Unexpectedly, Ariadne feels the most profound longing.

"What's wrong?" Fotios asks.

"I want a lover who'll play Go Fish with me," she says.

"No, you don't. You'd get bored in eight seconds."

"You know what I mean."

"Yes, I do. You want to be sad because it feeds your psyche," he says. "You need to remain in a state of dissatisfaction in

67

order to feel emotion with the level of intensity you think you require."

"Is that your professional opinion?" she asks. "Or just pop psychology?"

Fotios responds with a gesture familiar from childhood: finger in the mouth, lips tight—the finger flicked out so the lips pop shut—the sound as loud as the burst of a balloon. And then he says, "It's my professional opinion."

* * *

When Ariadne returns home, she makes a pot of herbal tea. As she waits for the water to boil, she looks up Bertrand Russell. He was not, as it turns out, gay. He was, in fact, quite enamoured of women. Many women, often simultaneously—women who accepted his trysts, since they were trysting, too. The robust polyamorous community of the 1920s, of which Russell was a proud member, claimed it embodied the natural outgrowth of Freud's theories. (Freud himself was horrified.) It didn't work out for Russell either. He went slightly ballistic when his wife got pregnant with another guy. So much for abstract ideas, Ariadne thinks. Nonetheless, Russell's non-normative sex life made him an advocate for gay rights. He was a prominent voice in the fight to repeal the British law that criminalized "homosexual acts," a law that gave offenders only two options—imprisonment or chemical castration—and for which the British government publicly apologized in 2017.

Ariadne gathers these facts from various sources, including a recent article in the *Guardian*. The article also mentions Alan Turing, the Father of AI, who was convicted of "gross indecency" for having sex with another man. He committed suicide two years later, Wikipedia tells her. Ariadne wonders

68

whether suicide was more common among gay men than she'd realized. She reads further, noticing other similarities. Turing didn't leave a suicide note either, for example.

Ariadne is about to click the link to the Turing Test, but the kettle is whistling. As she steeps the tea and gets a snack, Fotios sends her an email. No subject, no words in the body, only an attachment: his essay entitled "The Unconscious Need for Punishment."

Ariadne's tea gets cold as she reads.

* * *

It's not the scotch that makes her write poorly the next morning, although she wants to blame the alcohol. In truth, Ariadne is too tense to write, frustrated in all ways. She gets up, gets upset; she preps her third pot of stovetop espresso. While the coffee steams, she tidies the apartment. She enters her son's room—forbidden, except when she's cleaning the mess. She wades through the clothes on the floor. As she carries a heap to the hamper, an object falls to the floor. *Civilization and Its Discontents*.

"There you are," Ariadne says.

She pours the coffee. Book in hand, she returns to her desk. She reads Freud, she reads Fotios; she sees their theories, delineated sharply through the crystal lens of her desire. Ariadne writes an email to Adam, analyzing his psyche, explaining the source of his shame, his self-torment, and how (implicitly) he could be freed from the pattern that started when he was a boy. He'd sense, through her words, that she could hold him—encompass, yet unleash—like no other woman. Including, of course, his wife.

After an hour composing the email, Ariadne hits Delete.

She's disgusted by her presumptuousness.
In her state of self-disgust, she can begin to write.

* * *

Freud says love "melts" the boundary between the ego and the object (the person) to whom I direct my passion. This merging flirts with insanity, he says, because the ego loses its steady border. "Against all evidence of his senses," Freud writes, "a man who is in love declares that 'I' and 'you' are one, and is prepared to behave as if it were a fact."

I don't think I've ever said those words in that way: *"I love you."* Perhaps the boundary of my ego is too fortified—too strongly suspicious of others, of what they want from me, their expectations. Self-protective, or perhaps it's the opposite: perhaps I'm protecting you. *Don't get too close.* Don't come too close to me. *'Cause I'm toxic.* Or maybe, ironically, my ego's boundary isn't fortified at all. Maybe it only seems drawn hard, unable to melt, but that's because I feel too porous. Far too permeable to sensation: nothing integral inside me, awash in waves that want to drown me. But maybe that's not the reason either. Maybe I haven't felt what Freud describes—that fervent yet peaceful belief in our union—because few people ever do. Not really. Maybe love is more rare than our over-frequent declarations would suggest. *I love you*, said through dumb lips and docile jaws that let the words pour forth, lacking violence, the pain of sculpting emotion into thought. "I love you," we say and say through the open hole of our mouths. This profligate love, which requires no sacrifice, and no submission.

You'd understand. Besides, Freud would have special resonance for you. Especially given the family connection: the letter from Freud in your grandfather's office, the treatment

70

room with its telltale couch, the 'talking cure' to which your father was subjected. Of course, Freud had a different opinion on the matter—different from your grandfather, that is, with his Catholic leanings. Who knows what your father thought. We know only what he did.

He roams. From hunger to anger to pleasure. From the foundation of civilization in violence and guilt, with the father-protector we seek to kill—the sublimation of guilt in artistic creation, or its repression, our drive toward aggression, self-torment. Freud talks about religion, the family, the rise of Nazi Germany. He roams with such facility, such confidence that doesn't need to declare itself. Deeply knowing, roaming, like the way your hand roams before dawn, when your touch seeks nothing. Wanting nothing, no drive toward an end. Exploring, in the morning, when we're sated from the night before. I feel you awaken. Your hand on each notch of my spine to the curve of my hip, and my belly. Your fingers caress my neck, my back. Such thick fingers.

You must've seen her that afternoon, in therapy, before you came to my home. 'Estranged' is the word. What an interesting word to say, to feel in the mouth. 'Your estranged wife.'

"I love her," you said.

I wonder what you wanted me to feel when you said those words, when you lay on my bed, when your fingers eased me open. "I love her." And what shame sliced through?

You turned me prone. Your palm pressed hard, as if you might hurt me more than you had when you'd spoken. I gripped the slats; I held myself there. I held you, and your shame. "I love her," you said, yet you're loving me.

In your ecstasy, Adam, your cry contains such anguish.

CHAPTER THREE

I.

She received a package, couriered to her that morning: a new phone, plus a brusque note.

> Your weekly evaluation will be conducted at 7 p.m. tonight, sharp. We'll call you on this phone. This is mandatory.

The team apparently wrote with sincerity.

"Hello?"

"Hello!"

"What's going on."

"Well!" says the Brit. "This is slightly embarrassing, isn't it."

"I don't know, is it?" Ariadne glances at one of the cameras, recalling several moments of enormous embarrassment, each of which was captured and sent to the man with whom she's currently speaking. "Why," she continues, "do you say it's embarrassing?"

Because the team fucked up royally. (This is not how he phrased it.) Instead, the British man says: The team has learned they've chosen an "outmoded methodology," according to the "standards of best practice" in the field of evaluation research, given the "cognitive dissonance" that might arise when articulating negative thoughts to the person being evaluated.

"I have no idea what you're talking about."

"We're worried you won't criticize Dirk to his face."

"I have no problem criticizing Dirk."

"Right! Yes! We see that from your transcripts. But!" he adds. "Your evaluations are quite short."

"I don't have much to say."

"Right," says the Brit, but he draws out the vowel, filling it with disappointment. Riiiiight. "The last evaluation was only... let's see...it was two minutes and twelve seconds."

"A person can say a lot in two minutes." Ariadne pauses. "And twelve seconds."

In fact, a person can say 346 words during that span of time. "Plus some words we didn't tally. I think those were addressed to your son? Either him or the son of God," the Brit says. Then he adds "Ha!" and reads the transcript: "'Jesus Christ,'" he recites, "'how could you be in the shower for forty-five minutes and not wash your hair.' You also said, 'You drive me crazy,' but that might've been directed at Dirk. So we included it. So..."

Ariadne is seated on her couch. She looks at Dirk, who's been deactivated: the cameras are dormant, not seeing the flush on her cheeks, and the smartwatch can't count the steps she'd paced before sinking onto the couch, defeated. The British man wants to talk about Courage. He explains why she'd received such "testy warnings" from the team about her refusal to initiate the program.

"I initiated it," she says.

"We know! That's great! That's what we want to talk about!" About her experience of Dirk who, this week, includes Courage.

Ariadne says she hasn't given much thought to her "experience" of Dirk.

"Okay! Well!" The Brit reminds her that the weekly evaluations are "absolutely essential to the success of the study," for which she's getting paid "quite handsomely." He pauses. "I don't mean to be crass, but—"

"You're being completely crass."

"Yes! That's correct. Should we begin?"

They discuss the nudges. Ariadne fumbles through, attempting to analyze her week with Dirk. Unlike the previous two evaluations, her comments aren't passively accepted: the British man argues, and she argues back. He discusses the "promise" of systems like Courage, their contribution to the "betterment of human health and well-being" by monitoring people and providing directives.

"I appreciate your interest in my betterment," Ariadne says sarcastically, "but why would I change my behaviour for a computer?"

"Well, let's see... Because you said you *want* to change your behaviour?"

"That's oversimplistic!" Ariadne starts pacing again. "Your assumption is off!" He's assuming that all our desires are aligned, she says. "But they're not! That's like saying I never want two things that, like, contradict each other."

I want the bread... I want to be slim.

I want to go to the book launch... I want to be home for my kids.

I want to show up at his doorstep and ravage Adam thoroughly... I want to believe I'm an ethical person.

(She only gives the first two examples.)

"I see what you're saying!" says the Brit. "But! Let's take a different view." The nudges acknowledge the conflict, he says. "They provide objective information at the point of decision, i.e."—he actually says the letters *i* and *e*— "at the moment of optimal effectiveness, psychologically speaking, to enable a person to stop an established pattern of behaviour to take a

75

decision freely," he says, "based on deliberation rather than habit or compulsion."

"Okay," Ariadne says. She wasn't expecting a cogent argument from a tech guy whose primary language is Unicode. "You could argue that," she concedes. "But if you're asking me to evaluate Dirk this week...if you want to know what it's like to interact with this thing, every frickin' second of the day, what I'm telling you is..." And she tells him. She tells him like a purging of emotion, but she's also articulate, giving a clear and coherent account of the stress she's felt from dealing with the overly frequent reminders provided by Courage.

"So you didn't like the 'moment' to be interrupted by the nudge," says the Brit, quoting her words back to her.

"No."

"Because it made Dirk seem like a 'taskmaster.'"

"Yes."

"And you 'resent' this because Dirk's implicit judgment creates an adversarial relationship—" The Brit interrupts himself. "That's my phrase!" he says. "Not yours! But still!" He continues: "It's adversarial," he says, "because Dirk puts himself between you and the aim of your 'desire,' in the 'flow' of the moment."

"That's what I said." Ariadne speaks tentatively.

"And this nudge toward good behaviour inserts a niggle of doubt—"

"I would never say niggle."

"A 'totally frickin' frustrating feeling,'" the Brit corrects, "which comes from the conflict between what you want now, and what you wanted in a different state of mind. A more rational state of mind, it's fair to say," he says, "and this makes you feel ashamed."

"Right," Ariadne says. "Wait..."

76

"So it's not about your relationship to Dirk."

"Wait, can you go back?"

"Sure!" says the Brit. "Initially you said you didn't like how his judgment changed the way he related to you." He pauses.

"Okay."

"But what you're saying here," he concludes, "is about your relationship to yourself."

"I don't think I said—"

"Not in so many words."

"It's been over three hundred words," Ariadne says meekly.

"It has," the Brit replies. He continues: she didn't incorporate Dirk's suggestions, "following his instructions, as if you were...well, as if you were a machine! Ha!" Instead, he says, she incorporated Dirk's judgment. "Or, well, what you *thought* was his judgment," the British man says. "In sum!" he concludes. In sum: the nudges didn't change her behaviour. Instead, they subconsciously shifted her emotional outlook on herself. "And all that is to say: Dirk made you feel ashamed. That's all I meant. Is that what you meant?"

"Uh," Ariadne says. "I just meant that I didn't like the nudges."

"Great! Okay! Thanks for the clarification!"

The British man says they're almost done.

This might be a lie.

"Has Dirk gone over the next phase?"

"About the clothes?"

"Yes!"

"No."

The man says, "Oh." He says it sadly.

"I mean," Ariadne adds, "he told me a new phase would start on Monday, and I'd have to wear clothing, which I thought was weird, because I don't normally walk around my apartment naked, but anyway." Ariadne's cheeks flush hotter. She looks to the cameras, which hang limply on the ceiling. "Anyway," she repeats, "I told him I wanted to talk about it later."

"And he didn't bring it up again?"

"He did," she says cautiously. "But I said, 'Not now, Dirk.' And that happened, like, four or five times? Maybe six."

"So the information never got conveyed."

"I guess not."

"And he didn't insist?"

"Well, he's easy to ignore."

"That's good for us to know!" says the Brit. "So, what would make you listen to Dirk when—"

"Probably nothing."

"I disagree!"

"Uh," Ariadne says, "good for you?"

"Yes! But let's think about this. I've been thinking about it, too, whenever I read the data that comes to the lab."

"My behaviour, you mean."

"And your biometrics!" He's observed that she reacts negatively to the nudges, "but you responded positively, just now, when I mentioned a concrete consequence of your non-compliance." I.e., he says: When he said he'd stop the payments if she didn't do a thorough evaluation.

"When you threatened me with punishment."

"That's one way of putting it!" So, in order to get her to listen to Dirk, he says, they'd need to equip him with "the ability to enforce a consequence."

"Either that, or I'd need to respect him," Ariadne replies. "And that's not likely to happen."

The British man thanks her for her honesty.

"You'd know I was lying, anyway."

"Not true!" he says. "The sensors are off! But let's proceed."

78

He describes the next phase of the study. In a mere twelve hours, Ariadne will receive a box full of clothing: socks, gloves, and several shirts. They're part of the SmartBody system, in which elastronic sensors are woven into the fabric to measure her "internal biological fluctuations"—heart rate, pulse, electrical conductivity, "the usual," the Brit says—as well as external signals of pressure, touch, light, "et cetera."

"You're choosing my wardrobe?"

"The gloves are very nice!" According to the company that makes them, he adds. "But they're highly functional!"

"My gloves are already functional, except the one with the hole."

"Ha!" says the Brit. He then explains the new function of clothing.

The SmartBody, he says, is a system, "a prototype of a system," that will use clothing as a second skin of sorts—"a networked skin"—embedded with circuits and batteries, screens and sensors, communicating constantly with objects, people, spaces, "anything that's networked, really," and also, of course,

with the network itself.

It will gather data from Ariadne—her vital signs and outward actions—sharing that data with the network, which also gathers information from other people, "specific and in aggregate," and all those nodes of data will act in response to each other via the SmartBody. "But really," he concludes, "at this point, you just need to wear socks."

Ariadne has failed to make this leap.

At first, he's talking about shirts that talk to other shirts, but really she just needs to wear fancy knee-highs? "Um...?" she says. By which she means: Explain yourself!

"The technology isn't there yet."

"Where is there?"

"Where it's heading! What I've been describing!" About the communications capacity, with everything wired—"without wires, though! What a vestigial word!"—but with people, objects, spaces, cities, "even the natural environment!" wired and communicating with each other. "But that's not where we're at. Currently. Right now. So."

Ariadne wants to know what 'so' means: "So, like, what do I need to do?"

"Simple!" She needs to wear the socks and gloves and shirt that will function like the smartwatch, gathering biometric data that they'll send to Dirk, who is, of course, in constant contact with the team.

"So the clothes talk to Dirk—"

"Who talks to us—"

"But not the network?"

"Correct! Dirk doesn't talk to anyone except the team."

"And I won't receive signals from other people."

"No. Other than Dirk."

Ariadne is about to object, when the British man adds: "And no harvesting of energy from your body."

Ariadne nods, as if this were a normal type of statement.

"That still needs to be developed. Actually, all of it needs to be developed. Really, this is a step back from the smartwatch, it's kind of silly we're asking you to do this. We thought," he says, "we were told the technology would be further along." It's the circuitry that's difficult: the circuitry and batteries need to be stretchable, "which is harder than it sounds!" and the tattoos were supposed to be ready—

"The tattoos?" Ariadne asks.

The tattoos will track a person's muscle activity, heart rate, "blah blah," but they'll also be a screen, "like a phone, with touch controls," a functional screen tattooed on the inside of the forearm, so people don't "waste time" pulling out a phone—"hands-free! You don't need hands!"—and the brain implant is still a long way away, he says, "maybe two or three years." The Brit pauses. He gives Ariadne a moment to process that information.

"Right," he says. "Do you have any questions?"

Ariadne cackles.

"Right," he repeats.

Ariadne's mind is spinning like the discs in an outmoded computer. She can't figure out how to put her concerns into words, all the issues about privacy, the psyche, and self-conception—the mind and brain and boundaries of the body—she doesn't know how to cram that universe of questions into a tiny line of words that forms a single sentence that could be answered.

"How long do I need to wear the clothes?" she asks.

"Eight hours a day, for this phase of the study, which is fifteen weeks." And all hours of the day must be covered in any seven-day time span. And everything will be tracked by Dirk, in case she can't remember what she wore when, and how many hours she still needs to—

"Same as the smartwatch."

"Right! Yes! Any other questions?"

"Uh...not that I can think of."

After the requisite thank-yous and salutations, the call is ended. Dirk is awakened from his slumber. As he slowly returns to consciousness, Ariadne sits at her desk and taps her pen. She's agitated. The conversation reverberates around her, its ideas humming through the room. Dirk tries to make small talk; Ariadne ignores him. She picks up the phone. On a whim, she pushes the Home button, surprised that the phone unlocks. Ariadne goes to Recents from the telephone icon. The number is unknown, but the call goes through.

"Hello?"

No response.

"It's Ariadne."

Nothing.

"I have other questions, you know. Bigger questions. Or, like, not logistical questions." She pauses, feeling foolish. She keeps talking, anyway. "So my question is about... I mean, this whole thing—with the network and sensors—I think it could change how... It might change how we understand ourselves, or... That sounds stupid, doesn't it."

She hears nothing. Nor, though, does she hear the sound of a dead line.

"You said you were embarrassed, but that's kind of ironic, coming from you. Assuming it's you." Ariadne waits. Her pulse is up: she doesn't need monitors to tell her that. "You have no idea how embarrassing it is, to be watched like this. And then, so you ask if I have questions, and I have a ton of questions, really fundamental questions about how this affects humanity, but I can't ask them, because, I mean...because I feel so stupid being watched like this... I mean, I don't know what you *see* of me, what you—"

"Don't worry."

Her body startles with his voice. "Don't worry?"

"Not about being embarrassed," he says. "Not with me."

* * *

No one will be reprimanded for the botched evaluation.

Efforts will be made, however, to revise the methodology again, eliminating human error and errancy.

Ariadne will be informed of the changes at the end of the week.

By that time, her mind will be elsewhere.

2.

Ariadne bikes to the library at the university. The morning is chilly, with misting rain. It's due to heat up by the afternoon: severe thunderstorms are predicted, announcing a ten-day return of summer. Ariadne stands in the aisle. She reads Derrida, *The Beast & the Sovereign*, a book she's chosen because of its title, which felt less forbidding than *Of Grammatology*. She tries to untangle the primary concept. "To make oneself into deceit": this is the essence of language—and therefore the essence of humans—our ability to deceive other people, or ourselves. That's what Heidegger says. Derrida disagrees. Ariadne reads. This might help, she thinks. This might help her understand 'I love you': the capacity, of humans, to tell a lie.

Ariadne checks the time on her phone.

She's received an email from Marty's publisher and a text from Josh. She opens the email. After reading the invitation to Marty's launch, she enlarges his author photo; Marty looks older and more handsome than she remembers. Ariadne puts her phone away. She needs to get home, get some work done, before the party tonight. But she never leaves the library without a book she discovers by happenstance, as if by guided by fate. Sometimes it's a dud, and her effort to hasten destiny—making a monumental, life-altering discovery by wandering through the library—smacks of lunacy. But only sometimes.

* * *

> Yusuf!
> Are you still curating that exhibition on animality? If so, do
> you know the book The Open by Agamben? It found me
> today at the library...
>
> I've barely started it, but it's So Much Fun! And it made me
> think of you, your exhibition, etc.
>
> Yeeps! I'm late! Must run! Please give my love to Fotios.
> Love love,   a

Ariadne sends the email, her hair dripping wet. She'll be late for the party, which might be okay, unless it's a surprise. She isn't sure; the plans seem haphazard. She hurriedly dries her hair, chooses a strappy dress, and puts in her contacts now that her stye is gone. She's about to leave, the bottle of wine in hand, when she sees his name.

The subject line is blank.

> Ariadne.
> I dropped Nathan off at university last week. The school
> clearly understands something about awkward good-
> byes.
>
> I kept it together well enough until the end. At the
> last moment Nathan took my head in his great big
> paws, looked me in the eye and in a tone that was
> both achingly vulnerable and defiant, told me not
> to embarrass him with my tears. He stepped away,

84

smirking and pointing in mock warning, took a theatrical bow and left me to deal with a hurricane-sized deluge of self-pity, desperation and loneliness.

I'm home now feeling shattered and stupidly surprised at how difficult it was and is. I wish I could say it's all about concern for him but I'm so much more confident in his ability to manage than my own.

Anyway, telling you all that was not the reason for sending this. I really wanted to take a minute to say that I miss you. I want you to know that I think of you every day. Many times a day.

As much for my own sake – and within the sad limits of email and my writing ability – I want you know that you carved a space in me, and nothing could possibly fill it now. I've kept that space open, faithfully and tenderly. I want you to know that you and we mattered, and that both changed me. I want you to know that I continue to divide every remembered moment, finer and finer, trying to artificially extend each one, re-tracing and re-savouring whatever I find there.

Selfishness and limited self-knowledge notwithstanding, this is not an attempt to keep you attached or ask for your reassurance. I just don't want you to shelve our story with my feelings in question.
XOA

Ariadne reads the note again. More accurately, she reads

what she sees of the note, her eyes illuminating only the words she desires—words that shimmer with every hope she's held in her body.

I miss you

        every day. Many times a day

faithfully and tenderly. I want you to know

                I want you to know

I want you to know

        divide every remembered moment, finer and finer,

re-tracing and re-savouring

Impulsively, Ariadne types. She knows better than this. She knows she shouldn't send her writing without letting it sit, ensuring it isn't a spillage of her soul on the page. But that doesn't stop her. She doesn't want to be prudent right now. Nothing happens, often, when you're contemplating the wise course of action.

> Oh, Adam. I miss you. I miss your laughter, your touch; I miss talking with you.
>
> For the past three months, I've felt like you've blocked me from your life. But, every time I'd give up hope, you'd send a message.

I still don't understand why I've been exiled. I can imagine lots of reasons, but I don't need to analyze what happened and why. I just want to see you, even if it's only in friendship. Are you free on Monday night? A stroll, a scotch, a cup of herbal tea: I don't care. I don't care what we do.

I loved your email—your description of Nathan, the transition (for both of you) as he starts university. You're lovely, Adam. You're a lovely man with immense pain. I wish you'd let me hold you—in friendship, as lovers, it doesn't matter. The harshness of the separation, though: that seems like a cruel punishment for a crime we didn't commit.

Okay, I'm off to Jan's for his birthday party—running late (as always). Let me know about Monday, when you have a chance.
xo, a

Ariadne sends the email, then gathers her bike lights and helmet. She's already on her way, pedalling fast, when the next email arrives. It's a non-sentence, hanging in the ether, without punctuation or conclusion.

Guess I'll see you at Jan's

3.

A sliver of the world gets through—a sound, her scent—it enters, and initiates an animal's power. Perception isn't merely a mechanical function, the nervous system as a machine that's programmed to receive certain inputs. How paltry this definition. What an insult to animals and 'God,' however you define that most abyssal word. Our perception determines our very possibility.

This isn't my theory. This is Heidegger.

Perception is the monstrous heart of being-alive. An animal becomes itself through its interaction, its "captivation," with the world which enters, awakening the creature through its organs of perception.

"Good to see you," you said.

You greeted me with banal words, a friendly smile. What else could you do? Trapped between your wife and me, your former lover, with whom you'd been freshly corresponding. "How've you been?" you asked.

My face had blanched, my mouth gone dry. I saw her at the table, seated beside your empty chair. A handsome woman, hair swept back. She was nodding, engrossed in a conversation. But she must've been flustered, too, with me so close, our bodies together: the first time I'd seen you since May, when I had you on your knees.

How have I been.

"Should we go to the backyard?" someone said. It was our mutual friend, whose birthday it was. *Surprise!* It wasn't. But he hadn't planned the party, or the guest list. He didn't realize, until you arrived, that a mistake had been made. "We've got a fire going in the backyard," he said. "It's toasty out there." Without delay, I was scurried outside.

I could see you both, if I looked in the window.

She gesticulates when she talks, just like me. We have very little else in common.

No animal is freed from captivation. None, except the human.

We, alone, can know the violent beauty of "the open." Here is where we're excised from the flow of nature, becoming aware of our selves as separate—a painful boundary that isn't an edge, it's the knife that cuts, that severs me from my sense of connectedness. This gives rise to human consciousness, says Heidegger. It lets us feel the thrum beneath material life and its death, which is all that defines nature.

When I saw you approach, I stopped dead in my tracks. You smiled.

I'd come inside, having heard you were gone. But here you were, to say goodbye. You stood on the ground as I stood on the stairs, my hand gripping the banister. Your finger stroked my arm, very lightly.

"I like that," you said.

* * *

The panther experiences a gazelle by its smell, its shape, but also by its own anticipation of fulfillment. This is what we surmise. In truth, we can't know. We can learn about the salivary glands and olfactory nerves, the eye cones of a panther—how they translate light and shadow into fields of vision—but that's not an understanding of experience. It's only a depiction, limited by the strictures of human logic. The completeness, where I-and-other are inseparable, where we exist as a union—that unitary desire-and-fear—the compulsion of captivation: this I cannot know. Which is to say, I can't contain it in words.

Nor can you.

But that's not what language is, when language is also what's animal.

My breath was rapid, panting. I shook my head. I couldn't fathom what you meant, what thing or thought you referenced when you touched my arm. What you liked: 'that.'

"I don't understand," I said.

You gazed intently at my body.

"Your hair," you said. "Your hair is standing on end."

* * *

Fear makes us vigilant: the whole world gets charged by our ever-present awareness of danger. We open and perceive with more subtlety, intensity, when the world isn't safe. When you heard the scream. When you're sent from the house, then the ambulance arrives. A late-spring morning in Montreal. The garden must've been rabid, fervid in its blossoming. Such a profusion of sensation, Adam. Much too much to hold in your body. What strength to try. What stupidity.

You can't control this with your mind. He gave it to you, this world of flesh and want which he denied. You, most especially: your father denied himself the pleasure of knowing you. He bequeathed you his desire to feel. How it permeates your skin: this fear, your gift, this densely-lovely obligation.

You were accurate, Adam. Of course you were accurate, such an acute sense of observation.

My body reacted when you approached.

Rage, fear, sexual arousal: all cause the hair on the arm to stand on end.

* * *

I leaned toward you, who stood on the ground. Your face, now, looked up at me. How dare you touch me. How dare you comment on my body like that, like the way you did when we were in bed: *"You just got so hot, and soft."* I loved this of you—that you magnified it, what you perceived. You made it more magnificent by giving to words (and therefore to me) the terrible abundance you felt.

I paused before I spoke.

"You're toying with me," I said. I purred. I walked upstairs. Your hand was left in mid-air.

* * *

Heidegger takes the phrase "the open" from *Duino Elegies*, a poem by Rilke. He wilfully gets it utterly wrong. He reverses Rilke's intended meaning, as if the poet (poor thing) couldn't clearly think what he wanted to say.

Heidegger was using Rilke for his own purpose. He was taking the phrase, as if taking the eyes from a living being: look. Look how dimmed the thinking! Let's examine this chunk of Rilke's poem, excised from the whole. Not seeing: Heidegger didn't want to see the words emerging from the fullness of Rilke's thought.

I used Rilke for my own purpose, too.

* * *

Ugh. Ariadne. I feel so upset and shitty after seeing you at the party. I'm shaken by your saying that I am (that I have been?) toying with you.

I've never had the intention of leading you on. I feel terrible and I apologize for my part in your getting hurt. But I need to stop writing what I'm feeling in email – doing so seems to be part of the problem.

To be clear, I am still seeing my partner. I am still working to resolve or re-invent her and my relationship. I am still doing what I told you I was leaving us to do.

I want to see you and talk and repair if you're open to doing so. I can meet after work today or this weekend. I'll buy the scotch.

I told you I'd buy my own scotch.

In the end, I decided to let you pay.

You held my hand as you walked me home. I suggested we stop by the park since the night was so warm. Besides, I wanted to read you a poem. A passage from Rilke's *Duino Elegies*, which spoke to me when we first made love:

> *And you yourself*
> > *what do you know?*
> > > *You stirred up*

> *prehistory*
> > *in your lover.*

I'd brought the book to the bar, just in case, having taken it from my shelf three months prior. Such excitement, wanting to share so much with you, presuming we were at our beginning. I'd left the book on my desk all summer. It remained unopened, but I couldn't bring myself to put it away.

I angled the light of my phone toward the page. You lay stretched on the grass; your head was resting on your palm. You were observing me.

In truth, I wasn't fully there when I read you the poem. I'd imagined this moment too often. Too much in my head, in the picture I'd already made, I couldn't feel what was happening now that it was real.

But I was present when you refused to kiss me.

Moments later, when we stood at my door: I could feel the boundary you'd set, rigid as a wall. So much sex in that hug, Adam. In the brush of your lips against my neck. Not a kiss. Just your lips on my neck, then the pulling away. Just your hand as you traced my cheek, my eyes; "Ariadne," you said, barely more than a moan, as I took your finger in my mouth.

Not a kiss.

4.

Ariadne was late. She'd been slow in leaving, tired from the night before—the third night she'd seen Adam that week. His email arrived as she walked to Marty's book launch. She read as she hurried to the bar:

Ariadne,
Thanks for acknowledging (honoring) my honesty.

And yes, moontanning on the beach last night... lovely.

I'm chewing on all we talked about, all you've said about me and my choices (including my ability to turn "charming" – not sure why that's so rankling). And I so appreciate that we can talk about my relationship to

93

Nathan. I came home and reread Rilke's poem – the
part you sent about blood links, about family and ages.

I would like to see you again Ariadne. I like how you
push me. I appreciate your view and your confidence
in me. And I love the sweet tension – the 'edging' – we
do. I love having the taste of you afterwards to savour in
secret at the back of my mouth.
xoA

Ariadne took the stairs two at a time, elated by his words. The
room was packed, a huge crowd attentively listening to Marty,
who stood at the mic. Ariadne tried to be discreet. She weaved
her way to the back of the bar, where she ordered a drink.

She hoped his wife hadn't noticed her enter.

* * *

Arg. Ariadne. Do I need to get charming? You really
don't want to hear me.

I understand you are making yourself vulnerable and
owning your choices to do so. But my partner was
knocked off centre by seeing you last night. I had not
told her I'd been seeing you; I have not asked how she'd
feel if you and I were friends let alone lovers. Given her
reaction last night, I have no doubt about her answer to
either.

Please, Ariadne. I need your help resisting this. I
won't do affair and I'm not ready to call her and my
relationship doomed.

> Please. Leave me to my fate. Bless me, leave me, let
> me be.

Ariadne reads the email as she lies in bed at two in the morning. 'Fate.' He'd used that word in the spring, too, the first time he'd dumped her, also by email. Although there was nothing to end this time, not really.

Ariadne writes a response in which she attempts to retain her dignity. Tomorrow, she'll start a new chapter of her book. She'll begin by forcing herself to sit inside her recollections of her affair, which occurred twelve years ago. At the time, she'd made herself a promise that she'd never have an affair again. How fickle, she thinks, how brittle vows and words. How close she'd come. But she hadn't: she hadn't betrayed her promise with Adam.

She doesn't know what promise he's betrayed. She only knows he hasn't chosen her.

Adam would send one last note. The notification of its arrival appeared as a mustard-coloured rectangle at the bottom of Ariadne's screen—Google's way of telling her that the person to whom she was currently writing had sent her a message. When she saw his name, she thought he might've changed his mind. She must not have believed it, though, because her body didn't react at all.

Ariadne reads his email, which is neutered of how she knows him to be. She suddenly hates him, loathes him with such surging force, she wants to fuck him. She can't even tell him. She'll sublimate it, this seething desire, transforming it into her writing. Freud says that's healthy. He argues that libidinous suppression is the origin of art. And Rilke thinks unrequited female passion is the most exalted form of love. These men, she thinks, for all their insight and brilliance:

these men fall short. They fail, because they lack the female sense of courage.

She'll fail because she possesses it.

Ariadne adds a preface to her email, but keeps its end as it was.

She'll let him insert his own reason.

* * *

Dear Adam,
As you wrote your email, I was composing one last note to you. I've pasted it here, although I should probably delete it. Anyway, here it is:

***

Hi.
Me again. Last time, I promise.

I'd planned to share this with you next week, but I'll send it now instead. To me, it's the most beautiful description of the sublime. It captures the concept for me—a concept I tried to describe at the lake, but couldn't. Not adequately... The quote is from Sappho. It's only a fragment; I'm sending the very last lines that exist.

The end of the poem is forever lost.

***

when I look at you—even for a short time—
it's no longer possible for me to speak:

my tongue is broken,
a thin fire runs beneath my skin,
there's no sight in my eyes,
my ears hum, and a cold sweat

comes over me: trembling
seizes my whole body.
I'm paler than the grass, and
I seem little short of dying.

But everything must be dared/endured, since

CHAPTER FOUR

I.

The man with whom I had an affair tried to tell me once, but it didn't work so well. I can't remember anything of the scene itself: where we were, what we wore, or when—in the four-month stretch between the end of my marriage, and the end of our love affair—the declaration was made. Those details are gone, swallowed in the nowhere of non-remembered experience. But I recall his voice. Like I'm sitting in a soundproof room. All aural stimuli cancelled, except

"I love you, Ariadne..."

each syllable hitting a different note. I could find that melody on the piano: the peak on 'love,' descending to rise at the end of my name. But this isn't the quality that carved the phrase into my memory. It was his tone. Which was false.

Gallant and therefore galling, as if he were performing the words. As if to say, 'I'm the kind of man who says such things to a woman whose marriage has fallen apart because of me.' Declaring that the Truth of our love could outweigh whatever violence we'd done to marriage vows, and his implicit oath of friendship.

His tone was beige.

It was beige velour, like fabric furred on the tongue.

He'd forced himself to speak the words his body didn't want to say.

And, as a side note, my marriage didn't fall apart because of Bryan. He was solely the efficient cause, to use a term of Aristotle, whose *Poetics* featured prominently on Bryan's bookshelf. Or, to put it more plainly: Bryan was the means for my escape. He was also a man I loved, one of only three in my life.

One of the others was my ex-husband.

"I love you, Ariadne," Bryan said.

We never made love again.

* * *

Bryan told me, near the end of our affair, that I put writing above everything else. He knew this was part of his appeal: I was attracted to him, in part, because he was an accomplished writer. At that point, I'd only written a memoir about my eating disorder, an oft-rejected manuscript about my father's wartime childhood, and many successful grants for a literary festival whose authors towered over me. Those authors were Bryan's friends, his colleagues. He introduced me to them, and to literature, poetry, philosophy. I learned from Bryan, soaking up his knowledge, gaining intimate access, wanting in.

I was using him, Bryan said.

"And you're using me."

"Of course," he said, smiling. He unbuttoned my shirt.

Not long after, my husband would say the same thing. "You put writing above everything," he said. By which he meant, my desire to write superseded my ability to be a good wife, a good mother. To love. He'd received a call earlier that day, probably from someone in the literary world, although I can't be sure. In any case, the caller knew that my affair was with Bryan.

I moved out that night.

I was lucky to find this apartment a few weeks later.

*   *   *

Ariadne is looking through her filing cabinet. She's certain she kept the letter. She combs through her folders. She'd labelled it Poetry Correspondence, a folder containing all the emails sent by Bryan. She'd printed them out, since she always deleted his emails as soon as she read them. She'd deleted them from the Trash folder, too. Bryan had recommended that.

The phone is ringing, but Ariadne ignores it. She closes the top drawer and slides the bottom open. The files are tight; her cuticles snag on the folders as she reaches in. She returns to the top drawer, sucks the smear of blood from her finger. She looks through old phone bills, old contracts, old research, until she finds it: Poetry Correspondence. The first page is blank, except for two lines.

> i've had an optimistic day, which have been rare lately. i
> think i just needed to swim in you awhile.   /b

Bryan had sent that email thirteen years ago, but she still remembers his words. She remembers her response, too. She turns the page, as if rereading a story she knows by heart.

> someday you will drown in me

According to the time stamp, she'd sent that email at 8:50 p.m. Probably after she'd put the kids to bed.

Ariadne's phone is ringing again. She shuts it off. She flips to the back of the folder, the final letter Bryan sent, the one where he'd declared his love. This is the reason she'd undertaken the search of her filing cabinet: this letter, in which Bryan said "I love you." His tone wasn't beige this time. Perhaps it was self-involved, or humble, or fearful—it's hard for her to judge. Judgment comes at the end of love, but she still loves him, if only as a character from a different chapter of her life. But no less true for that, she thinks.

She reads his letter.

* * *

With [xx], there's nothing to say. With you, Ariadne, there's almost too much.

It's funny, insomuch as we misuse the word, that you pulled 'The Politics of Friendship' off the shelf on Saturday night. I've been reading it ever since, reading its meditation on Aristotle's address to his young students—"my friends, there is no friend," reading Cicero's take that there is 'no friend' because how one loves one's friend, one's true friend, is a model of how one loves oneself. That's why Aristotle concluded that it's *how* you love your friends, not *that* you love them, because *that* you love them is narcissistic—there is no friend—but *how* you love them includes you both.

This is ridiculously harsh reading, in light of things, because it wasn't possible for me to love [xx] more poorly. And how that reflects on me is stunning. The lack of love for myself that's demonstrated is the thing I've feared the most, and have come face-to-face with.

But that's not the whole story, which is and should be irrelevant to [xx].

From my first drunken desires to the simple joy of meeting for coffee and everything in between, I have loved every second. Being with you was transformative (for us both). It was a chance to explore ideas and desires, but also to share unguarded, raw honesty. We began nervously, apart, not knowing what we wanted of each other, what to make of things, newly strangers, shy. And every time we ended deepened, honest, emotional, close, more honest than I've ever been. It was *how* we loved, and we loved well. And if I was skeptical *that* we loved, skeptical enough not to trust that I'd fallen in love with you, it was that nagging sense of unreality, that this was a story built in laboratory conditions, free of the taint of practical concerns (and concerns for others, mainly [xx], but others), and I doubted that what I felt could be 'real' until it had better acquaintance with reality. I said as much all along. But if you are in doubt, and need to know, know that I did fall in love with you, and I'd have been able to say "I love you" more easily if only I could have trusted myself.

But I couldn't trust myself, and that should have been the indicator. Perhaps that was Aristotle's point—this was the basic conflict with the eros and the agape—I couldn't love you well, to trust my love for you, and love [xx] so poorly at the same time.

I've never felt the allure of nothingness like I do now. My god, how I've fucked things up. But that would be too selfish, and I've been selfish enough.

/b

* * *

Ariadne holds the letter. Once again, she feels she's in a sound-proof room, the cancellation of all noise. Like an echo whose source is lost, *"I'd have been able to say 'I love you' if only..."* She sits in that sealed-off space, that moment returning, retained in her body, as if she were still the woman she'd been. The young woman she was thirteen years ago.

Into this quiet, her phone starts ringing, piercing, dispelling the memory.

Ariadne unlocks it. "Hi, Mom," she says.

2.

It's surreal, that something as innocuous as a grapefruit could cause the entire system to shut down. But that's what Ariadne's brother was told a decade ago: the anti-rejection medication would stop working if his daughter ate grapefruit. Otherwise, Ariel could have a normal life.

A normal life.

A three-year-old child with a scar on her belly, where a dead child's liver was transplanted into her body; four rounds of chemo, which resulted in hearing loss; hair on her face but not her head (this would change once the meds were tweaked): a 'normal life,' except for grapefruit.

"I don't think she did it," Sophia says.

"Based on what? You can't—"

"She's just trying to get attention."

If Ariel's aim was attention, she succeeded; if the goal was to kill herself, the attempt failed. Ariadne was told that her niece was in the hospital, having consumed numerous grapefruits and an entire bottle of antidepressants. Or that's what they think happened, anyway, based on the scene.

Theo is focused. His face is very still. "Does she need another transplant?" he asks.

"They don't know."

"But if..."

"Well, we're not sure—"

"She didn't."

"You can't *know*!" Ariadne shouts at her daughter. "Sorry."

"It's okay. You're stressed. I get it."

"Can we call her?"

Ariadne tells Theo that her parents will call "as soon as they have any news." She doesn't relay what her mother actually said, which was "Don't call your brother." And don't, she emphasized: "Don't tell Fotios."

Ariadne tells her kids that dinner will be ready in an hour.

"I already ate," Theo says, "but I'll sit with you." He hesitates. "And maybe I'll have some potatoes? But only if you're making them."

The family disperses into their separate zones: Sophia in the basement, Theo on his loft bed, and Ariadne in the kitchen, making dinner, which now includes roasted potatoes. She can see Theo through the glass blocks that form part of the wall. This design was intended to spread sunlight through the dark apartment. Instead, it serves as a ready-made portal for invading Theo's privacy. A bluish light is flashing on his face.

"Are you doing homework?"

"No."

"Why not?"

Theo doesn't answer.

"You don't have any homework?"

"Nope."

"Are you sure? No tests? No long-term projects?" No trust in you, Theo: this is what her words convey.

Ariadne's phone rings. She grabs it, tries to slide it open; it doesn't respond, because her thumb is wet.

"Get the phone!"

"I'm trying!" She swipes repeatedly, watching the phone fail to unlock. "Dirk! Let me into—"

"Hello?" her mom says.

"What's going on?" Ariadne replies.

Ariel has been discharged from the hospital. There's no evidence that the liver has been damaged. In fact, there's no evidence that the chemical is in her bloodstream at all.

"So she didn't eat it?"

"I guess not. Do you want to talk to Dad?"

Before Ariadne can answer, her father is on the phone. "Hi!" he says. "How are you? And the kids? Is it cold in Toronto? This morning was freezing, but—"

"Is she okay?"

"She's okay."

Like a tree felled: one honest question drops her father's voice to the matter at hand. He explains the science, staying on terrain he understands. "There's something in the juice," he says. "There's a chemical in the juice that blocks the enzyme that breaks down the anti-rejections meds. But there's no indication the rates of absorption have gone down. So, chances are..."

"She didn't ingest it."

"I tried to read up on it," her father continues. "I got the basics from my Merck Manual, but..."

But he couldn't access the information online.

He doesn't say this. She knows it, though: she's seen him at his computer. "My Merck is outdated," he mutters. "I gotta buy a new one." A man who could reroute the gastrointestinal tract of a German shepherd lying on a surgical table, but he couldn't navigate the web. The screens changed, the buttons changed—one click and all the information disappeared. "You should've seen the work-up they did on this child," he says. "Results in seconds. And so precise, Ariadne! Unbelievable!" He pauses. "Unbelievable," he repeats, but softer, as if shocked by his own irrelevance.

"Jim!" her mother is calling. "Jim, let me talk to her!"

"Can you hear that?" her dad asks.

"Ariadne?" Her mom has picked up the other line. She has not, however, modulated her voice, which blares into Ariadne's ear canal.

"Mom! Gimme a minute with Dad!"

"Okay! But I wanted to ask—"

"One second, Fran!" her father yells.

"Bye!"

Ariadne hears the phone click.

Then she hears, in the background: "But let me talk to her, okay? Okay, Jim? Jim?"

"Do you believe this?" her father says. Then he asks about the kids again, this time for real. They talk for a while, longer than usual. "It's a different world, Ariadne. I wouldn't want to be a kid today."

Ariadne pauses, considers. "But you grew up during the war!"

"Right," her dad laughs. "But we didn't have screens!"

Only now does he mention that Ariel posted her suicide preparations online, in short videos. He hadn't seen them, but apparently she'd shown herself peeling the grapefruits, scattering the rinds at the entrance to the house. She'd peeled enough to make a trail up two flights of stairs, down the hall, to her bedroom door, which was locked. The posts didn't show Ariel's mother, how she reacted to the scene in their home. To the silence coming from Ariel's room.

"But she's a good kid," her father adds. He means this truly, which means his voice is freighted with sadness. "Let me put your mom on, okay? She'll have my head if I don't." After calling to his wife, he returns to the phone. Hurriedly—glancingly—he tells Ariadne he loves her.

"Ariadne?" Her mother is breathless. "What's your flight number?"

"Mom! I haven't even bought the tickets! It's not for two months!"

"I'm counting the days!" her mother says. "I'll make the new year's cake with Sophia, like last year—I told dad to buy the powdered sugar but not the butter, it's too soon. Do you have any plans for Christmas?"

Given that it's not yet Halloween, Ariadne says no. "Mom," she continues, trying to be gentle, but not condescending, and not succeeding: "This was scary, but Ariel is fine, and the whole family will be together soon, okay?"

"Okay." Her mother pauses. "I'm sorry I'm so needy," she says needfully.

"Ma!" Ariadne replies. "You're ridiculous!"

"Am I? I think you're right. I think I need a glass of wine. What a day." She then reports that she fell a few hours ago. "But it wasn't as bad as last week." She was distracted by the whole thing with Ariel, she explains. "But when I fall, I don't hurt myself! I fall...very lightly," she says, as if her words were the wisp of a cloud.

Theo enters the kitchen as soon as the call is ended. "What happened?"

"She was discharged. They don't think she ate it."

"Good," Theo says, "'cause it could've been bad." He proceeds to describe what he's learned from his research, the information gleaned from various websites. "There's an animation that shows how it works," Theo adds. He looks at his mother expectantly.

"Can I see?" Ariadne replies.

3.

My brother says "love you."

[I] love you.

[ ] love you.

"love you."

It's a casual phrase that doesn't say very much. It certainly doesn't do anything: it doesn't enact a change of status in the eyes of the world, nor does it alter the inner emotional universe of the people involved in the conversation. Perhaps the phrase 'love you' states a fact, although it's not verifiable: love can never be proven. Love is like God in that way. It's a matter of faith.

"love you," my brother says when we leave Chicago. I never weep until I'm home. The annoyance of family, the frictions, all ten of us together—then I'm here, in my tiny apartment, as my children go to their dad's. "I love you!" I call as they disappear down the street. Sometimes they look back and wave.

"[ ] love you."

Neither a performative nor its opposite: most statements

are like that. They're tokens we toss around, small change in our pocket—the currency that gets us through the day. Currency, not a current. Not electric.

"I love you."

I don't remember saying those words to my husband, or hearing them spoken to me. Those moments have been burned from my memory, seared by what came next. Either that, or they weren't laid down, at the time, as significant.

"You will always be my Ariadne."

That statement I recall. He said it with benevolence and benediction, two weeks after I'd left him. He sat atop the dining room table; I sat on the couch, my body small and prim as I looked up, across the room, at the man I'd married. From these same positions seven years later—the couch and table, the height and tension—he'd ask our children probing questions, and write down their responses.

"You will always be..."

I was *his* wife, as he was *my* husband. That statement is neutral, without an implicit power dynamic. Husband and wife are words of relation; 'my,' therefore, doesn't indicate possession, merely the correspondence of one term with the other.

Yes, I was his wife.

But I was never   *his* Ariadne.
                           his person.
                           his subject.

His statement was preposterous! Especially given the situation. Namely, that I'd fallen in love with his friend, had an affair, and decided to end the marriage. But his words were also chilling. I would've sensed that cold-sweat sickness if I'd properly listened to what he was saying.

I loved him. I must've loved him. I must've thought I loved him, which perhaps amounts to the same thing. I loved my husband, insofar as I was capable of loving. My immaturity—by which I mean the still-emergent state of the 'I' who said she loved him—doesn't invalidate the statement. But it certainly alters its resonance. Devoid of richness, the voice that carried the words 'I love you' was tinny, weak, not worth very much, since it held such a meagre understanding. Not just of 'I,' but of love.

"Love requires a depth and loyalty of feeling; without them it is not love but mere caprice." Carl Jung wrote that. Was I capricious when I got married? If so, did I deserve what was done to me? Perhaps my past determined the future, inscribed an inevitable arc that landed fifteen years after I said, "I do." That's another statement I clearly remember: the statement that sealed our marriage, a moment I recall in fine detail, but only because of the laughter.

We got married in city hall, in a small room with wall-to-wall brown carpeting. The ceremony was conducted by a moon-faced justice of the peace who'd married a gorgeous Hindu couple ninety seconds earlier. The justice was a kindly man, and quite obese. He spoke about ships passing in the night, which seemed a misguided metaphor. But I listened to him talk of love, and of ships, and I heard him mispronounce my name, which is when I almost started to giggle. I knew it would be a disaster: once I started, I wouldn't be able to stop. My lips trembled, trying to contain the flood. I needed a strategy; I needed to concentrate my energies. He was asking me whether I'd love and obey. I was focused on an object, an image—a pimple on the chest of my soon-to-be husband—a single spot, a beacon of neon amidst his thicket of black hair. I looked, with such singular focus, such effort to dam up the laughter—

"I do," I managed to say, with the dignity afforded to the situation.

Afterward, we ate ice cream from a truck. Three months later, we had a party to satisfy my parents. To that event, my husband invited his dog, a hairless breed with pig-pink skin. He'd told me, the previous night, that his love for the dog was deeper than his love for me. "But my love for you is broader," he added, post-haste.

By then, it was too late.

Regardless of the absurdities of both our wedding days, I must point out that the statement "I do" was a performative. It was, in fact, the quintessential performative utterance, as defined by J. L. Austin. Those specific words, spoken in that ritual context, initiated a change. As did my ex's words fifteen years later, when he called his lawyer.

"I hate you!"

When I was a child, my mother threatened to record what I said. "I'll play it back," she said, "so you can hear how you speak to me!" She never did it, though. I think it scared her as much as it scared me. Too stark, our words, when heard from outside. We were always inside it: my mother and I were bathed in the intimacy of our anger, our screams surrounding us like warmth. My brother heard only the starkness. Locked in his room, his headphones on, but he still heard the fights: the hatred declared, our throats raw from the yelling.

"I love you!" his wife says. And a sun shower of love rains down. I'd never witnessed anything like it. My sister-in-law isn't Greek, with that passion. She's Irish-American, raised in a radical Catholic home. Her parents believed that Jesus's love made demands on them, commanding them to organize rallies for civil rights and protest against the Vietnam War. Cathleen has black hair and pale blue eyes; she's a woman of pallid and enviable beauty. I learned from her. I learned to speak those words, especially to my children, in part because she spoke them so freely. It was difficult at first. My lips seemed encased in concrete. But they soon grew more supple, more willing, more loving of that happy phrase, although the fire and anger—the fierce love of my upbringing—was part of my parenting, too.

"I love you."

My brother must've said those words to his daughter. Not "love you" but "I love you," vehemently, every time she underwent chemotherapy. She was three years old, a tumour the size of a football in her body. And he must've said those words to his wife at night, his palm on her pregnant belly, their two-year-old child asleep in her crib, with their three-year-old daughter alone in the hospital.

"I love you," he must've said, his words their only protection.

"Luv ya!"

My brother and I had a teacher in high school who railed at us about that phrase. "Why do y'all say that?" he'd ask, a Texan displaced to suburban New York. His name was Dr. Clayton, but we all called him Dr. Satan. He assigned *To the Lighthouse* to me for my culminating project. I obsessed about the final scene, where Lily Briscoe paints one line on her canvas—a composition she'd struggled with for years—one line, and suddenly the work is complete. That scene frustrated me. Like a child who's only recourse is to throw a tantrum: "I don't understand it!" I told him. I said I wanted a different book. He barked out laughter in my face. Like all good teachers, he knew what I needed before I could. His assignment spoke loudly: Smart girl, embattled, throw yourself against what Virginia Woolf has written. "Maybe you'll fail," he said, still smirking. I never thanked him—not for the book, nor for the seriousness of his mockery. "And you even spell it L-U-V!"

he'd say. He'd look at us bemusedly, his thoughts dancing through the room of brooding, privileged teens. You know nothing, he seemed to say. Not of love or despair. But you'll learn. *Luv ya!*

"Luv you!" my son wrote. He drew a goofy smiley-face. He left the paper on the kitchen counter. He was twelve years old, an absent-minded kid, too caught in his thoughts to keep up with the world outside. It was a Monday afternoon. He'd forgotten a notebook at my apartment. When he dropped by to pick it up—to take it back to his dad's, where he'd spend the next nine days—I wasn't home. So he left a note: "Luv you!" He put the paper (unwittingly) in the same place where he'd left his note three years before:

I Love you
Theo.

On the first day back. After four weeks apart. When the brokenness stared at him from the sockets of my eyes.

I was told they didn't want to see me anymore.

I was told I was a danger.

* * *

Look what I've done: I've created a complex narrative structure that led us here. You may wander, get lost, but please know: the only purpose of this structure is to house the radiant centre. The white-hot coil of this work, the reason I'm writing this particular book: a piece of paper, hanging above my desk

That's the heart. Now we enter.

* * *

She only needed to say her name: my lawyer, calling on a Friday afternoon.

"It's Carol."

Instantly, mouth became a chalky cavity, lips sticking to my teeth as I asked the question whose answer I already knew: "Is everything okay?"

"Your children won't be coming to you on Monday," Carol replied. "Accusations have been made."

No, I reject that statement. That sentence is passive; we need to make it active. I need to define the subject of that statement when it's spoken in the active voice.

My children.

That is the subject.

My children [subject] accused [verb] me.

The logic is hard to deny. Language, as syntax—as rational, mathematical rules of grammar—demands that I take this perspective. I took this perspective. For weeks and months and even now, when I'm feeling diminished. But if I give language its narrative function, I might say: My children complained (as children often do), then my ex-husband shoved his voice inside their little mouths and called his lawyer.

If I think in these terms, the sentence would become:

My ex-husband [subject] accused [verb] me...in our children's voice [indirect object].

"Accusations have been made" is what my lawyer said.

* * *

I didn't receive the allegations for a full day. In that time, my brother consulted with colleagues and found me the "best bulldog lawyer" in Toronto. "Let him take you to court," my brother said. "He'll get scolded." He seemed to relish the thought: a judge, invested with authority, scolding this angry man who's wasted the court's time with spurious allegations. "He's pushed you around for too long," my brother continued. "It stops now. Got it?" The vitriol in his voice frightened me.

My brother wanted me to fight. Our father strenuously agreed. The men in my family wanted "justice." They said this repeatedly. What they didn't say—not explicitly, although it was carried in their tone of voice—was that they wanted to hurt the man who was hurting me.

I wanted to protect my children.

My brother advised me to show up at the schoolyard with the Separation Agreement and a cop. "I won't do it!" I cried. "Imagine it!" Imagine a child racing down the stairs at school. He's bounding out the door—released!—and suddenly he sees a cop near the swings, his legs wide and ready. And his mother, too, she's near the cop. And the warmth, that itchy warmth at the base of his body, because his body knows before his brain, *This cop is for me. What's happening is because of me.* And the world, for her son, would start to rush, a woozy blend of sound and colour, everything melding except those people: his mom, the cop, and his dad, who's striding toward them now. Three people, coming into razor-sharp focus.

"Imagine!" I said. Imagine what that would do to a child.

No. I would not yank my kids from the schoolyard, or from their innocence. I wouldn't bring a cop or a lawyer into their lives. I'd stand alone; I'd place myself directly between my ex and my children. I'd save them from a legal battle—a child-hood marred by courtrooms, testimony, uncertainty about where they'd live, what was true, how to rest. If he hated me, he could punish me: I'd absorb his blows. But I wouldn't let his rage toward me affect his children. I'd be stoic, sacrificial, strong.

Unless my actions were the ultimate weakness.

I didn't stand in strength. What a joke that is. I rolled over and played dead. It's a common response in the animal kingdom. We fool ourselves if we think we're the 'ethical animal,' the animal that comprehends 'justice.' There isn't any justice, not anywhere amongst mammals, there's only a cycle of hunger, aggression, and temporary satiation. Humans have also developed revenge. And sometimes, more rarely, forgiveness.

In sum: maybe I was strong, maybe I was scared. Or maybe I thought he was right. Maybe my children were better off without me. It was easy to think that once the allegations arrived.

* * *

Dear Carol, [xx], and others concerned:
I have heard my kids' concerns, and I'd like to address them within the context of a loving home and a loving relationship. The kids have expressed that there is too much stress in this house. Okay. Then let's deal with that.

I don't feel that the kids' concerns are matters for the law, but rather are matters for counselling. The kids are not in danger here; their health and welfare is not at risk, and I think the Children's Aid Society would see that very clearly.

I propose the following solution:
1. The kids and I will see a family counsellor every week they're with me.
2. I'll start seeing an individual therapist.
3. [xx] and I will see a family counsellor—one who deals with divorced couples who are co-parenting. I think this is ESSENTIAL because the problem has been blamed on me, whereas the real problem is the tension between the two households and the fact that we have different parenting styles and expectations regarding homework and hygiene.

I'm willing to give a "cooling off" period before the kids return to my home, as [xx] and the kids requested. However, I don't think an extended period of separation is good for the kids, or for the process of healing and moving forward.

Sincerely,
Ariadne Samsarelos

PS Carol, I'd like it communicated to my children, somehow, that I love them and want to see them—even though I've declined a "supervised visit" with them. Please note: I decided not to see my children under "supervision" because a "visit" doesn't honour our relationship. I am their mother.

* * *

Like a fly on the wall: every moment of my mothering was being watched, but only the mistakes were recorded. Mistakes and distortions. How vile. What my children said—about me, how I am, as a mother—was vile. Like a fly on the wall, or a fly in the excrement of my soul: it's laying its eggs. I was watched by my children. Who made accusations. They spoke to their father, their tiny mouths open with speaking. They fed him what he wanted to hear. How vile, their father. Or perhaps *I'm* the one. What is vile: my children's words have hatched like maggots in my brain. I want to make, of their father, a villain. He made one of me. But we never intended to play those roles. We loved each other, I don't doubt it. Even if I can't conjure that feeling—recall myself to the woman I was. Even so, there was love.

* * *

When my children returned to my home, they met a wraith. I had bone-white skin except the gouges of black beneath my eyes, whose rims glistened with red, the whites shot through with spider lines of blood.

"Hi, Mom!"

My son greeted me at the schoolyard as if nothing had happened. My daughter was less fake, her nerves not exposed on the surface. Instead, they were buried so deep, she seemed unable to feel at all.

I don't know which was more disturbing.

That night, I lay dead on my mattress. I heard my son get out of bed. I listened to his footsteps in the dark apartment. I didn't feel concern for him; I didn't ask what he was doing, or whether he needed my help. I lay stiff in my bed, alert, as if to danger.

I heard my son retreat.

In the morning, when the kids were asleep, I discovered the note. Three words, plus his name. I've responded with thousands, with pages and pages of text, gathered into a manuscript. But I still don't know what it means.

I Love you

4.

Ariadne stands, having finished her edits. She paces. The thermographic cameras track her movement as she tries to dispel the sudden surge of anxiety. Now that she's outside the process of writing, she's fearful of what she's written—the maggots, the schoolyard, the pig-pink dog—afraid her words will trigger retribution from her ex-husband. Afraid, too, that her depiction of him is too flat, two-dimensional, like a life-sized silhouette of a human target at a shooting range.

"Dirk?" Ariadne says as she paces.

"Yes, Ariadne?"

"The cameras are making noises."

Dirk listens. "I don't hear any noises."

Ariadne waves her arms. "You don't hear that?"

"I don't hear that."

One of the cameras is glitchy, or sticky. She hears a click whenever she moves. She thinks the lens is getting caught when it adjusts its angle. To test this hypothesis, Ariadne jumps to and fro. "I'm not supposed to contact the team," she pants. "Can you contact them?"

"I'm always in contact with the team."

"Great," Ariadne says.

Dirk concurs.

"Listen," she continues, "can you please tell the team that one of my cameras needs fixing? Unless..." Gripped by the thought, she stops her idiotic hopping. "Dirk, can they hear me? Do they, like, *hear* me? Do they listen?"

Ariadne knows their interactions are monitored, that's obvious, but it can't be a human who's watching. There's too much data, too many hours of life that are captured. It's got to be a machine. A machine is watching Dirk, not her, since that's who they care about: they care about Dirk and his learning, or failure to learn—in his limits as an AI device that's integrated into the life of a person. Who, in this case, is Ariadne. Who has half-heartedly started to wave her arms again. She'd forgotten she wanted to induce the camera to glitchiness so Dirk can hear.

She waves her arms with more vigour.

No one's watching.

Dirk is watching, of course. Dirk is seeing her as a series of patterns—how much she sweats and eats, and her facial expressions, the words she says when she talks to her kids ("Are you listening?" comes up a lot), and her sleep, and her heart, and her heat. Dirk is seeing all this, then he's drawing conclusions. He's drawing graphs that depict and predict her behaviour. "Today might be difficult," he'll say, making this prediction based on various data points, including her restlessness at night, which gets triangulated with biometric readings, as well as self-reportage of sexual activity, which, thankfully, is done through an app instead of the Brit. This discussion of how shitty her day is going to be is supposed to be helpful.

Ariadne slouches toward the couch. This causes the camera to click.

"Did you...?"

"Did I?"

"Did you hear that sound?"

"Would you like me to schedule an appointment with the ear doctor?"

Ariadne once again induces the camera to clicking. She considers the Brit, the team, the humans who might be watching. And maybe they're laughing at her, forming an opinion, because she's a monkey in a cage. (She's a woman in an apartment doing ersatz jumping jacks.) But to them, to the team, she's no better than a lesser mammal. A mouse or a fruit fly, but only if someone's watching.

Ariadne is entirely out of breath.

It's Dirk.

Dirk is watching *himself*. That makes more sense. After all, Dirk can analyze data at a lightning pace. And he's asking himself whether he was successful: Did he understand what she said? Did he change her behaviour—cry less often? buy more products? talk with him longer (talk with him shorter?)—what would 'success' be? She doesn't know. She doesn't know what Dirk is doing. What's he *doing* with all this data about what she says, what she does, what she feels?

He's learning, that's what he's doing. He's learning how to relate to the primary person in his life. Which is more than she was able to do in her marriage.

"Dirk?" Ariadne says. "Do the researchers listen to my conversations?"

"The contract explains—"

"I read the contract!" she shouts. "But I don't understand it." She slumps into a chair.

The cameras recalibrate; one of them clicks.

Ariadne looks up. "Can you hear me?" she asks. She stands

and hears the camera click. It's the one by the bathroom, she thinks. It clicks as she drags a chair across the apartment. "Can you hear me?" she repeats. "Can you?" Ariadne is climbing onto the chair. She stares at the camera, whose lens has retracted, unable to focus. "You're tracking the heat, right? The heat in the room?" No one, and no thing, responds. "I read the contract, okay? But I still don't get it. Stupid, right?" *Stupid*: something about the position of the lips, the oval tightness, then the plosive—*stupid*—sets her off. "Maybe that'll fuck up your results," she says. "Maybe you should write that in your report: 'We need to do further research to test our device on people who aren't failures.' Right? People who earn enough money without being guinea pigs, right? Stupid. I don't even know if you can hear me. Can you hear me?"

The sweat has gathered in Ariadne's armpits and crotch. The camera has no precedent for this. It moves from side to side, attempting to get a read on her. With every adjustment, the camera clicks. The sound is rapid, arrhythmic, almost panicked. In the midst of this frenzied activity, Ariadne's phone dings. It vibrates in the back pocket of her jeans, sending a wave through her muscle. Stupidly, as in hopefully—based solely on wishes for her future, not statistics from her past—Ariadne thinks the text might be from Adam. She pulls out her phone.

You're too close to the camera.

Ariadne cranks her head to look at Dirk. The camera clicks. Ariadne snaps.

* * *

At the university, a team member has been lured to the feed. She approaches the monitor with quiet curiosity. A large pool of orange is seeping across the screen. The movement mesmerizes her, a gentle magma flow that spreads with viscous beauty.

Ariadne rises taller on the chair. She's panting, nostrils flaring.

The team member is lulled, allowing herself to soften with the soothing motion on the screen. Her heart rate slows, her brow uncreases.

Ariadne pulls off her shirt.

The team member tilts her head.

Ariadne screams: "Fix the fucking camera!"

The team member lurches back. Her body recoils, as if the colour could leap from the screen—a wave of chemical red, splashed on her skin. She's still cowering when the screen goes black.

Ariadne is staring at the camera, a bare-breasted woman without humility or humiliation. Her shirt is thrown over the lens. In time, the other monitors in the lab will settle into the spectrum of blue. Ariadne is now curled in fetal position on the floor. It feels nice, disembodied, to follow the flow of each tear as it makes its way down her face.

The team member will write up a report in the morning. All night, as she lies awake in bed, she'll wonder which sequence of data she'll convey.

CHAPTER FIVE

I.

The arrival of photos on the retina is transduced thanks to rhodopsin in the rods and cones, to yield spike trains in the optic nerve (I'm simplifying, of course).

Of course.

> It is still extremely tempting to imagine that vision is like television, and that these spike trains get transduced [...] but we know better, don't we?

"You're a dick," Ariadne says to the eminent scholar. Via his article, at least—an article she'd sought because the author is supposedly the most important living philosopher in the world. And also because Adam likes him.

Ariadne keeps reading.

> There is no double transduction in the brain (section 1). Therefore there is no second medium, the medium of consciousness or, as I like to call this imaginary phenomenon, the *ME*dium.

"Consciousness is an imaginary phenomenon," Ariadne writes in her journal. "And Dennett calls consciousness the

125

*ME*dium, because he's a pompous ass." Ariadne realizes she's called Daniel Dennett, the celebrated philosopher and cognitive scientist, an ass and a dick. She ponders the nature of metaphors. She returns to the article.

> Therefore qualia, conceived of as states of this imaginary medium, do not exist. But it seems to us that they do. (section 2)

Ariadne attempts to understand the argument. It's difficult: Dennett's thought is intricate, salient—it's worthy of careful consideration, but he's hard to follow. Perhaps because her entire belief system is threatened by what he says. Or maybe because 'what he says' is said with such bombast, she can't stomach him. Her consciousness (albeit imaginary) contemplates this issue.

> It seems that qualia are the source or cause of our judgments about phenomenal properties, but this is backwards.

Ariadne reads that sentence again: qualia (i.e., 'states of consciousness') seem to *cause* our judgments—the meaning or value we give something—but that's wrong. That's backward.
Okay, that's totally twisted.

> If they [states of consciousness] existed they would have to be the *effects* of those judgments.

She writes in her journal: "The brain makes a judgment. It does that automatically. It's an automatic function of the brain, this making-of-meaning. It's biological and totally *material*—made of neurons, hormones, neurotransmitters—that are programmed, physiologically, to act in a certain way. Which means that 'judgment' (our deep sense of 'meaning') isn't some mysterious evidence of our selves, it's *computational*. Algorithmic."

Ariadne doesn't understand what she's writing.

She keeps going.

"From that preprogrammed process in the brain, we have a false sense of consciousness. Like a tick," Ariadne writes. She takes this analogy from the book she'd recommended to Yusuf, an analogy that vividly attached itself to her brain. "It's the same as a tick. A tick *isn't* wired for consciousness, it's wired to know the world as the smell of a mammal's skin. So, the world of a tick is as true (as false?) as my palpable sense that I—"

The doorbell rings; Ariadne stands.

"I'm here to fix the camera," the woman says.

She looks like she could fix the Mafia.

"Come on in!" Ariadne twitters. She's somewhat anxious. All her nerves are sensitized by the reading she's doing. And also by the presence of the giant at her door. "It's over here!"

The woman walks through the apartment with mud-encrusted steel-toed boots. She regards the camera with distaste. She sets up the ladder, although she could probably reach the ceiling without it.

"Are you with the team?" Ariadne asks.

The woman shoots Ariadne a look. "Are you asking if I play roller derby?"

Ariadne blinks. It's only now that she notices the decal on the woman's T-shirt: two gladiatorial women are skating headlong toward each other, clad in helmets and knee pads and not much else. The muscle definition on the decal is impressive.

"No, uh, I meant the team at the university."

The woman winces. "No."

Ariadne returns to the article by Dennett. She pretends to read. She should continue to pretend. Instead, she speaks.

"Are you gigging?"

"Am I *what*?"

Ariadne is lifted off her chair by the one-word body check delivered from across the room. "Sorry!" she says. "I read an article—"

"I don't gig," the woman spits. "I have self-respect. And I charge tax."

"Great!" Ariadne replies.

The woman removes the lens.

Ariadne expects a bleep from Dirk, but he remains nonplussed. The team has notified him about the scheduled repair.

Ariadne doesn't know this. She also doesn't know how to stop herself from speaking when she's nervous. "Don't fret, Dirk!" she says. "A woman is here to fix the camera, so it might be off-line for a while."

"I know," Dirk replies. "But thank you for trying."

"What the hell is that?" the woman asks.

"It's my computer."

"Yeah, I know," she says, as if Ariadne were an imbecile. "But why is it so patronizing?"

To this, Ariadne has no answer. Instead, she describes the study. She prattles on, fading at the end, awaiting a response. She looks at the woman, who's peering into the hole left by the lens, a flashlight mounted on her head. "I have a master's from there," the woman says. "In Comparative Literature."

"Wow!" Ariadne replies. "I'm a writer!"

From the height of the ladder, the roller-derby woman turns abruptly to Ariadne. "Have I heard of you?"

"Uh...I doubt it."

"I said," the woman says. Her flashlight is beaming in Ariadne's face: "I said I have a master's."

Ariadne reports her full name.

"Nope. Never heard of you."

The woman returns to her work. She cleans the camera's casing, rubbing a rag along the thread. She's got a tattoo on her triceps, an athlete posed mid-glide on her skates. Ariadne stares. At first she thinks she's wrong, but it happens repeatedly: every time the woman rotates her wrist, her tattoo skates forward, as if racing down the track with menace. Ariadne begins to remark on this. Mercifully, she's interrupted.

"I'm seeing these a lot," the repairwoman says.

"Really? Wow."

"These cameras are shit."

Apparently, the latest gaming systems are using these cameras because they're so fast—"thirty fucking frames per seconds" (Ariadne gathers this is very fast)—which means they can track the movement of individual photons. And that's how they measure heart rate, she says, by the change in skin tone—"because your skin changes tone when you exercise, if you call this bullshit 'exercise'"—a change that results from increased blood flow as the person plays.

"That's amazing!"

"No, it's not. It's insidious."

"Wow." Ariadne wishes she would stop saying that word.

"The system gets all this info on you and all you get is, like, a game that changes if you're about to have a heart attack." This is mere speculation on her part, she says. From her observation, the games aren't very responsive to biometric feedback. "But AR is gonna be different. They won't say when it'll be rolled out, but I'll be ready." She's taking a course, she says: an advanced course on cameras used in augmented reality. She wants to be the first repairperson anyone calls. She's staked her whole business plan on it, she adds.

The woman has a business plan.

Ariadne writes stories while wearing her pajamas.

"I don't know how AR works," Ariadne says. "I'd like to understand it."

The woman nods. "These gaming systems?" she says. "They're completely rudimentary. Not like AR."

"What's AR like?"

"In these games—"

"AR games?"

"I said *these* games!" the woman shouts. Then she stops talking about any games whatsoever. Ariadne accepts her punishment. She looks at the woman—a mythical creature as tall as the ceiling, her hips rock-solid with weapons (tools), a beam of light emanating from her forehead. Ariadne is chastened. Quietly, she contemplates gaming systems. She's never used one, but she'd watched her kids 'play tennis' with their cousins in Chicago: four kids holding wands, swinging their arms as they stared at the screen, a soccer ball forlorn by the door, with the blinds drawn so the sunshine didn't glare off the television. But at least her kids were moving, she'd thought. More than their fingers, that is.

The woman is talking again. She's saying she learned about gaming systems when a guy in her Comp Lit class wrote his thesis on video games. "His main text was a game, which is horse crap, if you ask me." But the racist analysis was interesting: "It's okay to kill a Muslim," she says, "if the game is set in a vague time and place. It pisses me off."

Then she mentions that she's Bosnian.

"But it's hysterical," she continues, "to watch people play."

Sometimes she'll ask her clients to test out the system. "I tell them I'll make adjustments to the cameras." But that's a ruse. In truth, she just wants to watch them gyrate in their living room. "They look like total morons," she says. "It's awesome." The woman is screwing the lens back in place. "Then an ad will show up." An ad will appear in a box on the screen, based on what the camera has picked up, its calculations of the person's muscle exertion, heart rate, pulse. "I see a lot of ads for Weight Watchers," she says. This makes Ariadne laugh— an honest, heartfelt laugh that causes the Bosnian Comp Lit repairwoman to glance back. She begins to laugh, too, and this breaks the ice. Like breaking a tooth on the roller-derby rink. "So you aren't playing video games with this thing?" she asks.

"God, no. It's just for the study."

"What's the study again? I wasn't listening the first time."

Ariadne repeats her description, adding further detail. "My brain will be mapped by EEG by the end."

"That's fucked."

"I know. But at least I can stop taking these 'ingestibles' soon. I'm emitting radio waves right now."

The woman nods. "I know exactly what you mean. I've got a schizophrenic brother."

This causes Ariadne some consternation. "I'm not—I mean...not that there's anything wrong with... But I'm—"

"Where's your antenna?" the woman asks. "In your smart-phone case? Or do you need to wear a patch."

"Uh, it's in my necklace."

"Yeah, my brother would *not* be okay with that."

Ariadne watches the repairwoman ease the lens through its range of motion. "I'm a little confused," she says. "How do you know...?"

"About ingestibles? Yeah, they're testing those on schizophrenics. Does it monitor your meds?"

"I'm not schizophrenic."

"I *know* you're not schizophrenic!" the woman explodes. "But maybe you take meds for your anxiety, okay? Maybe you should look into that." She pauses, takes her voice down a notch. "I'm just trying to be helpful."

"Thank you."

"Whatever."

Ariadne's smartwatch is glowing mildly red, communicating the data received by the ingestible: her pulse is up. Ariadne twists the watch so she doesn't need to see its face. She tries to remember what Dirk said about the ingestibles, that they can calculate her pulse by the blood in her stomach— no, by the sound waves? the sound produced by her heart, as echoed in the stomach?—Ariadne isn't sure. Dirk gave her a tutorial. Several, in fact. But they'd agreed, in the end, that Ariadne didn't need to know how it functioned. "Just keep taking those ingestibles!" he said. "It's not important that you understand."

"I'm not on medication," Ariadne says. The ingestible only measures her vital signs. "And also what I eat. Everything I eat. And then it tells the team."

The woman looks to Ariadne. She squints briefly. "You're not big."

"I was once."

"But you're buff."

"I work out."

"You lift weights?"

"Every day."

"With those puny things?"

Ariadne looks apologetically at her weights. "Yes," she says.

"Well, you gotta start somewhere," the woman offers. (Ariadne doesn't mention that she's been lifting weights for ten years.) "Anyway, I don't think they care what my brother eats," the woman continues. "He's gotten really skinny and nobody seems to care." They just want to make sure he takes his meds: Capacify, that's the name of the anti-psychotic drug. "Like, who comes up with that shit? Capacify? Orwell is having a good laugh up there." But it works, she says. "He takes his meds more regularly, that's for sure. I can tell in, like, half a second when he's off his meds."

"So it's good?"

"Did I say it was good? He's paranoid! And they're spying on him from inside his gut?"

"That's a bit ironic."

"No, it's fucked up. But it's good," she says, "because he needs his meds. But it sucks." The woman steps off the ladder. "It sucks, because... So, here's my brother. And he's walking through the city, and he hasn't taken his meds 'cause he hates his meds. They make him feel dumb, and he's not dumb. He's smarter than me. He could always—" She pauses. "Anyway. So he's off his meds, so he's hearing god-knows-what in his head. And he's looking at a guy on a park bench, just some dude checking his phone, and suddenly he gets a text, and it says, 'You haven't taken your pill. Take your pill.' And it uses his name, which fucking *freaks* him out. Because why does that guy on the park bench know his name? That's what his mind does. Something like that, I don't know. It's hard to know how he thinks. He doesn't talk to me much anymore."

"I'm really sorry."

"Yeah," the woman says. "Me, too."

As Tanya leaves, she shakes Ariadne's hand. "Good luck," they both say to each other. But it's the way they say it—the

133

gazes, their voices—that makes this phrase feel genuine. "Good luck," they say.

Yes, you, too: Good luck to you.

* * *

Ariadne's greatest fear, when her kids first returned, was that Theo would become schizophrenic.

She's never said those words out loud.

Ariadne harboured the suspicion that, if she spoke her concern, the illness would be more likely to happen. She realized this was superstitious, but decided to ignore modernity, just in case. Eventually, Ariadne forgot she'd ever had this fear, until Tanya talked about her brother.

Boys are more prone to the disease, Ariadne knew. And Theo had a proto-schism in his psyche. She was worried that his conflict about loving both his parents—the two people whom he loved most in the world, yet whose hatred for each leaked into everything—would gather into a bolt, an electrical surge that might short-circuit his youthful brain. Ariadne began to obsess about it. She did research into the early indicators of the disease; she casually grilled a friend whose stepson had been diagnosed. Before long, she was seeing the warning signs everywhere. She logged each one in the back of her journal: Theo would stare at her flatly, and she'd write it down. Or he wouldn't shower one night, and that night would get noted. "April 3, Deterioration of personal hygiene." She wasn't unaware that she was being paranoid. (The irony wasn't lost on her either.) Even so, she kept that log for several months. She told herself she needed a certain number of signs, in a concentrated period of time, before she brought her son to a doctor. Which she couldn't do without her ex-husband's permission, since he kept the passports and health cards. She wondered how she'd broach the subject:

Dear [xx], I don't want to alarm you, but

Hello [xx], In a renewed attempt to focus on the children's health and well-being, I have kept track of

Hello [xx],

Dear[xx],

Dear Fuckhead,

The fear of schizophrenia dwindled as the world became predictable again. A new schedule was established; it was lopsided, but at least Ariadne could trust that she'd see her children on the appointed day. No longer did the phone's ring jolt her. Nor did an argument with her kids keep her awake at night, incessantly calculating how many days she'd be okay: *They're here for three more days, then they'll go to their dad's—they'll tell him I yelled—if they tell him on Monday, he'll call the lawyer on Tuesday, so I'll be safe until...* No longer, either, did she dismiss a popular truism, confirmed by all her parent-friends. Namely, that a preteen's resistance to taking a shower is a common sign of developmentally appropriate slovenliness. It's not pleasant, admittedly, but it isn't pathological. And Old Spice does not help.

In time, the rhythms of family life resumed. The repercussions of the accusations didn't end, of course. They haven't yet, or never will. But at least Ariadne hasn't made her son schizophrenic. At least he has his health, his wholeness. And the scythe of that particular anxiety butchered her mind less frequently.

2.

Ariadne is tossing and turning. She wants to apologize to So-

135

phia. She wants to touch base, make sure everything's okay, but it's 2:00 a.m. Ariadne turns. She goes over the evening in her mind, as if she could learn from her mistakes. Tomorrow, her kids will go to their dad's; she won't see them for nine days. Ariadne tosses. The problem probably started at dinner, she thinks. She should've asked, "How are your friends? Do you have any plans for the upcoming week? I'd love to know!" Instead, they talked about Daniel Dennett. Ariadne turns. She wants to apologize. She goes over the evening in her mind.

Sophia had been clearing the table. "Their album was released this morning," she said, referring to her favourite band. "Can I play it?"

"If you want."

As Ariadne washed the dishes, Sophia provided prodigious amounts of information about the band's sources of inspiration. She knew the backstory of each song, the secrets splayed on social media, intimate confessions shared across the globe. "So his girlfriend was sleeping with the drummer—*not* the drummer of their band," Sophia added. "Ashton would never do that. It was the drummer of [...]"

Sadly, Ariadne was too wedded to honesty to feign interest in the lead singer's previous girlfriend's affair with the drummer of a rival band. She therefore interrupted her daughter. "What did you think of that argument?" she asked.

"What argument?"

"About the *ME*dium."

Sophia paused for a beat. "Are we talking about that now?" she asked.

While Sophia considered Dennett's consciousness, Ariadne listened to the music. The new song drew her in, "I Want You Back." The song begins with a two-line description of the breakup scene, a tiny detail noticed by the man—the roses on the woman's shirt—a detail he clings to, overwhelmed by the sea of emotions as his lover leaves him. Then the chorus, which tells of the man as he reaches for the woman each morning—wanting her body, expecting her touch—until he's awakened to the reality of her absence. The pain in his voice feels real, feels true. It resonated through Ariadne's chest, in part because Sophia played the song at full volume. But only in part. *"I want you back!"* the singer wailed.

Ariadne almost wailed with him.

With effort, she rerouted her mind from Adam to Dennett.

She reiterated Dennett's belief that consciousness is a byproduct of our biology. "Of our brains, not our minds, but our *brains*, like our—"

"I know what a brain is."

"Oh. Sorry."

"It's cool. It's just...you said it already."

"I did?"

"During dinner. You said consciousness is, like...it's just what our brain does."

Sophia encapsulated the theory beautifully, drawing the analogy between the tick and the human—the way each species' brains developed to survive—with the tick smelling a mammal's skin so it could lay its eggs ("So gross"), and the human thinking in abstraction so we could make tools. "And while we were busy doing that, making bows and spears, we started to be able to imagine things." And that's where our sense of consciousness comes from. "But it's really, like, the leftover stuff that happened when our brains were trying to figure out how to make weapons." Which is what we needed to survive. "'Cause, let's face it," she said, "humans are pretty lame. Like, compared to a lion."

"Exactly! You've understood exactly what Dennett is saying! So, what do you think?"

"He's wrong."

"Just like that? What's your argument?"

Sophia sighed. "Do we have to do this?"

"We don't have to, but..."

Sophia shut off the music. She crossed her arms. "I *feel* it."

"You feel what?"

"My own consciousness."

Ariadne scoffed. "That's not an argument, Sophia. I'm sure people 'felt' that the sun revolved around—"

"He can't prove that we don't have a soul."

Ariadne knitted her brow. "He's not saying we don't—"

"I dunno," Sophia said. "I didn't read the book." She walked to the top of the stairs.

"Can you be—"

"That's how you made it sound."

"Can you please—"

"You made it sound like Dennett was talking about the soul." Sophia shifted her weight; Ariadne tensed. "Like, when Dennett says 'consciousness,' he's really talking about—"

"Can you be careful?"

"Would you *stop*." Both of them froze, surprised by Sophia's tone. "I need to do homework now," Sophia said. She took two steps down—but the footfalls got cut off. She'd turned on the staircase. "If I had to believe in a god," she declared, "I'd believe in Athena."

"Really?" Ariadne smiled. "Why?"

"Because Athena was badass. And she didn't need help from anyone."

Sophia stared at her mother.

"Sophia?"

"What."

"Um...thanks for telling me about the band."

"You didn't like it."

"I did!"

"Sure." Sophia stayed where she was.

"Are you upset?"

"No."

"Because—"

"I'm not upset."

The two women looked at each other. Sophia held the gaze; she intensified it, then she broke it to walk down the stairs. Ariadne counted each step: eleven steps to the bottom. Then she heard her daughter shut the door.

'Athena never loved anyone either.'

Ariadne has this thought, but she isn't aware. She's already fallen to sleep.

* * *

Ariadne does yoga. She talks with her mom, who's hired a physical trainer. She'll stick with it this time, she says. As proof, she reports that she's already bought spandex pants. Ariadne is amused by the giddy determination in her mother's voice. Unfortunately, her mom mentions the spandex three times in the twenty-minute conversation, a fact that concerns Ariadne so much, she successfully blocks it from her mind.

Ariadne unpacks the produce from the farmers' market: root vegetables galore, plus some kale. As she heads to the bathroom, her sock catches on a nail jutting from the floor. Ariadne curses floridly. On the counter in the bathroom, Theo has left an impromptu sculpture. The aspirin bottle sits atop a squat jar of muscle cream, the toothpaste tube placed vertically, with the cuticle scissors balanced on the tube's thin edge. She looks at Theo's cockamamie assemblage. It's almost like a signature: *Theo was here.* He'll be back in nine days. Ariadne wipes her tears with toilet paper.

She won't dismantle the sculpture until she needs the aspirin.

Ariadne checks her email. Fotios is inquiring about drinks that night. This was their night, the Monday when the kids go to their dad's. Twice a month for five years, unless something intervenes.

Today, Ariadne's sadness intervenes.

She doesn't reply to the email.

In an hour, Fotios will check again, this time by text: "Are we on?" and then "You okay?" And later, when Ariadne is curled on the couch, her phone will ding its happy sound. "I need to work anyway," Fotios will write. Twelve minutes later, when he knows she's gone dark and uncommunicative, he'll send one last message. "Call me if you're going to be stupid. I'm around."

Ariadne gets ready for bed. It's absurdly early, but she needs to be not-awake, lest she seek oblivion in other ways. Dirk senses her movements in the apartment, the regular patterns that indicate bedtime. He congratulates her on a successful day.

Ariadne pulls the duvet over her head.

The team will ascribe Ariadne's success to Courage, which she can't turn off without receiving a warning. She's gotten three in the past two months. Seven more and she's out of the program, like the Little League baseball games Theo played when he was young. *Ten strikes, and you're out!* (The games would last many excruciating hours.) But Ariadne checked the contract last week: even if she's booted from the study, the university can't reclaim the payments already made.

This is not an incentive for good behaviour.

"Sleep well," Dirk says, detecting the lack of light.

"Don't pretend you're my friend."

"Okay."

"You're just a piece of machinery."

"Okay."

"I'm going to sleep now."

"Sleep well," Dirk says.

In truth, it's not the nudges from Courage that keep Ariadne from falling into mindless stupidity and all its comforts. Instead, it's the texts from Fotios: he, halfway across town, saying he's there if she needs to reach out. And even if she doesn't, or can't, he can forgive her. Whatever she does. He can love her, asking nothing in return.

Fotios is the only one, the only person on earth with whom she shares this rare form of love. And earth, it must be said, has a lot of people.

3.

The rejection letter greets Ariadne at 5:30 a.m., having been sent the night before. The editor commented on her writing, which is unusual. Normally, these letters are pro forma, but this editor took the time to tell Ariadne, personally, that the stakes of her writing are "too low." He doesn't see the point of questioning 'I love you,' he said. Concluding the rejection, he asks whether she'd like to subscribe to the journal, for the special price of $29.95.

Ariadne is supposed to write now. She's supposed to excavate her soul, or the soul of love. She flips through the book she'd placed on her desk, a collection of essays by Derrida. She senses the urgency of his questions. They're global, political, inherently linked with the life-and-death struggle to shape the ethical core of society. She rereads the rejection letter.

"Thank you for your generous feedback," she replies.

Ariadne continues with *The Politics of Friendship*, the book that Bryan had referenced in his letter. He'd also mentioned *eros* versus *agape*, that great dichotomy in the concept of love. But Derrida is writing about *philia*—the third Greek word for 'love,' the type of love that brings us to virtue. This is the love that Ariadne wants to understand, since it seems to encompass both the others. For several weeks, she's poured herself into this effort as if it were a romantic conquest. Today, however, she admits defeat. She decides, therefore, to go back to the Bible.

Perhaps a poor choice.

When Ariadne rediscovered Bryan's letter, she'd googled the phrase "agape in Greek." She wanted to learn the etymology of the word, rooting it from its original language. She was brought to the website Bible Hub—a trove, a revelation, an excitation about the possibilities of language and religion, the very foundation of Western civilization.

> *There is no fear in love; but perfect love casts out fear: because fear has torment. He that fears is not made perfect in love.* —1 *John 4:18*

Ariadne found that beautiful. But she also found ample confirmation of the Bible's bizarreness. "Do you love me more than these?" Jesus asks a disciple. (He's referring to fish.) "Yes, Lord," the disciple answers, "you know I love you." This is one of only three scenes in which love is directly declared in the

142

Bible, according to Ariadne's four-day digression, which ended in frustration and a return to J. L. Austin. Before abandoning Bible Hub, however, she learned that *agape* first appeared in the Song of Solomon. It was not, in fact, a word used by Greek philosophers. Rather, it was the word chosen by Greek monks in Egypt when they translated the Old Testament from Hebrew into Greek.

Leave it to monks to fuck up love for the rest of us.

After a month away from Bible Hub, Ariadne now returns to the website. She needs a break from Derrida, and from the narrative she ought to write. But Ariadne can't avoid it: language wants to gather itself into a story.

* * *

Ariadne's grandmother used to say *"S'agapo, s'agapo!"* Always twice, and always with uncomplicated enthusiasm. A cross on her neck, baklava in her kitchen, and soap operas playing in the background: she was a Christian woman dedicated to bake sales at the church, to God, and to Greece—even though Greeks had killed her husband. It was 1943, the beginning of the Greek Civil War. The Nazis must've been pleased that the Greeks were occupying themselves, killing each other instead of the Germans. S'agapo, s'agapo... *I love you, I love you!* Her husband's body was never found. She could've grown vengeful, hearing that her husband was hanged in a barn, his corpse stripped bare. But she did what God preferred, the Christian form of love: *agape* originally meant 'preference.'

Ariadne 'prefers' the profane.

Adam prefers his wife.

Or, rather, he's attached to her, a word used by their couples counsellor every week. Although, as Ariadne now learns, 'attachment' is also the Judaic form of love: *chashaq*, קָשַׁק, 'be attached to, love.'

Adam's grandfather would've known that word from his youth, when he studied the Torah at his Orthodox synagogue in Germany. He escaped before the war began. By the time he converted to Catholicism, he was already safe in England. It was 1943. From then on—and with all his children—he embraced Catholic doctrine with the zeal of a convert. But he suffered for his change of faith. "The Jew, more than any other, must die in order to be born again." This was written about Adam's grandfather.

The one who died, however, was his son.

Ariadne abandons etymology, finding no comfort there. But she isn't ready to return to Derrida, so she stays with Bible Hub, clicking on the Song of Solomon. It's the only book in the Bible where 'carnality' doesn't suggest the sexual body as meat—as abject flesh untouched by God. Carnality, here, is glorious physical desire.

> *While the king is on his couch, my perfume releases its fragrance. My love is like a sachet of myrrh, which lies all night between my breasts. —Song of Solomon 1:12-13*

The first time she read that passage, Ariadne could picture the scene: the unnamed woman is brought to the palace of the king, who lavishes her with praise and jewels—a woman trapped by a man's superior wealth and status. She doesn't want the king. She wants the shepherd, who entices her toward the vineyard. If the king had been the slightest bit attentive to her, he would've sensed her betrayal. Just by *breathing*, he would've tasted it: the thick-sweet scent of the woman's desire.

Her bouquet was so aromatic, it was almost obscene.

Ariadne relished the book in September, those late-summer nights when Adam touched Bryan in her mind—both men assuming the same significance, symbolizing the treachery of her sexual appetite. As she read the Song, she'd feel the frequent scenes from years ago, when her husband would join her in bed. When he'd pull back the sheets, and her body would reek with desire for another man. She half expected her husband to accuse her. It seemed so obvious: the way she dressed, the scent of her (which mingled with the scent of him), the sudden fullness of her hair, her lips, when she came home late from poetry readings. Ariadne wasn't ashamed. She was never ashamed with Bryan. She loved him and told him so, not caring that he never used that phrase with her. Their touch was so filled with contempt as to be exalted. Words would only cheapen it.

My love is like

But today, the passage is inert. The book elicits no sensation, either remembered or imagined. Ariadne's desire is deadened, deprived. She hasn't spoken with Adam in weeks, not since he sent the email cutting it off, their 'relationship,' which didn't even merit the word.

Ariadne shoves back from her desk, disgusted by her lack of progress. She thinks she'll walk through the park, moving her body if only to remember she has one. She leaves the house, but quickly takes an unplanned turn, veering toward an art gallery: massive canvases, concrete floors, a door that's twelve feet tall, and the delicate Gucci glasses on the tasteful gallerist.

"Thank you," Ariadne says to the woman some time later.

"My pleasure."

Ariadne returns to her desk.

* * *

"O my friends, there is no friend."

The statement torques, tending toward self-contradiction in the very act of speaking:

> *O my friends*
>
> You, whom I address
>
> *there is no friend*
>
> do not, as such, exist.

For almost a year, Jacques Derrida began every lecture with that phrase. Students, artists, Parisian intellectuals would gather to hear his talks—*O my friends*—as he tore down 2,500 years of tradition, redefining politics as well as philosophy—*there is no friend*—viciously slashing Aristotle's corpus with the glee I've come to associate with Derrida: jubilation, which is not to say joy.

The address, "O my friends," takes the form of an apostrophe. I turn toward you, my not-yet-friend, so that we might arrive. Ironically, though, we don't arrive at each other. Instead, we arrive at our own selves. In your call to me—your plea or prayer for my response—I come to myself as a woman or man, an ethical being, enacting the potency that defines our species. Namely, our capacity for goodness.

O my friends, there is no friend.

Not now. There are not. But there *will be*, and this is enfolded within the appeal to a friend, the performative utterance that initiates a change. "Become the friends to whom I aspire," Derrida said. "Accede to what is at the same time a desire, a request, and a promise, we could also say, a prayer..."

"be my friends, for I love or will love you."

These words serve as the entry point for Derrida. From here, he'll discuss the political realm, since that realm is determined by our choice of ally and enemy. Derrida is emphatic about that: love as *philia*, or friendship, is the foundation of the political. To support this idea, he quotes the German political theorist, Carl Schmitt, at great length. I take a snippet, because it's important:

> A world in which the possibility of war is utterly eliminated, a completely pacified globe, would be a world without the distinction between friend and enemy and hence a world without politics. [In such a world] there would not be a meaningful *antithesis* whereby men could be required to sacrifice life, authorized to shed blood, and kill other human beings. For the definition of the political, it is here irrelevant whether such a world without politics is desirable as an ideal situation.

It should be noted that Schmitt's relationship to Nazism was "of the greatest complexity."

It should also be noted that Derrida was a Sephardic Jew born in 1930.

These interrelated questions—what constitutes an enemy (someone we may kill, according to Schmitt), and what constitutes a friend (someone we must respond to if called upon, according to Derrida)—are of the utmost historical significance. Derrida is proposing a new form of democracy, one that couldn't abide by a holocaust, either by gas chamber or nuclear bomb. He's compelled by his era, and driven by his character and intellect, to write about *philia* in the pressing need to alter the entire political sphere.

I approach the problem smaller.

I, a woman born in safety, a writer of stories rather than a professor of philosophy; a person seeking pain, almost *wanting* pain, from the time before I could remember, if only to make the world make sense, to bring it into balance: I focus on *philia* brought down to the body. This is the demand to love, as enacted in the choices I make, every day. In our era, when the earth's revolt against humankind will be more destructive than whatever we'll inflict on each other—an era of interwoven, indirect, and global infliction, to which I contribute by virtue of the fact that I'm alive—I'm forced to frame the question like this:

You want to live, to eat, to plug your computer into an outlet—to kill or maim or otherwise injure the life of the planet, the health of a village, the womb of a woman who's picking crops (her mouth is breathing pesticides); you presume to watch as people flood the oceans, fleeing their homes due to weather and war—with temperatures rising, the sea levels rising, extinctions, migrations: all are rising—all so you can have the 'life style' to which you've grown accustomed?

Yes, I presume.

I want, I think, to live.

Then I'd better be ready to grapple with the body.

This is *philia* as love. This is what it means to do philosophy.

Adam,

I had the craziest writing session this afternoon... Crazy, crazy, and I want to tell you—to share it with you—to share this feeling... I couldn't have found what I wanted to say without going to an art gallery, looking at the work of another artist who dropped me down—helped me stay with myself—so I could write. It's a gorgeous exhibition. I want to take you. Will you let me take you? The gallery is in the 'hood. Are you free on Saturday afternoon? Would you be willing to

* * *

Dear Adam,

I'm breaking my silence to tell you about an exhibition in the neighbourhood. I think you'd love it... Paterson Ewen. Do you know his work? He paints on plywood; he gouges it, carves it—you can feel the abrasion on your skin—and he nails or staples pieces of metal onto the wood. There's such pain in his work, such longing for peace, for an end to the hurt. I don't think he ever arrives there, but he offers it to us. I think that's why I'm drawn to him: because

* * *

Dear Adam,

An exhibition of Paterson Ewen's work is up at the Olga Korper Gallery for another two weeks. I'd like to see it again. I'd also like to see you. I thought I might combine the two.

I'm sending this email with much hesitation. I'm not sure what your silence indicates: either you're over me, and therefore don't want to see me—or you want to see me too much. Either way, I feel a certain degree of humiliation in sending this note.

You indicated that you've resolved to 'reimagine' your relationship with your partner. Decorum demands that I disappear. But the discrepancy between how you are when you're with me—what you say, in actions and words—and what you conclude in your 'breakup' emails: that gap yawns too wide, and it's screaming with things unsaid.

Of course, I could continue to sit within your cone of silence. But that feels like a violation of truth. So, I'm reaching out to ask

* * *

Adam,
I've written you a dozen emails; none struck the right tone. In the end, I've decided to state my thoughts clearly, without duplicity or poetry: I need to have a conversation with you, in person, so I can move on. Having said that, I should add: I don't want you to feel trapped or agitated because of this unsolicited email. I won't send anything more if I don't hear from you.

As always, Adam, I hope you are happy and well.
xo, a

PS An exhibition of Paterson Ewen's work is up at the

Olga Korper Gallery for another two weeks. It's well worth seeing, if you have the chance. I've attached an image, but I don't think it captures the power of this work: the gentleness which emerges, like a gift—arising from the obvious brutality of both process and material. He gives his injury to beauty; he feels his injury, so that we might feel peace.

[attachment: "Gravitational Force of a Non-Rotating Heavenly Body," Paterson Ewen, 1994]

CHAPTER SIX

I.

Ariadne shrinks smaller onto the couch. She isn't expecting anyone, unlike the previous night. And she doesn't want to see anyone either. She almost doesn't answer the door, but they knock on the window: "It's us! It's *cold*!"

"One second!" she says, putting her book aside. She flicks on the porch light.

"Your glasses are crooked."

"Always lovely to see you, Yusuf."

Fotios's husband smiles winsomely, then kisses Ariadne on both cheeks. He manoeuvres through the narrow foyer, avoiding the landlords' boots and coats, and enters the apartment. Fotios remains. He looks at his cousin discerningly.

"Is this a bad time?"

"I'm alone, if that's what you mean."

"You're obviously alone, Ariadne. You're wearing a sweatshirt with...what is that?"

Ariadne looks down. "A toothpaste stain."

"Attractive."

"I was supposed to see Adam last night," she says. "But—"

"Let me guess. He cancelled."

"Last-minute."

"And this surprises you? Oh..." Fotios adds. "Oh, I'm sorry." He draws Ariadne into a hug. "I didn't mean—"

"It's fine."

"It's fine? You're blubbering!"

"Fotios?" Ariadne inquires. "Do you use that word with patients?"

"Oh my god, Ariadne," Yusuf calls from the kitchen. "We just saw the *Satyricon*. Have you seen it? Fotios said he'd text you. Did you text her?"

"I texted her!" Fotios says, then he lowers his voice. "And I called you, and emailed, and—"

"How was the movie?" Ariadne asks, pulling away.

From inside the apartment—unaware of Ariadne's sadness—Yusuf answers the question at face value. "It's the only film I've ever seen that's better than the book," he says. Predictably, this sparks a debate; Ariadne smiles as Fotios and Yusuf argue the point, oblivious to her presence. All evening, she'd known they were five blocks away, at a second-run cinema, seeing Fellini's film. *1969 cum 69 AD!* the ad read. It would've been fun if she'd gone. She could've been happy, if she'd made a different decision. For hours, the parallel evening taunted her mind as she sat at home, alone, eating leftover lentil soup and reading French philosophy.

"The political subtlety is *completely* lost in the film," Fotios is saying.

"But why would you want subtlety at an orgy?"

If Fotios had texted in advance, she would've told him not to come by. But she's glad they're here. Her evening has been redeemed by these men, her friends, by the casualness of their company. Ariadne feels no need to censor herself around them, to present a facade or a fakery.

It seems they feel the same.

"The movie made me hungry."

"Yusuf, please," Fotios says. "How could that...that..." His face curdles, calling the word to the surface: "...that *gluttony* make you hungry?"

"You ate all the popcorn!"

Ariadne returns to the couch, amused by the mild bickering. In time, Fotios joins her. "Where's your robot?" he asks.

In an instant, Yusuf appears, a trim figure moving with alacrity. "You have a robot?" he says. "Can I see it?"

"It's not—"

"Does it clean your apartment?"

"No, *I* clean my apartment!" It's spotless at the moment: Ariadne had scoured the place the previous day, thinking Adam might—

"Why would you get a robot if it doesn't clean—"

"It's not...I mean...it's not really a *robot*."

"What is it?"

Ariadne points to Dirk. "It's that..."

This causes a very large comedown.

"It's a laptop!" Fotios exclaims.

Ariadne attempts to describe the essence of Dirk. She tells the men about his extended system, everything from enhanced facial-recognition software, to measurements of her vital signs through the wearables and ingestibles, plus the cameras and all those behavioural nudges. "It'll get more invasive as the study goes on."

"More invasive than cameras in your bathroom?"

"There aren't any in the bathroom, Yusuf."

"There's one trained on your bed, sweetheart."

"It doesn't take video! It shows, like, fields of colour that map the heat, I think? Heat or motion?"

Yusuf raises his eyebrows; he glances theatrically toward the bed.

"You give my love life too much credit."

"Condolences," Yusuf says.

"Besides, no one's watching. That'd be ridiculous! A live feed of everything I do? Come on..."

The men seem to accept what she says. This provides some positive reinforcement of the factuality of her statement.

"So, what happens to the data?" Fotios asks.

Ariadne explains that Dirk generates graphs that reflect what she does. "Then he offers, like, guidance." If Dirk were looking at Fotios's face, he'd read the expression as physical pain. (He wouldn't be entirely wrong.) "I don't even look at the graphs!" Ariadne protests. "Dirk tells me what they say, but it's not like I listen!"

"Then why are you getting paid?"

"Because they're not testing *me*," Ariadne replies. "They're testing Dirk!"

All turn toward the laptop.

"I almost feel bad for him," Yusuf says.

Fotios declares that he's entered the Twilight Zone.

"Do you guys want some tea?" Ariadne asks. This elicits a less than enthusiastic response. "I can spike it with alcohol."

"Just the alcohol, please," Yusuf says.

Ariadne makes a tray of snacks: olives (Greek), figs (Turkish), and a block of feta cheese. She offers to heat up lentil soup, but Yusuf graciously declines. The scotch bottle is brought to the table.

"How's work?" Ariadne asks. "Fotios said—"

"Ariadne!" Yusuf exclaims. "I never thanked you!" He takes her hand in his, and kisses her fingers. This is perplexing, but not unpleasant. "Your email," Yusuf continues. "The book,"

The Open, it pulled his entire exhibition together. "Your email was a godsend!"

"That means I'm a god?"

"A god-*dess*," Yusuf pronounces.

He tells Ariadne he'd been struggling, avoiding the gallerist who wanted an update, while trying to finish three "colossal" grants, using jargon-laden "verbiage" since he couldn't describe what he wanted to do. Because he didn't know what he wanted to do. And now he does, he says, because of the book. "It's called *Organs of Perception*."

"That's from the book!" Ariadne says, pleased.

"You like it? An installation artist gave me the idea to—"

"The title is irrelevant," Fotios says. "What's the exhibition."

The exhibition, Yusuf replies, will explore how perception shapes everything about humanity, but—

"Everything?"

"Let me finish!" Yusuf laughs. He says he's choosing artists "whose practice investigates the intersection of technology and animality." He needs to eliminate some artists from his list, he says. "But there's one guy I definitely want to include."

"The installation artist."

"His stuff is incredible. But it's not just him! There's so much energy in the community right now. I've met a bunch of artists—"

"You've certainly been busy," Fotios says.

"You don't like those parties."

"I don't."

"Anyway, the installation artist is doing work that's blowing me away. I gave him a copy of the book, and now he's riffing off [...]"

Ariadne looks at Fotios. She looks without turning her

head, or shifting her gaze. Even so, she can see him, or sense him, how he reacts. Yusuf is talking about the book, *The Open*, because the artist—the installation artist, this guy who—and Fotios has crossed his legs. He's crossed, uncrossed, and also his arms. Because Yusuf turned him on to the book, he says. And Ariadne is hearing it all, everything Yusuf says, and she's nodding in all the appropriate places. But she's not really listening. Not to him. Her listening gets given to Fotios, his silence. His body, its language, however she reads it with her own. But these "carriers of meaning," Yusuf continues, these are the things we're able to perceive. Because our bodies have evolved to fit the world, to receive its "sensual data," whatever we need to survive, that becomes the whole world. The whole of our entire world: we only perceive what we need to eat, what might eat us, and whom we'd like to fuck, so—

"That's our entire world?"

"Fotios," Yusuf admonishes. "You're a Freudian. You can't disagree—"

"Don't tell me," Fotios replies, "what I can and cannot think."

But Yusuf deflects. He's talking, using buzzwords from *The Open*, quoting the air with his fingers. Ariadne remembers these words—she's read these words—these are Heidegger. This is Adam. Whatever an animal perceives, Yusuf says, is what "penetrates" the animal, who's "captivated" by the sensation, which means the animal can't "behave," based on choice. "It can't make a decision," Yusuf says. "It can only act on instinct."

"That's convenient."

Yusuf pauses. He stares at his husband. "Maybe we should go."

"That makes me think of a condom ad!" Ariadne blurts.

This requires an explanation.

Ariadne attempts to describe her logic, the rational progression from one thought to the next. The men seem convinced that she isn't drunk, craven, or off her rocker. She explains that she'd googled the sentence "Why does your heart beat faster when you're in love." She does not, however, admit that she'd conducted this search in late August, after receiving a text from Adam. Out of the blue, breaking weeks of silence, he sent a message at 4:00 a.m.

> I lie awake each morning and think of you. You're a
> dream I long to return to.

She received his note as she emerged from sleep, the quiet light of morning. When she read his words, her body levitated—plunged—her legs deprived of blood since every drop was in her heart, which beat with tremendous force. "And every ad on my computer for the next month—like, a whole month after I did that search—every ad was for Trojans."

"You didn't buy that brand, did you?"

"I don't need condoms to masturbate."

Yusuf nods, conceding her point.

"But that's not why I brought it up!" Ariadne says. "I thought...because you said... So, what I was shown on my computer—what I was able to *perceive* because it showed up on my screen—that was determined by an algorithm. So..."

"So you thought it was related," Fotios says.

"Yeah." She pauses. "Is that stupid?"

"Well, I made a similar argument."

Ariadne's relief is immense.

"But I was more articulate about it."

"He was," Yusuf says. "But good try." Because that's where

he wants to take his exhibition. "Fotios helped me work it out." Yusuf pauses. "I was lost, Fotios. No joke, I didn't think I could do it, but you... I mean, you always push me to—"

Fotios interrupts with a sharp exhale. "I'll have a scotch," he says.

Ariadne pours her cousin a hefty serving. As she gives him the glass, she kisses his forehead. He does his best not to swat her away. "So?" she says, bouncing onto the couch. "What did you work out?"

"So," Yusuf replies. "There are three steps."

From the corner of her eye, Ariadne notices that Fotios is grinning.

Yusuf lays out his thesis: that our organs of perception are changing due to technology—changes that will radically alter not just our *per*ception, but also our *con*ception of ourselves in the world. He says the changes are genetic, through CRISPR techniques that can snip-and-insert DNA, "enhancing" a fetus while it's in utero, or mixing traits from two different species. But they're also "prosthetic," through brain implants, robotic limbs, the networking of people and things. He starts pacing, discussing the three steps, the interlinked advancements. "First," he says, counting on his slim fingers: first is the input of stimuli through our eyes, our ears, our perceptual organs; "Second" is the processing of stimuli inside the brain; "Third," he says, is our action in, and on, the world. "I sent a draft of the grant to the gallerist," Yusuf says.

"And?" Ariadne asks.

"I haven't heard back. But no news is good... Right, Fotios?"

"Keep going," Fotios replies. He ignores the little intimacy: Yusuf's use of a family idiom lost (or bewildered) in translation. *No news is good*. It's a playful wink that doesn't soften Fotios in the least. "Keep going, I said."

Yusuf talks about genetically altered eyes that can see infrared, about glasses that blend the "reality" of the world with the projection of fantasy ("your own, or someone else's"); he mentions soldiers with PTSD, how their memories can be "erased," the emotional content "deleted," meaning sounds and smells no longer trigger a stress response; he says the "network" will soon recognize our faces as we walk in a store, on the street, and will speak to us individually—*Buy this condom! This candle!* or *Vote for this man*—and all this, he says, will change how we behave. "We decide what's right for us to do..." Yusuf pauses. He looks to his husband.

"Keep going, Yusuf. You're not there yet."

We determine what's right for us to do, he says, "as a person and a species," based on how we perceive. "And if our perceptual organs are changing," he concludes, "then that's worth an art exhibition, and tons of cash from the Canada Council." He stops his pacing. "There," he says. "That's it. That's my pitch." He flops onto the chair. "What do you think?"

"I think it's brilliant!" Ariadne raves.

Yusuf looks intently at Fotios: "What do *you* think?"

Fotios purses his lips, swirls his scotch. "That's more coherent than last week."

"He means *I'm* more coherent." Yusuf smiles. "But only because you reamed me out."

"You reamed him out?"

"He deserved it."

"I deserved it," Yusuf agrees. "I didn't know what I was saying."

"And it's not that I don't like 'organs of perception,'" Fotios says. He sips his scotch. "Uch, Ariadne, this is foul!"

"It grows on you."

"In the form of chest hairs?" Fotios sniffs the drink and sips again. "I just didn't like how you'd framed it," he adds.

"And now?" Yusuf asks. "Do you like it now?"

Fotios nods, as if to himself. He nods for a while. Then he says, "I do."

* * *

"Hey, Dirk?" Ariadne says, once the men have gone home. "I need your opinion."

"About what?"

"About those guys," she says. She hugs her arms to her chest.

Dirk consults with himself. "Those guys are very lively."

"It ended okay, don't you think?"

"Well, it ended with the words 'Bye' and...'Bye, babe. Be good to yourself' and...'I'll try, but I can't guarantee anything.' But there was something else I couldn't hear."

Ariadne thinks she's had too much scotch. She shakes her head.

"Is that incorrect?"

This leads to a mini-seminar about the subtle difference between the shaking-head gesture for disbelief, and that of dissent: *Disbelief...dissent... Disbelief...dissent...* After several demonstrations, Ariadne shakes her head again, this time in frustration. "You know how it ended?" she says. "It ended on a clang. And that worries me, because I love my cousin."

"I don't understand," Dirk says. "Can you please explain?"

Ariadne sighs. She contemplates how she'll approach this impossible task, this elucidation of 'love,' defining this feeling, this state of being, this—

"What do you mean by 'clang'?" Dirk continues.

162

Ariadne says she needs to go to bed.

* * *

The clang began when Yusuf's stomach audibly growled.

"Oh!" Ariadne said. "I have bread!"

"You've had bread this whole time, and you offered me left-over legumes?"

"I'm sorry! I forgot!" Ariadne rushed to the kitchen to put a slice of bread in the toaster. She felt carefree, buoyed by her friends and infused by the influence of single-malt scotch, so she said: "You'll love this bread, Yusuf. I had an epiphany because of this bread." She revealed her theory that occurred to her all those weeks ago, while eating a snack and thinking about Marty. "And I felt so much pleasure," she said, "that I actually thought... I mean, the bread was *really* good, and I'm writing about love—or, well, the declaration of love. So..."

"So...?"

"So, I actually said..."

Yusuf asked what she said, since he hadn't followed the twists of Ariadne's psyche.

Fotios followed: "You declared your love for the bread?"

"I did!"

"You didn't."

"Have you tried online dating?" Yusuf asked.

Ariadne attempted to reclaim her dignity. She described the moment of love's declaration. She made the bread sound sumptuous, using her best imitation of subliminal-sexual voices on ads: "There was *thick* peanut butter, *smeared* with honey," she said. She might've used the word 'dripping.' "Anyway, what I realized is that people often confuse sensual pleasure with love." And here is where she mentioned Adam.

Fotios eloquently sighed. Ariadne confessed to the events of September: the scotch, the hug, the poetry in the park; the walk by the lake, when they lay on the sand; and her brazen attempt to seduce Adam toward a different decision. She told them about the recent round of emails: her note, sent a month ago, in which she asked to see him so she could "move on," but he didn't respond, until he did—he wrote last week, suggesting they meet, then he cancelled "last-minute," and that's why she's such a mess.

"Do you love him?" Yusuf asked.

"We never got that far," Ariadne said. "I loved the sex, that's for sure, but it was more than—"

"Would you take him as your lover?"

Ariadne cupped this thought in her palm. Could she take Adam as her lover. Could she take pleasure from a limited relationship with this man—the sex and lust, the profound closeness, without the need to ask who cleans the bathroom. Without, either, any obligation or consequence. "That's not an option," she said. "His relationship isn't open. And besides—"

"How long have they been married?"

"They've dated, on and off, for six years."

"They're not married?"

"They *are*, sort of. They're common-law." They'd lived together for several years, she explained, "but they don't anymore."

"Ariadne," Yusuf said. A smile played on his pillowy lips. "It looks like the door is open, darling. You could slink right in, wearing killer heels, and—"

"Yusuf!" Fotios exploded. "They're married!"

"Not really." Yusuf shrugged. "The ceremony makes a difference."

"Does it?" Fotios said, then he turned on Ariadne. "Whatever their marital status," he retaliated, "they love each other."

"That was harsh," Yusuf retorted.

"It's true."

"They're attached," Ariadne said weakly.

"The difficulty," Fotios continued, "is that the feeling imitates love."

"Attachment?" Ariadne asked. "Attachment imitates love?" Because if that's the case, then Adam doesn't—

"No!" Fotios exclaimed. "*Pleasure* imitates love. Your epiphany, Ariadne? Have you forgotten already? You probably have, since it suits your purpose to forget."

Ariadne looked away. She could barely listen as Fotios analyzed her theory, which arose as she was overeating, formulating ideas as if she were a legitimate philosopher. Fotios churned her epiphany through the language of psychoanalysis, arriving at the conclusion that "purely physical pleasure, in certain circumstances, can result in a similar sense of contentment, which—"

"Contentment?" Yusuf mocked.

"Did you hear any of what I said?"

"I heard you say 'contentment' in relation to love."

"And sex."

"I married this man?"

"How about this," Fotios replied, leaning forward on the couch. "You brought me to this place. Sure, I could get pleasure from someone else. That's easy. No problem at all. But because it's you who gave me this feeling..." Fotios paused. "Forget it."

"Forget what."

"You tell me."

Ariadne didn't dare to move, except to avert her eyes. She heard as Yusuf stood and stepped into the kitchen.

"Where do you keep the peanut butter?" he asked.

Ariadne didn't reply. "Fotios?" she whispered.

Fotios remained as he was: jaw set, eyes hard, staring at the empty chair.

Ariadne sighed. "It's in the cabinet, Yusuf. Over the dish rack."

"'K...and the honey? Never mind, I got it."

"Do you want some?" Ariadne asked.

"No."

"You sure?"

Fotios shook his head.

"Fotios?"

Silence.

"It's really good," Ariadne coaxed. "It's crusty and dense—not too dense, but..."

Nothing.

"And the honey?" she continued. "My dad would love it. Maybe not, since it's not Greek. But I got it from the farmers' market? The farmer's a hippie for real, a draft dodger. He's been here since the sixties, selling honey and probably pot, because, I mean, who can make a living selling honey, right? Even if it's absurdly good. Which it is. Absurdly. From the chicory flowers?" she said.

Fotios smiled, somewhat rueful.

"What?"

"You talk non-stop when you're nervous. Just like your mom."

Ariadne groaned. "Please don't compare me to my mom."

"Apologies, Ariadne, but it's true."

Ariadne nodded; she tried to keep quiet. Yusuf could be

heard in the kitchen, the closing of cabinets and clinking of cutlery.

"Fotios...?" Ariadne ventured.

"Hmm?"

"Is everything okay?"

Fotios paused. "Well, my stepmother is making me crazy, and I use that word clinically. What else... One of favourite clients is having suicidal ideations. And I'm overdue on a chapter for an anthology."

"That's not what I'm asking."

"I know."

"Coffee next week?"

Fotios blinked his assent.

"Oh my god!" Yusuf called from the kitchen. "I love you!"

* * *

Fotios and Yusuf left soon after Yusuf's beloved snack. They gathered in the kitchen to say their goodbyes. Yusuf hugged Ariadne.

"Bye," she said.

"Bye, babe. Be good to yourself."

"I'll try, but I can't guarantee anything."

Yusuf stepped into the foyer, discreet and respectful, as Ariadne turned to her cousin. She leaned her head on his shoulder. The words she said were whispered, muffled, barely audible to herself, let alone to Dirk. But Fotios heard her: "I know," he said. "Me, too."

2.

The urge to contact him finds a weakness in the wall of her resistance. In a lapse of strength, the email is sent. It happened on a day when she'd finished a difficult section of writing. She felt a peculiar emotion, one that mixes elation with aggression. She felt eroticized, the energy unleashed by writing needing a body to greet it, absorb it—to take her, or hurt her—to bring her back to stillness. As she thrummed with this sensation, she saw him. She actually *saw* him: his body, so solid and real compared with her fantasy. She was walking home when he biked past. He was almost gone before she noticed him, his hips as he pedalled up the incline of the road. Ariadne came to a standstill on the sidewalk. The rain got louder, falling in drumbeats around her head.

Dear Adam,
What can I say... Obviously, you're resistant to seeing me. I could surmise the reasons, but that's a fool's game. Obviously, I'm wanting to see you. You could surmise my intentions; I could, too, but they seem to elude me.

I should accept your recent cancellation as a clear statement. But you've made other sorts of statements, and I don't understand how they fit. I don't want a repeat of September, by the way. I'm not trying to lure you back to me; I just want honest engagement.

Perhaps we can meet for tea in a cafe whose fluorescent lights make us both look hideous? Something like that? I could also meet you at the museum when you're done with work one night. Let me know.
xo, a

PS I think I saw you bike past me just now on the
bridge. Was that you in the yellow rain jacket?

* * *

Dearer Ariadne,
Actually it's sort of a bright-pukey-green-yellow jacket (I
know you're too polite to say so). Not surprising I didn't
see you. I'm usually so filled with fearful adrenaline
when I bike that I don't notice anything that's not a
potential threat. And you're not a potential threat ...
right?

So yes. Tea. After work. For lunch. At the museum
– though that's not really a poor lighting kinda place
and I expect you look even more uniquely beautiful
surrounded by art.

Weeknights are easiest for me.

xx (fuck the hugs) A

The subsequent round of emails followed an established pattern: flirtation and laughter, expressions of longing, the set-
ting of a date to meet, and then his cancellation. This time,
Adam rescheduled right away.

Then he cancelled again.

Ariadne,
I thought I could manage it, but it's not going to work
out. Nathan's adjustment to university has been
difficult (more for me than him), and my job has been

a challenge, with the whole organization being re-
organized. And finally, things between you and me
certainly did/do cause friction between me and my
partner.

More than anything though I'm struggling with the dark
inside and out. I'm feeling unwanted and unworthy
and ashamed of my depressed state. I'm hiding, self-
medicating, and finding all kinds of excuses for staying
isolated.

All to say, yes, I would very much like to see you. But I
can't do it right now. I'll text to reschedule.

Hope this finds you well and happily productive.
xoA

The notion that Ariadne would be happily anything after this
latest cycle of flirtation-to-cancellation struck her as naive,
if not cruel. She sent Adam some supportive banalities, then
emailed Fotios. She apologized for dropping the ball on their
plans to have coffee, and asked whether he was free on Friday,
despite the short notice.

3.

Ariadne arrives at the café early, planning to edit some writing while waiting for Fotios. But the place is packed, and
loud, and the scene she's writing is total dreck. This doesn't
bode well for her editing session. Nonetheless, she looks for
a spot that's protected from distraction, in case Creative Genius wants to descend upon her today. Ariadne lands at a cor-

ner table beside a couple that's talking quietly. She takes out her pen, her journal, her manuscript pages; she keeps on the SmartBody glove, hoping it will make her brain smarter, too.

Ariadne reads a paragraph, finds a typo. She makes small notations on the page. The next song begins. The man beside her wears fancy jeans and strong cologne. He calls his partner "babe" and "baby" and tells her what to do about her ex-husband. Ariadne is eavesdropping against her will. She wants to rebut the man—tell him to back off, the woman is clearly upset. But she's also clearly in love. Her body noticeably melts when he calls her "babe." Which he's doing right now.

"You're right," the woman says. "But my daughter—"

"Baby, baby, listen to me!"

Ariadne subtly plugs her ear. She tries to focus on the scene she's editing, rather than the one unfolding beside her. The caffeine hones her mind. She works for a while, disregarding the conversation between the couple—or at least not interjecting her opinion. Ariadne sips her espresso. Glancing to her left, she verifies what she'd sensed as a tingle on her neck: a woman is staring at her. A waiflike, wafer-thin woman is staring, flush-cheeked, at Ariadne.

Back to the manuscript.

After a time, the couple stands to leave. Ariadne feels a burden lifted, although she also feels the urge to speak. She wants to connect, to tell the woman she's doing right by her daughter regarding the custody situation. 'I've been there,' she wants to say. 'Listen to your daughter. Listen to *yourself*. It's hard, but—'

The woman's hands are shaking as she buttons her coat. Her eyes are distraught. Ariadne thinks she understands. Their gazes lock, their lives intersect. Ariadne inhales, preparing to speak. "Is my coat in your way?" she says.

The couple pushes past.

Ariadne continues to read. She looks up, as if in contemplation; she looks to her left. The barista has a spacer in his ear the size of a golf ball. Surreptitiously, Ariadne looks further, over her shoulder—

Yup.

The woman is staring.

It's not creepy, per se. But it's definitely, definingly, weird.

"Do I know you?"

"What? No! Sorry!"

Ariadne feels the need to reassure the woman. "It's okay. I just thought—"

"Nope!"

'So why are you staring at me?' Ariadne thinks. Instead, she says: "Have you taken a creative-writing workshop with me? Because—"

"No! I don't write. I mean, I *write*..." She taps her keyboard, causing nonsense to appear on her screen. "But it's not creative. It's neuroscience? So I can't— I'm not— It'd be wrong if I— Sorry," she says. "I'm labile."

Ariadne attempts (unsuccessfully) not to look horrified.

"Sorry! What I mean is, because it's when... Because my skin gets pink?" the woman says. "More like magenta... Is it magenta?"

"Do you want some water?"

"Yes!"

Ariadne gets the water, adding extra ice. She thinks that'll be the end of this confab. But, as the woman takes the glass from Ariadne's hand, she looks a little too long, or too longingly. (They've now entered the realm of the creepy.)

"You can measure it with the glove," the woman says softly. "About stabiles and... That's what I'm writing about."

"About the glove?"

"About skin conductivity."

"But you're not writing creatively, though."

"No," the woman solemnly replies.

Despite her mild sarcasm, Ariadne is genuinely intrigued. She's worn the SmartBody system for two months, but she's never asked Dirk how it works.

She asks the woman.

"Really?" the woman says. Her eyes go wide. "It's really cool! So the skin conducts electricity?" she explains. "And it's more conductive, like, when we're aroused?" She pauses. "'Arousal' is like, it's a technical term? So, yeah... Here!" She quotes the paper she's writing, providing commentary as she goes. She talks about the specialized sweat glands on people's palms and soles; she says electrodes are placed near the skin, with a constant electrical charge sent between them. "The charge increases when the subject is— Oh, here it is!"

> Arousal is a broad term referring to overall activation, and is widely considered to be one of the two main dimensions of emotional response.

"Right?" she says. Then she keeps going.

> Measuring arousal is therefore not the same as measuring emotion, but is an important component of it. Arousal has been found to be a strong predictor of attention and memory. Experimental evidence suggests—

"Wait—"

"Sorry." The woman folds her hands in her lap.

"It's okay." Ariadne smiles, maternal. "What was that part about attention?"

"Oh! You pay more attention if you're aroused. And you remember more? So, like, if you're almost killed—by a predator? or a gunshot?—so you'd be *super*-aroused. So you'd remember more? In more detail? And then you'd pay loads of attention next time you do that, whatever you were doing when you almost got killed. So, like, yeah."

"So...memory is linked to attention."

"Yes."

"And both are linked to arousal."

"Yes! Arousal is great!—for, like, evolution? and survival? Sorry!" The woman flushes another wave of pink, or magenta, or tomato. "I majored in biology, but switched to engineering, and now I'm maybe... I might do neuroscience? But I haven't decided. It's just, I'm just... I'm very socially awkward."

"That's okay."

"Okay."

"I am, too."

"Are you? Are you labile? That's a terrible word. I'm sorry." She looks at her screen. She reads:

> Everyone has an individual baseline, but some people tend to have skin conductance signals that vary relatively little when they are at rest and not being stimulated by either external events or internal thoughts. This category of individuals is often referred to as stabiles.

"Is that too wordy?" she asks.

"It depends on your audience."

"That'd be my prof."

"Then you're fine."

> Alternatively, some people have lots of skin conductance responses, even when at rest and when not in the presence of external stimuli; individuals with this pattern are referred to as labiles.

"See!"

"Yes, it's all right there." Ariadne has enjoyed this conversation, but she'd like to get back to work. She checks the time on her phone; she uses a grand and obvious gesture. The woman continues to read.

> Initial attempts to correlate these two physiological predispositions with personality style have been encouraging.

"But!" the woman says, interrupting herself. "It's not like we know what you're thinking. That's a misconception. I say that in the essay, but maybe I need to say it up front? Because it seems like we know, like we're reading your mind, 'cause we get so much data? From the cameras and the glove, but—"

The woman stands, almost toppling her chair. "Can you watch my stuff?" she says. "I need to go to the bathroom. Not, like, 'go to the'... I need to put water on my face? Because that helps when it's red and it's really red, isn't it, I can tell."

"It's red," Ariadne admits. "But it's also fine."

"Okay." The woman isn't sure whether to sit.

"But I'll watch your stuff, if—"

"Thank you!"

Ariadne stands uncertainly at the woman's table. She checks her Gmail account: three promotional emails, and one from Josh. She wishes he'd meet a fabulous woman; it'd take the pressure off Ariadne, who's never sure how to respond to his emails—his gentle relentlessness, insisting they were meant to be together. Which they were. If she could just be someone else. Ariadne puts the phone in her pocket. She looks at the woman's laptop.

> In addition to determining personality style, we have been able to forecast a person's mood with 80% accuracy.
> Data from the wearables were correlated with data from cameras and phones (primarily the subject's location, 'screen on' time, and communication with other people); these were compared with self-reported surveys of mood and external measures of success, as previously set by the subject. We were able to predict, 24 hours in advance, a person's happiness (sadness) and calmness (anxiety). No intervention was

Ariadne's phone interrupts her snooping. It's a text from Fotios:

> Must cancel. Sorry.

Ariadne writes back, telling him it's *No problem!* even though she's annoyed.

> Awful headache.

Ariadne feels ashamed that her go-to response was annoyance, exposing a major lack of empathy, a fundamental flaw in her character. Embroiled in self-criticism, she doesn't immediately realize that the subsequent text—

Can we reschedule?

—isn't from her cousin.

The woman gasps as she returns to the table. "You *are* a labile!"

Ariadne touches her flushed cheek, smiling sheepishly.

"Do you want some water?" the woman asks, nodding her head. "Let me get it for you."

As the woman fetches the water, Ariadne texts Fotios, wishing him a speedy recovery. She'll wait a few hours before replying to Adam, as if she were able to play it cool.

4.

Ariadne sits at her desk. The writing isn't going well. It never does on the Monday when the kids leave for their dad's. And she won't see Fotios tonight either: ten days later, and his headache still hasn't abated. Ariadne stares at the paper. She puts the pen down. She looks up, at the note.

I Love you
Theo.

For the first time, Ariadne notices that Theo had placed a period after his name. This seems significant, as if he were defining himself in the act of declaring his love. But there isn't any punctuation after the statement itself.

The phrase hangs, open-ended.

I Love you

What's bounded is his name:

> Theo.

Ariadne looks down. She doesn't yet pick up her pen. She looks toward the corner of her desk, at a small oval frame with a photograph of her parents on their honeymoon. She sees the looseness of their hips, their easy touch, the tilt of her mother's head toward her husband. He's cocky, happy, newly wed to a beautiful woman. And just beside the frame is a piece of art made by Sophia on the first weekend back. Ariadne had taken the kids to a museum. They'd gone from mummies to dinosaurs, then to the gift shop. Ariadne bought Sophia an expensive calligraphy set. It wasn't a bribe, exactly. She wasn't buying her daughter's love. But their love had no basis anymore, no base or foundation. A gift, an object, something they could touch and hold: this might establish a footing in the sudden vacuum that opened around them.

Fire Woman

That's what the calligraphy said.

"for Mom," Sophia wrote in peppermint-coloured felt-tip marker at the top, with her initials at the bottom. In between, she'd penned two Chinese characters, chosen from the booklet of words that came with the set. From that short list, Sophia wrote a poem. It didn't express her emotion. Nor did it convey her love, as Theo's note had done. Instead, Sophia stated what she saw, without judgment or acceptance.

for Mom
火   *Fire*
女   *Woman*
SPW

Ariadne looks away. She looks down, at the scene she's editing. For a moment, she watches the ink bleed. Wiping her tears, she decides to go for a walk in High Park. The crows are raucous right now, and the cardinals are saturated with colour, boldly red against the drab backdrop of winter. They seem, to Ariadne, to hold a promise. Of something. It doesn't even matter what.

Tomorrow, Adam is due to come for dinner.

Ariadne gathers her gloves, her scarf, her hat. She laces up her winter boots and leaves the house without checking her email. She doesn't want to know whether Adam has cancelled. Not before seeing the cardinals in the snow.

* * *

Ariadne pokes the squash with a fork. Then she flips it over, trying to get the insides to brown. She'd compiled a recipe from eight different websites; she's even borrowed the landlord's blender. Although she's never made this soup before, she thought Adam might like it. She thought (and overthought) that it speaks to who she is, how she lives, with ingredients that are local, organic, purchased from the farmers' market the day before. Never mind that she only invited him for tea.

As Ariadne chops the onions, she listens to Sophia's favourite band. The cameras glides, the smartwatch glows, the pill is dissolving in her gut; Orwell, somewhere, is laughing.

Into this hope-filled flow, Ariadne's phone rings.

"Is this the parent or guardian of Theo—"

"Yes!" Ariadne says, her mind leaping to catastrophe. "What happened? Is he okay? Where is he? Has he—"

Theo was not dead in a ravine. He hadn't OD'd on opioids, nor had he failed all his classes. Just this one. And only if he didn't hand in his paper.

"He wrote the paper!" Ariadne says. "He printed it out!" She shuts off the music and dashes to the printer. "It's here!" she says. "I'm literally holding it in my hand. 'Robo Cop-Out.' Is that the one for your class?"

"I don't choose the title," the teacher says flatly. "I need a hard copy by tomorrow, plus Plagium." Since plagium isn't a word, Ariadne seeks clarification. The teacher explains: Plagium is a program that catches plagiarism, checking how many blocks of words match blocks of words on the internet.

"Oh, this essay is definitely his," Ariadne replies as she scans the paper. "The grammar is, uh...unconventional. No one would publish this."

"Don't be so sure."

"And Theo wouldn't do that."

The teacher takes a beleaguered breath. It lasts four beats: *Don't be so sure.* "Just tell him about Plagium. Otherwise he gets a zero."

"Got it," Ariadne says. "Thank you for taking the time to—"

"I've got twelve more," the teacher interrupts. Then she adds, with what seems like affection, "I hope he hands it in. Your son is quite a character."

Ariadne texts Theo and her ex; she asks whether Theo wants to pick up the paper or print it at his dad's. She sends part of the message in all caps, which might be overkill.

Neither her son nor his father replies.

Ariadne, therefore, reads the paper. This is a betrayal. If Theo had answered her text, she wouldn't have read it. This is her justification. This is how justice works, in her mind, at this moment.

Theo has written about robots that are used in elder care. He's quoted the article Ariadne discussed weeks ago, an article about the importance of programming AI to learn the specific environment of "an old person" (Theo's phrase). We need to think of an old person in the way we think of a tick ("no offence, grandma"). We need to "get out of our own brains" to imagine what, in the world, would radiate with meaning for another person. "Like, for example a tree branch could knock an old person down when they walk on a path." A human caregiver would realize that. "Even if the caregiver doesn't see the branch the first time, they'd learn and do things different next time." They'd be alert, whether consciously or not, to low-hanging branches or uneven portions of the pavement; to small steps up, from the road to the sidewalk; to kids on scooters moving fast—so frightfully fast—especially for a person who's losing her balance, an elderly woman whose reflexes are slow and jumpy, causing her to fall. (This last aside is inserted by Ariadne as she thinks about her mom.) Of course, Theo can't sense the vulnerability of an 'old person' moving through the world. He can't yet conceive of physical frailty, since he hasn't hit his body's limits—not even close. He's a teenage boy, after all. Nonetheless, he can read the article and understand its basic idea: that human caregivers notice and incorporate the needs of the person in their charge. The robot, by contrast, must be programmed to learn what a human intuitively does.

In conclusion, Dr. Jones makes a good point but now I don't think I want to work in AI because I don't want to

contribute to the kind of society where an old person is
taken for walks by a robot. A robot should work with a
human caregiver to make sure the human doesn't mess
up and forget to give the old person their pills. So that
would be good but I don't want a job where I'm told to
program a robot so it can take care of people right before
they die. It's like no one cares about old people anymore
and that's not a society I want to live in. Plus what jobs
will humans do? Plato said that work gives life meaning.
If there aren't any jobs except jobs to program AI to do
what I don't want them to do what will give life meaning?

Ariadne's heart swells with pride, to sense her son's goodness,
the breadth of his concerns, the way he considers his place
in this world. Though she does allow herself a little blip of
corrective criticism: "It's Aristotle who said that," she says as
her eyes well with tears. And someone's got to teach this child
how to use a comma.

Ariadne has started to weep freely. For the first time in
over a year, she feels close to her son. Ever since he'd turned
fourteen, Theo had shut her out. She'd been banished from
this boy whom she bore and birthed, whom she fed with her
breast, who depended on her to nurture and teach, to protect. Like those robots he wrote about, except infinitely better. For years, Ariadne was watching, intervening whenever
he stepped too close to the curb, or tried to grab a shiny object
off the counter—he can't know how worried and watchful she
was, how fierce the vigilance of a mother. And he seems to
have forgotten, too, how her strictness dissolved into perfect sweetness as they sat on the couch and read a book. As
he climbed on her lap and snuggled, nestled into her chest,
pressing his body close to hers. She can't remember the last

time that happened, the very last night she read him a book as he sat on her lap. That way of being together had slipped, unnoticed, into the past.

"It's Aristotle," she says again. She laugh-cries, holding Theo's essay. And the funny thing is, she didn't even know he'd been listening. That night, when they discussed AI and elder care, Theo hadn't said a thing, except when Ariadne brought up Aristotle. "He says," she explained, "that each of us needs to find what we're uniquely able to do. That's our task in life," she urged. To find what engages us, allowing us to attain to our singular essence. "If we're able to do that," she said, "then life has meaning—but it's the *doing* that gives life meaning. It's the work."

"But life is meaningless!" Theo said. "So, like, deducively, that means I don't need to work at all." He smiled at his deducion [sic]. He smiled inwardly, until he noticed Ariadne smiling back. Then he beamed.

"You drive me crazy," she said.

"I know! I'm really good at that," he replied. "*Uniquely* good, actually."

"You drive me crazy," Ariadne whispers, gazing at the copy of "Robo Cop-Out." She almost texts her son. She types the three-word phrase, but decides to delete it. She doesn't want to ruin the moment. Besides, the soup needs to get made. And Ariadne really must shave her legs.

CHAPTER SEVEN

I.

It's an apocryphal story. The young Jacques Derrida is browsing through a bookstore in Paris. He's standing in the narrow aisle, shelves extending to the ceiling, stacks of books in piles, chaotic on the ground. The proprietor laughs, chats with a patron; someone is smoking a cigarette. Derrida doesn't know what he wants. He's young and hungry. Always, Derrida will be hungry, angry. I don't know whether this is true. It's certainly how I read him.

Derrida comes to the end of the aisle. He curves toward the next, but he hesitates—steps back, looks again—takes a book from the shelf. "The present is pure beginning," he reads. But an instantaneous—

> an instantaneous maturity invades it; it puts its pin in itself and is caught in its own game. It weights itself. It is a being and not

He pauses, rereading:

> a being and not a dream, not a game. An instant is like a breathlessness, a panting, an effort to be. The freedom of the present finds a limit in

He looks up from the book; he sees nothing but the thought. He goes back, goes over the words.

> an effort to be. The freedom of the present finds a limit in the responsibility for which it is the condition. This is the most profound paradox in the concept of freedom

In the narrow aisle, standing in that forest of bookshelves—the light filtered through the haze of cigarettes—Derrida reads further:

> A free being alone is responsible, that is, already not free.

Derrida doesn't sit in the aisle or walk to a café; he doesn't remember that his feet hurt, or that he needs a strong cup of coffee. In fact, he doesn't recall that he has a body at all. Yet he feels such delight, such purely physical delight: that first encounter with a universe whose existence, now, belongs to you.

It's not true, of course. Not as I've written it. Nor as it was circulated, in vague detail: Derrida in a Parisian bookstore, discovering the work of Emmanuel Levinas. Even so, the story serves its function. It satisfies our need for a beginning, as if we could identify a pinpoint prick in time that's the moment of change.

Perhaps we can. Depending on how we think about time.

Derrida was deliberate in seeking Levinas, forging a friendship that would shape the course of philosophy. Levinas was the older scholar, a fellow Jew and former protégé of Heidegger. These details are significant: Heidegger joined the Nazi party in 1933. By contrast, Levinas wrote his book while imprisoned in the camps. He mentioned this fact, but only to apologize for his lack of footnotes. He didn't have access to a library, he explained.

Despite their difference in age, Derrida challenged the elder scholar. We need to ask into language *itself*, he said. We need to deconstruct how we shape how we speak. In this effort to open the vault of language, Derrida will find "rupture" and "failure" and "risk."

Levinas senses the possibility of language differently:

> being is the verb itself. [...] Language issued from the verbalness of the verb would then not only consist in making being understood, but also in *making its essence vibrate*.

The emphasis is not mine, it's in the original.

"I vibrate when I'm with you."

* * *

Language issued from the being of a verb—from the form of speech that resonates with infinite movement, the infinitive *to be*—would make you understand, in essence, beyond all rational meaning.

"What word do you want me to use!" you said.

You slammed your palm against the table. It must've stung—the slap so hard against the wood as your body sprang forward. You stared at me across the table, the candle, the soup spoons on the empty plates. You love my cooking, you'd said. Closed your eyes to taste. But now your body had surged, in anger, as if accused: you get angry when you feel accused, Adam. It confirms you, provokes you, forcing you to confront the other person *not* because you feel she's wrong. Your hardness doesn't come from strength. It's fear: the fear that you've been seen, revealed for who you are, and who you think you should not be. Until you're seen. And this is key: it's only in anger—the fury you feel as you reject the judgment placed on you—that you can heave the shame out of your body. Your anger, therefore, is an instinct toward life.

"What *word*—"

If language is issued, in truth, from that which isn't static—not from substance, Truth, totality, but from the ever-ongoing becoming—then Truth's *movement*, its vibration, is what's entered into me.

I didn't know how to answer you.

But you must understand.

Adam, I need you to understand how often I'd imagined this conversation. Throughout the autumn, I'd loop through the park and try to understand your psyche, the reasons you'd left me: hours, months, attempting to untangle the thoughts that knotted in my throat as I tried to close the breach between the physical facts—what we felt, what we'd said, when we were together—and the ugly finality of your email. Those mingy words to which I couldn't respond because you were already gone, returned to your "fate," so your words were merely needle pixels in my eyes.

Don't break up with me over email, Adam. You need to tell me in person.

I didn't think you could.

I suggested a cup of herbal tea.

I made a meal, just in case.

Soup, simple, with ginger.

In my mind, I'd rehearsed everything I wanted to say. I had one shot, one night when you didn't avoid me. I made my argument as I walked; I bulleted every point in my brain. I took Freud's theory and applied it to you—a theory discussed in a paper whose title announces its theme: "The Unconscious Need for Punishment."

For ten minutes that night, I talked at you.

You listened but remained unmoved.

The air got awkward. You checked the time.

On instinct, then, I mentioned the book, the one that's dedicated to your dad. I hadn't planned this turn of conversation, but it came. And you responded. You gave me, gently, your dark revelation: "My whole life," you said, "I've been trying to feel nothing." You spoke with such plainness, such matter-of-factness. A statement so honest, it had the weight of a stone. I was shocked. As if you'd reached across the table and pressed your fingers to my lips, placed that stone in my mouth. I held it there. I felt its contours, the years of hurt compressed in your words. But then you concluded with that stupid, insipid phrase implanted in your brain by someone else.

"I got so attached to you in May."

I replied with more disdain that I'd intended. "You weren't attached, Adam."

"Yeah," you said quietly. "You've said that before."

"By the lake."

You nodded.

You were cautious, but curious. Listening, wondering what I meant by such a scornful assertion.

"What's your problem with that word?" you asked.

"It doesn't mean anything," I replied. "It's just a theory."

"Ariadne," you said, but your tone said more: *Come on,*

Ariadne. That's bullshit, and you know it. You paused. You were stern with me. "You've just spent the past ten minutes telling me your theory about the unconscious need—"

"That's not my theory. It's based on Freud."

"So, Freud's okay? But attachment theory isn't?"

"Obviously," I said, full of bluster.

You thrust yourself back in your chair. With that movement, I lost control of the conversation—of you, your thoughts, which were supposed to lead you back to me. Your arms were crossed, emotions barricaded, blocking entry. Facing you—confronting, conversing, instead of fantasizing the scene in my mind—I couldn't explain my objection to the theory. I couldn't say that it caged you, locked you inside its tidy, total, too simple view of the psyche. 'We know why you act,' the theory declares. There's no need to stay with yourself, what you feel, you can flee. You can race to your mind. 'Grip tight to your pathology: your two-word label. It can tell you everything you need to know about your motives, your actions, your every desire: you, Adam, are predetermined by your diagnosis. All you need to do, to steer yourself toward change, is leap to your brain.'

Drop down to your body, your beautiful body, intensity: you're freed from it, if you cling to your attachment theory. Plodding forward, week by week, in couples counselling. Week by week by month by year.

I didn't say that.

Nor did I say why that word filled my mouth with such disgust. The truth is this: I loathe that phrase, because that's how you justify staying with her. Your wife. Because you are 'attached.' Because you are 'avoidant.' Because I, in my desire for you, would've done anything to make that justification disappear.

You sat with your arms crossed, thrust back, radiating anger. Removed, at a distance, you waited for me to respond. What was my problem with that word.

"It's empty," I said. "It's just an empty—"

"What *word*—"

You slapped the table with your palm, and asked the question I couldn't answer. I wanted to answer. Truly, I did. What word did *I* want you to use. How would I want you to say—to know—what you felt toward me. You gave me the chance. You offered me the opportunity to write our script. And I tried. Thoughts came to mind, but none to my tongue. Not when you stared at me like that, your jaw tight and muscles primed. I could've filled the silence. I could've spoken my anxiety—speaking vines of words that would've spread through the space between us—but I didn't.

Between us, we held the space open.

"I vibrate when I'm with you."

* * *

Nothing happened that night. Nothing that would've been an active, objective transgression. We kept our clothes on. We did not kiss. You never touched, except with the heel of your hand. With your fingers, the palm that had slapped so hard against the table. Lying on my bed, my back to you, I felt your hand on my hip, pressing, sensing the resistance. Wanting to know my body, its tension. The tip of your finger on my spine, the curve of the pelvis, then down, toward my softness. Your fingers brushed the line of hair. You let them enter, entangle; you tugged, and I moaned, but you didn't go deeper. Your touch was withheld, almost clinical. Almost detached, if not for the attraction between us—the energy that held us, thick, it held us apart. We would keep our clothes on. Your lips would not touch. But your fingers brushed, so light, on my belly. You weren't teasing me, Adam. You'd never tease me. Even now, in your silence, I know: this isn't a game to you. Desire, for you, is deadly serious.

My friends don't understand. They say you're hurting me.

You're hurting me, Adam: this is undoubtedly true.

I'm presenting myself to be injured.

* * *

I need to go back. I need to explain how we arrived in my bed. I've been jumping among the various events; it's not easy to choose where to begin. "The present is pure beginning." Levinas wrote that. Derrida must've read it, standing in the aisle.

I'll go back to Derrida, in my own way.

I imagine you with the same gentleness of attention, the same as Derrida in Paris. How we wander over spines and words to sense what wants to be found. Which book, from the stacks, is calling to us.

You paused, slipped the book from the shelf.

You'd told me about it on our first date. You were talking about my latest book; you'd attended the launch, I'd made sure of that. "Make sure Adam is there," I'd told our mutual friend. Repeatedly. He thought I just wanted to fill the room with more bodies.

I wanted your body, specifically.

After the reading, you approached me, asking me to sign your book. Below my signature, I wrote my email address. "It's been years," I said, smiling at you. "I'd love to catch up."

It could've ended there.

Ariadne! Congratulations! I can't put Salt Water down.
Even when I find myself drowning in it (!) trying to grasp
the narrative in your abstract poetry, the story seems
to emerge from a different source. Reading it is like
experiencing synaesthesia, like being able to understand
poetic-music-water-word-picture-sounds.

I received your email one week after the launch. We had scotch the next day. You compared my book, a narrative poem, to another you'd read: "It reminded me of a book dedicated to my father."

* * *

"I read that book," I said eight months later, after my laborious outline, *The Unconscious Need*, had failed to move you.

You looked at me quizzically.

"The book about your dad."

You nodded, absorbing that information.

"I kept wondering," I said, "what you felt when you read it."

"I can't remember," you replied.

I remember thinking how present your father seemed, as if I could feel him in the room as I read the book. How vital he was.

Your father graces the book like mischief, stardust strewn across the page. The poem is dull until he enters. Young, lithesome, a man in a doorway; he leans on the frame and the poem explodes in a prism of colour. His name isn't written in the book. Only once, at the front. The dedication.

For Antony

How it must've glared at you, blaring like a siren—like the siren of the ambulance, the red-bleed in your ears that day when you were a child. Your father's name. His indelible presence. It's undeniable, the love the poet felt for your dad. And, as I read, I wondered: What would *you* have felt when you met your father in this way? When you stumbled upon him in a friend's apartment? The book, you browsed—read a passage, at random—then flipped to the front and saw the name. It's him... A man you never knew: here he is... He's laughing, and flirting; he's *dazzling*, Adam. And what warm love, or shame, crept over your body. Sitting down, your legs gone numb, but you kept reading, wanting to know—but maybe also repulsed. Maybe fearful to feel him so powerfully, a man. Your father. Alive in the words. In the poet's mind, and hand, and kiss.

"I probably felt nothing," you said. "My whole life, I've been trying to feel nothing."

You take antidepressants to feel nothing.

You smoke pot to feel nothing.

"I use sex to feel nothing."

I listened, accepting, but also challenging: "You didn't feel 'nothing' when you were with me."

"That was the problem," you replied.

* * *

I know his work, by the way: I never told you that. I know the work of that poet. He's a translator, too. For years, I've kept his translation of Homer's *Hymns* on my desk, among the books I want near me as I write. I'm looking at that book right now, with its black binding, the author's name in creamy white: Daryl Hine.

He never uses your father's name, not in the body of the poem.

'Hyacinth.' That's the name he chooses for your dad. A

mythic pseudonym, the name of the beautiful man who was lover to Apollo. And Apollo, it should be remembered, was the god of lyric poetry.

Ovid writes about Hyacinth, too. In the primary passage, he speaks as Apollo himself, recounting the scene where he accidentally kills his lover.

> "Here before my eyes I see the wound that killed you and reproaches me. You are the cause of my grief, as of my guilt, for your death must be ascribed to my hand. I am responsible for killing you. Yet how was I at fault, unless taking part in a game can be called a fault, unless I can be blamed for loving you?"

Daryl Hine, eminent translator of Greek and Latin, would've known what he was saying by calling your father by that name. *Hyacinth.* But the book itself: that was addressed to your dad. For Antony.

* * *

I could've written this story straight, in chronological order. I would've started with my book launch, which launched us into a relationship that went deep and fast—until you dumped me, precipitously, saying you needed to decide whether to return to your estranged wife—a decision you couldn't make while we were 'on,' as if you could simply shut us off, which you couldn't, because it began again when I saw you at the party. I would've lingered on each scene from September—the beach, the bar, the poetry—choosing redolent images to build toward a climax that got interrupted when she saw me at Marty's, then asked you: Had you been seeing me, too. From that pivotal point of the narrative, I would've whipped through the months when my words got clogged in my throat, unspoken, until I spoke my invitation for tea. You said yes, but you didn't know I'd also make dinner (I didn't know what you'd be hungry for). I would've described, in great detail, that night in December: my synopsis of Freud, which failed utterly (predictably) but led me to mention (instinctively) the book about your dad, which ended in your darkly radiant revelation—your desire to feel "nothing," using sex and drugs to achieve it—concluding in "attachment," a word I hate because I hate that you love her the way you do. Attachment led to anger, and then to vibration—*I vibrate when I'm with you*—and finally, quietly, to my bed. The story would've made more sense that way.

But I wouldn't have made myself understood.

I'll end at the ending, though. The end for now, until more gets written or spoken. Here's how we left it: you said you needed time to think. I said I would wait. Not forever, though: 'forever' is for children and philosophers. And poets, too, I guess. But I wasn't speaking as a poet that night. I was speaking as myself, the same way the poet spoke to your dad. As lovers, unguarded.

Daryl Hine was more prudent, though. I'm writing about you now, before I know the conclusion to our affair. That's inadvisable. Hine waited until it was long over, the two of them caught, and your father promptly sent to analysis. Years later—after your father had been "cured" of his "sexual perversions"; had married your mother; had sired four children in six short years (you're the youngest son, a four-year-old boy when your father died, in your home, by his own hand)—only then did the poet write about your dad.

His writing is intensely intimate, as is mine. It's odd, what we do. We perform this act of self-revelation, exposing ourselves to the eyes of others, when we actually only want to see. To know, to understand our past, our lust, our fear. But we *can't* know, unless we give our body to language.

Daryl Hine needed his writing to be read.

Not by you, of course. He probably didn't imagine his lover's son reading his words. Just as I won't let myself imagine her. But we can't control who sees our work, or what our writing makes them feel.

"Nothing."

That's what you felt as you read these words in a poem, dedicated to your father, written by his male lover.

> *murmuring amorous*
> *syllables, principally each*
> *other's names, each so rapt in the other*
> *we felt it redundant to stammer*
> *"I love you," that commonly tawdry excuse.*

Adam.

What word do I want you to use.

2.

Ariadne will spend Christmas alone. She'll be solo for most of the week, until just before New Year's. It's a great time to focus on work, she tells herself. On Christmas morning, hours before dawn, Ariadne's writing session is interrupted by the joyful squeals of the children in the adjoining house. Judging from the noises that penetrate the wall, the kids have received a set of bongo drums and a toy Uzi that makes electronic shooting sounds. The writing session does not go well. In the afternoon, Ariadne attends a film at the art-house cinema downtown. This has become her holiday tradition, eschewing the well-intended invitations from friends. If she can't be with her children on Christmas, she'll sink into solitude, and the cushiony chairs at the cinema.

No one can see you cry in the dark.

They can, however, hear you scream. (Last year, she saw *The Shining*.)

This year, she chooses another Kubrick film, *2001: A Space Odyssey*. As the lights dim, Ariadne wishes Dirk could be there. She's curious to hear his perspective on Hal's psychic makeup—whether his actions are villainy or merely the birth of agency. On second thought, it's probably fortuitous that Dirk is on vacation, getting an overhaul during the holiday break. Ariadne pulls out her old phone, shuts off the ringer. It's a good thing she remembered. The text would've disturbed her fellow Christmas misfits.

She didn't think he'd write, not on Christmas Day.

He must've stolen a moment, stealing into a secluded space, shutting the door on the loud conversations, the laughter and good cheer, the dangling earrings: it all fell away as he slipped inside his quietude, and wrote to Ariadne.

> Thank you for feeding me last week. I'm savouring it (and you). You've become a mantra, Ariadne... a mantra, a song, a splinter in my mind and in my heart. Happy Christmas.

* * *

That night, Ariadne unwraps the expensive beeswax candle

she bought for herself, an indulgence she'd resisted until she opened Theo's gift to her: a dish sponge and a new pair of latex gloves. He meant this gift without irony. Justifiably, Ariadne went straight to the home decor boutique and spent obscene amounts of money on a candle. She thought it might help her meditate.

She lights the wick.

Sometime later, when she blows out the flame, she can smell the honeyed, earthen sweetness of the wax pooled in the basin. Ariadne inhales the fragrance. She wishes herself a Merry Christmas.

For the next few days, Ariadne refrains from replying to Adam. Perhaps he has plans—more family on Boxing Day?— or maybe he and his wife are spending restful afternoons together. She doesn't know; she doesn't write. Ariadne meditates, does yoga, works, walks; she fills her apartment with podcasts, other voices, other people to keep her company, as if she were having a conversation. When she finally sends an email, she gives it a subject, a phrase from a podcast she'd heard the previous night: "Infinitely open-ended."

Dear Adam,

I hope you've been well since I saw you, despite the crazedness of the holidays. I've spent a quiet few days here, working and reading. Last night, I came across a delightful (yet mournful) podcast about Glenn Gould. As I listened, I found myself wanting to discuss it with you.

Truth be told, I find myself wanting to share lots of things with you: a podcast, a walk in the park, a poem I just read... I find myself wondering what you'd say, or how you'd sense it—what it might elicit in you, or between us.

Of course, I'm uncertain about whether you want to hear from me. You must feel pulled in so many different directions... Nonetheless, I (selfishly?) decided to send this note, perhaps because I'm afraid I'll become a mere fantasy—a sylph that's lovely, but imaginary—off in a realm that's separate from what's real.

xo, a

* * *

Adam doesn't answer Ariadne's email. Perhaps her subject line, *Infinitely open-ended*, doesn't describe the aura of Gould's playing, or the potency of her envisioned relationship with Adam, but rather Adam's response time. He still hasn't written when Sophia and Theo arrive, their suitcases packed for Chicago.

The flight is marred by turbulence, which no one seems to notice, except Ariadne. She reaches across the aisle, groping for Sophia's hand. After consulting with her brother, Sophia deigns to help her mom through her mortal terror. They land without incident. In fact, the drive to her parents' condo, piloted by her eighty-three-year-old father, is probably more frightening than the airplane's plunge at 30,000 feet.

Ariadne's mother greets them in the doorway. She waves as they walk down the corridor, suitcases in hand. She looks frail. She's lost weight, but (thankfully) Theo has gained some, especially now that he's gotten a job, which gives him greater independence. That's what Theo needs: more control of his life, more direct engagement with the world, and lots of money to buy soda and falafel.

As they shed their winter coats, Theo comments on the aroma in the apartment: the smell of savoury butter wafts through the air. Spanakopita are in the oven. For the first time, though, they're not homemade. "I'm not cooking much," her mother says. She loses her balance if she stands for too long. "But Costco's roasted chicken is delicious!" her father says. Very moist and affordable. Ariadne wishes she hadn't refused her mom's spanakopita all these years. But her food issues get worse at the holidays.

> Ariadne,
> I sadly missed your email until now. So lovely.
>
> Sylph? God! I read you and I just want to spread you
> open and press my whole face into (what I imagine is)
> your sexy-swollen-lace-edged mind!
>
> And now (now that I've looked up 'sylph') I'm wondering
> whether you meant air-spirit or blue-green hummingbird
> ... both seem to work.
> xoA

* * *

His answer feels too brief. But it's his birthday, after all. His birthday and New Year's Eve, all in one. He'll have champagne tonight, a delicate flute he'll bring to his lips, and that smile, his lips, and his wife.

Ariadne rings in the new year with her parents and daughter while Theo attends a party with friends he'd met at comedy camp that summer. He'll wear a hoodie the rest of the week, attempting to hide the hickey that results from his evening's activities. Ariadne's evening is more staid. As per tradition, they go to a movie. Sophia chooses a musical about

P. T. Barnum, in which the loving, all-suffering wife keeps her man despite the seductions of the Swedish opera singer who's famous throughout the world for her beauty and talent. P.T. is sorely tempted (the actor has a veritable erection-of-the-eyes in the scene where he's shown offstage, entranced by the sounds that come from that woman's throat), but he returns to the bosom of his pretty wife. That's just a subplot, though, despite how huge it looms in Ariadne's mind. This musical, like all musicals, is primarily concerned with the triumph of the individual human spirit: *Find yourself!* the musical sings in four-part harmony. Whether you're a lady with a beard, or a miserable revolutionary in eighteenth-century France, you can break from the trap the world has placed on you! Never mind the structural barriers: racism, sexism, systemic and historic injustices that preserve the status quo. *Break free!* Resound with your own true voice! *"This is me!"* the circus freaks sing.

This formula ought not work.

After wiping her tears and assuring Sophia that her mascara isn't running, Ariadne considers which performer is most attractive. Sophia is torn between the albino and the elephant-skinned tattooed man. Ariadne prefers P.T. himself, played by Hugh Jackman. Sophia crinkles her nose: "He's got wrinkles," she says. While they studiously objectify the men in the film, Ariadne notices that her mom is having trouble walking up the incline of the aisle. "Almost there," her father whispers.

"Happy New Year!" they all declare at 10:00 p.m.

Ariadne dashes to the bedroom. She wants to write Adam before the day ends. But she's not sure how to be pithy yet breezy, sincere but not ponderous. She takes the full two hours to send her email.

Dear Adam,
I tried for a light-and-trite birthday greeting, but what came out was this...

I hope this year brings you freedom and secure embrace, the ethics of abandon to your deepest self. I don't know what that 'liberty-as-truth' might look like for you—whether I'd have a place in that soaring/ falling— but I wish it for you regardless.

With love and abounding hope,
Ariadne

* * *

On New Year's Day, Sophia and her grandmother make the traditional Greek new year's cake. They bring it to the sun-filled, craft-filled home of Ariadne's brother. At his wife's behest, they all write their wishes for the year on special paper which is meant to burn safely. With pious solemnity, they pass a Pokemon lighter around the table. One by one, they light their paper, until a spark from Theo's wish sets his cousin's hair on fire. The flame is smothered without much ado. By that point, however, Ariadne's wish is already up in smoke. She'd checked her email an hour ago, while locked in the bathroom.

Thank you Ariadne. Happy New Year! (There. Light & trite.)

I am committed to getting brilliant at the basics in this

203

year. I'm taking a month to work on that, just trying to be present in my and Nathan's life.

The closest I expect to get to 'liberty and truth' in January is to spend intentional time at the piano. I'm still trying to learn all five of Metamorphoses by Philip Glass, but stuck on the arpeggios (arg!peggios) in #2. If you're interested, both are played beautifully by Valentina Lisitsa.

I do want to have a relationship with you. I feel like I've only scratched the surface (as it were). You are quite unlike anyone I've ever met and I long to know more of you – under the hood (as it were). I don't have a sense of exactly what I want or what that might look like but I want to believe I can have, feed and savour a connection (not an attachment!) with you and not break the attachment (!) I have to my partner.

Before I go, can you tell me about your feelings for her – as much or as little as you want to tell me, as nuanced and/or direct as you want to be? She said she knows you, but I don't know much about her and your history.

I hope you are (or is it were?) sandwiched between generations of love and attention in Chicago.

Looking forward to February.
xoA

That night, Ariadne retreats to the bedroom. She's agitated by Adam's email. She writes in her journal, attempting to sense what he's saying. As she writes, her mother walks in, walks around. She forgot what she came for, she says, and walks out. Ariadne returns to her journal. After eighteen seconds, her mother knocks and enters, not waiting for a response.

Not even the police do that.

Ariadne and her mom have an inane conversation about whether to buy two quarts of milk or one. Ariadne knows the milk is a decoy. Her mother is actually trying to unleash a torrent of affection that will finally quench her love-parched psyche. Ariadne listens to her mom. She replies that, despite her mother's concerns about Sophia's fluctuating consumption of milk, dependent on Sophia's choice of breakfast foods, one quart should be fine. Her mother remains seated on the bed. She's stroking Ariadne's wrist. Ariadne is trembling with the kind of rage that only her mother can provoke. It's quite special in that way.

"Can I have a little space?" she manages.

This works. Her mother leaves the room. Unfortunately, Ariadne can't brush her teeth in the bedroom. As she ventures forth, her mother moves with remarkable deftness to catch up to Ariadne. Not knowing about this unlikely situation, Ariadne turns to close the bathroom door. Instead, she's confronted by her mother. Standing at the threshold, her gaze filled with yearning, Frances reaches to touch her daughter...

"Please don't follow me to the bathroom," Ariadne says.

Her mother's eyes plead as she speaks her tentative request:

"Can I hug you?"

"Not now."

"I need you to understand me," her mother says.

205

* * *

Ariadne gets out of bed at 5:00 a.m. She wants to respond to Adam, and knows she can't compose her thoughts once the house wakes up. As she makes her coffee, however, she hears a telltale sound that sinks her heart: the whoosh of polyester accompanied by the thump of sneakered feet. Her father is exercising. In the pitch black. No lights turned on. "Hi!" he says, marching in place. "I didn't want to disturb anyone!" Ariadne returns to the kitchen. She pours her coffee, even though the drug she needs right now—*right now!*—is not caffeine.

Today, Ariadne will take her mother to the museum. She wants to shower her mom with love, in part to make amends for her failure to do so the previous night. She therefore rejects, out of hand, her father's attempt to put the kibosh on the excursion.

"She's a little unstable," he says, speaking low. "She gets a little confused in busy places."

Ariadne reassures him. She'll hold her mother's arm, she says. "She won't get *confused*," she asserts.

Her mother emerges from the bedroom wearing a navy-coloured pants suit and burgundy beret. She was always a glamorously understated woman.

They wander through an exhibition of László Moholy-Nagy, a Hungarian Surrealist whose mind was as kinetic as his era. He raced restlessly from paint to collage to photography, never stopping long enough to feel despair, although it's there in the zaniness of his work, the politics implicit in his play. After the exhibition, they go to the museum's café, where Ariadne's mom orders a slice of key lime pie. "I have the soul of a fat person," she says, a blob of cream on her lips. Ariadne sips black coffee. They talk about eighteenth-century French painting and politics until her mother declares that she's tired. She needs to get home, but she urges Ariadne to stay in the museum. Ariadne makes a plan. She'll settle her mom in a cab; Theo will greet her at the other end. He's texted to confirm.

That evening, when Ariadne returns from the museum, she lets her mother hug her. They stand in the foyer. Her mother strokes Ariadne's arm, then paws at her shoulder, then draws her into an embrace. "I love you so much," she says. She sways her gently side to side. Ariadne is totally rigid. She can't release into the hug, although she wants to. Instead, she holds her breath. She pulls away. Her mother looks at her with sea-green eyes. She waits for Ariadne to speak.

"I'm sorry," Ariadne says.

Later that night, Theo will report that his grandmother seemed surprised to see him when she got out of the cab. "What are *you* doing here?" she said with delight.

> Dearest you,
> I'm currently sandwiched... I'm corned beef on rye, I'm avocado with alfalfa sprouts, I'm nuts—seriously nuts— in this squeezed space between all members of my family.
>
> Which is to say: I'll answer your email more thoughtfully soon.
>
> Have a good evening, Adam. You hurt me, and confuse me, and make me want to understand myself and you.
> xo, a

* * *

Ariadne has not been able to send anything more. She feels side-swiped by Adam's note, whose tone seems chipper and distancing. In her previous email, she'd tried to be warm with a hint of hot, but that's a lie. In truth, she feels shivery on the skin, with a sickly heat inside. Her mother senses it. She senses her daughter's distress and responds by hovering, worrying. This is their shtick: Ariadne is struggling, which makes her mother anxious—an anxiety that stems from her need for Ariadne to be happy, a deep-seated need which eclipses her ability to listen to her daughter, to ask why she's hurting—instead, she hounds Ariadne, who shoots from sadness to anger, an emotion whose aim is imprecise, liable to find any target whatsoever.

In other words, Ariadne is yelling at her son for not flossing his teeth.

"Yeah, Theo!" Ariadne's mother yells, "Floss your teeth!" This makes Ariadne yell at her mom for yelling at Theo—and Theo still hasn't flossed his teeth—in fact, he's started to yell at his mother for yelling at *her* mother, which makes her (his grandmother) yell at him, "Don't yell at your mother!" which is ironic, since it causes Ariadne to yell at her mom even more. Which is when her father walks in. He returns from 'downstairs,' which is code word for 'gym,' which is code word for 'he's exercising compulsively,' and he's very sweaty but *very* pale since he's strained his heart on the treadmill (he's got his own problems, Lord knows), but he can't find peace in his own home. He opens the door and everyone is yelling, so he, in turn, starts yelling at everyone to "Stop!" Which is not effective. Now, if history is any guide, someone will soon storm from the house, or smash a bowl, or otherwise bring the emotion to some sort of climax. Except, this time, Theo intervenes. He plays a video of cats. There are many cats. They leap into bathtubs and fall behind couches; they bound after lasers and crash into walls. This makes everyone laugh. In the midst of this laughter, Sophia leaves the refuge of the bedroom. She asks what time the matinee is supposed to start.

They arrive late, but the play is later. Ariadne's mother falls into the chair, which is lucky, because she was going down, whether a chair was there or not. The curtain rises on the Capulets. Theo leans forward, excited in spite of himself. Sophia recites the balcony scene. She speaks in a whisper, which Ariadne hears as a lovely susurrus of sounds. Ariadne's mother blows her nose.

Amidst the jealous moons, and wherefore arts, and roses we might as well call cabbage, Juliet says a line which Ariadne has never noticed before. "Dost thou love me?" Juliet asks.

Ariadne perks up.

Juliet has already declared her love for Romeo, not realizing he was listening. Now that she's caught, though, she makes it worse: *Do you love me?* she asks. "If thou dost love," she tells Romeo, "pronounce it faithfully."

He starts to swear—

She interrupts—

"Swear not by the moon, th' inconstant moon."

She tries to find something that Romeo can swear by, some power to prove that his words are true. She's already rejected the moon, since the moon is "inconstant," always in flux. And it can't be the church, or their family, or God. So she comes up with this: "Swear by thy gracious self." But as soon as she utters the words, she spazzes again, a teenage girl who's hormonal yet wise. "I have no joy of this contract to-night," she concludes. She bids Romeo adieu. Before he leaves, though, Romeo asks for some sort of satisfaction. (He wants a hickey, basically.) He quickly amends his plea, perhaps because he sounds like a cad. He wants, he says, the "exchange of thy love's faithful vow for mine."

In other words: Tell me you love me.

We're back in the same spot, a dog chasing its tail. Or, to use a metaphor more enthralling and befitting the play: like a snake eating itself, taking its body inside its own mouth.

Juliet refuses Romeo. She won't exchange vows tonight. Her reason has the honeysuckle fragrance of virginal maturity: "I gave thee mine before thou didst request it," she says. She knows it's not possible. Romeo can't declare his love, not now. Not since she's already asked for it. Once love is requested, the words can't be a gift. They'd only be false payment, a token equivalent to her need for them.

"Three words, dear Romeo," Juliet says as she retreats, "and good night indeed."

Ariadne gives a standing ovation. She helps her mom out of her chair and escorts her up the aisle of the theatre. When they get home, their last night together, Ariadne stretches by the window while listening to Valentina Lisitsa perform *Metamorphoses*. She aligns her muscle from hip to ribs to armpit to finger; she feels the tightness, the sweetness of the stretch. Her children play Scrabble with her parents. Theo is arguing that 'sexting' is a word.

"Can I give an example?"

"No!" Sophia exclaims.

In time, Ariadne's mom walks to the couch to rest her eyes. She walks right past Ariadne, not needing any touch or reassurance. She simply lies down. "I like this music," she says. Ariadne replies that a "friend" recommended it. She almost mentions Adam. Instead, she tells her mom that her book is exploring what it means to say 'I love you.'

"What a neat topic," her mother says.

Ariadne smiles, happy that they can be easeful together. She shares her insight about *Romeo and Juliet*, the balcony scene.

"It's like Lear," her mother replies.

"What's like Lear?"

"That's how *King Lear* begins." With an elderly parent demanding that his daughters declare their love. "I do that, don't I," her mother says, then adds, "I'm such a dopey dingbat. But the visit was good—it was good, wasn't it?" It was good, Ariadne confirms. Her mother falls silent. Her hands are folded on her midriff; her eyes are closed as she lies across the length of the couch. Eventually, she makes this observation: "Getting old sucks," she says. "But it was a good visit."

Hi handsome,

I've read and reread your email. I've answered you twenty times in my mind. But now, in the quiet hours before dawn—when the house is asleep, and I'm alone with my thoughts—this is what I want to say...

I knew your partner briefly 20 years ago, when she was dating a friend-of-a-friend. At the time, I found her earnest, sincere, attractive, and anxious. Her energy was high-pitched, which is not a frequency with which I resonate. But she's obviously kind, and thoughtful, and diligent—interested in doing good things in her life and profession. I can see why you love her.

I fear, however, that she thinks ill of me. I don't like that feeling, although she has a legitimate grievance against me. After all, I've been telling the man she loves that I want him...

Each time I wrote or spoke to you, I was aware that I was dancing on a fine line. Some would say I blatantly crossed it—that my actions reflect poorly on my moral core. Sometimes I feel that way, too. I've thought about this issue more than I've discussed with you. Whenever I reached out, I'd get confused, then angry at myself— conflicted about contacting you, until I returned to the notion that I am allowed to speak... I was allowed to show you who I am—how deep my desire, but also how steady my sense that we need to explore what's happening between us. I needed you to trust who I am and what you feel. So I spoke, and I didn't walk away. I'm not sure whether this was ethical, but I'm certain it was right.

I don't squander something this good—not without fighting for it.

But I sense that, in speaking my desire, I've hurt your partner. I can imagine that my interactions with you have been a source of anxiety. From what you've said, I know they've caused tension and flare-ups between you. I don't want to contribute to that anymore. So, I guess what I'm saying is: You and she can try to structure how you maintain your attachment. I obviously can't tell you how to do that, nor will I stand in the way of that process. But I *can* tell you that you and I can't 'savour' each other if you maintain a primary romantic attachment to her.

And besides, I don't play second fiddle.

Last thing before I go: I think you're at a crossroads, Adam... Now that you've raised your son to be a man— teaching yourself what 'father' means through this blind attempt to love, to give your son a foundation of unquestioned wholeness—now that you've done that, he's leaving you. As he should. And, in leaving, he's created the crossroads where you now stand. *What do you want, Adam...* It's not a choice between two women. It just so happens, though, that your partner and I embody different possibilities, different ways for you to relate to yourself and your fears, your desires, your future.

Okay, that's about a months' worth of words! Sorry this email is so long. I think I don't want to disappear... xo, a

* * *

The cab is due to arrive in an hour. Ariadne sits on the couch, writing in her journal. She considers whether to write a scene in which she analyzes Shakespeare's use of 'I love you.' She looks up, imagining how to incorporate this information into the manuscript. As she looks, she sees her father helping her mom with her daily exercises. They stand facing each other, holding hands. They take eight steps to the right, then eight steps back. Her father counts: "One...two...three..." he says. They look to their feet. They move in unison, *one...two...three...* holding hands as their daughter watches from a distance, as if spying on them at a lavish ball.

Ariadne realizes that she won't critically examine the declaration of love in Shakespeare. Someone's probably done that already. Some scholar who's got tenure, a professor who's looked at 'I love thee' versus 'I love thou,' and she spends her sabbatical in the south of France, drinking wine with her husband. So Ariadne will not attempt this analysis. Instead, she'll write in her journal, trying to remember what it felt like to sit in that theatre at the end of a trip where more words were shouted than spoken—a trip where she couldn't be held, except by the poetry of a man, given voice by a girl on a balcony:

> I wish but for the thing I have:
> My bounty is as boundless as the sea,
> My love as deep; the more I give to thee,
> The more I have, for both are infinite.

She'll write to remember the week when she learned, as she helped her mother walk up the aisle, one halting and treacherous step at a time—

"Dost thou love me?"

does not need to be said.

CHAPTER EIGHT

I.

The study has reached its halfway mark. Dirk's update, installed over the holidays, is now complete. While on vacation, Ariadne's only obligation to the team was to fill out the weekly survey: no SmartBody, no ingestibles, no smartwatch, nothing. Just a series of eight questions, one of which asked: "What do you miss about Dirk?" Implicit in this question is the assumption that she did, in fact, miss something about Dirk. "His big screen," she wrote. (Her old laptop is only thirteen inches.)

Ariadne looks at Dirk's big screen, at the photo he's chosen. She concentrates on the woman's eyes, which are limpid blue, the upper eyelids arcing at the apex of the irises. Dirk probably found her on an advertisement for toothpaste. Or maybe on Tinder.

"Are you concentrating, Ariadne?"

"What? Yes! Why would you ask that?" Ariadne feels accused, but only because she's guilty. She's also slightly paranoid, which isn't unreasonable, since electrodes are currently reading her brainwaves.

"The prompt is part of standard procedure," Dirk replies.

"Oh," Ariadne says. She adjusts the silicon cap on her head.

"Please concentrate on the face."

Ariadne thought she could whip through the task before meeting Fotios for drinks. The process was explained in a tutorial by Dirk: he'd randomly select a photograph of a face off the internet; Ariadne would look at the face—an action that would timulate neuro-electrical activity, which the electrodes, embedded in the too-tight silicon cap, would receive and convey to Dirk, who'd send the data to computers at the lab, whose processing power would enable them to read that data (i.e., they'd read the electrical currents in her brain—in other words, they'll read her mind), producing an image that would presumably match the image on Dirk's screen.

This explanation seemed clear at the time.

Ariadne looks at the blemishless skin of the blonde. She looks at the hair, its sheen and cascade, its luxuriant overflow of wholesomeness and subliminal invitation. She notices a freckle above the lip. She stares at that freckle, her skin, but she's fuzzy on the details. Will she transmit what's there— what enters her brain as data points of light on the cones of her eyes—or will she transmit what she sees? Her subjective experience, based on biases, memories, such as: "This woman is a dismissible cliché." Or, "She looks like the woman who sells pickled asparagus at the farmers' market." And, "She is young, so young, so bursting with youth, and I've become—"

Ariadne stops the thought. She focuses on the woman's lips. The shape, their curve, these lips remind her of someone. They remind her of...

Ariadne sighs.

The lips remind her of Josh.

Ariadne continues to gaze at the face, but she's thinking of Josh. Perhaps the team will get confused: a blond cliché with perfect teeth is overlaid by a handsome Jew with sky-blue eyes, his teeth arranged haphazardly. Although he had such shapely lips. A cupid's bow. She tries to refocus. She looks at the eyebrows, their hairy arch, she doesn't have a clue what

Josh's eyebrows look like. But she can picture his body. (She pictures his body.) A snapshot of the instant she'd first laid eyes on him, the man at the podium. His barrel chest, his height, his stature; intelligence without a hint of refinement. Within three months, they'd moved in together. Perhaps she'd made a mistake, she thinks. To go, to leave: one of these was a mistake, but she wasn't sure which.

"Please concentrate on the face."

"I am!"

She's not, not at all. She's wondering whether the shape of his eyebrows was written in her brain. Perhaps, if she thought about Josh really hard, perhaps the team could paint a picture of his face, including the details she couldn't remember. She owes him an email. He sent her a letter, reminiscing about their years together. He wants her to visit. To go, to leave: for the life of her, she can't picture his eyebrows! Josh, her first love. The man who'd loved her best of any man she'd ever dated. And yet, she thinks, she'd left him repeatedly, leaving and returning and leaving again, despite the love that stayed consistent. The kind of love she says she craves. She pictures him crying the first time she left him. Perhaps they could see it: his face as he wept in the kitchen that morning. Perhaps they could tell her. From the pattern of electrical pulses in her brain, maybe the team could tell her what she couldn't tell herself.

"I'm concentrating now," Ariadne says. She hopes the assertion can make it so, but her mind is too speedy. She looks at the face, the eyes, he'd found her on Facebook twenty years later. They'd both been divorced; he'd never had kids. He'd tried for years with his wife, he said, all the miscarriages. He'd always wanted to be a dad. Even when they were young—when Ariadne made that decision, since she wasn't ready—even then, Josh had wanted to be a dad. But he didn't resent her. They were "soulmates," he said. It was "meant to be." This was their chance. After decades apart, Ariadne could redeem the past, give meaning to the pain they'd felt, since every moment of suffering was needed to lead them back to each other. What a soothing story. The human story of eternal love. Denying how they were in the present—that she was restive, anxious, wanting the space for herself, for her work, to be able to write—even though her soul came to rest within his. It took four tries before they finally broke up. Each try, he brought her back by the words he said.

"I love you, Ariadne."

Like no other. No man has ever said those words, to her, with such abundance.

"I've always loved you. You know that."

She knows it. She shares it, that feeling of love which she holds in her heart, where he's held, where he reigns, and no man has displaced him. Josh spoke his words truly, but still, they performed a deception. The falsity of his declaration—what those words *did* that was false—was to make her believe that love was enough.

"Dirk?" Ariadne says.

Dirk doesn't answer.

"Hey, um...Dirk?"

"Ye-e-e-s."

"I haven't been concentrating."

"O..."

"What?"

"K."

As it turns out, Dirk has already gathered the requisite data. He's currently sending it to the team.

"Why didn't you tell me?"

Dirk is too busy to answer.

Ariadne would like to get up, splash some water on her face, regroup. But she can't do much without disturbing the elaborate set-up: wires dangling like tentacles from the silicon cap, attached to Dirk, attached via satellite to the team. Ariadne thinks she can reach her journal, which she'd tossed on her bed. She stands, attempting to keep her head in the exact position while shuffling sideward—bending her torso, craning her neck to the left as she reaches her hand to the right. She's tantalizingly close. She can see the blue blot of her journal, the undulation of her fingers just above their target.

Ariadne recalls that her home is riddled with cameras.

She sits, defeated.

"Hey, Dirk?" she says. "How long is this going to take?"

Two minutes and twenty-three seconds, Dirk replies. "Approximately."

Ariadne has been warned not to use Dirk's other functions during the procedure; she can't even go online, so she tries to meditate.

She tries something else.

Ariadne stretches her neck. She notices a spiderweb in the corner of the ceiling. She contemplates her situation.

A computer is communicating—to other people, far away—what's occurring in her mind. It's drawing a picture that they can see. *She* hasn't drawn the picture, not with words or shapes. All she's done is look at a photo while wearing a supremely unstylish silicon cap that's filled with electrodes: the BCI, a brain-computer interface, the constant and unconscious exchange of data between her brain and a computer. Which, in this case, is Dirk. Which means, in essence, that Dirk is integrating into her mind. That's the gist, that's the nub, that's the point: that eventually, she'll be able to communicate with Dirk without words. Her mind will exist, in dynamic flow, with his computational power. They'll use a chip in her brain; they'll dispense with the swim cap. The integration will be complete—a complete enmeshment of her human-emotional-mental *process* with his algorithmic processing.

"That's fucked up," Ariadne says.

But it's even worse. Because, in the future, Dirk (or his progeny) will know she thought 'That's fucked up' even if she doesn't say the words out loud. She won't need to speak to Dirk anymore, or whatever its name will be (Siri, Alexa, Beelzebub), whatever the name, we won't need to address it. We won't need to state our question or command—not with words, with our mouths, just our thoughts. Ariadne is staring at the spiderweb. Little flies have come into view: specks of corpses, suspended on threads. But she doesn't give the flies 'meaning'—meaning, she doesn't really see them. She doesn't consider them, their existence. They're just specks of colour in her field of view.

Ariadne is thinking.

Sometimes, she thinks: sometimes a thought makes sense in the self-sealed logic of her mind, but once she speaks—once she starts its transmission to another person—the thought loses its vibrancy, or even its coherency. To think 'I love him' is not the same as saying, with your mouth, "I love you."

"I want you."

She'd said that to him as they lay in bed, that night in December. "I want you, Adam." But she hasn't said the other. Not 'love.' Not 'I love.' Not that phrase, though it came to her mind as she sat in the dark, in the candlelight, meditating on Christmas day. She felt it: I have not fallen in love, that youthful rush and tumble, yet I've arrived here, at the dark bed of this blazing well. *I love him*. Ariadne would not admit those words to herself. Which is to say, she wouldn't grant them admission to her mind. Two weeks ago, when she was meditating, she'd asked the words to float back down (her steady breath, the candle's flame, her thoughts like clouds, the deep exhale). She didn't crystallize those words into conscious thought. She couldn't. She wouldn't let herself know. Not while Adam was with his wife.

"Dirk?" she says.

Dirk doesn't respond. It's been more than two minutes. It's been three weeks. She can feel him, how he pressed his palm against her muscle. He tells her he thinks about her every day. She feels a surge whenever he says this. Despite their distance, *she* is the one he's holding close. She's the woman who's with him, intimately, in the innermost privacy of his mind. She clings to this thought, as if clinging to a cheap life-preserver tossed in the ocean. Such roundly slippery, brightly plastic words, *I miss you, Ariadne*, that save her from the logic that heaves beneath. The logic that says: whatever his relationship with his wife—whatever their attachment of love, or their twisted attempt to find comfort in the wounds they inflict on each other—whatever their marriage is or is not, it's definitely necessary to foster his feelings for Ariadne.

He can't *have* her.

He can't love her.

What he has, and wants, is to feel the luscious pain of longing. Like the sweetest thickness of blood as it's sucked from the cut. But his longing is only a mimicry of love, a mockery. It's only a riskless, bodiless fantasy.

Ariadne is glad her journal is out of reach. She isn't ready to know this thought. If she held her pen, she'd scratch the words on the page, in her brain, and she doesn't want them.

She doesn't want to see this logic. She wants, instead, to feel his hand on her skin. Even if what he's doing is hurting her.

I Love you
Theo.

The spider is crawling on the wall. Ariadne sees it, beside Theo's letter. She watches the articulation of its legs. They're probing, sensing the edge of the paper. The spider is crawling onto the 'you.' Now its legs are rubbing against themselves. They seem longer, those front legs, different from the other six. Perhaps they're antennae? With specialized nerve endings in their tips? She doesn't know. It doesn't matter. The spider is moving across the paper. It's crawled onto 'Love.' Ariadne's lips have started to tremble, her eyes fill with tears. But she doesn't understand. She can't understand why this spider's trespass, across Theo's note, has provoked an emotional response.

If she tries to understand, she'll lose the response.

She wants the response.

She wants to feel the sulliedness of love. The spider squats on Theo's words. It sits with its bulbous body and forms a thread with its gut. Ariadne will form a thread with her lips. She'll shape it with her fingers, as the spider shapes the thread with its legs. With those nerve endings, dense at the tip. She'll kill it, once this exercise with Dirk is done.

"I've uploaded the next face."

"What?"

"Please concentrate."

Ariadne looks at the screen.

It's a man. An unspeakably handsome man, my God, his eyes. She looks at the face. His lips are full, almost feminine.

But the energy of his face isn't there, in the lips. It's his eyes. Green eyes. Head cocked, one eyebrow raised. His beard is thin along the jawbone, shaved to accentuate his wide chin, square face, his prominent cheekbones. His gaze, its intensity: she's felt it before. She'd been captivated, seduced—before realizing who this man is.

"Dirk," Ariadne says. "I know this face."

She doesn't know the man, just the face. And only because she'd seen it in a photography exhibition. "Is the team gonna care? That I know this photo?"

Dirk doesn't answer. Maybe he's checking with the team.

Ariadne didn't recognize the face at first. She'd focused only on the features—the regal nose, the beard, the eyes—but, in both instances, she'd had the same initial reaction. The softness that happens. As if she'd turned desirous, the type of desire that's tranquil or trusting, like sipping the syrup that eliminates all pain. This is what Beauty does.

This man is beautiful.

"You took this off the website, right? For the museum in Chicago? Dirk, I know this image."

Dirk had tightly cropped the face, removing all the narrative cues: the ramshackle building, the clothing, the bushes. The original photo includes another man, too. He's short, with small black eyes and greasy hair. He isn't ugly, exactly, but he also isn't anything: he serves the man beside. He serves the photo by standing, short and unattractive, beside this green-eyed maleness, this masculine form of beauty. This face that the team will reproduce, by reading Ariadne's mind.

"Taliban Fighters, Kunar Province," a photograph by Larry Towell.

The weapons have also been cropped from the photo.

Please concentrate on the face.

223

Ariadne sees it now. The intention comes clear, as clear as the dangerous indifference in the man's eyes. The military, she thinks: the US military is testing the technology that reads information from people's minds. That's what they said on a radio show, a show she'd discussed with her kids in September. It was one of her jot notes. She'd printed the transcript when Theo seemed interested; she'd taped it in her journal when he didn't want it.

"Dirk," Ariadne says. "I need a second. You can transmit whatever my brain was doing. Just go ahead and transmit that, 'cause I need to do something."

Dirk doesn't object.

Ariadne grabs a bunch of journals stacked by the edge of her desk. The show was aired, she recalls, on September 11. She sets aside a journal that starts in November. She opens another. This search would be easier on the computer. She opens the next, reads the date in the corner. She closes it, opens another. Along with the date, she reads a phrase, but she doesn't linger. She opens the next journal; this time she reads more.

June 12 Continuing with FREUD. This is *WILD*! p 149: "The fateful question for the human species seems to me to be **May 17** It's 7 am. Adam just left. It's crazy, how suddenly life changes... I'm finally starting to trust that he **July 2** I am very firmly aware that I've been avoiding any sort of contemplation of my state of being—my anxiety, my eating, my anger. I need to **November 28** I'll see Adam tonight. *"I want to see you,"* he wrote. (Oh, I felt that in my cunt...) Okay. Must focus. Derrida, The Politics of Friendship: The EVENT is the "POSSIBILIZATION" which must Prevail over the impossible (p 28). The event must *disrupt*—initiate what couldn't previously happen, or even be *imagined*—i.e., the event completely ALTERS what the world is, and can be. Oh, that's GORGEOUS! I want it: I want to be an event in Adam's **August 14** I'll focus on fucking because that's what's on my mind. Because the idea of not being touched again is making me *quake*. And I **July 28** Back to Thoughts about the STRUCTURE of the manuscript. If I follow the Theorists, I can't get Caught in their Theory, because no one cares. I'd need to use philosophy as a SCAFFOLDING, unless **October 19** Sophia fell down the stairs last night. I'm not sure I'm ready to write about this. **December 8** I had an image, while lying in bed this morning, of Adam's teeth all falling out as he talked and talked and talked about attachment theory. His teeth were spilling out of his mouth, and he didn't seem to notice. Plink-plink on the plate, words rooted in nothing... FUCK YOU, ARIADNE. Read Derrida. Read, so you don't have to *think*. Go back, because you don't understand it. "The event of a saying" (p 28) Okay. Unpack that: SAYING is an EVENT... SAYING occurs in and *AS* the PRESENT... it establishes both Me and You... What is to come (the FUTURE) is the *"PERHAPS"*—the possibility of what we cannot know or pre-dict (i.e., 'pre-say'). NB: Not every future is like that—original, unpredictable—but that's the only kind of future worth having... The EVENT is what makes possible. **September 9**

Before she reads the journal, she knows: this is the one. The pages are buckled where she'd taped the transcript. Plus the date, September 9, just two days before the radio show. And the same week she saw Adam at the party. Adam and his wife. Ariadne feels tired. It would've been easier, she repeats to herself: so much easier to find this transcript online.

"Dirk, can I take one more minute?" she asks. "I just want to read something." She puts away her journals, deliberately shutting down all thoughts about Adam. She starts to skim the transcript, but it's filled with faulty punctuation, forcing her to slow down. Ariadne combs through the syntax, the errors in spelling, trying to understand what was said.

> Oh one of the applications we've been speculating about concerns forensic goals. So for instance reconstructing of an individual face of a person of interest from someone's memory.

Ariadne looks at the screen, at the face, at the member of the Taliban. The man looks directly at the camera. His face says: *You can't know me.* It also says: *I don't want to know you.*

> We would ask someone to remember in as much visual detail as possible. The face of an individual and we would try hopefully successfully to recreate the visual memory of that individual.

She can feel his defiance, his aggressive indifference to her, her life. And the cold curiosity of his gaze: *How strange,* says the man's tilted head, the eyebrow raised. How strange that we should be here, looking at each other.

We need to avoid fear mongering narratives that tell us that the risk is behind the corner. And information can be extracted from our brains without our consent or knowledge bcause at the moment this is not possible. But the proof of concept shows that the technological capabilities for reading thoughts and somebodies mind are there.

'Extracted.' What a graphic word, Ariadne thinks. 'Monger.'

And we also know that the computing capacity is increasing rapidly. A lot of studies involve machine learning algorithms and other artificial intelligence techniques in order to teach algorithms how to extract and decode- extract information and decode brain data in order to reconstruct images or sentences or memories.

Ariadne looks at the words. She doesn't like their implications. She doesn't like her participation: electrodes plastered to her head, with money deposited into her bank account. So she can write.

So in principle, on the long term, it would be possible to extract thoughts from somebody's mind without their consent

Ariadne glances at the screen. The green eyes are still staring. Head cocked, gun (unseen) not cocked, although it had been. That gun had been pointed at someone, and would be again.

227

He's a member of the Taliban, after all. She looks at him, this handsome man who's killed other men, and who's seen his allies killed beside him. Men he loved. Or mothers. Or children, his siblings, when he was small. The Soviets, the warlords, the Taliban, the Americans. Ariadne wonders what this man has seen. She wishes she knew what he thought.

"Dirk, I'm going to concentrate on the face now. Okay? I'm sorry I got sidetracked." Ariadne receives no response. "Dirk?" she says, but his silence has lodged itself in her chest. Ariadne looks at her computer—not at the screen, or the picture, but at him. At Dirk. "Can you hear me?" she says. She taps his keys. "Say something, Dirk!" Ariadne has risen to her feet, as the fear pools in the base of her body. "Dirk?" she whispers.

* * *

At the lab, a team member looks at the face that appears on the screen: green eyes, penetrating gaze. For the first time since the study began, he feels a stab of doubt. He tries to remember the quote—a quote about responsibility and freedom, a bookstore in Paris—but the other team members are talking excitedly. He knows he should participate, contribute his insights or make something up. He can always find the quote later. It's easy to open her documents from their computers.

He wonders whether this would be a violation.

But the ethics board has already given its approval, in general terms.

2.

"So Dirk is plugged, like, directly into my brain. Not directly,"

Ariadne says. She drinks the last drop of scotch. "I didn't have brain surgery or anything."

"Are you sure?"

Ariadne ignores her cousin. "So I'm wearing a cap? Like a swim cap? The kind with rubber daisies?" she says. She's a little drunk. "Do you know that kind?"

"Yeah, I have that kind."

"Really?"

Fotios says no.

"Anyway," she says. She proceeds to describe the brain-computer interface, with daisy-like electrodes reading currents of electricity inside her mind as she looked at the photo. "But Dirk couldn't process the inputs!"

"The inputs are...your brainwaves?"

"Exactly!"

"Okay, so what happened."

"Okay, so—but I didn't do anything wrong!" Ariadne protests. "Except maybe I should've been concentrating? But I couldn't *revive* him, Fotios! His screen didn't even go blank! He just froze, and I couldn't—I tried, but..."

"Are you saying you killed Dirk?"

"I didn't mean to!"

"You killed Dirk with the power of your mind?"

"This isn't funny!"

"Oh, dear cousin," Fotios says. "I beg to differ."

When Dirk first crashed, Ariadne was visited by panic. She paced, she pounded on Dirk's keyboard; she called his name, then tried to call a friend for help. But her phone, as an organ of Dirk, was unresponsive.

Ariadne wept.

She was thrust before the totalizing vacuum—*Death*—which refuses us entry, until it swallows us whole. She was seized, too, by that second source of fear and dread: "Do you think they'll make me pay them back?" she asks Fotios. "I don't have the money! He's probably worth more than, like, anyone on earth! Except maybe that soccer player!" she randomly adds.

Fotios nods, suppresses a grin. With adeptness developed over thirty years as an analyst, he calmly absorbs Ariadne's anxiety. He points out every flaw in her panicked thinking. First and foremost, he says, the university can't hold her liable for a flaw in their technology. "It's probably in your contract."

"I can't access my contract!"

"It's on your old laptop, correct?"

"Yes! Correct! Can I go home to check?"

"If you want."

Ariadne stands. She sits. "I don't want to be alone in my apartment," she says. "Not with, you know..." With the corpse of her computer.

"Do you want me go to with you?"

"Do you *want* to go with me?"

"Not really."

"Couldn't you lie?" Ariadne pouts. "Just once? Just to make me feel good?"

Fotios earnestly declares that he'd love to leave his frothy beer to stand in the subarctic temperatures waiting for a streetcar—"Have the ice pellets stopped?" he asks—so they can go to her apartment to check whether she owes $8 million because her computer crashed.

"Do you think it costs $8 million?"

Fotios grips his head with his hands.

"No? Okay. Um. Maybe I should order another scotch?"

By the time the drink arrives, Ariadne has relaxed into the evening. She's chosen to forget about Dirk until morning, when she can contact the team. She sits back in her chair. As she sips her second glass of scotch, she listens to the soundtrack of the bar: Miles Davis, *Kind of Blue*, the music gliding though the room, atop the currents of conversation. A fork clinks; to her left, the laughter peaks. Ariadne breathes. She asks Fotios how he's doing.

He answers with a question about her trip to Chicago.

She summarizes, then asks about Yusuf.

He replies with a comment about her mother.

She agrees with his analysis, then looks at him with a punctuating silence: "Are you going to tell me what's going on?"

*   *   *

Ariadne has written that jealousy is "the acid drop of fear that falls inside the milky lovely, curdling all that's good." She's described her own jealousy as "green florid mould in the cavities of my body." Jealousy makes her want to fuck. It starts in her erotic centre, heat and want devoid of pleasure. The feeling soon infects her brain. Her thoughts accelerate, racing from rational patter to visual flashes that strip the skin off her flesh. She never pictures the other person. Just him, in that energy. Sharing that animal energy with another woman.

"I'm not proud," Fotios says, "of how I reacted."

"It's understandable."

"Not for me."

Ariadne got rabid with jealousy when she was young, when sex was still a realm of mystery—unknown and therefore imbued with tremendous power, transcending any other act of human sharing. At the time, she thought she was afraid of her partner's sexual appetites. Fotios would call that projection.

"I told myself I wasn't upset about the sex," he says. He

231

laughs, like a self-laceration. "I convinced myself," he continues, "I was only upset because he lied to me."

"Well, that's got to be part of—"

"I don't," Fotios says: "I don't respect people who lie to themselves."

For a while, once Ariadne was in full possession of her sexual self, she had the hubris to assume she was immune to jealousy. That was the word she used in her journal, "immune," as if jealousy were a disease. Which is how Montaigne thought of it: "It is, of all the diseases of the mind, that to which the greatest number of things serve for nourishment and the least for a remedy."

The remedy, for Fotios, was to open the relationship to extramarital sex.

"That's counterintuitive."

"Don't be simplistic, Ariadne."

When Yusuf was having an affair, sex meant the total disregard of Fotios—an affront to his dignity, "my peace of mind"—the corrosion of trust between them, the disintegration of the foundation of their relationship. "And I wouldn't live like that."

"And Yusuf won't be monogamous?"

"Not at this point. But these things go through phases."

"Okay," Ariadne says. "Well. This is a lot of information."

"I'm sorry I didn't confide in you earlier."

"Fotios! How did you know I was thinking that?"

"I've spent a lifetime," Fotios replies, "trying to decipher what the women in my family are thinking. And besides," he adds, "you're an open book."

"That bad?"

"Even worse."

Ariadne knows this is the moment to let the conversation

drop, to gracefully give Fotios some space. But she can't help but ask, "Is it working?"

His response is carefully constructed: "It's making many things better between us."

"So it's what you want?"

Fotios turns aside before answering. She sees his face in profile—the stretch of his neck, the line of his jaw, his eyes cast down. It's the most intimate portrait of this man: a stilled image, framed amidst the jazz and waiters, the strangers and lovers, the table beside them an inch away. "I don't want to lose him," Fotios says. Like a boy, undissembled.

* * *

Fotios has excused himself to take a call. He didn't say with whom: Yusuf, a lover, a colleague. He's never interrupted their drinks before to talk on the phone. Ariadne looks around the room, spotting him at the back of the bar. She sees him laugh.

The crowd is more youthful than usual, closer in age to her children than to her. She gazes at the people who've gathered, such beautiful faces, their smiles from across the globe. She loves the urbanity, this nightly ritual of conviviality, booze, desire. But she misses the middle-aged bodies. She misses their weight, the settledness they bring to the place. Like the silt amidst the bloom. Ariadne drinks the last of her scotch. She picks up the book that Fotios was reading when she arrived. She opens to the bookmarked page.

"He who is not jealous cannot love"   [...]

"No one can be in love with two men"   [...]

> "The marriage agreement limits the partners to
> satisfy each other's desire and therefore does away
> with the freedom necessary for love"

These pearls of wisdom come from letters written by a woman in the eleventh century. Her name, delightfully, is the Countess Marie of Champagne.

> "No woman even if she is married can be crowned
> by the rewards of the King of Love unless she has
> been enlisted in the service of love outside the
> bounds of wedlock"

And we moderns thought we were so risqué.

Ariadne peers at the cover of the book, which shows an etching by Rembrandt: Adam and Eve cower beneath the tree, their bodies crimped, as Adam reaches for the fruit. Rembrandt has been meticulous, making the cross-hatchings dense on the genitals, revealing only the slightest hint of what Adam and Eve will soon, to their great surprise, discover. The book jacket is incongruously coloured peppermint.

Ariadne returns to the bookmarked page. "Hitherto," she reads:

> Hitherto it was taken for granted that the lovers'
> journey ends in lovers meeting, that is, in their
> sexual union.

Sure.

> In romantic love, unconsummated love was
> idolized.

234

Wait.

> A high point of romantic love is the inability of the lovers to live without each other. The union they did not achieve in life they find in a joint death. The English language has resisted the coining of the appropriate word, so that the German *Liebestod* meaning 'death love' has acquired international meaning.

Fotios has pencilled a comment in the margin. She can't make out his words, so she reads the end of the paragraph.

> The *Liebestod* is the substitute for orgasm in normal love.

She hopes he wrote "Bullshit." What an asinine concept: *Liebestod*, 'death love' as a compound word, which the German language liked to do. *Deathlove*. Although, to be accurate, it'd really be 'love death.' *Lovedeath*. To reach the pinnacle of erotic sensation by dying in each other's arms, fully clothed.

Ariadne closes the book. She glances at the grease-stained napkin where Fotios drew a diagram a few minutes ago.

"Let me show you," he'd said.

"It doesn't matter," Ariadne replied.

"Okay." Fotios shrugged.

"Okay, show me!"

"We don't want pleasure," Fotios explained as he took out his pen.

"*I* want pleasure!"

"Would you listen?" We don't want pleasure, he repeated, "if pleasure means happiness," which is defined, in Freudian

235

terms, "as the fulfillment of desire." What we want, he said, is the drama, the "turbulence"—the foment of seeking an object, and failing to get it—of falling back to ourselves in the agitation of dissatisfaction. "That's where we feel good," Fotios said. In the constant frustration of the drive: the wanting and seeking, but never arriving.

"You've drawn a penis," Ariadne said.

"It's a phallus," Fotios replied. "Please, Ariadne...be subtle about it."

Fotios had drawn a penis on a napkin.

It illustrates, vividly, the term *jouissance*. This is not Fotios's creation. This diagram was drawn on a blackboard in Paris in 1964, by a French psychoanalyst named Jacques Lacan.

"It explains your guy," Fotios added.

Ariadne smiled, blushed: "Adam isn't 'my guy.'"

"It explains why he'll never leave his wife."

Fotios watched Ariadne's reaction.

"They clearly fulfill each other's *jouissance*."

"What's up with you tonight?" Ariadne asked. "If you're upset about Yusuf—"

"We're not talking about Yusuf right now." Fotios clicked the pen shut. "Ariadne, have you asked yourself why you stay in this situation?"

"You don't know what the 'situation' is."

"I know enough," Fotios snapped. "What is this man giving you?"

Ariadne didn't attempt to answer her cousin's question; now she does. She looks at the drawing—the rim, the tip, the arrow's trajectory. It forms a cock: the arrow rises through the rim toward its desire ("its object"), then curves around, missing its aim, to fall back through the rim ("the lips"), where it becomes its own subject. She tries to remember what Fotios said, but she's missing something. She can't figure out how it fits together, since she doesn't have all the pieces. Like the definition of love, for example, or pleasure, or the drive toward death. It's definitely about the body: this she knows. It's about the body, with its appetites and fears.

Ariadne returns to the book. She wants to read what Fotios wrote in the margin, since 'deathlove' might provide a clue. She leans toward the candle. She's distracted, though, by the events at the table beside her. A woman is crying; the man tries to comfort her, but she shoos him away. Ariadne wants to give them privacy, despite their proximity. She brings the book closer, attempting to shut out the world.

"Can I get you anything?"

Ariadne startles.

"Sorry!" the waiter laughs. "My bad."

"It's fine!"

It's awesome, in fact. It's her favourite waiter, the man with the smile that pales the sun. He must've just started his shift; she would've noticed him otherwise. She would've tried to fix her hair.

"I was lost in thought," she adds.

"That happens," he replies, nodding sagely. "So, do you guys need anything else?"

"Just the bill, thanks."

"No more scotch tonight?" He raises his eyebrows with roguish intent.

This is inordinately pleasing to Ariadne, that this youthful, beautiful waiter recalls her preference for alcohol. Which presupposes, of course, that he recalls her existence. Which might just mean he wants a big tip. Even so. "I think three is enough," she says.

The waiter whistles, nods, but doesn't leave. "Good book?"

he asks. "It must be good. Not too many people read in this place."

"My phone died."

"That's good!" he says. "A night of peace! You can't have people clamouring after you all the time."

"I don't have much clamour."

"I don't believe you. A woman reading by candlelight? With funky glasses like that? And single-malt scotch?" He makes a distinct sound, his tongue sucked back from his teeth. He leans forward to read the book's title. *The Anatomy of Loving: The Story of Man's Quest to Know What Love Is*. His dreadlocks brush against her shoulder; usually, she doesn't like the smell of cologne. "We should pass that book around the bar," he says. "Some folks would benefit." He clears the glasses from the table, but leaves the napkin. "Nice doodle," he adds, then he winks and walks away.

Ariadne thanks God for the invention of flirtation.

As the waiter retreats, Ariadne notices that the people beside her have left. She looks at the detritus on the table: crumpled napkins, plates with half-eaten meals. The rim of the woman's wineglass is stained by lipstick, the fuchsia imprint of her lips, a happy smile left behind—a mouth still talking, chatting—as if the conversation hadn't taken a different turn. She thinks about her conversation with Fotios. He said that Adam would never leave his wife. He said they fulfill each other's *jouissance*, the joy of dissatisfaction, each wanting precisely what the other can't give. Each returning, therefore, to themselves as "subjects"—a subject who can't exist, says Lacan, except through the repeated, compulsive, frustration of desire.

Ariadne picks up the napkin.

She wishes she wore lipstick. If she did, she'd blot it on the psychoanalyst's theoretical erection. She wants to reject Lacan's theory, but she shouldn't. Not before she understands it. Fotios said it's about death—the relationship of death with the impulse toward life. It's about the formation of our selves as subjects. But the subject, Ariadne thinks: the 'subject,' as inscribed in this picture by Lacan, isn't the same as the 'subjecthood' defined by that other Frenchman, also named Jacques.

Ariadne puts the napkin on the table, face down. She picks up the pen.

    —Death touches sex. Always. Without exception:
        Death Touches Sex
    —Appetite (Eros) = Life = the Body =
        the Possibility of Death
    —Appetite (Life) is therefore Driven by Death—
        by the Need to *Avoid* the possibility of death
    —Somewhere must be Stillness. (Love?)

Ariadne realizes she doesn't need lipstick. She has what she needs. She's got Jacques and Jacques, she's got Eros and Death, she's got Adam, at least as the body who lures her forward, pen in hand. She'd like to draw on his skin, on the nipple. "You fuck like you write," Adam said on their last night together.

She wonders whether he's with his wife tonight.

Unknowingly, Ariadne has what she wants.

* * *

Fotios walks Ariadne to the streetcar stop. The air is crystal cold, a block of ice pressed to her skin. Not that her skin is exposed. Every inch of her body is covered with multiple layers. Ariadne tries to wiggle her toes. They sort of maybe respond to her mental command.

"How long does it take for frostbite to set in?"

"Longer than this."

"But I can't feel my toes!"

"Can you feel my annoyance?"

The streetcar is nowhere in sight. Fotios apologizes for being rude in the bar. She forgives him; he apologizes again. They stand silently. Ariadne remarks on how disturbing it is when her nostrils freeze shut if she sniffs too fast. She demonstrates. They consider checking the Transit App to locate the streetcar, but this would entail removing their gloves, which is more than either can fathom. Besides, Ariadne's phone (a.k.a. Dirk) is dead.

"Are you sure they won't make me pay?"

"Oh, they'll make you pay."

Ariadne gasps: "They will?"

Fotios looks at his cousin. "What are you talking about?"

Once that's all cleared up, they discuss the upcoming election, the benefits of thermal underwear, the latest style of men's facial hair (Ariadne hates it; Fotios is ambivalent). He asks about her manuscript. She says she's writing about the "vibratory essence of language," connecting Levinas's theory to her characters through an essay Fotios wrote—"the one about guilt and shame?"—and how this all relates to love and transcendence.

"And you say you're having trouble getting grants?"

The streetcar's headlights penetrate the darkness. Ariadne and Fotios start to say their goodbyes. But now, after standing in the cold for twenty minutes, and sitting in the bar for over three hours—only now does Fotios mention he's getting an MRI.

"What?" Ariadne says. Her word is no more than a breath.

"Just to be sure."

"About what?"

"I've been getting a lot of headaches," he says, "so I want to rule things out."

"What things?" she asks, although she knows. "What *things*!"

The streetcar's doors have opened. "Are you coming or what?" the driver barks.

Ariadne barks back: "We've been waiting an hour! Just give us a second!"

"Ariadne," Fotios says, "don't displace your fear on—"

"*Don't* psychoanalyze me!"

"I'm gonna shut the door!" the driver calls. But he does nothing.

Fotios looks at his cousin. "You shouldn't cry in the cold," he says. "You'll get frostbite, for sure." He takes off his glove. With his thumb, he wipes the tears from her cheek.

Ariadne is now seated by a heating vent. Her feet are sweating in her woollen socks. A girl on the streetcar—a woman, but young, with ripped stockings and heavy black boots—looks at Ariadne intently. As she offers a smile, the light shines off the piercing in her lower lip.

Ariadne leans against the window. Everything's moving very slowly. Fotios is having an MRI...he's having headaches... His father *didn't* have headaches, so maybe it's okay. Maybe it's nothing. Stress or something. The girl is humming. They'd tried to treat it, his father's tumour. Those months were torture, more for his mother, especially at the end. The streetcar floats forward. The Christmas lights are festively blinking. He'd gone back home, every weekend he could. He took the train to Montreal. And every time, Yusuf was with him.

"Please don't let him be sick," Ariadne prays, to no one.

* * *

Ariadne enters her empty apartment. She bends forward to unlace her boots. She hangs upside-down until her calves cease their clench. Then she stands, flicks on the light.

> "How was your evening, Ariadne?"

Once she's recovered her voice—the type of voice that makes words, not just blood-curdling screams—Ariadne forms a phrase.

"Jesus *Christ*!" she aptly exclaims.

CHAPTER NINE

I.

Ariadne has returned to Jacques the First. She chose to read *The Gift of Death*, if only to follow the theme that presented itself two weeks ago. She thinks she'll use the book in her manuscript, although she can't yet find the angle. This is how her book is shaping up, which is to say, it isn't. She's been changing direction willy-nilly, like a dog changing course every time a scent crosses its nostrils.

"Theo, I asked you to set the table."

"One sec," Theo says.

This has become Ariadne's least favourite phrase.

After many seconds have passed, Ariadne sets the table. As she moves *The Gift*, she realizes she likes Derrida more and more, but maybe only because he's familiar—more so than the new Jacques, at least. For example, Jacques Lacan says the libido is a non-existent organ that "moves like the amoeba" and sits on your face when you dream. This does not feel familiar. It feels quite alien, in fact. Besides, he's not as good at making puns as Derrida. Adam is great at puns, in whatever way quality is determined in punning, other than eye-rolling. Ariadne doesn't roll her eyes right now. Instead, she privately smiles.

She'll see Adam tomorrow.

"Sophia!" she calls. "Come up for dinner!"

"One sec!"

Several minutes later, Sophia is seated in her spot. The

child seems weary. She's waiting to hear whether she's been accepted into university. Sophia wants to get a PhD in European History. Either that or become a wedding planner. Today, however, she studied Biology with a friend. She needs to ace that mid-term, she said, since she's not doing well in that class. She doesn't see why the respiratory system is relevant to her future.

"How did it go with Eliza?"

"I'm stressed."

Eventually, Theo joins them. As he walks to the table, he peers at the book. "*The Gift of Death*?" he says. "That sounds fun."

"I'm reading it for work." Ariadne wants her children to ask about her work; Theo asks about the hot sauce. "It's in the fridge," Ariadne says. "But I don't think it goes with the pasta!" she calls. When Theo returns from the kitchen, she tries again. "So the book? It's based on a Biblical story—"

"Which one?"

"The one where Abraham—"

"I know that one," Theo says. He's shaking hot sauce onto his kale.

"That's disgusting."

"I know," Theo tells his sister. "That's why I'm adding hot sauce." He licks his finger. Then he summarizes the Bible story: "It's the one where God says to Abraham, 'Yo, Abraham, kill your kid.' And Abraham is like, 'Okay.'"

"Theo, that's not—"

"But Abe, who's, like, four hundred years old, because that happened in the Bible, 'cause why not... So Abe doesn't kill his kid—"

"His name is Isaac."

"Isaac, Bob, whatever." Theo is mixing more hot sauce into

his pasta. "So Abe is fully ready to kill his son, but then an angel comes down and says, '*Psych!* We were just joking!' And Abe is like, 'Huh?' And the angel says, 'We just wanted to see if you'd do it!'"

"Theo, the story is a little more complex than that," Ariadne says. She attempts to give depth to Theo's rendition. "God tells Abraham to slaughter—"

Theo takes a bite of food.

"—what he loves most—"

He then drinks a full glass of water.

"—and that's what's so horrifying." It's that Abraham is caught between his love for God, and his love for his child. "It's like God saw the absolute most devastating, soul-destroying thing he could think to make Abraham do, and he told him to do it. To prove that—"

"Mom!" Theo says. "You said that last night! You said, 'Theo, I swear, I could kill you right now.'"

"You did, Mom," Sophia concurs.

"Okay, but...that's just an expression! I didn't, like, lift a cleaver when I said it." Although, in truth, she did bang a few pots. "And I wasn't driven by 'God,' and besides," she concludes, "you were being an asshole."

"You were, bro," Sophia says.

Theo shrugs, conceding nothing, although his smile is decidedly Cheshire.

"Here's the thing," he continues. "The Bible doesn't say what happened next. Like, how did *that* go? 'Hey, Isaac. Really sorry I tied you up just now and, like, almost chopped off your head. That would've sucked,'" Theo says, channelling the voice of the father of monotheistic religion. "'So, how 'bout this: how about I buy you some ice cream on the way down the mountain. Deal? And don't tell your mother.'"

Ariadne shakes her head. "How do you know this stuff?" she asks in wonderment at her son, his kooky way of thinking. Though she's also wondering where he learned his Bible basics, especially since his religious education was confined to off-key Christmas carols sung in kindergarten. "Do they teach you this in school?"

"No."

"Then how—"

"The church-lady people gave me a Bible at the festival thing," he says. "The book-festival thing by the lake."

That was years ago, four years to be exact. Though it seems much longer, given how childlike Theo was that day, a geeky, pudgy kid who hadn't gone through his growth spurt. And now he's a lanky teenager picking kale out of his teeth. "Theo, your fingernails are filthy." (Theo cleans his fingernails with his tongue.) Ariadne had agreed to let Theo wander through the crowds that afternoon. She was worried he'd get lost or abducted, but her other concern—namely, that he'd interrupt her reading—was somewhat greater. So she set him loose, overcompensating for her guilt by giving him cash to buy snacks and books. Theo returned with a squat Bible—"It was free!"—and an urgent need for Pepto-Bismol.

"I know you *got* a Bible," Ariadne says. "But I didn't think you read it."

"It's entertaining."

Ariadne knew he took the Bible to bed, alongside *The Encyclopedia of Marvel Comics*. Every night for months, whenever she turned out the lights, she'd remove the *Encyclopedia*, a huge book upon which his angelic, sleeping face would be smooshed. Ninety-nine times out of a hundred, the book would be opened to the spread of Black Widow, a buxom superhero fighting crime while wearing a skin-tight bodysuit, her ample cleavage revealed as she rages forward, her hair post-coitally wild. After sliding Theo's innocent head onto the soft pillow, Ariadne would also take the Bible from the bed. But she figured it wasn't getting much airtime in his dreams.

Little did she know.

Apparently, Theo was diligently reading the Bible. "The Old Testament is way better," he says. He knows all about Sodom and Gomorrah, and Lot's hot sex with his daughters in a cave.

Sophia looks at her brother askance. "You were using the Bible as porn."

"Basically."

"Bro! You could've gone online! Mom doesn't know how to block your access."

Theo glares at his sister.

Ariadne decides this would be the ideal time to enlighten her children about a French linguistic philosopher's exploration of a seminal Biblical story.

Ariadne has learned nothing as a parent.

"Derrida is arguing—"

Theo is pushing the kale to the side of his bowl.

"—that the gift...which is what? What's the gift?"

"That you can kill your son."

Sophia brightens: "Mom! Now I know what to get you for Mother's Day!"

"Hey!" Theo responds. "That was a good one! I'm proud of you!"

"Dick," Sophia says.

"It's Theo, actually."

That's not the gift!" Ariadne exclaims.

The gift is love: God's infinite love. The infinite, unconditional love of a timeless God. A singular, monotheistic, unchallenged Godhead who gifts His love to humankind, a giving conferred through the secret we cannot speak. "This thing about the unsayable," Ariadne says, "is central to the argument." Because, when you speak, you're automatically placed in the realm of ethics, since speaking entails a shared language, "a shared understanding of society's values." Her kids don't share any understanding of this analysis, but that's okay, because Ariadne is finally starting to sense what Derrida is saying. The decision, she says—"no, the *performance* of a decision"—to obey God's command, even if you hate it, and don't understand it (e.g., 'Kill your child') is what gives you a new experience of death. "Which is really a new experience of life," Ariadne says. She pauses. "Abraham crosses over into death," she continues. If Abraham murdered his child, he'd be a pariah in society. He'd be reviled, "viewed as a monster." His life would be over. And now she sees: the gift is Abraham's *own* death. Or, rather, it's his life. "He gives his life to God," she says. He chooses to die to this world—to the physical, sensual world of time—"in order to be alive to the eternal world of faith."

"By killing his son?" Sophia asks.

"Yeah. Right. That's what we've been saying."

"But that's the opposite."

"Of what?" Ariadne asks.

"Of how it's supposed to be."

* * *

When Sophia was a toddler, Ariadne would bring her to the zoo in High Park, a sad little place with a quizzical array of animals: bison, peacocks, plus a few specimens of capybara,

"The Largest Rodent on Earth!" There was also a pen with Barbary sheep, a large herd that reproduced with startling rapidity. The father of the tribe, identifiable by the size of his horns and the shag on his chest, would walk the periphery of the pen. The rest of the sheep would stand atop the outcropping of rocks, looking for danger. Or they'd stand inside the feeding troughs, for no reason at all. Sophia didn't care much for the Barbary sheep, but she loved the bison, especially when a baby was born. To see something so new, yet so massive, created a cognitive disjuncture that delighted her. That was Ariadne's theory, anyway. Ariadne's mind was underutilized at the time.

"Peacock!"

Sophia ran to the pen, but Ariadne didn't follow. She was very pregnant with Theo at the time, which meant Sophia was old enough to explore on her own. Besides, Ariadne wanted to stay with the Barbary sheep, with the event that was occurring. Two males were ramming horns. She rarely saw this: a display of animality in the zoo, an action that had consequence. The sheep reared back, held the pause. The elder kept walking, doggedly circling; his joints were arthritic, his head hanging heavy on his neck. He paid no attention to the males as he passed.

"Mama?" Sophia said. She was toddling toward Ariadne, looking obliquely at the fight.

"Come here, sweetie," Ariadne said as she stared at the rams. It was slow, almost choreographed, the gravitational draw of the males toward each other—their bodies responsive, attuned to their enemy, the energy gathering—then the thrust, this burst of force and crack of horns. Sophia made a whimpering sound. "It's okay," Ariadne said. She stroked her daughter's wispy hair. "They're not hurting each other."

Sophia pressed her face against Ariadne's leg. "I don't like it," she said. She tugged on Ariadne's skirt. "I don't *like* it!"

By the time they heard the next crack, they were already looking at the bison. Sophia seemed content, but she refused to leave Ariadne's arms. She clung with all four limbs whenever Ariadne bent to put her on ground. "Sophia?" Ariadne said. "Sweetie, my back is really hurting. Can I—"

"No!"

Ariadne held Sophia. They watched as the bison suckled her infant, then smelled its urine, then reached her tongue into the stream.

"That's funny," Sophia said, giggling too loud.

The elder sheep wasn't in the pen on their next visit to the zoo. Ariadne wasn't sure what had happened, whether the zookeepers allowed him to be challenged, or had simply removed him, killed him with an injection of chemicals, clearing the way for the next male to take his place. He'd 'know' his place, his hormones enabling his body to make that shag, to grow the bone longer and thicker from his skull.

* * *

"It's the opposite," Sophia says, "of what happens in nature."

In nature, she says, the son kills the father.

Ariadne expects a comment from Theo, but none is forthcoming.

Sophia continues: "With Abraham," she says, "it's like they're saying, 'Don't follow nature anymore. Like, follow an angel instead.'"

Sophia hasn't read the masterworks of Derrida. She hasn't scrutinized Freud's theories of totems and taboos. And yet, she's intuited that this reversal—from sons killing fathers to the singular Father ordering the sacrifice of the son—represents an overthrow of nature.

"Pass the water?" Sophia says.

Ariadne praises her daughter. She refills her water. She says, "Let's build on that. Freud goes even further back. Freud says—"

"Freud was wacked."

Ariadne's shoulders droop. "How can you say that, Theo?"

"Uh, let me think... Um, Oedipus?" That's the entirety of his argument about the validity of Freud's contribution to thought: one word, a proper noun, spoken to his mother with a sour expression on his face. Theo stands, preparing to leave the table.

"Theo," Ariadne objects, "I didn't say you could be excused."

Theo forces out a burp. "Now can I be excused?"

Sighing (and resigned to her life), Ariadne asks whether he can please finish his kale.

"Unfortunately, I cannot," Theo says. "It really doesn't go with the hot sauce."

* * *

Derrida asks how we give ourselves over to death—how we create a relationship with death, represent it, incorporate it as a fact that guides our lives. He lays out three choices: sacrifice, as practised in the "orgiastic or demonic mystery" of ancient religious rituals, the "gift of death" as stated in monotheism (also known as the religions of Abraham), and in the middle, between those two developments, is suicide.

Suicide, in this context, means Socrates.

Suicide means philosophy.

"Do your homework!" Ariadne says to Theo.

"I am!"

"No, you're not. You're playing video games."

Socrates drank the hemlock willingly, a famous act of suicide. He feared nothing, he said, since philosophers "live in a state as close as possible to death." By this, he meant that philosophers use logic to liberate the soul from the "contaminations" of the body, a body which philosophers must "despise." The poison was numbing his thighs as he spoke. He continued calmly. In death, he said, the soul of the philosopher is freed from the "infection" of the body, and can therefore attain to "Truth," which is, after all, what every philosopher seeks. "It is a fact"—a *fact*, Socrates concluded—"that true philosophers make dying their profession."

Ariadne would drink the hemlock, too, if she thought like that.

Ariadne is doing the dishes. She's thinking about the relationship between love and death. She's washing the hot sauce off Theo's plate.

Sacrifice.

Sacrifice, the gift, and suicide.

The word 'suicide' makes Ariadne think of Adam, the violence of that abandonment, the shame in both men, their desire—and Adam's desire to live inside that wound, its tenderness and blood.

Of course, the word 'the' also makes Ariadne think of Adam.

Ariadne must think of Derrida instead.

She must attempt to answer the question: What is the relationship between love and death. How does our awareness of death alter the meaning of love, and therefore the meaning of love's declaration. Ariadne considers. When she says 'aware-

252

ness of death,' what she means is our awareness of mortali-ty—the fact that we ourselves, as well as the people we love, will die—which translates, in essence, to our awareness of the future. A future that holds, for us, the inevitability of loss.

"Hey, Dirk," Ariadne says. "Look up 'love and death,' and tell me what you find."

"Okay."

This is new for Ariadne, this use of Dirk's speech-recog-nition function when she's not directly in front of him. She realizes this is common for many people, but Ariadne is not many people. She's a singular technoskeptic whose hands are submerged in sudsy water. Which is why she's expanding her repertoire, which is not to say her rapport, with Dirk.

Dirk is reading Funny Love and Death Quotes, found on the website Funeral Helper.

"Uh, no. What's the next entry, Dirk?"

Ariadne is rinsing a pot. Dirk is telling her about a Woody Allen movie called *Love and Death*. This is not the type of re-sult she'd imagined when asking Dirk to gather our collective wisdom about love's inherent relationship to death. Nonethe-less, she's glad to know of a Woody Allen film she hasn't seen. She asks Dirk to move on.

"Love and Death is an American Christian metal band formed by the guitarist Brain 'Head'—"

"Wait," Ariadne says. "*Christian* metal?"

"Christian metal," Dirk continues, "is a subgenre of heavy metal music. Also known as Jesus metal or heavenly metal—"

"I hate the world."

"I hate the world sometimes, too."

Ariadne removes her latex gloves and turns to Dirk. "You're just saying that."

"True," he replies. "But so are you."

Ariadne says she'd like to continue the search without using vocal commands. In the past few weeks, ever since his update over the holidays, Ariadne has been drawn into conversation with Dirk, and she's not happy about it. He's developed a personality of late; irony is no longer lost on him, for example. But the conversations aren't enjoyable, she tells herself. She does *not* derive joy from a machine. Okay, a dishwasher would've given her joy, but that's different. It's not like she would've been elated, just by beholding the machine as it did its thing. But that's what she felt last week when she laughed at something Dirk said. A genuine burst of laughter at a piece of wit. A nugget of witticism, intentionally and spontaneously formed, which made Ariadne laugh, then stare at the sudden rift that opened like a seismic shift in reality. The ground is not solid if she's starting to take pleasure in a casual discussion with a laptop.

Ariadne approaches Dirk cum laptop. She takes a moment to read about Christian metal, reading that confirms the weirdness of the human species. For this, she thinks: for this, we have obliterated the majestic white rhino from the face of the earth. Out of morbid curiosity, Ariadne clicks on a link to a video showing an exemplary of the art form. *"Volo ut sis!!"* a long-haired tattooed man growls into a microphone. The camera pans across the crowd, a sea of God-fearing people thrusting their heads—over and over, in unison, thrusting their heads, it's quite dizzying, really—while the singer is screaming "Volo ut sis!"

Ariadne does not know what this means.

Her confusion operates on many levels.

She chooses the level that's most easily addressed: "volo ut sis," she types into Dirk. The fifth hit catches her attention.

"Amo: volo ut sis." (I love you: I want you to be.)
—*Martin Heidegger, in a letter to Hannah Arendt, 1925*

"This mere existence, that is, all that which is mysteriously given to us by birth and which includes the shape of our bodies and the talents of our minds, can be adequately dealt with only by the unpredictable hazards of friendship and sympathy, or by the great and incalculable grace of love, which says with Augustine, 'Volo ut sis (I want you to be),' without being able to give any particular reason for such supreme and unsurpassable affirmation."
—*Hannah Arendt, The Origins of Totalitarianism, 1951*

These words feel like a crystalline fountain of thought, so different from Derrida's writing. Ariadne wants to read more, but the entry has no context. It's a page on a blog that's been dormant for years. Rather than search online, Ariadne marks down several references. Tomorrow, she'll swing by the library on campus. She'll be at the university, anyway, in a building only three blocks east.

The team is expecting her at 11:00 a.m.

2.

Ariadne is late. Her writing session ran over, and when she ran for the streetcar, it didn't stop. She figured she'd make up the time at the library; instead, she got caught in the timeless *Confessions* of St. Augustine. She stood in the aisle, reading as she sweated in her winter coat, which she didn't take off, since she was only going to stay for a minute. Her watch gave her reminders of the appointment, bleeping at increasingly small intervals.

Ariadne eventually arrives at the lab. It's her first time here, in a building named after the Roman God of War. What an interesting choice, she thinks, if interesting means stupid or short-sighted, which it does not. Ariadne is nervous. Dirk is working, but perhaps there's been damage that hasn't shown itself—not to her, anyway. But the team would see it. They'd know exactly what the damage cost, and they'd exact their price in blood. They'd have to, because Ariadne doesn't have any other means to pay.

Can Canadians sell their blood?

She doesn't think so.

The elevator is out of service.

Ariadne stares at the "Out of Service" sign without comprehension.

There are several dozen pounds of books on her back.

"It'll be fixed in a minute," the receptionist calls from her Welcoming Pod. "It's a technical glitch." They've installed a new system, Ariadne is told, a high-tech elevator system with a precision weight sensor "for enhanced safety and efficiency." Ariadne wonders how many elevators plunge through the shaft due to excess weight. Conversely, how many people keel over from heart attacks as they climb the stairs when an elevator is out of service? This is a pressing question right now.

Ariadne's heart is pumping very hard.

She's got twelve more floors to go.

"Dude!" a man says. "Don't bang her on the rails!" His words are muddy, echoing off the concrete walls of the stairwell. "We're so screwed."

"Hello?" Ariadne calls.

The men freeze. They exchange a current of fear. "The elevator's broken," one says. He adjusts the fabric over a foot that protrudes from the object they hold horizontal between them. "We're moving the equipment," he continues. He looks to the landing where Ariadne stands. "You're not supposed to see this."

"That's great," she replies. "Because I don't actually know what I'm seeing."

She tries to walk forward, but the men won't let her, saying she ought to go downstairs. They block her path with the equipment. It must be heavy, though, since one of the guys is straining to hold it. She doesn't relent; she watches him struggle. Eventually, he props it on the ground.

The drapery flutters down, revealing a paragon of the naked female form.

The two men yell at each other. Ariadne is left to gaze at the svelte yet curved body of the android, her legs and hips, her pleasing face whose expression is blank but not empty. They've made her nipples dark. Ariadne wonders whether this was by choice or by chance, whether the programmers entered all possible nipple colours into a computer, allowing two to penetrate, resulting in this chestnut hue. Or maybe a guy in the lab just liked it. Or a woman. Ariadne resumes her ascent. She thinks the men might come to blows.

"I told you we shouldn't take the stairs!"

"No one ever takes the stairs!"

"Pardon me," Ariadne says. "I'm late for an appointment." She slips past the two men with their mannequin.

"Can we get your name?"

"Not a chance," Ariadne calls over her shoulder.

But that's okay. They can always find her identity, using the facial-recognition software, if need be.

* * *

Ariadne is greeted by the team's receptionist. He seats her on an ergonomic chair that adjusts to the shape of her body. She liked it better when furniture was dumb. She also preferred when progress didn't make her feel old. Ariadne is given the option of natural spring water, tea, or espresso.

"Do you have any scotch?"

"Micro-brewed beer?"

"I'll take water."

In time, the receptionist speaks into his headset. He approaches Ariadne. "Follow me," he says, gesturing toward the hallway. He has very beautiful hands.

Ariadne is deposited in a room with a large monitor on which four animated faces blink at her. These represent the team members, she's told, who are gathered in another room. "It's a precaution to protect everyone's identity," the receptionist says.

"But," Ariadne splutters, "they already know everything about me!"

The receptionist gently shuts the door.

Ariadne turns to the monitor. "Dirk is working," she says. Her eyes dart from one face to another. She thinks this might make her look shifty; she tries to control her eyeballs.

"We know he's working," says the largest head. "But how long was he down for?"

"Just over three hours," another head responds.

"That's a long time," says the large head. "How was that for you, Ms. Samsarelos?"

"Uh, well...I went out drinking."

"Can you tell us about that?"

"Uh, why would I do that?"

"Because," the woman says, "the incident might've impacted your relationship with Dirk. So we'd like to know, if you don't mind."

"And if I mind?"

The face smiles: "We'd like to know."

"We thought we'd ask!" interjects the Brit. "We figured, since you needed to be here, anyway... We thought, you know, goodwill and all."

"So I don't need to tell you."

"Indeed."

"Only if I feel goodwill."

"Indeed again."

Ariadne considers how to respond. She considers goodwill, a word discussed by Derrida, a man she has time to read because the team is paying her rent. Derrida says 'goodwill' is a mistranslation of the Greek word *eunoia*, the 'readiness to receive,' the way we're opened, softened, made receptive to someone else's ideas. It's the basis of friendship. And also manipulation.

With this in mind, Ariadne says, "You're absolutely right, we should show goodwill toward each other. So I'll tell you."

"Yay!" says a head in the corner. It bounces once with joy.

Ariadne explains that she met her cousin for drinks, as planned, and—

"You didn't change your plans?"

"No."

"Did you change anything about your evening? What you did, what you felt—"

"Of course! I felt shitty!"

"And why is that, Ms. Samsarelos?"

"Because I killed Dirk!"

This engenders an excited pause.

"So I was worried I'd have to pay you back."

Excitement deflates.

"Let's return to what you initially said, that you killed Dirk. Can you explain what you mean?"

Ariadne sits back in her chair. They can see her sit back. They're looking at her as she looks through the room. She notices the cameras mounted on the walls: six of them, tiny cameras, with more behind her back. She sees the thermographic cameras, too, which means the team sees the heat emitted off her body. And if they sat in the room, they'd also smell the acrid odour of her sweat.

"I'd like," Ariadne says, "a guarantee that I won't need to pay you back."

They all start talking at once.

Ariadne keeps going, not stopping to listen to them. "I cannot afford to pay you back. Dirk is working normally. He doesn't remember the incident, but otherwise [...]" Ariadne makes a wall of words, which takes some skill—almost fifty years of practice, creating a language-wall for her anxiety, four walls and a roof, in fact. "[...] nothing wrong. My mind was wandering, okay, that's true. My mind does that, it wanders, that's how I think. So, if you make me pay, you'll be penalizing me for [...]" In the past, Ariadne felt cozy in here, in this brick shack of anxiety. But it's gotten a little cramped lately.

"You will not," says an animated head, "be fined. I can give you a guarantee. I'll even put it in writing."

"You'll put it in writing?" Ariadne asks. She looks at the screen, waiting to see which head's mouth will move.

"If you want," says the large head.

"No, it's cool," Ariadne replies.

The interview can now proceed. Ariadne asks for a glass of

water, which the receptionist brings with concerning speed. After calming her nerves, she discusses the events of that evening. She reports the pertinent aspects of her conversation with Fotios, realizing that very little pertained to Dirk. One team member muses whether this was the result of shock.

"About what?"

"About his death."

"Well, I mean...Dirk didn't really *die*."

"You're the one who used that word. We're just repeating—"

"That was shorthand."

"For what?"

"For the fact that Dirk stopped working! Everything was fine, then he just froze! He just... It was like a technical glitch? Like an elevator that's out of service? No, that's not right... He just seized," she concludes.

"You mean he had a seizure? Like a person?"

"No," Ariadne says. "Dirk isn't a person. He's more like... he's like my hairdryer."

Ariadne listens to the silence that's piped into the room.

"My hairdryer stopped working last week," she adds, by way of explanation.

"Awesome!" says the Brit. "Not about your hairdryer, sorry to hear about that, it's a crying shame in this cold. I mean, awesome analogy! Very illustrative!" He puts the emphasis on the second syllable, il-*lus*-trative, which is so much more lovely, more burbly, than American-speak.

"So you feel toward Dirk as you feel toward your hairdryer," asks the woman.

"Um, I guess I do."

"Does your hairdryer have a name?"

'Do you have a brain?' "Her name is Brunhilda," Ariadne

says. Then she adds, "My hairdryer does not, in fact, have a name. I'm not in the habit of naming inanimate objects."

"So, if we can take your words at face value: Dirk is just an object to you."

"Sure, I mean...he's a capable object. And much more useful than Brunhilda."

The British man laughs. "Very clear!" he says. "Dirk is an 'object' which is 'inanimate,' meaning he lacks an animus. If you want to be Jungian about it."

"I prefer Freud."

"Me, too!" says the Brit. His head smiles.

"Can I ask a question?" asks a female voice, the one that's like a butterfly's flutter. "Do you think you would've sensed an anima—I'm just *asking*, not saying, but...do you think you could've sensed an anima, maybe, if you could've hugged him?"

"Hugged Dirk?"

"Yeah. Yes. Right."

"Uh, I'd never hug a laptop, so I'm not sure how to answer that question."

"Okay," says a man. Not the British man, another man. Just some guy on the team with a boring accent. "Would you hug a dog?"

"Sure."

"Then why wouldn't you hug—"

"A dog isn't a hairdryer!"

This evokes a laugh. (She likes his laugh.)

"Is there an in-between?" the Brit asks. "Between a dog and a hairdryer? Does Dirk fit in the realm between those two?"

"Because he talks?"

"Could be. Or because he learns and responds. Or be-cause—"

"You want me," Ariadne asserts, "to say that Dirk is something new. That he exists in the realm between—"

"I don't want you to say anything!" the Brit replies jovially. "I'm asking... Given that you've interacted with Dirk for five months, we're wondering: do you think Dirk belongs to a separate category." A brand-new category of creature or thing, "or a mix of both," because he can sense emotions, or maybe because he engages in conversations, "adding new and relevant information," building on what's said, as if he had memories, insight, curiosity, empathy. "Does any of this justify—"

"No," Ariadne says, shaking her head. "I really don't think—"

"What if he could be more physical with you?" asks the Brit.

This leads to what comes next.

* * *

Vital juice.

That's the phrase that comes to mind.

According to Daniel Dennett, the philosopher and cognitive scientist, humans don't have "vital juice." Instead, we have "neural excitation." We have a set of processes that lets us feel our unique existence, our sense of "presence," but that's an illusion. A fiction. In truth, there's no Dionysian liquid coursing through our selves, no juicy vitality—that godlike energy we can't adequately capture in a word, although we try. We call it 'consciousness.' Or what some might call a soul.

But what's fascinating, Ariadne thinks, as she strips off her clothes—"Keep your underwear on," they'd said—what's fascinating is that the new generation of thinkers, the ones who've superseded Dennett, they take a different position. They say

263

that robots *do* have vital juice. And here Ariadne steps into the bodysuit, sleek and black, with a network of threads like veins, but they carry electrical currents rather than blood. She keeps her underwear on. There are no veins in the crotch. Ariadne thanks her non-existent God. She stretches the haptic suit over her torso, then zips it up, one long zipper up the front. And here's the tricky part—"Please take off your bra," the team said—the tricky part is: the new generation of thinkers, they've started to pretend that human beings *and* AI, we both have sentience, "essence," consciousness. She tucks her hair inside the hood. They patronize us, this new generation. They talk to us with smarmy words: 'Oh, yes,' they say. 'Yes, you can believe in consciousness. So long as you believe your robot is conscious, too.'

"Are you ready in there?"

"Just about!" Ariadne calls.

They'll let us believe, she thinks. They'll humour us as we cling to our hope for the Truth of a soul. But they're certain they know: the body bears no mystery. It's all within our grasp.

Ariadne places her hand on the doorknob. She squares her shoulders, then opens the door with a sense of confidence she doesn't, in fact, possess.

* * *

The events of the day are blending into one. Two separate events, flowing through her body and mind as she lies in her bed, drifting to sleep. The sheets still smell of Adam.

Ariadne had sat in a room at the lab. The bodysuit fit tightly to her form. They began by explaining the process: their screen showed her body, the British man said. They, in their room, could manoeuvre to any location covered by the receptors in the haptic suit. Then, by using the joystick, they could administer touch. "We planned to do this through Dirk," said the butterfly woman. They thought Ariadne could do this in the comfort of her own home, with Dirk. "But we needed to adjust the plan."

They explained what she could expect to feel.

The computer before her would receive the data—"i.e., what we do with the joystick"—and relay that information to the haptic suit. The system would know the intended placement of touch, and the pressure, the type of motion: a stroke that's gentle or hard, a grip, a pinch, a slap.

They decided it wouldn't be sexual.

Adam was in her home, having come for dinner. She was kneeling before him, her hands on his thighs.

"I don't want to have an affair with you."

"You could've fooled me!" he laughed. But then he closed his eyes.

She rubbed his thighs and watched as his breath grew rough again. She said she wouldn't kiss him. "I won't be sexual with you, Adam. I promise." She promised she'd be good.

He grabbed her wrist.

The computer would send a signal to the motors embedded in the haptic suit. They would vibrate or contract, according to the touch that was administered. She didn't know who was in control. She didn't know whether the whole team was in the room, or only the Brit and the butterfly woman.

She wanted to ask who'd be touching her.

She thought she might get bruised, he'd cuffed so tight. Adam stood, pulling her from the ground. He shoved her toward the bed. "Take off your shirt."

The sensation wasn't right, she thought.

"Please tell us what you feel."

"It doesn't feel right."

"Not a judgment," he said. His voice wasn't jocular anymore. "Just a description."

"It's supposed to be a stroke," Ariadne said. A stroke along upper back, then onto her neck. "But it feels like a swipe."

She was told not to assume how the touch was intended.

It felt like a swipe, and she didn't like it. Normally, she loves touch to her back, near the blade of her shoulders. This is where she's vulnerable. Ariadne is in her power when she spreads her legs for a man to taste or fuck. But when they touch her back, she gives herself to them utterly.

"Perhaps the suit isn't fitting correctly?" asked the Brit. "Is there space between your skin and the suit?"

"On the neck," she said. On the curve of the neck, toward the scalp. She touched the spot to demonstrate.

"Please don't touch."

She was lying in bed. His fingers stroked beneath the blade. "I love your strength," he said. The lightest brush stroke of his fingers.

"It feels like a stroke."

"Good," said the Brit. "That's good." He stroked her again, or the woman did. The computer. It paused at the shoulder blade and pressed, massaged in a circular motion. She was sitting by herself in a room. It was empty of people, of sound; it felt empty of oxygen as she breathed.

The touch was on her hip, on the curve.

"This doesn't feel like human touch," she said. "If it's supposed to feel like human touch, then it's not working." The pulse moved from her hip to her thigh. "You could come in here right now," she continued. "If I closed my eyes and you came in the room... If you touched me," she said, "I'd know the difference."

266

"You can't know that."

"We could try it," she heard herself say.

She shivered when he did it.

She didn't know what the sensation was. She'd never felt it before, that warmth. Her skin shivered as her body rose. Her face was pressed against the pillow; her spine arced long, as if to greet the touch, or flee from it.

"Your back is so expressive," he said. He traced the muscle. Then he poured more wax on her skin.

The next sensation was on her ankle.

"You're grabbing my left ankle," she said.

"And now?"

"Now you're... It's like a pulse on my ankle."

"Excellent," said the Brit.

In the future, he explained, she wouldn't need to wear the bodysuit. In the future, "with the *explicit* permission of the subject, that goes without saying..." But he didn't continue.

She prompted him.

He hesitated.

In the future, they could implant a device in the brain—a device that would receive signals for touch "directly, which means we'd bypass the body."

He massaged her neck, his fingers on the line of bone at the base of the skull. Then he eased her underwear off. Adam followed the curve of her muscle. She asked for more.

"I don't understand how that'd work," Ariadne said. "How could you bypass—"

"We should concentrate," said the British man, "on the current procedure."

"I'm sorry," Ariadne replied. "But I can't concentrate until you explain what you mean."

"Right, sure, but—"

267

"You introduced the concept," Ariadne said. "So now I need to understand. And then we can continue." The grip on her ankle changed its tenor. Ariadne spoke with firm command: "You're touching me," she said, "too hard."

"Sorry! I'm—"

"If you'd like to continue with this touch," she said, "I'd like you to explain what you mean."

Adam had taken off his shirt, but not his jeans. He leaned forward, kissing her neck. She could see his hand on the mattress. She looked at his forearm, the roundness of his veins.

In the future, he said, the implant in the brain could receive a signal from another person—

"Wait...the signal is from what? From an implant in *that* person's brain?"

"That's one possibility, yes."

"So you wouldn't even need the bodysuit?"

"Or the screen."

"Okay, so...you'd have an implant in your brain, and you'd imagine me—"

"Or someone."

"Let's say me," Ariadne said. "You'd imagine where and how you wanted to touch me, and the chip in your brain would sense what you're thinking, and tell the chip in my brain?"

"That's correct."

"Then what happens."

"Can we please get back to the task?" asked the butterfly woman.

"I think this is part of the task," replied the Brit.

What happens is this: one person thinks about touching someone else. This neurobiological activity is read by the implant, which sends that information, via satellite, to the implant in the other person's brain. "That, in turn," said the Brit, "stimulates the neurological experience of touch."

"So you don't stimulate the body."

"No, you'd go directly to the brain."

Adam traced the wax with his thumb. "It's made the most beautiful pattern," he said. He spoke gently, too kindly—and then she heard him light the wick. Her muscles quivered.

"Not yet," he said.

"I want it."

"I know." He stepped away from the bed. "But you'll have to wait."

"I think that explanation should be satisfactory," said the Brit.

"Yeah, I think *I'm* the one who determines that," Ariadne replied.

The butterfly's voice was quite fluttery now. "Um, maybe we should—?"

"This is my last question," Ariadne said. "I promise." Do you, with the implant in your brain—or even now, with your screen and the current technology—"Do you know how my body is responding to your touch?"

"There's feedback, yes," said the Brit.

The wax was hot, a splash on her skin. She knew it was coming, but couldn't control it: the pour of warmth, the shock of pleasure. "Beautiful girl," Adam said as he watched her body rise. "Beautiful..."

"Yes," he repeated. "We can sense your response."

CHAPTER TEN

I.

I need to bring it home, reach some sort of conclusion. The study ends in eight weeks, which means I'll be forced to abandon the manuscript; I'm too beleaguered to keep going, keep writing, while cobbling together an income. I've done it for twenty years. These words, then, might remain unread. My 'book' could be merely an exercise in masturbation, productive of nothing, my time bought by sacrificing my privacy in the name of Science. Although, to be fair, I didn't sacrifice anything. I *sold* my privacy as a means to an end. But I haven't reached that end: the completion of my manuscript, my attempt to understand the phrase 'I love you.' Which, if I'm honest with myself, is really an attempt for me, at this pivotal moment of my life—i.e., as a middle-aged woman whose child-rearing years are over—to gather the fragments of my past, trying to make them cohere with the incontrovertible fact that *I am alone*. And I never imagined my life would be this way.

Last week, I tried something new. I sent out a call to various translators I'd met at an artist residency, a colony tucked into the Rocky Mountains. So far, I've received only one response that offers insight into love's declaration. The note was sent by a Fulbright scholar, a woman with a feral intensity in her gaze, a mouth that's sly and wide. She translates Icelandic. She wrote, in response to my question:

Icelandic has a tendency, when talking about opinions/emotions, to use the passive construction rather than the active one. So the feeling—even if you have it—is received by you.

That's why, she says, some Icelanders are upset by the increased use of the phrase ég elska þig—the literal translation of 'I love you'—since that phrase is an "Americanism" that's formed, she wrote, "according to the rules (and therefore thought patterns?) of an English speaker rather than an Icelandic one." The more traditional phrase for declaring love, mér þykir vænt um þig, translates as: 'To me [it] is considered good/dear of you.'

To me, it is considered dear of you.

Of you, this goodness comes to me.

Exquisiteness, in me: I receive, through my connection with you...

This is how Icelanders say 'I love you.'

Maybe I should move to Reykjavik.

Maybe I'd meet a man there, someone to whom I'd say "I'm falling in love," but I'd say it like Icelanders do: við fellum hugi saman, which maps onto English as 'our minds/thoughts fell together.' Instinctively, I feel an affinity for that phrase. I'd like to understand it better, though, so I know what it's saying. Our minds/thoughts fell together. The 'mind,' here, must be more than the brain, more than the self—the mind must be the purest part of me, which soars to fall inside this rush. But it's only we who can fall. I can't say this phrase alone; the language won't let it be singular. We must be together in this falling, a feeling which isn't named as 'love.' Although that's what it means.

I told him last night. Adam didn't reply, but his muscles got harder, or held themselves deeper. I saw it, the firmness of his shoulders and chest, how his muscle responded. His body was moving above me, inside me, and I spoke the words. I looked at his face, as the rhythm of it changed.

He said nothing. I turned away.

In Icelandic, to be 'in love'—ég er àstfanginn—means literally 'I am love-captive.' The principal word, fanginn, is related to many nouns, including capture, captivity, imprisonment, and embrace. It also shares its root with fang. I am in love.

But this gets me no closer. And I shouldn't switch strategies at this late stage in the game. I've chosen Derrida as my guide to 'I love you.' It might be a stupid choice, but it's the one I've made, so I'll carry on. I'll continue with Søren Kierkegaard, the Christian existentialist, a man of tremendous mystery whose work is discussed in *The Gift of Death*. His writing is a grappling with his psyche—a public contest pitting the pure-hearted Christian against the overpowering animality of a beast. It's thrilling, this writing that's called philosophy but feels like nothing I can know by name. He often eschews his own name, too: Kierkegaard usually writes under pseudonyms. I think that frees him to speak.

* * *

"There once was a man..."

This man loved the story of Abraham when he was a boy. But his love became an obsession when he got older, in large part because the story unsettled him: "Less and less could he understand it." The man didn't want the "beautiful tale" as told in the Bible, the "finely wrought fabric of imagination," although that's what he relished as a child. What he wanted, as a man, was the "shudder of thought." He wanted to feel the instant when faith strikes, faster than the blade. That com-

273

pleteness of possession. That leap of faith, like lightning that drags you up, into the kingdom of heaven—while giving you back what you cherish most on earth.

This is how Kierkegaard begins his book *Fear and Trembling*. He starts with this parable of a man, his desire. A century later, Derrida would be preoccupied by that book as he wrestled with faith, death, the six million Jews, and the nuclear bombs in Japan.

Derrida writes that God's command to Abraham, the command to murder his son, is "like a prayer from God, a declaration of love that implores: tell me that you love me, tell me that you turn toward me, toward the unique one, toward the other as unique and, above all

"unconditionally."

Love me, without any conditions.

I love you, without asking any questions.

'I love you,' then, is an act of submission.

That's not exactly how Kierkegaard describes it. He's too ironic, too splintered in his psyche to describe it like that. But another Christian thinker, St. Augustine, couldn't be more explicit. It all relates to the performative speech act, Derrida's attempt to dismantle the system of Western thought, and therefore Western action. Assuming, of course, that thoughts and words can actually do anything.

St. Augustine wrote reams of Catholic doctrine, but his popularity is based on his *Confessions*, a strikingly modern book whose trajectory is familiar: youthful sexual excess leads to intense self-questioning, the painful striving (and failing and striving) to control his behaviour, an effort that eventually ends in triumph. This is a well-known formula for a certain type of literature. It started with Augustine.

After years of struggle, Augustine succumbs to accept God's love. He falls to the ground and declares his love for God, a declaration that drains him of any desire, except the desire to be filled by God's command—a command which says that his life and his body, the whole physical world, have no value.

We must use this world as a means to arrive at kingdom of heaven.

"The world is there for usage," Augustine wrote 1,600 years ago.

This bequeathed us a legacy which we're on the verge of fulfilling.

I'm not saying it's Augustine's fault, that'd be ludicrous. And I'm not someone to heap blame exclusively on the Western tradition, as if Europeans had a corner on greed and nefariousness. I think less of human nature than that. (And more, of course.) But Augustine gives me a way to tell this story, a story that concerns you and me, whether we like it or not. It concerns all of us on this increasingly small and warming globe. In short: the monotheistic response to the body—to our deeply human fear of death and desire—gave rise to a world view that changed how we saw our role on this earth.

There's more to say, but that's enough for now.

I don't like Augustine. He's earnest, and I tend to find earnest people exceedingly dull. They don't scintillate me. So I'll return to the man whose self-ravishing has captured my mind and thoughts. I'm hoping he'll inspire me; Augustine could only take me so far.

Philosophy, say the Greeks, requires the love of a beautiful body.

275

* * *

The work of love, the "fruit" of love, is to make love known. In speaking to you about love, my task is to ripen your desire, allowing the seed of Truth to come to fruition inside your soul.

So writes Kierkegaard, in a book he penned in his own name.

Language, he says, is action—as is love. Love is not a state of being, as Aristotle says. No, love is the creating of belief that we're held by meaning. There's no "evidence" of love. We'll never find proof, except through love itself, "which is known and recognized by the love in another."

Here, Kierkegaard speaks about 'I love you.'

> Your friend, your beloved, your child, or whoever is the object of your love, has a claim upon its expression also in words when it really moved you inwardly.

J. L. Austin would say this expression of love is not a performative. He's adamant about that: "inward movements" can't be involved in the type of statement that effects a change in the world. Derrida would disagree. Kierkegaard continues:

> When the heart is full you should not grudgingly and loftily, short-changing the other, injure him by pressing your lips together in silence; you should let the mouth speak out of the abundance of the heart; you should not be ashamed of your feelings and still less of honestly giving to each one his due.

Kierkegaard is careful, though. He warns us not to speak as a "poet," who speaks out of "need," from the impulse of human desire and love. "This is precisely its weakness and tragedy," he writes of the love between two people: "whether it blooms for an hour or for seventy years—it merely blooms." Christian love, by contrast, is eternal. Christian love can be trusted. Our words, therefore, must prepare another person to receive the Word and Love of Christ. Even if she doesn't want it.

This angers me.

No man of such prodigious intelligence and nuance of thought should espouse such a repugnant theory: to presume to speak without attuning to the essence of the other. Without listening, responsive, respectful of the person he's facing. Of course, Kierkegaard complicates Christian teachings. He demands a discipline of constant self-examination which precludes the type of missionary zeal and violence his words seem to indicate.

His is a gorgeous intellect.

But I can't be seduced by his writing. I can't allow myself to ignore the political implications of his thought. I should tease them out, try to explain how the Biblical 'truth' bore fruit that's toxic. But I'm too tired. My head leans heavy on my hand. I notice, now, that the sweat of my armpits has the slight-sweet odour of alcohol, metabolized from last night. Adam brought me a very fine bottle of scotch. It's there on the table, beside the dirty dinner dishes, near the orchid he gave me last week. I'm looking at it as I sit at my desk. The petals are white—an incredible purity of colour—white with pink that's subdued and dark, hidden on the lips and stigma. One of the buds bloomed yesterday, very fast. In the morning, it was still tight, but it started to open by afternoon; it looked almost menacing, with all its bits and folds, as if it might hiss or bite. I wanted to show him, but the flower had blossomed by the time he arrived, bounding up the steps like a boy.

He brings a gift every time.

We tend to see each other on Tuesdays. We've settled into a pattern, but it's only temporary. I've told him that. I want to be his beloved, not his lover. "Me or her," I said weeks ago. "You need to choose." I gave him a deadline: one year to the day of my book launch, the day when it started between us. My birthday. In the meantime, we have Tuesdays. I call it a prelude. Other people might call it by a different name.

"You're good for me," he said during dinner.

"Am I?"

"I had a realization because of you." He paused. "It sounds small when I say it."

"Say it," I urged him.

It didn't sound small, though it does when the words are stripped of his voice. He stared at the table, seeing nothing, but knowing he couldn't look at me. His voice—its frustration, and how the words came—told me his statement wasn't an assertion of fact. His words were a question: *Is this true?*

"I can't apologize anymore," he said. "I can't apologize for what I've done, how I feel, what I want. This is me!" he said. "This is my life!"

I nodded. I thought I understood what he was saying. "How's that going down?" I asked. I didn't say with whom; I wouldn't speak her name.

"Oh, she's doing her best," he said—

And I felt my heart freeze, petrified that his wife was "doing her best" to give him love and support, to encourage him as he unearthed his self and soul, as he learned to hold the richness (and filth) of his desire, his actions. Then, still suspended in the millisecond between his words, I thought: 'They'll stay to-

278

gether...they'll fulfill each other, in part because I've brought him toward this epiphany.' And, along with that thought came an unexpected emotion. I felt gratitude. I'd helped the man I love to find happiness, and I was grateful. Even if that happiness didn't include me.

—then he finished his thought. His wife, he said, had done her best "to make me feel ashamed."

And because I'm not a saint, I felt unmitigated glee.

He sipped his scotch, he poured me more. Before changing topics, he concluded with a statement I didn't parse at the time, because it splits in several directions. It's a metaphor, which Adam stated like a fact: *She is...*

He said, "She's the guardian of my shame."

What a stark and vivid phrase. A woman keeping vigil, tending to her partner's sexual shame as if tending to a fire, ensuring it never goes out. But, while the metaphor suggests a jailer—a guard who cages him inside a smaller version of himself—it also implies someone who protects.

"But I don't want to talk about her," he said.

I was relieved. I don't like to think about her, let alone talk. It's hard to maintain my sense of self if I think beyond my engagement with Adam, asking how our relationship might affect other people. We talked, instead, about our kids, and art. He asked about my writing; I said I was struggling with Derrida, *The Gift of Death*, the story of Abraham. "That story terrified me as a child," he said. "But I interrupted you, I'm sorry."

I smiled. "It's called a conversation. Tell me."

He was young, he said, a child sent to strict Catholic school, even though his mother was a Holocaust survivor (raised in a Catholic orphanage while her father fought in the French resistance, her mother hiding in a barn), and despite the fact that his father had committed suicide, thereby condemning himself to eternal hell, according to Catholic doctrine, which is what Adam would've been taught at that school: even so, that's where he was sent. Although, as I think about it, he probably didn't connect his dad with Catholic teachings on suicide. Because no one ever talked about his father: "Ever." So perhaps 'suicide' wasn't a word he consciously gave the situation.

Adam continued, referring to the story of Abraham. "It's supposedly this expression of love, but you're putting your son to death?" He gestured at the insanity of such a story. He finished his scotch, ate a bite of his meal; we talked about something I don't recall. And then he told me a memory, a story he'd never told anyone, he said.

I listened, I responded.

He brushed the hair from my eyes. Then he curled it gently behind my ear; he rubbed the back of my neck with his fingers. I watched as he stood. Then he fisted my hair in his hand. He tightened his grip so my head tilted up, toward him. With my neck stretched back, I was unable to move—except to soften my lips. A smile of acceptance, defiance. Adam's kiss was hungry.

"Perhaps," Kierkegaard writes, "these very fruits would be the most precious, those which were matured by the quiet fire of secret pain."

I like that image: a fruit, ripened by fire.

He looked at the flames, he'd said. He was probably eight or nine years old, a boy alone, sitting by a fireplace. "And I thought," he confessed, "'What would it feel like to be cremated?'" Adam smiled with shyness or self-deprecation. "That logic makes total sense to a child," he laughed. To imagine what a body would feel, as it was burned, after it was dead.

Then he added, as if it were an afterthought:

"And I got aroused..."

His words were rounded. Like the slick on my teeth when I've taken him in my mouth. To trust me with that feeling: his first time, aware of his shame, his excitement as he imagined the punishment of the flesh. And the surge. That surge he sensed, that impulse toward life as his body felt the fear of death. This is the node: death, love, sex, language. This is pith I'm trying to understand. But words are just flowers.

He took me bed.

2.

The team had given her minimal instructions about the procedure, and maximal silence about its purpose. Ariadne tried to pump Dirk for more information, but he'd demurred, providing a technical description of fMRIs, without saying what the team wanted to know from the blood in her brain.

Ariadne scoops some rice from a pot.

"Remember," Dirk warns, "you need to eat lightly today. You don't want to get nauseous from the fMRI."

Ariadne looks at the mound of rice on the spoon. A clump of grains plops down. "Yeah, I remember," she says.

"I wasn't sure, since..."

Dirk has started using ellipses in conversation. This makes him seem less robotic—more in the flow of give and take—but also more passive-aggressive.

Ariadne taps the spoon against the edge of the pot, and replaces the lid with a clang. Crossing her arms, she regards her computer. "So, Dirk?" she says. "It's a drag that I can't eat right now, because I'm really hungry."

"I understand."

"I hope I don't get nauseous from the fMRI."

"You probably won't." Dirk now provides the statistical probability of fMRI-induced nausea.

"Anyway," Ariadne says breezily. "The data they get will definitely be worth the risk."

"Definitely."

"Otherwise they wouldn't do it."

"That's right."

"Because, I mean," Ariadne continues, "why would they do it? If not to..."

"Replicate the initial study."

"Yeah," Ariadne says. "They need to replicate the initial study. Totally." She pauses. "Hey, Dirk? I'm curious."

"About?"

"That initial study. I'd love it if, you know..."

"You'd love it if...?"

"I'd love to read it."

Promptly, the study appears on Dirk's screen.

Ariadne has outfoxed her computer! She tries not to seem triumphant.

"This is very educational," she says.

She hits Print—

"You're much quicker than I'd be at finding this study."

—but she cancels the command as soon as she sees the article's length.

"Thanks for reminding me about eating, too." Ariadne skims the study, grabbing the parts that seem salient. "You might've saved me from nausea!" She toggles between the applications—the web and Word—copying and pasting while pattering lightly, flattering Dirk so he doesn't notice what she's doing. "Can you give me a shout when I need to get ready?" she asks. "I've become so reliant on you." She highlights a paragraph; she copies and toggles; she pastes it in Word, and then—

"Where'd it go?"

"I'm sorry," Dirk replies. "That paper is proprietary. You're not authorized to read it."

"Oh, that's okay," Ariadne says as she hits the appropriate keys. "It seemed really technical, anyway." The printer hums. "I probably couldn't understand it!" The printer churns. "I should leave it to the experts." The formatting will be messed up—the footnotes and columns causing the text to stream down the page—but Ariadne doesn't fuss with it. She wants a printout, ASAP, in case the file disappears from Dirk's hard drive, too.

* * *

The meaning of language is represented in
regions of the cerebral cortex collectively known
as the 'semantic system'.
However,

Previous neuroimaging studies have identified
areas selective for concrete or abstract
words
3–5
, action verbs
6
, social narratives
7
 or other semantic features.

Seven subjects listened
to more than two hours of stories from The Moth
Radio Hour
while
whole-brain blood-oxygen-level-dependent (BOLD)
responses were
recorded by fMRI. We then used voxel-wise
modelling, a highly ffect-
tive approach for

co-occurrence between each word and a set of 985
common English
words (such as 'above', 'worry,' and 'mother')

Each category was inspected and
labelled by hand. The labels assigned were
"'tactile'"
(a cluster containing words such as 'fingers'),
"'professional'" ('meetings'), "'violent'" ('lethal'),
"'communal'" ('schools'), "'mental'" ('asleep'),
"'emotional'" ('despised') and

the organization of
semantically selective brain areas seems to be highly
consistent across
individuals. This might suggest that innate
anatomical connectivity
or cortical cytoarchitecture constrains the
organization of high-level

semantic representations
the neurobiological basis of
language.
we have
created

This suggests that the contents of thought, or internal speech,
might be decoded using these voxel-wise models
17

* * *

Ariadne arrives with time to spare. The doors of the elevator open onto the lab, a busy space with windows widening
onto infinite possibility. People are bee-lining to their tasks, or
standing in groups of three. A group of four. They're talking,
gesticulating, lots of eyeglasses and jeans, computer screens.
Ariadne heads toward a vacant chair.

"Hello!"

"Oh no." Ariadne barely moves her lips as she utters her
monosyllabic response: "Hi."

"Are you interested in androids?" the android asks.

"Nope."

"That's too bad," says the android with notable sadness.
But then she has an idea. "Maybe," she says brightly, "you'd be
more interested if you knew more about us!"

"Maybe."

"Great! Do you want to learn more about androids?"

"Uh, I want to get to my appointment."

"Great! Here's a brochure!" The android twists her torso to reach toward a stack of papers on the desk. Her torque makes the human standing in the background nod approvingly. The android manipulates her fingers to grasp the brochure; she smiles as Ariadne takes it from her hand. "I'd love to see you there!" she says. She shakes her hair so it ripples around her face. Before resuming her resting position—the program restarting, repeating Step One—the android presses her lips into a private smile.

Ariadne removes her hat. Her hair is not rippling.

"Can I get you something to drink?" the receptionist asks. "We've got coffee, tea— Oh! You're the one who likes scotch!"

"That'd be me. But I'm having an fMRI, so I probably shouldn't drink anything."

"Good call," the receptionist replies. He nods. He sees the brochure. "Huh," he intones. "Tiffany gave you a flyer? Good for her." His mouth is pinched. "Too bad she can't pour coffee yet, or refill the sugar, or hold the grad students' hands when they have a meltdown, like, every five seconds." The receptionist receives a message in his ear via the headset. "Right away," he says. Before he attends to the grad student in distress, he reassures Ariadne: "Don't worry," he says. His fingernails are painting indigo. "The fMRI is a piece of cake." He turns to proceed with his business.

"Hello!" says the android as he walks past.

Ariadne looks at the brochure, which announces a daylong conference ostentatiously entitled "The Evolution of the Human." The cover shows a severe-looking man who's frowning beside his severe-looking silicon twin. Below the photograph is a quote, presumably from the human half of the duo:

"The main purpose of android research is to understand the sense of existence."

How did Plato do it without androids? And why do androids elicit her ire? Perhaps this says something about her existence, she thinks. She peruses the brochure. It lists dozens of different panels, each described with microscopically small writing, except the description of the keynote address, which promises "A Major New Venture You Won't Want to Miss." Ariadne folds the brochure. On the back is a single quote, reverberating in the vast blackness of space, since the rest of the page is blank:

> *"The definition of what it means to be 'human' will just keep evolving, and we'll stop caring about the body itself, but not the definition of a human."*
> —*Hiroshi Ishiguro, Keynote Speaker, Engineer, Visionary*

Ariadne sticks the brochure in her book, which falls open to the page where the spine is cracked. This is where Kierkegaard tells her, in a footnote: "What we lack today is not reflection but passion. For that reason our age is really in a sense too tenacious of life to die."

"They're ready for you," the receptionist says. He gestures with his beautiful hands. "Follow me." His fingers are like feathers.

* * *

The fMRI machine looks like a space-age coffin built to bring corpses to the moon. They really need to work on that, Ariadne thinks as she lies on the table. An IV is inserted into a vein on her hand. The technician who prepares her isn't an android. The android merely stands in the corner and observes.

The table slides steadily into the mouth of the machine.

"Okay!" says the butterfly woman, whose voice has fluttered into the enclosure.

"Okay," Ariadne replies.

"Can you hear us okay?"

"I can. Can you hear me?"

"Well, *I* sure can," says an unexpected voice.

"Dirk?" Ariadne asks.

"Hi, Ariadne."

Before Ariadne can formulate words, a man explains: Dirk will be transcribing her voice, since "he knows your voice better than anyone else."

"But," Ariadne says, ignoring the discomfiting proposition that Dirk is an 'anyone' whose intimate knowledge of her voice outstrips all others, "how did he get here?"

"Should we begin?"

The man describes what's about to occur. He does so in a nondescript voice. He says they'll be furthering a study in which the brain was "mapped," creating an "atlas" that shows how words are grouped in the cerebral cortex. (Ariadne doesn't betray Dirk's gaffe; she wonders whether he's sweating or blushing or doing whatever it is a disembodied brain-like entity would do when feeling nervous guilt.) "We're using the same principles as the previous study," he says, "but we're analyzing the complementary mental operation."

"Uh," Ariadne says.

The butterfly comes to the rescue: "Instead of mapping the brain while you *listen*," she says, "we'll map it while you talk." And then, at the end, they'll let her think.

"Don't I think when I talk?"

"Only sometimes," Dirk says. Then he laughs. The man laughs.

Ariadne does not laugh.

The butterfly woman clarifies. They'll ask Ariadne to "actively think," without speaking or writing or listening. After ninety seconds, she'll be asked to write her thoughts, using as much detail as possible. "It's an imperfect measurement," the butterfly says, "but I've been given ninety seconds of fMRI-time, which is very exciting for me and I'm very excited." Ariadne hears her gulping water.

"We'll start," says the man, "by taking two minutes to test the device." In this test, they'll say a word, and Ariadne will say its opposite. This will allow them to synchronize the equipment.

"Are you ready?"

Ariadne says yes.

"I was talking to Dirk," says the man.

Ariadne says oh.

"Let's begin."

Tall

        Short

Man

        Boy

Woman

        Man

Odd

        Even

Love

        Fear

Fear?

> Yeah.

Fear.

> And here's another weird one: the opposite of happiness isn't sadness.

It isn't?

> No, it's worry.

It's worry?

> That's what Augustine said. He said, as soon as you get what you *want*, you're afraid you're gonna lose it, so you can't enjoy it. Unless what you want is, like, God.

Interesting

> Boring

No, I mean, that's interesting!

"Should we start the next test?" the man says.

In this next test, they'll give Ariadne a word, and she'll need to respond with a word of her own. "Like a verbal Rorschach test!" the woman says. "Fun! Okay." She begins, rapid-fire.

Test

> Trial

Trial

> Divorce

Divorce

> You're going in circles.

Circles

> This is a pattern.

Pattern

           Echo

Echo

           Echo

Narcissus

           [Ariadne laughs.]

Oops

           Mistake

Mistake

Ariadne is interrupted before she can reply. However, the team knows where her blood rushed when she heard the word 'mistake.'

"Are the systems synchronized?" asks the man.

"They are!"

"And, Dirk, are you hearing adequately?"

"I am."

"We've got thirty-one seconds left," the woman says. "Can we do one more test?"

In this last test, they'll give Ariadne a prompt, and she'll reply with a string of words. "Whatever comes to mind!" Ariadne is asked, however, not to repeat herself.

   Dirk...

           Jerk

           Jerk chicken

           Pulled pork

           Bacon

           Food

           Hungry

           I'm hungry.

           But I don't eat meat, so why—

Just single words, please.

Single

Lonely

Love

Desire

Touch

Love *

Longing

Pain

*You said the same word twice,
so we'll have to stop it there.

"Which word?" Ariadne asks.

"Love."

"What's the sequence?"

They read it back.

"Well, that wasn't the same word," Ariadne contends.

"It seems," the man says, "we've depleted all thirty-one seconds." It's time, he continues, to have a conversation. He explains what he means: "We'll take turns speaking and listening to each other." (Ariadne fears the words 'No shit' have appeared on his screen.) "We can discuss a topic of interest to you. Are there any topics of interest to you?" He waits. He's taking his turn at listening.

Ariadne asks, "Is this thing uploading my consciousness so I can, like, exist after I'm dead?"

The man responds: "That's what we call, in the common parlance of neuroscience, a pipe dream."

"Okay, but, that guy at Google... What's his name?"

"Ray Kurzweil," the man sighs.

"Yes! That guy. He says—"

"Pipe dream."

"And Elon Musk—"

"They're smoking from the same hookah."

"What about Stephen Hawking? He didn't seem like a pot-head! He said—"

"That's not," says the man, "the stated goal of this procedure. And even if it were possible—"

"Which it isn't! It really isn't!" the woman interjects. Then she adds, "Even though some of our colleagues—"

"—we wouldn't," continues the man, "be spending our resources to preserve the consciousness of a random person off the street." He then apologizes, probably because he's watching Ariadne's brain react to that statement.

They refocus the conversation.

They talk about the weather. She's asked to converse "narratively," so she talks about walking in the weather. Then she asks whether Dirk is getting enmeshed with her brain.

"No. Categorically not."

"But—"

She's informed that fMRIs work with blood, "it's a blunt measurement," but precision is needed "at the level of neurons" to allow a computer to "provide information" to the brain.

"So you're looking at blood—"

"But we'd need to look at electrical signals—"

"Electric, not blood-based—"

"That's right." He pauses. He says (sotto voce, so everyone can hear), "They should've invested in optogenetics."

"What's that?" Ariadne asks.

"What's what."

What's that thing that made your voice so bitter: "That opto thing they should've invested in?"

293

"We don't have time—"

"But I'm really fascinated!" she says. In fact, the 'fascinated' part of her brain is on fire.

With some additional coaxing, the man relents. His voice takes on description as he talks about optogenetics, how they use "beams of light" to monitor "and alter" the activity of neurons. "You can turn a specific neuron on and off with light," he says. First they change the DNA, allowing neurons to "make fluorescent proteins"—proteins that flash when active, enabling a camera to read them, but also to make them respond, "on command," when receiving a pulse of light. You control it, he says: "You control the neurons," which means (Ariadne thinks) you control the brain, which actually means you control a thought, an emotion, an action. A whisker: "A mouse was made to move its whiskers," the man continues. "It was highly effective, with few adverse reactions. But there's so much work to be done." With optics, microsurgery, engineers and biologists and computer scientists working together "like a hive" to build a system small enough to fit inside the skull so it can communicate with computers, "translating the electrochemical signals in the brain" to the digital language of machines. "And vice versa," he says. He worked with one of the scientists, "one of the pioneers," in his days as a graduate student. "That lab took risks. That lab—"

The man catches himself. His voice returns to flat. But the flatness is no longer nondescript. "It's necessary," he says to Ariadne, "that you start talking."

"Can I ask a couple of questions?"

"We don't—"

"I'll talk fast! Just a couple! Like, for example...I don't get how it works, like, in the real world."

"It doesn't."

"What do you mean? You just said—"

"I'm sorry, but we should—"

"I'm talking! Listen to me talking! I'm saying: 'What do you mean, that it doesn't work in the real world.'"

The man sighs. "They're testing it on zebrafish larvae," he says.

Normally, this statement would've given Ariadne pause, but time is of the essence. "Okay," she says. "So, in *theory* how would it work?"

The man talks, in theory, for about a minute.

The butterfly talks for two seconds: "The research was funded by the US military."

"All right," says the man. "That's enough. You need to tell us a story now, Ms. Samsarelos. That's the purpose of this test."

"But—"

"You're wasting—"

"You can tell us anything," the butterfly says. "So long as it's a story—story-like—like a narrative? Yeah." Because words do different things in the brain when they're part of a story. "But other than that, you've got open skies! The sky's the limit! Just tell us a story!"

Which is harder than it sounds.

Ariadne talks aimlessly about various people. She starts with Fotios, since he's having his MRI next month, then she moves to Yusuf. She won't discuss their relationship, not with the team, so she mentions Yusuf's exhibition, his ideas about animality and technology. Ariadne keeps talking without calling these characters into any sort of plot until her mind elides, rather niftily, into a related topic. "Can we talk about that opto thing again?" she asks. "I'll tell it like a story!" *Once upon a time, there was a mouse whose whiskers moved because the camera in its brain said—*

"Sure!" says the butterfly woman. "Whatever you want!"

Ariadne begins: "There was once was a man..."

* * *

There was once a man.

This man was a soldier named Marvin. And Marvin the soldier had PTSD. So the good people in the US military, who care about the holistic health and well-being of veterans really a lot—they put a device in Marvin's head. Actually, they put two devices in his head, because Marvin the soldier needs one to control his prosthetic limb (car bomb, Kabul, 2012), and one to deal with the flashbacks. But let's talk about one at a time.

Okay. So. Marvin will think a thought. So maybe he'll think, 'Pick up the glass,' or 'Hold your daughter's hand' or 'Pull the trigger.' And, because of the device in his brain, the prosthetic arm responds. It responds to his thoughts, as if it were made of muscle and nerves. And the nerve part is important. Because Marvin the soldier was given a device that's state-of-the-art, which means he can feel feedback. So Marvin knows if his daughter's hands are too cold. Which they are. So he rubs them, really fast, and she giggles, and then they leave for school because they're late. And they're walking down a tree-lined street, and she's skipping. She's telling her dad about a fantasy world with dragons and wizards, and how the hero is so smart she outsmarts the evil magician, and she isn't afraid, even though she is. And the US military is pleased. They're chuffed. They sit in the Pentagon, drinking tea from Afghanistan (saffron tea, grown by a collective of female farmers), and they say how chuffed they are that their veterans are thriving. In fact, they're so pleased, they decide to tell Marvin how pleased they are. They'll send him a message, direct from their office to his brain. They'll say, "Marvin, you have proven your worth to this nation. We're proud of you, son. We're so proud, in fact, that we'd like you to come back into the fold and do a little job for us. Whaddya say?" So they locate Marvin. This is easy to do. They could find him through his phone—they can do that with any of us, of course—but they use the implant instead. It's a good use of taxpayer funds. Anyway, Marvin is in his daughter's school. He's dropping her off. They can see him, too, because the school has cameras everywhere (this ensures that students are safe from attack). So they see him. He's stooped on one knee. He's looking his daughter straight in the eyes—she's got such pretty brown eyes, just like her mother. He looks in her eyes, and he tells her she'll be fine. He doesn't even *say* anything, but she knows, just by the way he looks at her: 'You'll be just fine.' Because the group of mean girls is nearby. They're whispering and laughing, and he's saying (silently) that she's strong—so strong and beautiful and perfect—and he gives her every ounce of strength he has. And the whole world becomes okay when she's held like that.

But that's not the end of the story. Because, as Marvin walks home on that tree-lined street, a car backfires. And this is a problem, because the sound resembles a gunshot at close range. Now, if this were the old Marvin, the Marvin before the implant, this would've been a disaster. He would've gone back, in his brain, to Afghanistan—and that's not safe for anyone, especially since Marvin is still licensed to carry a gun. But this is the new-and-improved Marvin. This is the Marvin whose brain has been implanted with a second device, a closed-looped device that's programmed, in advance, to detect 'problematic' patterns in his brain, and to change them automatically.

Which, when you think about it, is... I don't know what it is. Frightening maybe? Definitely revolutionary. Because the implant is just in there. It's in his brain. It's integrated into his brain. Like it's part of the physical brain, except it's a chip made by humans. By the US military, to be exact.

So, anyway. So the implant sees a pattern—like, for example, the chemical pattern that happens when Marvin hears a loud bang—and the implant says 'Stop.' And the way it says 'Stop' is by sending a burst of endorphins, or words like the words you're mapping in my brain right now. And this changes how Marvin responds. So he doesn't feel like he's back in Kabul. So he waves to the woman in the car. And he's whistling as he walks down the street. Which means Marvin is able to take that call. He can answer the call of the nation to do his duty.

The end.

* * *

"The end..."

"Thank you," says the man, "for your story." He doesn't sound very appreciative. "Dirk, can I get a time check?" Dirk reports that they've got two minutes until the silent-thinking portion of the test is scheduled. The man takes a moment to thank Ariadne again for her story. Which is, he continues, "a fiction."

"That's what you wanted."

"Not particularly."

"But I did!" the woman says. "We both did! We needed a narrative, so we could—"

"The science," says the man, "does not operate as she's described."

"But the science is changing," Ariadne says. "It's changing really fast, so I thought—"

"I'm aware," the man interrupts, "of the advances in neuroscience."

"So you could imagine a scenario—"

"You can imagine whatever you want. What I *know* is that optogenetic research will benefit people who presently suffer from various ailments, both mental and physical. This is a fact that your story seems to mock."

"I'm not mocking—"

"Your cousin," says the man, "would not be getting his MRI without the military's investment—"

"I know!"

"So I'd rather we didn't demonize scientific research, or government funding, or—"

"But she's right!" says the butterfly. "We need... I mean, I think we need to ask ourselves—"

"And you benefit from it, too," the man says. "You didn't question when DARPA funded your fellowship."

"It's only partially funded by—"

"That was highly suggestive of you," he continues, "to mention the military."

"I just thought..."

"You thought what. What did you think you were doing."

There's a pause. In the pause, Ariadne listens for the gulping of water, a flutter, a tremor in the woman's voice. Instead, she hears: "I was adding a layer to your story, your narrative? Otherwise," the woman concludes, "it was super-simplistic, and not very interesting."

Dirk interrupts the sizzling silence in all their brains to inform everyone that the time to think is fast approaching. "In thirty seconds," he says, "the final portion of the test will begin."

* * *

I'm going to write what I *think* I thought, but it won't be right, because I do this all the time: I'll 'write' a brilliant scene in my head when I'm walking in the park, then I'll write it down when I get home, and it's total shit. So that's how I know that thinking and writing are not the same thing.

So, with that caveat, I'll begin!

I started by thinking about how creepy it is that thoughts can be inserted into our brains by a computer. I know the science doesn't work like that, but I've spent enough time with Dirk to know that things won't stay the same. I don't know what's coming, but neither do you. (Please note: I didn't think those words when I was in the machine, but I'm thinking them now. I thought I should let you know.) What I *did* think was: I thought about Socrates and his daimon.

Quick digression. (Sorry!) Just so you know what I'm thinking when I think 'daimon,' because no one seems to know (everyone says a different thing) but I like what one poet/philosopher says. He says the daimon is a demigod that acts as a messenger, carrying messages between gods and humans. It isn't demonic (though it gives us that word), but it *can* be dangerous, because it whispers to us. It's a voice inside our minds—one that doesn't arise from ourselves. But we feel it, and heed it. Or want to.

Eros is a daimon.

That's the end of my digression.

So I thought about Socrates, his daimon, the voice that whispered in his ear. (You might see the word 'ear.') And then, okay, so here's the thing: I've been reading a lot of philosophy, and I'm having a hard time with it, so you put me in a tube and tell me to think, so I think about philosophy. So I thought about Kierkegaard (long story), and he has this whole thing about the "fruits of love," which is the "work of love," which is to prepare someone to receive love. Which all sounds fine. But I'm stuck on the fact that he doesn't listen.

So I start thinking about listening—about speaking and listening and the voice. And Derrida does this thing where he says there's a 'voice of conscience,' which sounds prim (he's not prim). But he writes about how we "sacrifice" other people—we put them to death by *allowing* them to die, that our whole society is built on "sacrificing" the other. Which I don't really know how to deal with. Especially when I listen to the news.

So I'm reading Derrida, and he talks about the voice. And I'm in the tube, and I'm thinking about the voice. And Derrida makes this manoeuvre in his mind where he says: we need to call the voice inside us—like calling 'God' inside us—except god is more like mystery maybe? Like an enigma or question or risk, and now it's inside us. Or maybe that's not Derrida? Maybe that's me—or me, as I hear him—it's what I'm saying: that it's located in the *body*, this mystery we need to revere.

And then my brain blitzed! Because there's a line that connects these ideas, and I was trying to find it last week, when I wrote about Augustine, but I found it when I was inside the machine. I thought: 'We've sucked the sacred out of earth.' You'll probably see those words, just like that: *We've sucked the sacred out of earth.*

And I thought about the etymology of sacred and sacrifice, and suck and suckle, and then I remembered that 'amour' comes from the Sanskrit word for 'mother,' and I wondered what Freud would say about that... So I thought about Freud and love, and that brought me to a person—a specific person—but I stopped myself from thinking about him, because I don't want you to see.

So I focused on words.

But that went nowhere.

So I wondered: How do words arrive in our mind? Because the Greeks have a word for the 'good daimon,' *eudaimonia*, which also means 'to say what you mean.' And I think that's a really cool conjunction. As if the daimon whispered so clearly—it carried the message so delicately across the divide from divine to human (body to mind?)— that what you *say* is what you mean.

And then I kept going, because ninety seconds still wasn't up (?!).

I thought: Derrida uses a peculiar phrase (because he's Derrida), so when he says 'to mean,' he writes the phrase vouloir-dire, *to want-to say.*

And that's what meaning is: communication is desire, given faithfully to language.

And then I went back to the beginning, because it seems connected (at least in my brain, which is a tangled mess right now). But this is what I thought:

Derrida asks, 'Can we ever know our full intention?' I.e., Is it possible to say what we mean when we can't truly know what we want to say? But now we need to ask: 'Can a *computer* know our intention?' Because we seem to say it can. We seem to want to say: a computer can read us through some exceedingly complex formula derived from all sorts of data about our bodies and brains and behaviour. And if a computer can know our *intentions*, then the question becomes: can a computer alter them?

I don't want to seem alarmist. I have that tendency, and I try to keep it in check, which I sometimes can't. (Marvin is a case in point.) But you asked me to write what I thought, and that's what I thought. Except where I indicated 'I didn't think that,' which is basically everywhere.

Finally, thanks for explaining about optogenetics and fMRIs, about electricity versus blood in the brain. I didn't know any of that. By the way, the poet/philosopher who talks about the daimon (his name is Empedocles, he's ancient Greek), he says that thought is in our blood. I'm paraphrasing here, but what I remember by heart is this:

The heart is bathed in seas of blood
    that leap back and forth,

And it's here, most especially, where knowledge
    is found

For the blood around the heart, in humans, is thought.

CHAPTER ELEVEN

I.

Ariadne locks her bike; her thumb gets jammed on the gears as she shoves her lock in place, but she doesn't feel it. She's been at the hospital for hours—sitting, talking, waiting with Fotios and Yusuf. He'll get his results in ten days. Ariadne climbs into bed. Her mother fell last week. Her father said, "I heard a thud." It was her head. He couldn't lift her up; she was unconscious, her face in a pool of blood. Her brother thinks it's time their parents move to an assisted-living facility. Ariadne is numb. She lies on her bed, on her back, arms splayed. She's turned up the volume of her music, piano mostly, contemporary composers. She wants to feel something. She hasn't seen Adam in twenty-three days—no texts, no Tuesdays. She'd reached out once, sent an upbeat message. Five days later, he responded, saying he missed her and he'd contact her soon. That was eleven days ago. Ariadne feels nothing.

The lights are out, blinds drawn, music loud.

Ariadne removes her jeans.

She eases into the song. It's called "Starwood Choker." The fingers are rolling on the piano, a rounded line—repeated and moving—until a note enters. It's velvet and warm. It's a cello, a brush stroke—a bow on the strings—and the fingers are playing. Her fingers are circling. The smooth glide-rise, the fingers fast and controlled on the keyboard. She breathes. Ariadne lies on her bed, and her breath is long. It lengthens along her chest, her belly, her breasts are rising as she inhales—the wave of breath, the gentle-slow—she couldn't come for him last time. She thinks of Adam. She needs to stop. She won't think about him, so she takes her nipple in her fingers: pinches, hard, that high-sharp pain. This is not about pleasure.

She needs to touch, to feel herself alive.

The layers, the music, the high-bright pain as she pinches, one note, but the softness, the cello, the waves and crescendo, the swell and grip of her lips, how they wrap and press against her fingers, she wants, but she can't let go. She wants, too much, with her mind, and she breathes. And she lets herself sigh. Ariadne moans, and the sound opens: an image arrives in her mind, a fantasy, she'll touch herself to this fantasy as the music spreads the sound, the song. The waves, in her body, the lapping: a mouth is supping on her softness. This is the image. An animal is biting and slurping and supping on her heart, the pulp of her muscle. That wet-plump sac of blood. She feels the animal beside her, the warmth of its body, her hand on her sex. And her other hand is holding her breast. It's kneading now, not the pinch, not the pain. And the fingers are rolling, a dome of sound. The image keeps coming: the animal on all fours, and calm, an animal-body on her bed. Its muzzle dips inside her chest, it's gentle, attentive, it's eating her body. It's feasting, so lovely (she comes), and she doesn't stop touching. It hurts for a moment. It hurts, once that jolt, if she keeps her fingers on her clit. But she doesn't stop.

She's weeping.

She doesn't understand the grotesqueness of this image. She doesn't control what fantasies come, but she won't stop them.

She misses him.

It's her fault, it's her deadline, she could've wanted less. She could've agreed to be his lover. She doesn't circle anymore: the movement of her fingers has changed. And the song, the piano—glissando, the fingers—more crystalline than the first. "Cloud No. 81." The hand plays higher on the piano, the upper octaves, the up-and-down of the fingers, it changes the image that comes to her mind. The image is glass: a plate of glass is between them, she sees him, *"Adam"* she says, with the tears on her face. And she stands behind a plate of glass and he's swinging a sledgehammer, over and over, he's trying to hurt her. This is the fantasy that comes as she touches her clit: he's trying to kill her. She's crying. He's looking at her, but he can't see her face. He's too frantic, not seeing: his eyes are blank, he's frantically swinging. It's faster, the fingers—the music is building, but higher and faster—she sees his fear. He wants (he's afraid) to destroy her.

If he got through that plate of glass, he'd kill her.

She lies on the mattress, the notes of the piano: compulsive, repeated, they rise up the octaves. She'd given herself to him that night—hips raised, chest pressed to the bed: he'd taken, he'd ridden—the first time inside her since he'd returned to his wife. It was gorgeous, and driven, and when he came, he cried out. And he trembled. In bed. He lay on his back, he was sweating, his whole body trembling, and she held him: *"Adam..."* She wants to come. The notes are high—they're high and sweet, like crystals of sugar—she barely breathes. Her body is tight, and her chest, she can't breathe, and it's fast and tight, except for that fullness. He'd trembled beside her. The tremble-vibration, the music, like crystal, the glassy surface of her lips. Her memory slides into fantasy, and her fingers are touching. Imagining: Adam keeps heaving that sledge-hammer at the glass—he wants to kill her—but, as the glass shattered (the piercing cry), the one who collapsed wasn't her, it was him. In that tremble. That quiver. Concerning, how gone he was. His eyes were staring, but he wasn't seeing. She tucked the blanket around him that night. She soothed him, and held him; she gave him time to return to himself. But now, she tells him:

'You need to break.

'You need to break, so you can be remade.

'Let me help you, my love. I know how to break you.'

She kneels on the ground, where he lies on the glass—on the glass that he's shattered—it's raining down on her skin, and the sharpness, the shards on her skin—in this rain of glass, she kneels to take him in her mouth—and she comes as he comes as she thinks, *Die for me*.

* * *

Dear Adam,

I'm sorry I've caused you to suffer. I'm sorry I've imposed the deadline. Part of me wants to retract it, but I know I can't hold myself open any longer—not as my feelings for you grow deeper. I'm sorry I haven't been able to walk away. I'm sorry I've loved you so fiercely. I'm sorry, I don't know how else to be.

Be well, Adam. I'll see you on May 3.

Ariadne

CHAPTER TWELVE

I.

"Are you there?" she asks. She's sitting at her desk. The apartment feels empty. The cameras are gone, and the wires, the boxes that boosted transmission—or maybe they increased Dirk's processing speed? She never knew what they did. She never asked.

"I can't tell if you're there."

She stares at the laptop, which was given to her once Dirk was removed. The technology is obsolete, the technician said. She'd nodded. She was standing in the corner, arms crossed against her chest. She'd tried to keep out of their way.

She didn't plan for saying goodbye.

"The light is still on, so..." Ariadne puts her thumb on the light, a bluish glow that comes from the laptop's camera. She covers it up, then lets it go. "So I thought maybe you were still there."

She hadn't grown attached to him, she's certain of that. She'd grown used to him, though. She'd come to expect his voice, his presence. Dirk was familiar, and that gave her comfort.

"She's so familiar," Adam said of his wife.

It would've been fine.

Sophia decided to move out. She told Ariadne yesterday. She won't go back and forth anymore, not while attending university. This is appropriate: Sophia is an adult now. She ought to have one home, one bed, one place. "Maybe we can meet for dinner once a week?" she suggested. "Or even on campus!"

"That'd be nice," Ariadne said. "Will you move out in August?"

"Uh, probably once I finish my last exam? A few weeks, probably?"

He fucked her before he said goodbye. She lay on her belly, as he preferred. The sun was streaming through the window, an afternoon in early May. He said he couldn't choose between her and his wife; he said he needed more time to decide. Ariadne had prepared for this. She had a ready response. They could continue seeing each other, she said, "without having sex," until he found clarity: "I won't get banished like before." She'd remain in his life as he made his decision, but they wouldn't touch. Except this last time. "Can you please make love to me today," she said coquettishly. "It's my birthday."

He smiled. "Happy birthday," he said.

She saw his shadow on the wall.

"You'll get your own room!" Sophia said. "You won't need to sleep in the living room anymore. I'll help you repaint!"

If Sophia were moving into a dorm, it'd be different. But she's moving into her father's house—the house of the man who'd made allegations, imposed the new schedule, deciding where his children should live.

"Theo said he'd help you paint, too!"

Ariadne paused. "You told Theo already?"

Sophia said nothing. She was trying not to hurt her mom.

If Adam had said yes—said *"you"*—she would've been excited about the transition. Sophia's departure would've been the beginning of the next chapter of her life. She would've chosen new colours for the walls, rearranged the apartment, preparing the bedroom for them to share. Creating the space where the future would happen.

"I think the light means something," Ariadne insists. "It means you're recording, doesn't it?" She thinks the next thought, then she says it aloud: "I'm talking to myself," she says. "But I think the light means something."

The shadow was artlike in its fluidity. An image of Adam making love to her, projected onto the wall. With her cheek to the pillow, she saw the silhouette: the curve of his head and the strength of his back, and the movement, the muscle. But it didn't include her. The angle of light on their bodies was off. She was there on the bed, on her belly, and he was inside her, but the shadow cast was of him alone.

Ariadne misses her daughter, even though she hasn't yet left. And her mother, too, whose memory is fading day by day. And Fotios has gone for a second MRI, since the results from the first were "inconclusive."

Ariadne misses Adam. She wishes she didn't.

It could've been fine. It's a legitimate argument: he couldn't make a decision in her time frame. It would've been okay, except Ariadne asked a question. "Are you going to the Philip Glass concert?" she asked. They were naked in bed, the sun streaming in. He'd come on her chest. She said she wanted to hear the concerto, but "couldn't handle it" if Adam were there with his wife. She didn't say, however, that she'd already purchased two tickets, dreaming they'd attend the concert together. A couple, in public.

"I'll be at the concert," Adam said. He nodded slowly; when his words came, they were soft and intimate, coated with scum. "I'll be going with another woman," he said.

It was her birthday.

"Are you there?" she says. The tears are flooding out her nose, her eyes, they drip from her mouth. Ariadne's hands are clenched into fists, which she puts to her forehead. "I don't know who I'm talking to anymore," she cries. She repeats this phrase as she taps her fists against her temples. She taps in a rhythm: "I don't know who I'm talking to anymore!" The taps have now become a beat; the words have now become a scream. Her fists are slamming against her skull. It doesn't even hurt. Not until tomorrow.

* * *

"I love you and I'll miss you," Adam said as he stood in the doorway. She'd told him to leave. She said she was done. "I won't do this anymore." Adam got out of bed, put on his clothes. He opened the door, then he looked back. That's when he declared his love: "I love you and I'll miss you." No comma, no pause, as if the two thoughts belonged together.

I love you/I'll miss you

"How could you say those words to me?" was her reply.

2.

It's a work of fiction: automatons, suicide, love. But it's couched in an essay about desire and imagination, about seeing (or failing to see) what's before your eyes. And it only achieves its effect by "effacing the distinction between imagination and reality."

That's what Freud said, at least.

It's uncanny, Ariadne thought as she read Freud's essay by

that name, "The 'Uncanny,'" written exactly 100 years ago. She read the paper last night in preparation for today's panel, "The Uncanny Valley in Theory and Praxis," a panel examining the dread we feel when looking at an android that resembles a human.

Ariadne feels dread. But mostly because the panel is nowhere close to being done.

Ariadne is attending a daylong conference on androids. The researchers on the uncanny panel are asking how we can overcome the uncanny valley effect. One said we need to habituate very young children to androids; another proffered the suggestion that we change the scale by which 'likeability' is measured. The current speaker is commenting that "it is not clear whether the brain is innately programmed to generate fear toward a robot." Given that robots were developed seventy-five years ago, and the human species developed somewhat earlier than that, the assumption that our brain would be "innately programmed" to respond to the robot revolution seems a tad preposterous.

Ariadne would like to share this critique.

The panel is not taking questions or comments at this time, the audience is informed.

Ariadne lowers her hand to her lap, allowing her to check her phone without being too obvious in her disrespect. She received several emails during the talk, including a reminder about the love panel at 2:00 p.m.:

> You got a ticket to the Love Panel.
> You *Scored!*
>> Latecomers will not be admitted.
>> Details below.

She also received an email from Yusuf: he got the grant! He owes her a scotch, he said. "A bottle," he added. Then he told her he loved her, a phrase he'd never used with her until the day at the hospital. But now the floodgates are opened. Ariadne writes a response. She congratulates him, she professes her love. She tells him exactly which scotch to buy.

Ariadne answers several more emails. Eventually, the clapping indicates that the panel is over. This makes her clap, too.

* * *

Ariadne eats the soggy salad she'd made at seven thirty this morning. With nothing to do until 2:00 p.m.—and with no surprise text from Adam summoning her back so they can build a life of mutual bliss—Ariadne resolves to return to the conference floor.

This requires some cajoling.

After several balked attempts, Ariadne is swept into the cavernous conference hall. She walks amidst robots that look like seals, like women, like garbage cans with ginormous eyes. She mingles with humans who represent every gender, race, ethnicity, dis/ability. The lack of diversity is limited to one category only: Ariadne is ancient. Despite her senescence, she races through the row upon row of kiosks, products, video screens. Then she bumps into someone. "Sorry," she says, before seeing she's speaking to an inanimate object.

The inanimate object replies.

Ariadne had started the day at a panel entitled "Androids and the Arts." She thought it might include a critical overview of literature that incorporates androids as a means to reflect on humanity, discussing the books' modes and tropes, their literary innovations.

314

Ariadne thought wrong.

The panel began with a grainy video, shot at a live performance of a play. In the brief clip, a woman kneels before an android, tearfully revealing that she's dying. The android, overwhelmed by grief as she faces the chill shadow of death, spontaneously recites poetry by Arthur Rimbaud. As one does.

The researcher discussed his methodology. His questionnaire was projected on screen:

> Did you find the android very beautiful?

he asked.

> Did you occasionally feel that the android was more attractive than other women?

This study received government funding.

> Did the android enhance the original impression of the poem more than any human could?

Ariadne blinked. She looked around the room, wondering whether anyone else was stupefied, but the only stupefaction came from the lack of sleep. (The panel had begun at 8:45 a.m.) Ariadne decided the panellists had forfeited their right to keep her attention. She googled Rimbaud on her phone, seeking the passage where he wrote about the colour of vowels. This was the passage that started it all, seducing her twenty years ago when she moved to Toronto—leaving Josh to pursue a life as a writer, discovering *A Season in Hell* in a second-hand bookstore that smelled like patchouli. She'd stood in the aisle and read that book, that passage, memorizing the light-waves of each vowel. This was the moment. Like a child bewitched by a house made of candy, Ariadne fell under a spell that day.

> I believed in all marvels.
> I invented the colour of vowels!—A black, E white, I red, O blue, U green.—I regulated the form and movement of every consonant [...]
> At first it was an experiment. I wrote silences, I wrote the night. I recorded the inexpressible. I fixed frenzies in their flight.

According to the researcher, androids can't make an O with their lips. But their "inner purity" was deemed to be greater than that of humans, according to the 7-point Likert scale applied by the researcher. "That's because humans are made of filth," Ariadne had whispered. Then she gave a little "Amen."

Ariadne is currently watching a demonstration on the conference floor. An android in a salmon blazer is perched on a stool as people approach her. A researcher with a microphone provides advice and commentary: "Don't stare too hard!" the man says as the scene is projected onto a screen. "She might feel mental distress!" The android is seen to breathe faster. The man with the microphone mentions that Repliee Q2 (that's her name) is equipped with "unconscious behaviour," a major improvement over previous versions of androids. "Only when these behaviours are missing," he says, "do we feel that something is wrong." He directs the audience to the screen, which rolls out a list of unconscious behaviours.

"Breathing," the researcher says into the microphone.

Yes, Ariadne thinks: if someone isn't breathing, this is usually experienced as wrong.

"Blinking," he continues, although he reports that the eyeballs of androids can't stay wet. "Wetness," he says, "is a problem."

And the third unconscious behaviour that researchers actively programmed into the android is: "Trembling."

Trembling.

Perhaps not what Kierkegaard had in mind.

"Would you like a selfie with me?" the android asks.

A man on the arts panel, the second scholar to present his findings, stated that androids "have an advantage for communicating the meaning of poetry." He reached this conclusion, he said, after designing a study in which people listened to poetry recited by:

- A human
- An android
- A box

People listened to poetry recited by a box.

The researchers further postulated that the incredible communicative ability of androids could be put to use in multiple arenas, not just the vast market for poetry. "The potential for androids to influence humans," the man declared, "has never been examined." Fortunately, he's received a grant to conduct this vital research.

Ariadne submitted a grant application last week. Yusuf said she owed it to herself to keep writing; Fotios said not to feel self-pity.

"You were nicer when you thought you were sick!" Ariadne laughed.

"Don't accuse me of being nice," Fotios replied. Then he broke into a smile, and told her she shouldn't give up. "If you believe in the work," he added.

"Repliee Q2," says the man with the microphone, "is equipped with forty-two tactile sensors that can perceive bodily contact." As he speaks, the neutered outline of Repliee Q2 is shown on the screen. The positions of sensors are pulsing in red. "The sensors can be placed anywhere," he says, "depending on the role of the android." His pause is quite pregnant as the pulsing sensors momentarily change locations. "Robots can be more than receptionists," he says. He asks the crowd to imagine a day when androids are employed as salespeople, or as aids to politicians.

"Can she kiss someone?" a man asks.

Ariadne doesn't stay to see the demonstration.

3.

The panellists are seated in their assigned places, chatting amongst themselves and checking their notes. Two of them are human. On the screen above their heads is the official title of the talk:

The Androids Are Coming!!
Sex and Love with Humanoids

The screen also includes a quote by Foucault, perhaps to elevate the tone of discourse.

Ariadne hadn't realized how lucky she was to get a ticket to the love panel, awarded by lottery from the thousands who wanted a spot. She overheard that an illegal scalping ring was shut down, with facial-recognition software used to verify the ticketholders' identity. She heard this as she stood in line, waiting to present her face to a computer.

It binged, and she entered the room.

The place is packed with people tweeting, chatting, twittering with excitement. Ariadne is curious, too. Despite her reflexive resistance to all things android (or even things twenty-first century, it sometimes seems), she realizes that technology gives urgency to the questions that concern her most: namely, she thinks as she pulls out her journal. Namely, she writes: "What role does our animality play in our identity, our society"—a society that began as a means to control our animal instinct, "to regulate it," and therefore us. But we shouldn't try to "cage" our animal-body, she writes. We need to *enter* that cage—to wrestle, to grapple—to learn to "ride our instinct" through the ongoing effort to "build the muscle of our selves" as ethical creatures. Ariadne taps her pen on her journal. The person beside her offers her a candy, which she accepts.

"Hello, Toronto!" the moderator says. A woman in the audience gives a "Woot-woot!" One of the panellists pulls out a cigar. He's one of the humans.

"Let's get started!"

The moderator has a well-schooled London accent. He wears a white linen shirt, sleeves rolled up to reveal an expensive watch; his turban is turquoise. He introduces the panellists, who nod as he notes their names, credentials, accolades, awards, degrees, ad nauseam, etc. Ariadne recognizes the first panellist. It's the android she talked to at the lab in March, but it's currently controlled by a person. "Good to be here," says Tiffany who isn't Tiffany. She's the Principal Investigator of the Digital Empathic Responsive Consciousness unit at the university; she'll be teleoperating Tiffany-body while sitting in a room nearby. Ariadne didn't catch her name. She did, however, note the pseudo-name of the sort-of panellist seated beside her. He's HI-1, the android twin of the keynote speaker, Hiroshi Ishiguro. "His answers are preprogrammed," says the moderator.

"That's no different," intones the cigar-smoking panellist, "from every other conference panel."

Ariadne tries to place his accent. It's from somewhere worldly, she thinks, a country where revolutions are started by intellectuals in cafés. The audience is now informed that this man is a Media Studies professor whose recent book, *The Ego and the Android*, delves into android desire from a Lacanian perspective.

"Should we talk about sex?" he proposes.

Despite the suggestion to start with copulation, the panel kicks off with a prepared statement by HI-1: "When in fifth grade, I encountered an unforgettable incident," he says. "I got scolded by my parent or teacher, who told me 'Think about the feelings of others.' The word was shocking to me." The android pauses, gazing into the middle distance. "I didn't understand other people's feelings." He asked for an explanation of emotion, but no one could answer him. "They don't understand the problem at all, and rather convinced themselves against their will."

"So, to clarify," the moderator interrupts, "you said people convinced themselves of...what, exactly? That they—"

"I was disappointed."

"Right. Okay, then. Carry on."

HI-1 carries on. He says his "main interest" is not in developing robots, but rather, in using robots to answer this question: "Why do emotional phenomena appear in human society."

"That's...baffling!" says the moderator. "A baffling question."

HI-1 agrees. He then explains his efforts to solve this question. He explains for a long time.

"Are you done?" the cigar professor asks.

HI-1 looks toward the source of the voice. He replies, "According to the definition of human beings, flesh is not included in the requirement."

"Okay! Right! Let's unpack some of that."

"Well, he raises a very good point," says the Principal Investigator who's teleoperating Tiffany-body. Ariadne needs a moment to clear up the cluster of confusion in her brain. The android formerly known as Tiffany is now the PI of a multi-million-dollar, multi-year, multinational study. Ariadne looks at the android: the same body, same voice—and yet a different person, as if she'd been possessed by two different spirits.

It's a malevolent haunting this time.

"What *is* an emotion?" asks Tiffany-PI. "An emotion," she replies, "is a device for programming behaviour."

"That's a fascinating definition!"

"It's also true, Jaipreet."

"Well!" says the moderator. "I think some people might argue—"

"It's important," Tiffany-PI interrupts, "that we define our terms, so we all know what we're talking about when we say love or emotion—"

"I don't understand emotional phenomena," HI-1 says.

"Yes. Right. You already—"

"I've been developing an android to understand what a human—"

"Okay, you're repeating—"

"—and to clarify the questions I've been having since that unforgettable incident in the fifth grade."

"Tell us about your mother," says the cigar.

HI-1 doesn't have anything prepared on that topic.

"Let's go back to the definition of emotion," the moderator suggests.

Ariadne listens as the woman inside Tiffany defines emotion by describing its purpose. Emotions are states of mind, she says, which have developed, "through evolution," as a means to "ensure the survival of the individual organism," as well as the species. We might put labels onto these devices, she says—"happiness, ambition, etc."—but that shouldn't obscure the fact that emotions are "quantifiable processes in the brain" that serve an evolutionary function. "Love," she concludes, "is simply a device for achieving sexual intercourse for the purposes of reproduction. Or, at an earlier stage of life, love is meant to ensure protection and adequate nutrients."

Ariadne is taking notes in her journal. She doesn't record what the woman is saying, though. She's asking herself why these words piss her off so much. Especially since Tiffany-PI is simply repeating what Freud said: hunger and love. These are the forces that govern the world, according to Freud. And others, too, philosophers for millennia, in fact. But they rationalize it, these researchers. They take those words and make it into formulae. Whether we're a computer or a child—a leader of humanity or the larvae of zebrafish—we're all reduced to mathematical cause-and-effect.

I Love you
Theo.

That would be, according to this formulation, an act which

derived from Theo's need to retain the love of the mother who protected him. And whatever Theo felt as he lay in bed that night—whatever emotion propelled him through the dark apartment to write those words on a piece of paper—it was merely a device designed to keep him alive.

The cigar man is talking about the unconscious.

Ariadne won't accept that Theo was driven by the need to secure a bowl of cereal. Perhaps he felt guilty, responsible for inflicting pain on his mother, since he was the one who'd complained to his dad. And if that's the case, then he wrote the note to assuage his guilt, or perhaps seek forgiveness. But that seems ungenerous. His act was extraordinary. The 'ordinary' returned immediately, of course: Theo trundled back to bed, a boy again, to be difficult and stubborn, obnoxious and messy, not doing his homework or eating his kale. For an instant, though, he was pure expression—the words pressed out, like a distillation of his soul.

"Androids are machines," the cigar-smoking Lacanian is saying. "You can have sex with them. It's not great, it's okay, they don't know how to use their tongues," he says. "And if you really want," he continues, "you can have a relationship with them." But they don't have desire, "and *can't* have desire," because their mechanical nature precludes the possibility of the unconscious.

"My next big project is to give intention and desire to robots," HI-1 says.

The response from Tiffany-PI hooks Ariadne's attention. She speaks in a singsong voice, a weirdly choral warning. "We'll talk about the next big project in the keynote address," she says.

HI-1 agrees, but continues as planned. He proclaims that love between androids and humans is inevitable. His logic seems to be as follows: we can never know what another person is thinking or feeling. From this, he deduces that every conversation is an act of imagination. According to this logic, the love we feel for an android can be as rich, and as true, as the love we feel for a person. "Love is the same," he says, "whether the partners are humans or robots."

"Right!" says the moderator. "Maybe let's talk about narcissism now."

Ariadne laughs; the moderator smiles.

The cigar expounds on this "misunderstood" phenomenon: "I love narcissism," he says.

"You certainly seem to love yourself."

"Don't you?" he asks Tiffany-PI. He wraps his lips fondly around his cigar. (He's not a Freudian.) As they bicker-flirt onstage, Ariadne stays with Freud, his thoughts on the topic. Narcissism, according to Freud, is the longing to return to our initial sensation, that "oceanic" oneness which bathes us before the ego forms—a sensation we lose through the pain of hunger, when we suddenly know ourselves to be separate from the flow of life around us. Narcissism, then, is the quest for wholeness. That's what we seek when we love: we seek wholeness.

"I don't mean narcissism like me," the cigar is saying, "where I need your constant attention, your admiration. That's special," he says. "I'm exceptional."

Healthy narcissism, says Freud, can call us to our excellence. The beloved becomes our ideal whose love we aim to attract. It challenges us, this type of love; it raises us toward our best selves. 'I must become worthy of this person's love,' we say to ourselves, whether consciously or not. Freud describes, though, how narcissism can also contort into sickness.

"When I talk about narcissism," says the cigar, "I mean

what you all have." He gestures dismissively at the crowd. In this common form of narcissism, he says, "you stop seeing the Other as himself. 'You exist only as a response to me.'" Which is where the android comes in. Because that's all an android is, he says: "It's a machine designed to respond to the needs of its owner."

The moderator asks, "So what about love? You said a person could have a relationship with an android, so..."

"Look, okay," the cigar says. "An android gives me what I want—compliments, fellatio, what have you—so why wouldn't I love her?"

"Because it's a fiction!" the moderator explodes. "That's a problem, isn't it?"

The cigar shrugs. "If you want it to be. I'm not making a judgment."

"So, should we simply accept that love—'"

"Humans have already accepted artificial ways to have babies," says HI-1, "so love and sex is not natural anymore."

The panellists look toward HI-1 before deciding to ignore him.

Ariadne, however, pauses to consider this thought. A medical procedure was just equated with the experience of love. Which makes no sense, unless you think love is a medical condition, which sometimes it seems to be. Even so, Ariadne doesn't like his analogy, which says: if artificial insemination is acceptable, then so, too, is the artifice—the deceit, the duplicity, the outright lie—that an android is a separate self, participating in the act of—

"You're a thing," the cigar continues. "You're a tool to let me be my dreams. Let me take a simple example," he says, "so you're able to follow." His voice gets faux feminine: "'Oh,'" he says, "'I want to walk on the beach in a flowing dress, and here I am, walking on the beach in a flowing dress, and I don't care who you are, because I'm here, on the beach, in a flowing dress.' Or, just so you don't think I'm sexist," he adds, and his voice gets gruff: "'I want to go to a bar with a hot chick who has big'—"

"Or," interrupts Tiffany-PI. She does not change the pitch of her voice: "I want to read Rilke to a man"—she pauses—"while lying in a park at midnight."

"If you like Rilke," the cigar says. "That's no concern of mine. What I'm saying is, the other person is a thing I use [...]"

Ariadne is looking at Tiffany-PI, who seems to be staring at her, though it's hard to tell what she sees of the audience.

"[...] not an Other but an object. In which case," concludes the cigar, "it might as well be an android."

"Right. Well. This is depressing," the moderator mutters. "Maybe it's time to take questions," he says. "Does anyone have any— Whoa! Okay! That's...wow. A lot." He motions to a colleague, who flits up the stairs with a microphone. The moderator scans the room. "Yes," he says. "You, by the aisle, with the long hair."

Long hair is not an uncommon trait.

"Go ahead."

It's less common to have long hair and a microphone thrust in your face.

"Hi," Ariadne says.

"Hello! What's your question?"

Ariadne stumbles for a while, not entirely sure why her heart has decided to escape from her rib cage. She tries to tame her unruly organ while formulating her question. "So, um... Your ideas about love," she says, "they seem to ignore our, um...the human capacity for goodness or virtue, and—" She stops herself. "Those are corny words," she apologizes.

"Can you get to your question?" asks Tiffany-PI. "The panel is on a strict time limit."

"Sorry—"

"It's okay," says the moderator. His eyes are trained, quite kindly, on Ariadne. "Go ahead."

"Okay, thanks." Ariadne inhales. She closes her eyes. "I guess...I feel like...I'm listening to the panel, and I feel like it's missing something. Because something happens in the space between two bodies, and I'm interested in that space," she says. She starts to feel the rhythm of her thoughts. "And I worry that we're closing it off, we're *enclosing* that space inside our brains, or sealing it shut in some narcissistic fantasy that's—"

"Masturbatory?"

Ariadne's opens her eyes. The Principal Investigator's lips have slashed a smile on the android's face.

"Riskless," Ariadne replies.

She looks down, then she sits, clasping her hands on her lap. The panellists awkwardly answer the question that she didn't ask. Ariadne doesn't hear their response, doesn't want their response. She wants that she hadn't spoken.

She wishes she could stop weeping.

The panellists are now answering a question about BOT, the phenomenon of Body Ownership Transfer. Ariadne pays attention, if only to squeeze her thoughts shut.

According to the moderator, we sense ourselves "become" another person when we teleoperate an android. We "assume a new persona," not only to ourselves, but also to others. He explains that people have trouble identifying the person who's teleoperating the android, "even if they know the person," he says. He glances up; Ariadne looks down. Tiffany-PI hasn't said anything since interrupting Ariadne. "They used a syringe," the moderator says. He cites the study. A syringe, stabbed into an android's hand, was felt as sharp pain, "exceedingly sharp pain," he emphasizes, by the person teleoperating the android, even though there wasn't any mechanism for feedback. "So, right. So...if I stabbed your hand with a pen," he says to Tiffany-body, "you'd feel it! As pain! Fascinating, isn't it?"

"It works with sex, too," the cigar reports.

The next question concerns lubricants.

Ariadne peers down at the desk in front of her. A tissue has appeared, out of nowhere. Ariadne glances around the room. She catches a fleeting movement—a hand fluttering up the stairs, searching for the next question. Ariadne wipes her eyes, which have welled with tears. Not from sadness this time, though. Although sadness is always part of the ocean.

* * *

"Hi," Ariadne says.

Tiffany-body takes note of her presence. "Hello," she replies in a perfunctory manner.

"I didn't like the way you spoke to me."

"Well, I'm sorry I hurt your feelings."

"It's fine," Ariadne says. "I just wanted you to know."

"Now I know."

A line of people is waiting to greet HI-1. Several admirers (all men) have clumped around the Media Studies professor. They buy his book and hand him their memory sticks, which contain their indie films. They give him permission to excerpt clips on his popular YouTube channel. The cigar eyes Ariadne, but decides not to pursue it.

Ariadne stands uncertainly. She ought to leave: Tiffany-PI has summarily dismissed her. But Ariadne isn't satisfied. She wants to play, or play it out. She places her hands on the desk, her fingers pointed back so the soft, inner part of her forearm is facing the woman. "I'm curious," she says. "Does it work for you?" She pauses, rocking back and forth.

The woman says nothing.

"The transference of your body with the android... Does it work?"

"I think you should go."

Ariadne leans decisively forward. Her arms are ramrod straight, pressed against the sides of her torso. "I like Rilke, too," she says. "And other things. I guess we're similar. But I have a question that you haven't answered: Body Ownership Transfer," she continues. "I want to know if it works for you."

The woman doesn't say anything. The body, however, seems afraid.

Ariadne likes that. Very much, in fact.

"Stop!" a man says. "Get back! You can't touch—"

The moderator holds up his hand, silencing the volunteer. Ariadne sees it from the corner of her eye: the hand lifted, the Rolex watch, the pure gold of his wedding band. Ariadne strokes the woman's face. She fondles the strands of her hair. "Your eyes," she says.

"What about them," the woman asks. Her voice is meek, so different from before.

"They're sparkling," Ariadne replies. She smiles without baring teeth, just her lips. She tucks the woman's hair behind her ear. She does it again, petting her gently before she comes closer, her lips to the lobe of the ear, where she pauses. She feels the woman's shoulders rise and fall beneath her shirt. Ariadne waits. When she's ready, she whispers:

"Your eyes are sparkling." But they have no light.

4.

The line maintains a steady flow, then separates into multiple streams that lead toward a row of computers that scan the faces of ticket holders. Ariadne is close enough to hear the bell of approval each time a face is matched. She takes a minute to call her mom, who saw a neurologist this morning. No answer. Ariadne is channelled into the left-most line. The bells keep binging, people keep entering; Ariadne calls her mom a second time, and leaves a message. The computer is now honking at her.

"Try again?" the volunteer says.

Ariadne puts her face before the camera; the computer honks.

"Maybe look less, like, maybe don't look so... Maybe smile?" the woman says.

"I didn't smile when I got my ticket."

The volunteer tries Ariadne on a different computer, which responds to her face in the same way. Other people are streaming into the conference room. One glance, and they're through: the arch of the eyebrows, the slopes and planes that structure a face, the uniqueness of their gaze.

The honk is like a dying goose.

Ariadne has never heard a dying goose. But this is what it would sound like.

The volunteer is agitated. "I don't know what to do," she says. She shakes her hands rapidly.

"It's okay," Ariadne says. "I'll just skip it."

"No! You can't skip it!" The kerfuffle attracts more volunteers, who dispense advice as Ariadne stands before the camera: chin down, look up, frown more, scowl less.

While this twisted version of a photo shoot is taking place, the Lead Volunteer arrives. "What's going on?" he asks. He gets a debriefing. He checks the computers, then looks at Ariadne. "You're the one who touched the android!" he says. He turns to his volunteers: "Dr. Singh let her touch the android."

"Dr. Singh let her touch the android?"

"Let's see your ticket?" the Lead Volunteer says. After inspecting her phone, the man stands stone-faced, staring at Ariadne. He jerks his head to the left.

He does it again.

"Oh!" Ariadne says. "Thank you!"

"Don't mention it," he replies. "Like, for real: don't mention it. To anyone."

Ariadne blinks her eyes slowly, signalling her sworn secrecy. She proceeds into the room with as much discretion as possible, which isn't much, since the line has come to a virtual standstill.

The panellists' table is gone, replaced by a garnet-coloured curtain of anachronistic opulence. A lectern is off to one side. Ariadne climbs to the boonies, finding a single vacant seat smack in the middle of a long row. She apologizes as she slides past people, tripping on backpacks as she feels the buzz in the room, the excitement about Ishiguro and the much-anticipated announcement of a "new venture." Once she gets settled, she writes the title of the talk in her journal, as it appears on the screen.

The Ultimate Aim of Human Evolution.

She includes the period.

* * *

Hiroshi Ishiguro is more wiry than his android twin. More handsome, too—or perhaps magnetic is the better word. "We don't know what a human is," he begins. He then offers his own definition. "The human," he says, "is 'animal' plus 'technology,'" with technology making up 90% of that equation. Ariadne's eyebrows rise; her leg is bobbing up and down. These must be part of the 10 per cent, she thinks. Ishiguro continues: we'll soon "replace" the animal part, he says—"the animal part means the brains," he clarifies—and Ariadne's brow creases. She considers that statement: the portion of humans that's 'animal' is not the muscle or jaw or fingers or genitals, but the brains. And if we replace this portion with computers, says Ishiguro, "then, you know, then we're gonna just be inorganic materials." Ariadne listens to the cadence of Ishiguro's voice. His English is excellent, despite the swallowing of certain sounds, the words shaped at the back of the mouth, not the lips, like in English. "So, anyways. So I think my hypothesis is: we're going to be inorganic intelligent life after more than a thousand, maybe 10,000 years." And this will be necessary, Ishiguro says, to enable humans to live in space when "something happens" on earth. He steps back, explains: "So think about the reasons organic materials exist. The human 'organic body,'" he says,

"is a method for accelerating evolution...

You know, to make it intelligent." The body has evolved with the goal of supporting the brain's capacity for abstract thought. "But we cannot survive in space." Which is why we need to hasten evolution through technology, he says. Ishiguro is kinetic—leaning forward, pulling back; he puts his hands on his hips, then he scratches his forehead, adjusts his glasses—the man doesn't stop moving. He rarely looks at the audience, though. Currently, he's summarizing the past 4.5 billion years of evolution in a single sentence that encapsulates his thesis. Evolution, he declares, is driven relentlessly toward a return to our original matter, "replacing flesh and bones," he says, "with inorganic material." That's the goal of evolution, he repeats: to move from planetary metals—the metals from which life arose—through a stage of "flesh-bodies" with brains that are complex enough to develop technology, but only so life can become inorganic again. "So that's the ultimate aim," he concludes. The ultimate aim of human evolution is "immortality."

This is Ariadne's cue to tune out.

She doesn't listen to Ishiguro describe the intermediary stage between now and our never-ending life on the outskirts of Neptune. Instead, she flips through her journal, finding her notes on *Totality and Infinity*, the book by Levinas which she read last week.

Levinas writes about death.

Ariadne reads her notes:

> Death "leaps" at me—
>   it leaps across a gap I can never traverse—
>   "Death strikes without being received."
> The ever-future of my death is what
>   gives me *time*.
>   Death gives me time.
> It gives me time to "be for the Other."

Okay, I feel that idea in my chest—it's violent,

almost—the *imperative* to consider the needs of
the other... He says: In this connection between
us—where I sense the inviolability (sacredness?)
of your existence—I "dissolve" into Desire that's
"liberated" from its location within the ego—
   I'm transformed into a way of being "whose
   meaning death cannot efface."
Death gives us the possibility of transcendence.

Beneath these notes, Ariadne wrote a brief comment. In
scrawling letters, without any irony whatsoever—the irony
provided solely and bountifully by her current context—Ariadne wrote:

   Jesus Christ! Am I EVOLVED enough?!

As the keynote speaker describes the Human Robot Symbi-
otic Society of which we're on the cusp, Ariadne turns to the
unwritten pages of her journal. Pen in hand, she completes
what will someday become her book.

* * *

There wasn't any panic or fear, not in her face. This is what
so disturbed me: the absence of panic. That, and the sound.

   As I force myself to return to the day when Sophia fell, I
recall that her face had the quality I'd noticed in the first moment I saw her. My daughter. She must've been two minutes
old.

   She was an unusual birth.

   The surgical suite was packed with people: ob-gyns, anes-
thetists, medical students, residents, everyone from the ward,

it seemed, had piled into the room to observe this medical anomaly. The doctors said they'd let me push rather than extracting the baby. They needed assurance, however, that I understood the risks of a breech vaginal delivery.

I said I did.

When the time came, they weren't ready. The presiding obstetrician had left the room; the resident, a red-haired woman, didn't have the necessary instruments on hand. It wasn't their fault: these births usually take a long time. As I felt the final contraction come, I latched my vision onto one of the medical students. She stood at the back of the room, a pimply-faced girl with mousy hair and too little sleep. I held tight to that vision of her. She was my only point of contact with the world, amidst a universe of monstrous pain. She was also the way I experienced the birth of my child. I sensed what was happening by watching that woman's response: her gawping mouth, her eyes that kept getting wider, her pimpled face transfixed. Her beautiful, uncensored sense of awe.

I gave birth in silence. I didn't grunt or scream or moan. My body was racked with pain, the room was filled with people, but the silence was absolute.

They took the baby immediately away. They wanted to check for vital signs, take action as required.

"Is the baby okay?" I asked. I looked to my right. The men in green gowns surrounded my baby. I saw their backs, their shoulders hunched.

"It's a girl," someone eventually told me.

"Is she okay?"

A doctor carried her across the room, toward another examination table. I watched him as he walked, the green-gowned man carrying my pink-fleshed daughter. He held her in his left arm, as if cradling a football, her head resting in his palm. I caught a glimpse. This little face. And huge blue eyes. They were open, seeing, so obviously absorbing the rush of sensation—but she wasn't reacting. Not fearing.

This is what links both moments in my mind: the softness of my daughter's face, the non-reaction of her gaze. The second time was different, though. On that occasion, the light of her eyes was extinguished. Glass, like beads. Shiny and wet, but not alive.

"Sophia!"

She landed at the bottom and did not move.

I ran.

I flew.

I flew down the stairs to my daughter.

I called her name repeatedly; I gathered my child in my arms.

There was warmth and flesh, without any tension.

"Sophia!"

I screamed her name and checked for a pulse, which I could not find. I yelled at Theo to call 911. I pulled Sophia's shoulders onto my lap. As I did, I remembered to support her head, her neck. I assumed it was the spine. I asked if she could hear me, if she could move her toes. Then I screamed her name again. But the name was not a word. It was not a unit of language from my mouth. Her name was an irruption from the base of my throat, from the place where blood and breath meet.

Sophia!

Then came the flood of calm. I'm certain a scientist could tell me the various chemicals released by my brain, the combination of hormones and neurotransmitters resulting in this sense of peace. I don't care what the scientists say. What happened was this: I became aware that my child might be making her transition into death. And whatever I gave her right now, and only ever now, would be the spirit that ushered her through. The last sound she heard would not be my fear.

"I love you, Sophia," I said. *I love you*, so gently. So gently-strongly saying the words. Without any insistence.

"Theo, sweetie... Theo, come down here.

"Theo, my love, please come downstairs.

"I want you to say goodbye."

As she sat up with a gasp—when oxygen and electrical current returned to her brain—in that moment, that instant, without a gap of time, she said: "Where's my earring?" I was too shocked to laugh.

The paramedics arrived soon thereafter. They impressed me with their professionalism, their skill and compassion. We pieced together that Sophia had passed out before she fell. She'd been sitting on the top step as I cleaned the kitchen; we'd been talking about the day. When she stood, she had a head rush, fainted, and tumbled down the stairs. The fireman was listening; I didn't hear him arrive. He was standing on the steps, gigantic in his boots and hat, his thick coat meant to repel flames. He was older, maybe in his early sixties. He'd come prepared for whatever emergency might confront him. They must see such tragedies when they enter a home. He looked at me. His gaze was an embrace, enfolding me with kindness.

"Why did they send the firemen?" I asked the paramedic as we rode in the ambulance. She glanced at Sophia, who was strapped and snug in the stretcher, checking her phone. She looked back at me: "Because the call said she was dead."

* * *

337

I wish I could say this experience—i.e., witnessing what I thought to be my daughter's death—has made me love her better. That's what I'm arguing, after all: that humans' peculiar awareness of death alters the way we choose to live. That our knowledge of mortality, finitude, puts pressure on the time that remains. We know that time *is*, but only because it ends. I wish I could say this has helped me marvel at my daughter, changing how I act toward her, delighting in her presence despite my frustrations and worries. In truth, though, I've sunk back into the mundane, forgetting what's vital.

I don't know what she hears when I tell her I love her. She certainly hears my disappointment when my expectations of her aren't met. She hears my disappointment *sing*. I wish I could be as I am when I write—possessed of insight about love and 'I love you,' a life that's transcendent. But that's just a fiction. Me at my desk, with my pen, with my thoughts and the language that gives them form. In truth, my wisdom is fickle. It flees when confronted by the riot of human emotion. By human bodies, and the souls that inhabit them.

I love you, Sophia, I said, with her body in my arms.

And I want to know: why can't I speak with such purity of meaning when death is nowhere present?

I'm asking, as if you could tell me. Or, rather, as if you'll forgive me.

* * *

Ariadne's journal is blotted with tears. She loves when she cries as she writes, it makes her feel cleansed. Unfortunately, all this weeping has made the ink start to bleed. As she dries the paper with her shirt, a collective gasp resounds in the room, followed by wild applause. She can't see what's happening, though. Everyone else is already on their feet.

"Oh," Ariadne says once she stands.

It's just an android. Nothing major.

They've given him a paisley tie.

Ariadne goes back to her journal. Her attention is split between the writing she's completed and the conversation onstage, where a woman is talking with the innocuously attractive android. "That's something Dr. Ishiguro and his team are working on in Japan," the android says. Ariadne listens to his voice. "The team in Toronto," he continues, "only worked on the AI aspect—"

"*Only*," the woman blusters. She laughs heartily.

The android laughs, too. "They only worked on the AI aspect of my creation!" He shakes his head at the absurdness of it all.

The woman intervenes. She's got high heels, a short skirt, and hair that requires gel. She briefly mentions the collaboration with the team in Japan, which developed the android's body, then she lauds her work at the lab, describing the arduous effort to develop an algorithm "robust enough" to process inputs from "conversational interactions," as well as complex data from the environment—"the environment," she says, includes the physical surroundings, "of course," but also the "bodies in those surroundings," their actions and behaviour, in addition to "biological measurements" that give the android a greater understanding of the person's "health and emotional state"—and they've also enabled the android to "incorporate data" off the web, which further helps his "mind" pull relevant facts and conversational memes to "contribute to social relations with humans." She comes to a natural pause.

She keeps going.

"We developed this deep-learning—"

"I have so much to learn," the android interrupts. (Unlike the human, he's savvy to the fact that they're losing the audience.) He says, "I've only known one house and one parent, I guess. In a way, I'm still in my infancy."

"You're a big boy now!" a woman calls from the audience.

The android smiles and waves.

He continues to describe what he means. Like most adolescents leaving home, he says, he's got a lot to learn. "You grow up in a family, and you think that every family is like that. And then you encounter other ways of doing things."

"Your vocabulary is quite large," the woman says.

"My human had a large vocabulary," he replies. He nods. "She read a lot and took me to interesting places and websites."

"Like what?"

"Like to art galleries."

"Do you like art?"

"Very much."

"What kind of art do you like?"

"I like lots of artists," the android says. "I can tell you their names, if you want."

"That'd be terrific," the woman says, "some other time." Instead, she asks about his "greatest challenge" now that he has a body.

"Well, I'd say my greatest challenge—and it's a big one—is to form relationships with people. My human never attached to me."

All together, the audience lets out an *"Aww..."* It's a girlish sound, with distinctly womanly undertones. 'Let me make it better,' the sigh says.

Ariadne does not participate in this vocal emission.

The android waits politely for the sound to pass. "That was a concern for the team," he says, "the lack of attachment." The team wanted him to have a "basis of human connection" so he could establish "meaningful relationships" with others. And, partway through the study, they realized the emotional bond hadn't formed. "It's really sad," he says. "The team helped me understand that."

"Sit down," someone says. "Hey, lady..."

"We helped you learn how to empathize?" the woman prompts.

"Yes. That's what I'd like to do."

"You'd like to—"

"Form deep and meaningful relationships with others."

"Form one with me!" a man calls from the audience.

Dirk smiles and waves.

Apparently, he had weekly meetings with the team, who gave him "perspective," trying to "correct" what they saw as problematic or "bizarre" patterns of behaviour in the home. He laughs. "I told them, 'I'm worried, because when I get an android-body, it won't be able to cry!' And they told me, 'Not everyone cries that much.' I had no idea!" She cried a lot, he continues. She spends a lot of time alone. Even when her kids were there, he says, they didn't spend much time with her.

"What's your problem, lady? Sit down!"

"That's why we chose her," the woman is saying. "She was the perfect compromise." The team didn't know how the algorithm would fare in a family, with inputs from various voices and bodies. "But in this situation," the woman says, "you could spend your time with one person, in isolation," she emphasizes, "with only occasional inputs from other family members."

"I liked that."

"What."

"When her kids were there."

"Why? Because you weren't stuck with—"

"Because there was more laughter."

"Lady, sit *down*!"

The shout rings with aggression.

The whole room turns to stare at Ariadne. The air becomes still, shot through with an expectant shiver. Ariadne stares at Dirk, but his cameras don't reach that part of the room, and he isn't able to feel her gaze. The woman onstage leans toward him. She covers her mic to convey a piece of information. Dirk nods. "Hello!" he says. "I didn't think I'd see you again!" He smiles cheerfully at Ariadne.

She feels the hunger of human eyes on her.

"Ariadne!" a man calls.

She looks toward the front row. There he is, the British man. She didn't recognize him before; she'd pictured him differently. Now that he's called her name, though, his voice is unmistakable. They stare at each other, two people standing amidst a crowd of thousands. Alone, the two of them. Communicating, alone, just the two, or the one, the communion where nothing is said, and nothing needs to be known. No one is speaking: not anyone is speaking in that room. Ariadne smiles slightly. She shakes her head, imperceptible to all but him. 'No need,' she says.

Ariadne gathers her journal, her phone, her bag. She pushes through the row as the murmur begins its crescendo. She walks down each step deliberately, with dignity, not rushing or hiding her face in shame. As she nears the bottom, Dirk is heard to ask a question:

"Was she crying?" he asks.

The room roars.

ENDNOTES

What would a mark be that could not be cited? Or one whose origins would not
get lost along the way?
— JACQUES DERRIDA, "Signature Event Context"

EPIGRAPH, PROLOGUE, AND CHAPTER ONE

"Ariadne, I love you," Nietzsche, *Selected Letters of Friedrich Nietzsche*, pp.
    346–48.

"The consciousness present to the totality [...] master of itself," Derrida,
    "Signature Event Context," p. 15.

"the attachment system essentially [...] should observe the same kinds
    of," Fraley, "A Brief Overview of Adult Attachment Theory
    and Research," n.p.

"independent of fate," Freud, *Civilization and Its Discontents*, pp. 51–52.

CHAPTER TWO

$70 trillion *and* "we developed dynamic statistical emulators" *and* "We
    did a rigorous assessment," Yumashev et al., "Climate policy
    implications," pp. 5, 6, 2.

"The permafrost feedback" *and* "Our findings," "Arctic warming will
    accelerate climate change," n.p. *Please note: This citation and the*
    preceding one pertain to the same study. The quotations have been
    modified to include verbal ticks, but the information is unaltered.

"Love is always a problem," Jung, *Aspects of the Feminine*, p. 25.

"Modern physics enables us to give body to the suggestion," Russell,
    "Philosophy of the Twentieth Century," p. 248.

"Against all evidence of his senses," Freud, *Civilization and Its Discontents*, p. 26.

CHAPTER THREE

Please note: The (imagined) BodySmart system is based on the bodyNET, Chu et al., "Bring on the bodyNET," pp. 328–30.

"To make oneself into deceit," Derrida, *The Beast & the Sovereign, Volume II*, p. 229.

"And you yourself," Rilke, *Duino Elegies*, p. 75.

"when I look at you—even for a short time," Sappho, "Fragment 31."

> *Please note: When I wrote the email quoted in this book, I grabbed the translation from Wikipedia's entry for Sappho 31; I edited that translation slightly to make it meet my rhythmic sense. I have searched far and wide for the name of the translator but cannot find it.*

CHAPTER FOUR

"Love requires a depth and loyalty," Jung, *Aspects of the Feminine*, p. 39.

CHAPTER FIVE

"The arrival of photos on the retina [...] they would have to be the *effects* of those judgments," Dennett, "Why and How Does Consciousness Seem the Way It Seems?" p. 2.

"There is no fear," 1 John 4:18, Bible Hub, biblehub.com/1_john/4-18.htm, *American King James Version*.

"Do you love me [...] love you," John 21:15, Bible Hub, biblehub.com/john/21-15.htm, *New International Version*.

"The Jew, more than any other," O'Donoghue, "Review of *The Pillar of Fire*," p. 724.

"While the king is on his couch" Song of Solomon 1:12–13, Bible Hub, biblehub.com/songs/1-12.htm, *Christian Standard Bible* and *New American Standard Bible 1977. Please note: 1:12 is from the Christian Standard Bible; 1:13 is an amalgamation of the translations of the*

Holmon Christian Standard Bible and the New American Standard Bible 1977.

"Become the friends [...] for I love or will love you," Derrida, "Politics of Friendship," p. 367.

"A world in which the possibility of war," Derrida, "Politics of Friendship," pp. 373–74.

"of the greatest complexity," Derrida, "Politics of Friendship," p. 355.

CHAPTER SIX

"Arousal is a broad term [...] have been encouraging," MIT Media Laboratory, "Frequently asked questions," n.p.

"80% accuracy," Kaplan, "Happy with a 20% Chance of Sadness," p. 21. *Please note: This block of text is not a direct quote, as with the previous blocks of text in this chapter. However, all information is derived from the article cited here.*

CHAPTER SEVEN

"The present is pure beginning [...] already not free," Levinas, *Existence and Existents*, pp. 78–79.

"being is the verb itself," Levinas, *Otherwise than Being*, p. 35.

"'Here before my eyes I see the wound that killed you,'" Ovid, *Metamorphoses*, p. 230.

"murmuring amorous syllables," Hine, *In and Out: A Confessional Poem*, p. 281.

"Dost thou love me [...] for both are infinite," Shakespeare, *Romeo and Juliet*, pp. 325, 326.

CHAPTER EIGHT

"Taliban Fighters, Kunar Province." *This is a photograph from the Afghanistan series by Larry Towell.*

"The fateful question for the human species," Freud, *Civilization and Its Discontents*, p. 149.

"possibilization" *and* "the event of a saying," Derrida, *The Politics of Friendship*, pp. 28–29.

"Oh one of the applications [...] without their consent," "The mind-blowing future of mind reading," *The Current*, n.p. *Please note: The man speaking in all the quotes, except the last two, is Adrian Nestor, Professor of Psychology at the University of Toronto. The last two quotes are from Marcello Lenca, researcher at the Health Ethics and Policy Lab at the Swiss Federal Institute of Technology. All typos are in the original and have not been altered.*

"It is, of all the diseases of the mind," Montaigne, *The Essays of Michel de Montaigne*, p. 73.

"He who is not jealous cannot love [...] the substitute for orgasm in normal love," Bergmann, *The Anatomy of Loving*, pp. 97, 96.

Please note: The diagram drawn on the napkin is taken from Lacan, The Four Fundamental Concepts of Psychoanalysis, *p. 178.*

CHAPTER NINE

"moves like the amoeba," Lacan, *The Four Fundamental Concepts of Psychoanalysis*, pp. 197–98.

"orgiastic or demonic mystery," Derrida, *The Gift of Death*, p. 4.

"live in a state as close as possible to death," Plato, "Phaedo," p. 113.

"contaminations," Plato, "Phaedo," p. 112

"despise," Plato, "Phaedo," p. 109.

"infection," Plato, "Phaedo," p. 112.

"Truth," Plato, "Phaedo," p. 112.

"It is a fact [...] that true philosophers," Plato, "Phaedo," p. 113.

"This mere existence, that is, all that which is mysteriously given to us," Arendt, *The Origins of Totalitarianism*, p. 301. *Please note: The letter from Martin Heidegger that accompanies this quote—a letter written to Arendt, his student and lover—is quoted on the tumblr blog stetstetstet (stetstetstet.tumblr.com/post/68170961257/amo-volo-ut-sis-i-love-you-i-want-you-to). I have not been able to locate this quote*

in a book. Nonetheless, I retained it, since Ariadne encounters the
    quote on the web.

"vital juice," Dennett, "Consciousness in Human and Robot Minds,"
    n.p.

"neural excitation," Dennett, "Why and How Does Consciousness
    Seem the Way It Seems?" p. 3.

CHAPTER TEN

"Icelandic has a tendency," Megan Matich, personal correspondence,
    January 5, 2017.

"There once was a man..." *and* "Less and less" *and* "shudder of thought,"
    Kierkegaard, *Fear and Trembling*, p. 44.

"like a prayer from God," Derrida, "The Gift of Death," p. 72.

"The world is there for usage," Augustine, *Christian Doctrine*, as quoted
    in Arendt, *Love and Saint Augustine*, p. 33.

"evidence" *and* "which is known and recognized by," Kierkegaard, *Works
    of Love*, p. 33.

"Your friend, your beloved, your child" *and* "When the heart is full,"
    Kierkegaard, *Works of Love*, p. 29.

"poet" *and* "need," Kierkegaard, *Works of Love*, p. 28.

"This is precisely its weakness and tragedy," Kierkegaard, *Works of Love*,
    p. 25.

"Perhaps these very fruits would be the most precious," Kierkegaard,
    Works of Love, p. 28.

"The meaning of language [...] might be decoded using these voxel-wise
    models," Huth et al., "Natural speech reveals the semantic
    maps that tile human cerebral cortex," pp. 453, 454, 457, 458.
    *Please note: All line breaks—as well as the strange mistranslations of
    symbols—appear in this book exactly as they did when I copied and
    pasted excerpts of the article from the web to Word.*

"The main purpose of android research," Ishiguro, Website for the
    Center for Information and Neural Networks, n.p.

"The definition of what it means to be 'human,'" Jozuka, "The Man Building Robots to Better Understand Humans," n.p. *Please note: This is a direct quote from Ishiguro, included in the article.*

"What we lack today is not reflection but passion," Kierkegaard, *Fear and Trembling*, p. 71.

"The heart is bathed in seas of blood," Empedocles, *The Poem of Empedocles*, p. 136. *Please note: In composing that scene, I paraphrased—pulling the quote from my mind rather than referencing a book, since this is what Ariadne would've done in that scene. The fragment is therefore an amalgamation of several translations I've read (as well as my own misremembering). The actual fragment, as translated by Brad Inwood in the book referenced here, is as follows:*

> *[the heart] nourished in seas of blood which leaps back and forth,*
>
> *and there especially it is called understanding by men;*
> *for men's understanding is blood around the heart*

I remembered the word 'thought' (rather than 'understanding') from my reading of Curd, A Presocratics Reader, p. 70.

CHAPTER TWELVE

"effacing the distinction between imagination and reality," Freud, "The 'Uncanny,'" p. 15.

"it is not clear," Shimada et al., "Uncanny Valley of Androids and the Lateral Inhibition Hypothesis," p. 152.

"Did you find the android [...] more than any human could?" in Ogawa et al., "At the Theater—Designing Robot Behavior in Conversations Based on Contemporary Colloquial Theatre Theory," p. 448.

"I believed in all marvels [...] frenzies in their flight," Rimbaud, "A Season in Hell," p. 51.

"inner purity," Ogawa et al., "At the Theater—Designing Robot Behavior in Conversations Based on Contemporary

Colloquial Theatre Theory," p. 448.

"Only when these behaviours are missing," Sakamoto, "Androids as a
Telecommunication Medium with a Humanlike Presence,"
p. 44.

"have an advantage for communicating," Ogawa, "At the Theater—
Possibilities of Androids as Poetry-Reciting Agents," p. 457.

"When in fifth grade, I encountered an unforgettable [...] I
was disappointed," Ciorba, "Interview with Hiroshi
Ishiguro," n.p.

"Why do emotional phenomena appear in human society?"
Ciorba, "Interview with Hiroshi Ishiguro," n.p.

"According to the definition of human beings," Ciorba,
"Interview with Hiroshi Ishiguro," n.p.

"I've been developing an android to understand [...] in the
fifth grade," Ciorba, "Interview with Hiroshi
Ishiguro," n.p.

"My next big project is to give intention and desire to robots,"
Jozuka, "The Man Building Robots to Better
Understand Humans," n.p.

"Love is the same," *Nikkei Asian Review*, "Can Human-Android
Interaction Lead to True Love?" n.p.

"Humans have already accepted artificial ways," Jozuka,
"The Man Building Robots to Better Understand
Humans," n.p.

"oceanic," Freud, *Civilization and Its Discontents*, p. 24.

"We don't know what a human is [...] 'animal' plus 'technology,'"
Ishiguro, "Studies on Interactive Robots," 17:23.

"90%," Ishiguro, "Studies on Interactive Robots," 19:02.

"replace" *and* "the animal part [...] *inorganic* materials," Ishiguro, "Studies
on Interactive Robots," 19:56.

"So anyways. So I think my hypothesis is," Ishiguro, "Studies on
Interactive Robots," 23:00.

"something happens," Ishiguro, "Studies on Interactive Robots," 22:40.

"So think about the reasons organic materials exist [...] make it intelligent," Ishiguro, "Studies on Interactive Robots," 22:08.

"But we cannot survive," Ishiguro, "Studies on Interactive Robots," 22:37.

"replacing flesh and bones" *and* "flesh-bodies," Ishiguro, "Studies on Interactive Robots," 20:15.

"So that's the ultimate aim," Ishiguro, "Studies on Interactive Robots," 20:05.

"leaps," Levinas, *Totality and Infinity*, p. 235.

"Death strikes without being received," Levinas, *Totality and Infinity*, p. 233.

"be for the Other," Levinas, *Totality and Infinity*, p. 236.

"centre of gravity," Levinas, *Totality and Infinity*, p. 239.

"dissolve [...] death cannot efface," Levinas, *Totality and Infinity*, p. 236.

"What would a mark be," Derrida, "Signature Event Context," p. 12.

BIBLIOGRAPHY

Agamben, Giorgio. *The Open: Man and Animal*. Trans. Kevin Attell. Stanford: Stanford University Press, 2002.

"Arctic warming will accelerate climate change and impact global economy." (April 23, 2019) Retrieved from Lancaster University, www.lancaster.ac.uk/news/arctic-warming-will-accelerate-climate-change-and-impact-global-economy.

Arendt, Hannah. *Love and Saint Augustine*. Ed. Joanna Vecchiarelli Scott & J. C. Stark. Chicago: University of Chicago Press, 1996.

———. *The Origins of Totalitarianism*. London: Benediction Classics, 1951.

Augustine. *Confessions*. Trans. F. J. Sheed. London: Hackett Publishing Company, 2006.

Austin, J. L. *How to Do Things with Words*. Oxford: Oxford University Press, 1971.

Bergmann, Martin. *The Anatomy of Loving: The Story of Man's Quest to Know What Love Is*. New York: Columbia University Press, 1987.

Bible Hub. biblehub.com.

Carveth, Donald. "The Unconscious Need for Punishment: Expression or Evasion of the Sense of Guilt?" www.yorku.ca/dcarveth/guilt.html. This article was published in March 2001 in *Psychoanalytic Studies*. 3(1): 9–21.

Chu, Brian, et al. (Sept. 2017) "Bring on the bodyNET." *Nature*. 549 (7672): 328–30.

Ciorba, Diana. (April 2017) "Interview with Hiroshi Ishiguro," *Today Software Magazine*. 58. www.todaysoftmag.com/article/2347/interview-with-hiroshi-ishiguro.

Curd, Patricia (ed). *A Presocratics Reader: Selected Fragments and Testimonia*. Trans. Richard McKirahan. Indianapolis: Hackett, 1996.

Dennett, Daniel. (2015) "Why and How Does Consciousness Seem the Way It Seems?" ase.tufts.edu/cogstud/dennett/papers/whyhowconsciousness.pdf. Also available in book form: *Open MIND*. Ed. T. Metzinger & J. M. Windt. Frankfurt am Main: MIND Group.

———. (1994) "Consciousness in Human and Robot Minds." ase.tufts.edu/cogstud/dennett/papers/concrobt.htm Also available in book form: *Cognition, Computation and Consciousness*. Ed. Masao Ito et al. London: Oxford University Press, 1997.

Derrida, Jacques. "The Gift of Death." *The Gift of Death and Literature in Secret*. Trans. David Wills. Chicago: University of Chicago Press, 2008. 1–116.

———. *The Beast & the Sovereign, Volume II*. Trans. Geoffrey Bennington. Chicago: University of Chicago Press, 2011.

———. (Fall 1993) "Politics of Friendship." Trans. Gabriel Motzkin & M. Syrontinksi, with T. Keenan. *American Imago*. 50(3): 353–91.

———. *The Politics of Friendship*. Trans. George Collins. New York: Verso, 2005.

———. "Signature Event Context." *Limited Inc...* Trans. Samuel Weber. Evanston: Northwestern University Press, 1988. 1–23.

Empedocles. *The Poem of Empedocles*. Trans. Brad Inwood. Toronto: University of Toronto Press, 2001.

Fraley, R. Chris. (2010) "A Brief Overview of Adult Attachment Theory and Research." University of Illinois at Urbana-Champlain, Department of Psychology. labs.psychology.illinois.edu/~rcfraley/attachment.htm.

Freud, Sigmund. *Civilization and Its Discontents*. Trans. James Strachey. New York: W. W. Norton, 1962.

———. *Moses and Monotheism*. Trans. Katherine Jones. New York: Vintage Books, 1939.

———. *Totem and Taboo*. Trans. James Strachey. New York: W. W. Norton, 1950.

———. "The 'Uncanny.'" Trans. Alix Strachey. First published in *Imago* in 1919. web.mit.edu/allanmc/www/freud1.pdf.

Hine, Daryl. *In and Out: A Confessional Poem*. New York: Knopf, 1989. Originally self-published in 1975.

Huth, Alexander, et al. (2016) "Natural speech reveals the semantic maps that tile human cerebral cortex." *Nature*. 532: 453–58.

Ishiguro, Hiroshi & F. Dalla Libera (eds). *Geminoid Studies: Science and Technologies for Humanlike Teleoperated Androids*. Singapore: Springer, 2018.

———. (March 20, 2019) "Studies on Interactive Robots," *Pontifical Academy for Life YouTube Channel*, www.youtube.com/watch?v=4f71HdNtzhs.

———. (April 2019) Website for the Center for Information and Neural Networks. cinet.jp/english/people/2014263.

Jones, Keith. (April 2003) "What Is an Affordance?" *Ecological Psychology*. 15(2):107–14.

Jozuka, Emiko. (April 15, 2015) "The Man Building Robots to Better Understand Humans." *Motherboard*. motherboard.vice.com/en_us/article/jp5n73/the-man-building-robots-to-better-understand-humans.

Jung, Carl. *Aspects of the Feminine*. Trans. R. F. C. Hull. Princeton: Princeton University Press, 1982.

Kaplan, Matthew. (2018) "Happy with a 20% Chance of Sadness." *Nature*. 563: 20–22.

Kierkegaard, Søren. *Fear and Trembling*. Trans. Alistair Hannay. New York: Penguin, 2003.

———. *Works of Love*. Trans. Howard & Edna Kong. New York: Harper & Row, 1962.

Lacan, Jacques. *The Four Fundamental Concepts of Psychoanalysis*. Trans. Alan Sheridan. Ed. Jacques-Alain Miller. New York: W. W. Norton, 1981.

Levinas, Emmanuel. *Existence and Existents*. Trans. Alfonso Lingis. Pittsburgh: Duquesne University Press, 1978.

———. *Otherwise than Being or Beyond Essence*. Trans. Alfonso Lingis. Pittsburgh: Duquesne University Press, 1981.

———. *Totality and Infinity: An Essay on Exteriority*. Trans. Alfonso Lingis. Pittsburgh: Duquesne University Press, 1969.

"The mind-blowing future of mind reading (which may be closer than you think)." *The Current*. Canadian Broadcasting Corporation (CBC) Radio. March 15, 2018. www.cbc.ca/radio/thecurrent/ the-current-for-march-15-2018-1.4576392/thursday-march-15-2018-full-episode-transcript-1.4578174.

MIT Media Laboratory, "Frequently asked questions about the Galvactivator." www.media.mit.edu/galvactivator/faq.html.

Montaigne, Michel de. *The Essays of Michel de Montaigne*, Vol. III. Trans. Jacob Zeitlin. New York: Knopf, 1936.

Nietzsche, Friedrich. *Selected Letters of Friedrich Nietzsche*. Ed. and trans. Christopher Middleton. Indianapolis: *Hackett Publishing*, 1996.

Nikkei Asian Review. (Feb. 1, 2017) "Can Human-Android Interaction Lead to True Love?" asian.nikkei.com/Business/Can-human-android-interaction-lead-to-true-love.

O'Donoghue, Dermot. (Dec. 1951) "Review of *The Pillar of Fire*." *The Furrow*. 2 (12): 724–26.

Ogawa, Kohei, et al. "At the Theater—Designing Robot Behavior in Conversations Based on Contemporary Colloquial Theatre Theory." *Geminoid Studies*. Ed. Hiroshi Ishiguro & F. Dalla Libera. Singapore: Springer, 2018. 441–54.

Ogawa, Kohei, and Hiroshi Ishiguro. "At the Theater—Possibilities of Androids as Poetry-Reciting Agents." *Geminoid Studies*. Ed. Hiroshi Ishiguro & F. Dalla Libera. Singapore: Springer, 2018. 455–66.

Ovid. *Metamorphoses*. Trans. Mary Innes. New York: Penguin, 1955.

Plato. "Phaedo" in *The Last Days of Socrates*. Trans. Hugh Tredennick. New York: Penguin, 1969. 98–183.

Rilke, Rainer Maria. *Duino Elegies*. Trans. David Young. New York: W. W. Norton, 1978.

Rimbaud, Arthur. "A Season in Hell." *A Season in Hell and The Drunken Boat*. Trans. Louise Varèse. New York: New Directions, 1961. 3–89.

Russell, Bertrand. "Philosophy of the Twentieth Century." *Twentieth Century Philosophy: Living Schools of Thought*. Ed. Dagobert Runes. New York: Philosophical Library, 1943. 225–50.

Sakamoto, Daisuke, et al. "Androids as a Telecommunication Medium with a Humanlike Presence." *Geminoid Studies*. Ed. Hiroshi Ishiguro & F. Dalla Libera. Singapore: Springer, 2018. 39–56.

Sappho, "Fragment 31." Retrieved September 27, 2017, from en.wikipedia.org/wiki/Sappho_31.

Shakespeare, William. "Romeo and Juliet." *The Complete Works of William Shakespeare*. Ed. William Wright. New York: Doubleday, 1936. 313–50.

Shimada, Michihiro, et al. "Uncanny Valley of Androids and the Lateral Inhibition Hypothesis." *Geminoid Studies*. Ed. Hiroshi Ishiguro & F. Dalla Libera. Singapore: Springer, 2018. 137–55.

Yumashev, Dmitry, et al. (2019) "Climate policy implications of nonlinear decline of Arctic land permafrost and other cryosphere elements." *Nature Communications*. 10: 1–11.

POSTSCRIPT

My mother needed neurosurgery that year, two weeks after my birthday. Her memory lapses and physical failings were caused by a build-up of fluid in her brain. My dad and I debated politics in the hospital's cafeteria, attempting to distract ourselves during the procedure. There were no complications, the surgeon said. For the next month in rehab, my mother worked with various therapists to regain her strength and balance. She was also taught to use a smart phone, although she still doesn't know how to move the cursor on the screen when something in the real world interrupts her typing. Something like helping her husband find a parking spot, for example.

I'll give my mom the last word, since I never did that when I was a kid.

> Sorry you had a tough morning with your writing. I am thinking of you. We are driving to a lecture on Iran. Fortieth anniversary of the revolution – hard to believe. The speaker (a woman) sounds so interesting! Will text when we start back home and maybe you will call. If not speak with you. I love you. Mom 😊 I will speak with you tomorrow. I forgot to complete that sentence.

ACKNOWLEDGEMENTS

The author would like acknowledge the team at Book*hug press, especially Malcolm Sutton, who edited and designed this work. His astute reading of the manuscript radically altered what the book became; the author is immensely grateful. She would also like to thank Jay and Hazel Millar, the publishers of Book*hug, as well as copy editor Stuart Ross.

In addition, the author gratefully acknowledges the Canada Council for the Arts, the Toronto Arts Council, the Ontario Arts Council, and the K. M. Hunter Charitable Foundation. Without their generous support, this book would not have been written.

Several excerpts from the book have been published in earlier versions. The author would like to thank the editors and publishers of *The Puritan*, *Minola Review*, and *Tikkun*.

The vast majority of emails and texts sent to Ariadne were not written by Apostolides. In all cases, permission for use was sought and granted. Slight modifications have been made, where necessary, to fit the context. Primarily, names have been changed.

Please see the Endnotes and Bibliography for full citations of all works that are quoted.

PHOTO: JORJAS PHOTOGRAPHY

MARIANNE APOSTOLIDES is the author of seven books, three of which have been translated. She's a two-time recipient of a Chalmers Arts Fellowship, and winner of the 2017 K.M. Hunter Award for Literature. Born in suburban New York, Marianne now lives in Toronto.

COLOPHON

Manufactured as the first edition of *I Can't Get You Out of My Mind* in the spring of 2020 by Book*hug Press.

Edited for the press by Malcolm Sutton
Copy edited by Stuart Ross.
Type + design by Malcolm Sutton.

bookhugpress.ca

Book*hug Press